TENNESSEE BLACKBERRIES

MARK D. WOOD

20 Twenty
Literary Group

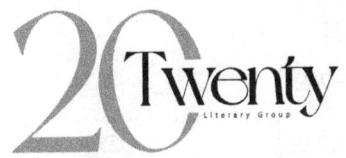

Tennessee Blackberries
Copyright © 2024 by Mark D. Wood

All rights reserved. No part of this publication may be reproduced, distributed, or transmitted in any form or by any means, including photocopying, recording, or other electronic or mechanical methods, without the prior written permission of the author, except in the case of brief quotations embodied in critical reviews and certain other non-commercial uses permitted by copyright law.

ISBN
978-1-962868-55-6 (Paperback)
978-1-962868-56-3 (eBook)
978-1-962868-54-9 (Hardcover)

For My Parents

Who Always Believed

PART I

CHAPTER I

1864
·················

The doctors in the camps weren't always the best, and in some cases, their behavior was terrible. Still, Charlie Barnham didn't figure that they ever killed anyone on purpose. They sawed arms and legs off with great frequency and, in some cases, speed. They probed for bullets with blunt instruments, changed bandages whenever possible, and prescribed whiskey and brandy for pain control as often as they prescribed laudanum and morphine. Some were gentle, some were indifferent, and all of them ignored the screaming, the pleas, and the cursing.

But until he met Doctor Sebastian Crane, he never figured that a doctor would kill anyone on purpose.

1985
·················

Sometimes, on long, interminable nights when the memories were my only friends, I would sit in the dark and remember how it was to live without fear.

Many years have gone by since then, the seasons rolling by as effortlessly as a handful of pebbles scattered into a still pond. In that time, I have become a different person altogether. I have lived a life of shadows and despair, have spent years locked away for the sake of safety—not only mine, but according to the doctors, others as well—and have known firsthand that Evil is a pervasive force that walks among us.

I suppose it was a blessing that until I was twenty-one, I had really never encountered such a force. But as Shakespeare says, when troubles come, they come not in single spies but in full battalions, and that was certainly true of my life the summer before my last year in college. Two men entered my life and changed it forever in that long ago summer of 1985, one of them a man who promised love and a future and a life… and the other, a monster with no conscience or hope of salvation.

The gods had cast us into the eternal roles of hunter and prey, and that was exactly what we were: a vicious, relentless predator who stalked his prey without mercy or honor, and my Bobby, the gazelle at the watering hole who had no idea he was even being pursued. I don't know if knowing would have made his fate any easier; his family had long known of the hunter and had hidden Bobby away since the day he was born, and *still* the hunter had tracked him down. As his grandmother had told me, "The insidious patience of evil can be relentless, my dear," and she was right.

And me? I was also a victim of what the military might call collateral damage. My role was innocent bystander, helpless girlfriend, witness for the prosecution… and many others, depending on the day and to whom the question was asked. At first, I was nothing more than a means to the hunter's end and certainly not considered an enemy of any consequence… but, later in the game, I became a hunter myself, a veritable Van Helsing with a terrible thirst for reprisal. I put a fear in my enemy that he had not felt for over a hundred years, and I did it in the name of vengeance and justice for so many fallen victims. I have chased him across the country, sometimes so close that I missed him by mere moments, but he is elusive, cunning, and has the luck of his father, the Devil. At the same time, after I declared war on him, he turned his attention to me, and so we are now locked in a fatal game of cat and mouse, neither of us relenting until the other is dead.

Had anyone even suggested to me that my life would turn out in such a way—scarred, chased and full of anger and purpose—I wouldn't have believed it. I was in my last year of college, fully grown but not quite an adult… I was young but not necessarily stupid, probably naïve and full of promise. Full of *hope*. Now, to be near my prey, I sleep during the day and roam the streets at night, watching and listening for his scent. I have come to read the newspapers differently, looking for strangely reported deaths or accidents, odd occurrences that seem to have no explanation. Sometimes these reports are given cute titles like *Weird News*, or *Filed Under Strange*, but I know better. I know these are my enemy's calling cards to me, letting me know he is still out there, still in the game… after all, there are a thousand ways to dispose of a body. It's the ones he leaves for display and speculation, that I know are his personal messages to me, a personal reminder for me alone. *"Come and find me, dear Beth… catch me if you can, before I catch you, and put an end to all this silliness…"*

So, is there a respect that resides between us? Absolutely not. Even respect is too positive of an emotion to waste on such a diabolical creature. And while it would be easy to almost become complacent with this kittenish communication between us, the trail of dead bodies and unexplained murders, I refuse to be complacent, and I refuse to soften my resolve.

For I am on a mission, and that mission is clear.

I will not rest until Sebastian Crane—Vampire—is dead.

CHAPTER II

1864
....

Private Charlie Barnham, of the Scarlet Tennessee Rangers, CSA, laid on his cot the first three days after being wounded, mostly uninterested in his surroundings. Stupid with pain and brandy, his head rested on an old bloody book that someone had supplied for a pillow, and with disbelief and horror, regarded the bloody stump where his left hand had been. He could hardly remember the explosion, but they had told him that the mortar had first exploded into the fencepost; all of the shattered wood had slammed into his hand, slicing off fingers, cutting and tearing, and when they had brought him to the field hospital, there wasn't much of a hand to save.

The bandage seeped pink and had to be changed every hour, except that there weren't enough bandages for the first twenty-four hours, and so the blood dripped off his stump and collected in a sticky, blackening pool. Flies buzzed and lit; their noises seemed alternately loud and soft to Charlie's ears. After others began to die off and bandages were more plentiful, did Charlie's bandages get changed on a more frequent basis.

The nurses were as attentive as possible, but there were too few of them, far too many patients, and even fewer doctors, so often hours would go by without anyone really checking on him. He had slipped into a hazy, unfocused cycle of restless sleep and painful awakenings... terrible dreams, often punctuated and interrupted by the screams and cries of men around him.

Early one morning, well before dawn, he was awakened by a gentle voice whispering in his ear, and he opened his eyes groggily to see a well-dressed man standing over him.

"Don't worry, I'm a doctor," the man murmured to him, gently holding the bloody stump in his hands. "Sebastian Crane, at your service. Are you in pain?"

"Some," he agreed, and a tear trickled down his cheek and into his hair. He was embarrassed to be caught crying, and even more embarrassed that this elegant gentleman doctor had caught him at it.

"Don't cry, mon ami," he said softly. "Pain is fleeting and reminds us how sweet the gift of life is. Don't worry, I will find you something for your pain." Charlie blinked rapidly at the man's soft, reassuring voice and tried to smile, though the effort was strained. He sought something intelligent to say, something of gratitude for this man, and weakly he licked his lips.

"Your hands are cold," he managed, and then realized it was a stupid thing to say. Still, it was the best he could do, with being awakened, and in such terrible pain, and he mentally forgave himself for such foolishness.

The man smiled thinly. "Are they? Perhaps you are still feverish, is all." With professional scrutiny, he studied Charlie's stump, holding up a lamp for a better look. Charlie took a deep breath as a fresh bolt of pain shot down his arm, and he closed his eyes tightly, submitting to the doctor's examination.

Time seemed to snag. The doctor said nothing, though Charlie noticed that the pressure on his wrist was increasing, and he opened his eyes again... only to be confused at what he was seeing.

Doctor Crane was staring intently at the rough stitches and bloody stump, but his eyes had suddenly gone very large and excited in the dark, and he had jutted his bottom jaw out a little, as if considering something of great importance. He made no sound, although his breath suddenly increased, becoming ragged and intense, and as Charlie watched, his confusion giving way to fright, the doctor's pink tongue snaked out and licked his lips. It was the same gesture Charlie himself would have given if he were gazing upon a *plate of his mother's sausage and eggs. Frightened, he pulled his hand away and stared at the doctor.*

With great effort, Crane seemed to pull himself together, and offered a weak smile. "I'll go find something for your pain," he whispered, and he turned to go.

The darkness seemed to swallow him as he disappeared down the row of beds. Charlie watched him go, confusion and fear spreading over his body like a thin blanket.

1985

It was the summer before my senior year in college. I was studying to be an elementary teacher—kindergarten or early childhood, to be exact—and my world was filled with primary things: sample lesson plans, diagnostic reading tests, picture books with simple tests, and counting blocks. I had done well in my theory and foundation classes, and I was set to take my last series of classes, the dreaded "methods" classes, which were the final lab experience before student teaching. It was a heady experience.

If things worked out, I would be the first in my family to graduate from college. My parents were long divorced; my father lived in another state, working as a security guard for a warehouse, and my mother was an assistant at a local preschool. It was from her that I learned to love the classroom and the joy of educating children, and I would help her from time to time on weekends and various vacations. Still, I quickly realized that even though she was impacting children's lives, it was not as fully as she could… in her capacity as an assistant and not the teacher, it was very much like the relationship between a waiter and a chef. The waiter got to carry the food after it was cooked, but it was the chef who decided upon the flavor. I knew I wanted to be the one who put the flavor, so to speak, in a child's education and not merely be a recess monitor like my mother.

But it was a daunting idea. College hours cost money, and that was something that was scarce in our home. In my senior year of high school, I worked hard on my grades and applied for a few scholarships. Most of them I didn't get, but I did win a few, and as my mother pointed out, every little bit helped. When I combined them with my small savings, I had enough to enroll at the local community college for at least three semesters... not actually live on campus, but commute there daily. As long as I kept my grades up, the scholarships were renewable every semester, and every time I wanted to skip a homework assignment, stay out late, or miss a class, I always thought of my mother on endless recess duty. This thought didn't exactly make me proud—I was never ashamed of my mother, not for even a second, but I thought she was wasted in such a capacity, and I in no way wanted to ever repeat her mistakes.

And so I played the educational game. I studied Piaget's levels of development, Maslow and his hierarchy of needs, and I learned how to write a lesson plan that was focused on best practices and manipulatives. I worked at providing differentiated instruction, and I worried about hitting all learning styles in a day. My supervising teachers and professors thought I had some promise, and I know I loved the children I worked with. They weren't all easy. Some of them were so damaged and unreachable, even at such a young age, that after some classes I was filled with despair. "You can't save all the butterflies," an older teacher once told me. "Just keep your net open wide, and hope that most of them fall into it."

I didn't date much in those years. Living at home off campus had its drawbacks, and I missed much of the social scene of college. While I probably wouldn't have ever pledged a sorority, I suppose I did miss the experience of having a roommate and living in a dorm. Most boys weren't really interested in girls who still lived at home because watchful parents and curfews made it clearly impossible to attempt to get into their pants. The occasional boy would ask me out, but no one ever special came along to sweep me off my feet, and so I drifted through the first few years of college the Eternal Virgin, solid in my commitment to my studies so I could maintain my scholarships, and definitely a loner, the quiet girl who blended into the back of the class.

I tried to tell myself that, really, I had no time for a social life anyway. I was balancing a hefty work schedule. Sometimes I worked two jobs, helped my mother at hers and worked around the house *before* I even touched my homework. It made for long days, late hours, and endless cups of coffee. Caffeine and MTV were my best friends, about the only ones I had time for.

And before I knew it, I was almost at the end, with no student loans to pay off, a fairly decent grade point average, and I was in the summer before my looming senior year. I took a job waitressing at a diner on the lake... not a chain restaurant, but a privately-owned place called Lou's Grill that attracted a pretty good summer crowd. I could work as many hours as I wanted; the tips were good, and while it wasn't the easiest job in the world, it was profitable, and my little bank account grew. My boss was a retired Marine who treated us well; in his earlier life, he had been a cook on a military base, and while his bark sounded rough, and the air around him was sometimes blue with his cursing, he really was a kind man, and I liked him a lot.

The clientele was easy, too. Fishermen, boaters, swimmers at the beach... "Summer People," Lou called them, people who were only passing through for a few days. Most of them were good people, families with children who would come inside the cool restaurant for a hamburger or chicken finger dinner after a long, sunburned day at the beach. Occasionally, a more elite group would come through—a bunch of fraternity boys fresh from a day spent water skiing, or rich old men swinging metal detectors around on the sand, and I would have to fend off wandering hands and phone numbers hastily scribbled on napkins and pushed my way. I would parry them with different degrees of tact and pleasantness, but none ever really got out of line, for Lou had a watchful eye and took care of his employees. He made sure to walk us out to our cars at the end of the evening, and on more than one occasion, I saw him cheerfully toss out any obnoxious diner who got too overbearing or refused to take no for an answer.

I worked long hours, many times pulling a double shift, but I was young and healthy, and I managed to keep up with the work fairly well. Still... I had to admit that it hurt me when people my own age, especially those that I recognized from some of my classes, would come into the diner. They were tanned and carefree, wandering in for a sandwich or a beer after a movie and serving them was more than awkward. Most of them were good about it, as embarrassed about it as I was as we exchanged pleasantries, but I still felt pangs when a laughing crowd of them would come rolling in, and even worse when they rolled back out. I longed to be with them, silly and troubled with nothing more serious on my mind than whose house the party would be held at that night.

One night, as I walked out to my car, I paused for a moment and looked out across the lake. Across the parking lot, two carloads of young people were screaming with laughter over something. I looked over at them and saw the typical scene of macho boys playfully punching each other over nothing and insipid girls playfully screaming with delight as their menfolk mock-charged and fought like silly gladiators. It looked absurd and ridiculous… and somehow wonderfully *fun*, and wistfully I watched them pile into their cars and, with wheels screeching, fly out of the parking lot.

And then I was alone again, except for Lou, who was silhouetted at the back door of the diner. He raised a farewell hand to me, and I waved back, but my heart was strangely sad, and I looked out across the lake again. It was a hot, still night; I could hear frogs peeping and grumbling in the reeds, and the gentle lapping of waves on the shore as a late-night boater made a final tour of the lake. It was a peaceful, beautiful picture… and yet inexplicably, I suddenly got the shivers, and it wasn't the first time. I felt I was being watched.

It had happened a few other times in the past few weeks—the odd feeling that someone was observing me and considering me from a distance. I would look around, certain that *something* wasn't right, but would never be able to find any reason to support my feelings of dread. I had simply shrugged them off, blaming it on being overtired and lack of sleep, but another part of me would whisper quietly, *no, it's not that, and you know it. There is danger here—a real reason to be afraid. Trust your senses, Beth… be aware, and be warned.*

Logically, the whole notion of being in danger was silly because things were actually going very well. I had a job, a good job I liked. My summer school class was easy, my mother was in good health, and my last table had left me a pretty good tip. Except for my nearly non-existent social life, I was doing just fine… and yet suddenly, my senses were alerted to some unseen presence. Despite the warmth of the night, goosebumps rose up on my arms as an uneasy feeling stole over me.

I increased my pace.

With every step, the feeling of eyes on me intensified. I looked around the parking lot again to see if anyone else had come out of the diner, but no one had, and I scanned the edges of the lot as well… but I saw no one at all. Taking my keys firmly in hand, my tennis shoes padding quickly on the pavement, I hurried to my car. A few moths circled the safety lights on their tall poles, buzzing in small, lazy patterns. With relief, I slid my key in the lock, turned it, and slammed the door tightly shut.

I had watched enough horror movies to know that when the young girl gets into the car, either she drops the keys, the keys wouldn't fit, or the engine wouldn't start. Not so here. My car started with a faithful purr, and Cyndi Lauper began to burble out of the radio about girls just wanting to have fun. I felt safe, much more secure, and I flipped the headlights on and pulled out, tapping my fingers in rhythm with Cyndi.

The arc of my sweeping lights caught the figure of a man standing at the edge of the lot.

So, there *was* someone there. I hadn't been crazy. I didn't even hesitate or slow down, and I immediately determined I was *not* going to stop for him, even if he got in the way of my car. I accelerated a little bit, pulling out of the driveway onto the road, and when I turned my head to look at him again, he was gone.

Cyndi gave way to Foreigner, who wanted to know what love was, and while I thought it was a pretty good question to ask as well, I had other things on my mind. I hadn't gotten more than a brief look at the man, and I really had seen nothing more than a figure there. No features, nothing I could identify, but then why should I? He wasn't doing anything wrong. Maybe it was just a last-minute patron coming out of the diner, or perhaps a night fisherman up from the lake, hoping for a cup of coffee. Totally innocent, nothing menacing at all…

And yet, my heart told me something else. Just the mere presence of the man, whoever he had been, had caused my innate defenses to rise, and I knew he had been watching me.

But as for who he was and what he wanted... I had no idea. Troubled, I drove home, where my dear old mother was tiredly waiting up for me.

* * *

The early morning alarm burned away most of my worries, and when I staggered out to breakfast, I found my mother sitting at the kitchen table, sipping a cup of tea. She wore the same raggedy, pink robe that I had gotten her when I was twelve, and though I had threatened to throw it away, she claimed it was the most comfortable thing she owned and wouldn't hear of ever getting another.

"Mornin'," I muttered, sliding into a chair across from her. "Or is it still night?"

She chuckled. "Well, sunlight means morning, unless I'm mistaken." She folded the newspaper and pulled off her reading glasses. "Breakfast, honey?"

I shrugged. "Nothing with syrup, please."

She frowned. "Beg pardon?"

"One of Lou's specialties on Wednesdays is pancakes... all you can eat. We must have served fifty plates yesterday. My uniform reeks of syrup."

"It just makes you sweeter." She smiled wickedly at me, and I scowled.

"Puns are the lowest form of humor, Mother, especially this early in the morning." I yawned and rubbed my eyes. "It would be awesome to just go back to bed."

"Corn flakes, then?" She waggled the box at me, and I nodded weakly.

She got me a bowl and then conversationally tapped the folded newspaper with one gossipy finger. "Did you hear the news?"

"Depends on what news you're talking about," I said, pouring milk over my cornflakes. "If it wasn't discussed over pancakes yesterday, I'm betting I didn't hear about it."

"You work too much," she tsked, and settled back into her chair. She suddenly looked sad. "I wish you didn't have to kill yourself. All these hours... you're a young girl, you should be out—"

I held my hand out, shaking my head. "What news am I missing?" Her eyes brightened, like those of a little girl about to share a juicy secret.

"Well, two boys disappeared last night, over in Cassler Hill. The police found their truck in the middle of the road, still running... but nobody inside." She snapped her fingers. "*Poof.* Just gone. But they did find blood all over the seat and windshield."

"Sounds like a job for Crockett and Tubbs." *Miami Vice* was our new favorite show, and I liked to tease her about having a crush on Don Johnson.

She made a face. "Go on, poke fun, but this is creepy, Beth. Two strong college kids don't just vanish... one of them was a football player, too, a big boy. Both of them are about your age, I think, and in fact, they went to your school. Do you know them?" She pushed the paper over towards me, and then poured herself another cup of coffee.

I stared at the headline and got a chill. Two black-and-white photos grinned back at me; one of them I had never seen before, but the other looked vaguely familiar, and I realized I *had* seen him around campus... and, as I thought about it, I realized he had actually been in my Sociology 240 class.

POLICE BAFFLED OVER UNUSUAL CRIME SCENE

The mysterious disappearance of two local college students has concerned police authorities. According to police spokesman Mark Cameron, the two young men, Christopher Giorgio, 20, and Scott Partridge, 21, were reported missing late last night after Partridge's truck was found abandoned at about 10:30 last night in the middle of an isolated farmer's access road.

"While we have no bodies or suspects in custody at this time, we do believe some sort of foul play has occurred due to the condition of the truck and general crime scene," Cameron said. "A great deal of blood was recovered at the scene, so we believe these two young men may have been the victim of some crime. Why was their truck still running? Where have these two young men gone to? These are just two of the answers we seek."

Both men are juniors at a local university. Giorgio, a sophomore, is a member of the football team, and Partridge is a member of Delta Xi fraternity and sits on the Greek Council as a student advisor. According to roommates and family, neither young man had enemies or was involved in anything illegal.

If anyone has any information regarding the disappearance of these two young men, police are asking they call 1-800-COP-TIPS.

My mother sniffed. "I suspect it was drugs," she said, as if she were in the know. "People don't care what Nancy Reagan says, they're just not saying no."

"Mom," I scolded, "you don't know anything about those guys. We don't know if they were on drugs or selling drugs. We can't jump to that conclusion."

"Well, you mark my words," she said imperiously, "when it all shakes out, you'll see that cocaine was involved in some way. Smuggling or dealing or..." She frowned thoughtfully, struggling to come up with something else, but that was pretty much the extent of her drug trade knowledge, and she cleared her throat. "Or something."

I snorted. "Mother, ever since you started watching *Miami Vice*, you've been seeing the Columbian cartel behind every tree. Seriously? Do you know how far from Florida and the ocean we are?"

She rolled her eyes at me, which was her way of saying that Young People Don't Know Nearly As Much As They Think They Do. I smiled down into my cornflakes, pleased that I had outdebated her this early in the morning.

But she wasn't done yet. She cleared her throat and looked at me curiously. "You didn't say if you knew them or not. Do you? They go to your school. I hope not, them being drug dealers and all."

I ignored this valiant attempt and thoughtfully looked at the pictures again. "Maybe I've seen them around, I'm not sure."

She frowned at this, pondering, as she spread marmalade over a piece of toast. "Well, you keep your ears and eyes wide open, Elizabeth, especially when you leave the diner at night. You have your pepper spray?"

"On my keychain, ready to use the instant I see a drug dealer." I pretended to give her a little whoosh of it the minute she took a bite, so she was unable to respond. "Besides, I think I have a different theory as to what happened to those kids."

Quickly, she chewed and swallowed, leaning forward eagerly. "You do? Tell me, what is it?"

I fixed my face into a solemn mask. "Alien abduction. I've been reading about it…"

She hesitated for a moment, wondering if I was serious, and looked uncertain. "Well… aliens? Hmm, that's a little far-fetched, maybe, but I suppose anything is possible—"

I dissolved into laughter, and after a moment, she did too. She pretended to smack me with the jelly knife. She turned back to the paper, flipping through the editorials, and I perused the comics for several minutes. After a moment, she said, "Well, aliens or drug dealers, I still want you to be careful walking out to your car tonight. Not until they catch the person who did this, or until they find these boys. You come out pretty late sometimes, and it scares me, thinking about you walking across that parking lot alone."

I suddenly remembered the man I had seen last night and the uneasy feeling he had given me. Goosebumps immediately rose up on my arms, and I tried not to shiver, not wanting to give my mother any more ammunition for her to worry about. "Well, Lou watches us leave every night. He's really good about it. And you know Lou, he's an ex-Marine."

"Beth." She was looking at me very closely, her eyes searching. "What's wrong?"

"What? Nothin—"

She frowned. "I know better. Who knows you better than anyone in the world?" Clearly, our moment of frivolity was over, and her face was troubled. "And I know when you're upset, and when you're hiding something. Is everything all right at work?"

I shrugged, trying to dissemble. "Well, besides all-you-can-eat pancake Wednesday, things are—"

"Elizabeth." She held her hand up, her tone serious. "Stop. I'm not kidding."

I sighed. She was good, I had to give her that. Of course, she was right; no one knows you like your mom, but with working in the classroom and dealing with thousands of children over the years, she had double the superhero powers as the average mom. She was a walking polygraph machine, and it was nearly impossible to ever get anything past her.

But what could I really tell her, and not sound like I was crazy? That I had been getting the jimjams over nothing? That I had seen some man in the parking lot... maybe doing nothing more sinister than merely walking to his car? After careful thought, I realized he had done nothing threatening to me in any way... he hadn't made his way over to me, he hadn't spoken to me, he had barely even looked at me, for that matter. Maybe, like me, he had just been looking out across the moonlight lake, admiring the pretty view. Taking it even a step further, if either of us had any evil aspirations, it was me who had considered the notion of running him over if he had even stepped in my direction.

I shook my head. "Really, just tired. Nothing more. And I've got a paper due for my summer class in a few days, and I haven't even started it." I tried to smile while she wavered, unconvinced. "And actually, I think I do know one of those boys..." I tapped the smiling face of Christopher Giorgio. "*This* one. We had a class together last fall. It's just... unsettling to think that someone I know might be... you know. Dead."

"Young people think they are invincible and bulletproof," she mused absently. "Did you know him well?"

"No." I shook my head. "Just to nod and say hello, that's all."

She studied my face a second longer and then glanced up at the clock above my head. "All right, sweetheart. I've got to get a move on, or I'll be late." She stood and took her dishes to the sink, where she rinsed them quickly and then stacked them in the dishwasher. "I'll see you tonight."

"Don't wait up," I said automatically.

"Of course, I'll wait up," she countered. "Don't be silly." She bent and kissed my head and pulled lovingly on my ponytail. "Take care, crocogator." I smiled. This was our usual farewell, coined years ago when I, as a very young but precocious child, had tried to impress my parents with colloquialism and had fallen short. "After while, allidile."

I watched her hurry down the hall to her room, where she quickly changed clothes while I finished my breakfast in silence, and then within five minutes she was giving me a final goodbye kiss and was out the back door. I heard her car pull out of the driveway, and then I was alone in the quiet house with my thoughts. Sunlight splashed into the kitchen like gold poured from a bucket as I considered the photos again in the newspaper and reread the brief article. While I was no detective, I was pretty sure those boys wouldn't be found again.

I remembered Chris Giorgio's arrogant little swagger as he would saunter into class, his quiet little laugh, and his cutoff Adidas shirts, which highlighted his muscles. The only time he had spoken to me was once he had taken a seat ahead of me and had to pass papers to the rows behind him. "Here ya go," he had said, his big hands brushing mine, but I had been unimportant to him… his dark eyes had scanned me for a second without recognition, and I could see him searching his mind, clicking through the files in his brain. Chris Giorgio only dated and socialized with sorority girls, girls of a certain social standing, and he was familiar with all of them on campus. He wasn't able to mentally place me in a sorority, and so he immediately dismissed me as someone not on his level. I remembered sitting in class that day as I struggled with that realization and struggled even more with the idea that I had been evaluated and judged and found not worthy of even further consideration. I had wanted to stab my pen into the back of his tanned, smooth neck even as he chatted with some little idiot of a freshman next to him, a giggling little creature with a side ponytail, proudly displaying her Alpha Phi letters on her chest.

They had walked out together at the end of class, and I had thought, *I hope he says, "Here ya go!" as he jumps on Little Miss Alpha Phi tonight… hope he crushes her with his stupid football self, and in the midst of passion, pulls that stupid ponytail right off of her head.*

And now he was probably dead, along with his buddy Partridge, whom I didn't know at all. What had they been doing on that mostly deserted road, and what had happened to them? Why was there blood found in the truck but no bodies?

Lots of answers, but no questions. As far as I was concerned, it was only idle speculation; it didn't really affect me personally, and I had far more pressing matters. I had my summer school class in an hour, and from there I would go directly to the diner, where I would work a shift and a half. At least I would be able to pick up both the lunch crowd and the dinner crowd, so hopefully, my tips would amount to something. Another full day.

I glanced at the pictures a final time and then picked up the newspaper and put it into the recycling bin by the stove. It didn't affect me at all.

I had never been so wrong.

III
CHAPTER

1864

The fourth day bloomed hot and muggy. In the tents, where the air hardly moved and the stench had begun to set in from the contaminated wounds, the patients who were lucid and coherent were four shades of miserable. Water was warm and scarce, food was dry and scarce, and death was plentiful. Charlie had been able to prop himself up on his good elbow and take a little food, the first he had eaten since the battle. It was only a biscuit: dry, tasteless, and full of weevils. But it was something.

For the first time, he was able to get a good look at his surroundings. As he munched, chewed, and flicked weevils onto the floor, he saw that the cots on either side of his were empty. Blood and urine stained, they both had had at least one occupant in his brief tenure, but he couldn't remember any specific details—not names, not hometowns, not wounds or times of death. It was all a void to him. Men had simply come in, broken and damaged beyond repair, and then they had died.

There was little activity in the tent. Most of the patients were asleep, snoring, or moaning in pain. At the other end of the tent, a male nurse was quietly copying a letter for the Parkinson boy. A moth bounced off the top of the tent, making tiny pap-pat-pat noises against the canvas. Charlie tracked it with his eyes, and as he was growing sleepy again, he looked over to see Doctor Crane standing in the shadows. His back was turned to Charlie, and he was making slurping noises as he drank. Charlie could see the doctor's head thrown back; he could see his raised arms. Water must not be scarce for him, he thought.

And then the doctor seemed to feel someone was watching him. He stiffened just the smallest bit, as if caught in a private act, and half-turned to see whose eyes had trapped him. As he did, the bloody bandage he had been sucking on dropped to the floor, and Charlie gasped.

Doctor Crane smiled thinly at Charlie, who lay frozen with disgust and fear. The doctor's eyes were the darkest blue, cold and deep. His black hair was slicked back off his head and fragrant with pomade, and the thinnest line of blood snaked down the side of his mouth. As Charlie watched, the doctor's tongue flicked out and caught the trickle, and then flicked back in, quick.

Doctor Crane tipped Charlie an intimate wink. "A Georgian boy," he said thoughtfully. "Thick, sweet... you can always tell, you know. Some of them have that bitter blood, like old pecans, but every now and then you get one who was raised on fruits. Makes the blood so much sweeter." He grinned, showing an exceptionally large pair of incisors, dark with old blood. He took several quiet steps, as silent as a shadow, and stood at the foot of Charlie's cot. Charlie felt his breath coming in short, panicked gasps as Crane's eyes flickered on his stump; the blue eyes widened in interest, and without taking his eyes off of Charlie, Crane asked quietly, "And where did you say you were from, friend?"

1985

Looking back on that faraway summer, I would come to remember it as a time when the nights seemed to go on forever and the days didn't last long enough.

When I arrived at the diner just before my shift, with barely enough time to change into my uniform—khaki shorts and a white Lou's Diner tee shirt; Lou liked to keep it simple, thank God—I found the topic of conversation was the murders. And it wasn't just the staff, either, that was discussing last night's events… as I moved from table to table, taking orders and refilling iced tea glasses, it seemed to be on everyone's mind.

Opinions ran the gambit from absurd to plausible. Some, like my mother, opted for the dramatic and immediately assumed the murders were drug-related. Rumors of Partridge selling pills and marijuana from his fraternity house and that he had failed to pay his supplier seemed to be the most common; other stories involved betting, or most salaciously, that the two had been lovers and it was a murder-suicide pact. This last one caused quite the stir. People love to believe the worst, and though there was not a shred of proof to back up such a claim, it was the one that was most circulated… albeit quietly.

Then there were the more bizarre theories. Dawnette, the hostess at Lou's, was just positive they had been abducted by a cult and taken out into the fields and sacrificed in some satanic or pagan sacrifice, while Miguel, one of the busboys, offered the theory that something called a chupacabra had bounded out of the trees and had carried them off. I wasn't exactly sure what a chupacabra was, but Miguel, who hailed from southern Texas, looked serious and quite upset about it. "It's like a Mexican devil," he explained, "kind of a monster that kills chickens and pigs and small children."

I blinked at him. "But the guys that were killed weren't chickens or goats or small children."

He waved me on as a disbeliever. "It doesn't matter. Their deaths sound just like a chupacabra attack."

I looked at him disgustedly. "Miguel, no one knows if they're even dead yet. All that's been found is their truck. They're just missing at this point."

"No, no." His dark eyes were very round, very intense. "I know they are dead. This is a chupacabra, you mark my words." He made the sign of the cross quickly. "When I was a little boy, my grandfather told me that one had attacked his farm. He said it had killed all of his chickens and his sheep. He saw it running from the barn with a dead lamb in his mouth."

I put some lemon slices into a little bowl and arranged it on my tray. "And just what does a chupacabra look like?"

He frowned thoughtfully. "Well... a rat-dog creature. With really long teeth." He scratched his chin. "And it also walks upright, like a man." I blinked at him, not sure whether or not it would hurt his feelings outright if I burst into laughter, and he continued, "Remember, it is a diablo, a devil. Claws, a tail—"

"Miguel." I hefted my tray. "I've lived here all my life, and I've never seen anything like that around here. I think the first time any creature like that comes out of the woods, some farmer is gonna blow it away with his shotgun and mount its head on the wall."

He firmed his chin up and looked offended. "Just because you haven't seen it doesn't mean it doesn't exist," he said stubbornly, and just then I saw Dawnette signal to us that she was taking a party to their table, and I patted him on the arm.

"I'll keep an eye out for your rat-dog man," I assured him, and then looked closer at the group Dawnette was seating, and I grimaced.

I had seen this group of boys come in before, a gang of about five or six of them. None of them was local... they were of college age, but they worked for the county, and had been hired with federal grant money to repair and repaint some of the historical houses in the area. They all wore blue and white tee shirts with the words GREAT PAINTING COMPANY printed on them, with baseball caps usually turned backwards. From listening to snatches of their conversation, I knew they had all rented an older home on the opposite end of the lake, in one of the coves, and the parties that had already been held there had been of epic proportions.

They were loud and obnoxious, and they usually took their lunch—and sometimes dinner—at Lou's because the food was better than fast food, and closer than the only McDonald's, which was out on the highway. Yesterday they had killed us at All You Can Eat Pancakes; even Lou had looked on in weary disbelief as this little band had kept calling for plate after plate. "Make sure they're actually eating them and not putting them in baggies for later," he had side-whispered to me, and I had assured him they indeed were. "Then they ain't human, they're machines," he had sighed, pouring more onto the griddle, and I had weakly laughed and taken more out for them.

None of us liked to serve them, though the first day they had come in, Paulina, the head waitress, had insinuated herself into my section with a warning glance at the rest of us and made a hasty advance forward in their direction. She was thirty-ish and acted like she was twenty-ish, and her flirtatious ways usually garnered not only tips but often relationships—or at least one-night encounters. With a mountain of blond, teased-up hair that would do justice to any Hair Band of the Day, she passed out their menus, smacked her gum with lusty promise, and chatted and flirted with them—only to be left with about thirty-five cents in tips when they left.

"You can serve 'em next time," she had grumbled to me, and I knew that she was not only disgusted by their tipping, but also because none of them had asked for her phone number.

I grabbed up a stack of menus and silverware and walked over to their table, ready to pour a glass of water down the neck of the first one who grabbed my butt.

"Well, we got something new on the menu," one of the boys cawed when I came over to their table. Several of them snorted and nudged each other, as boys will do in a group, but the handsome one with gray eyes just looked at me almost apologetically and smiled.

"Don't mind him, we'll push him off a ladder later, I promise," he stage-whispered, and I noticed how broad his shoulders were. The early afternoon sun glinted off of the stubbly whiskers on his chin, and I saw that he had paint splatters across his tanned forearms. He noticed me looking and grinned.

"Continental white."

"What?" I blinked.

He pointed to one of the dabs on his shirt. "Continental white. That's the color of the paint. We're using it on the old courthouse." One of the boys snorted again, and I heard the word "white." I must have blushed, but the boy with the gray eyes shot his friends a warning look, and they shut up.

"I'm Bobby Barnham, Housepainter Extraordinaire," he said confidently, and glanced at my nametag, waiting for the return introduction.

"And you are...?"

I slapped a menu down in front of him, trying to not look at his beautiful eyes. "I'm unimpressed *and* uninterested," I snapped, and while his friends clapped their approval and hooted with glee, I spun dramatically around and flounced off.

But the truth of the matter was... I was lying.

* * *

He was waiting for me after work.

It had been a busy shift. Flushed with victory, two softball teams had come rolling in after the dinner hour, ordering pitcher after pitcher of beer and more than enough nachos and pizzas to feed a small town. The jukebox was continually thumping, and the mood was light and fun; Paulina got more than a dozen phone numbers scribbled on napkins, which put her in a jolly mood, and even Miguel's dour temper about the chupacabra seemed to lift. I fended off two drunken marriage proposals, several more offers of a more obscene nature, and was given tickets to the next home game as long as I promised to sit in the dugout. The more the beer flowed, the better the tips were, and by the end of the night, I had made nearly forty bucks.

We finally pushed the ball players out the door after they gave us a final, drunken chorus of *We Are the World*, and I helped Lou with the cleanup while Paulina supervised the prep for the next day. By the time we were finished, it was well after midnight. I was exhausted, my uniform was splashed with beer and ranch sauce, and as I did a quick wash up, I suddenly remembered the murdered boys and my mother's worries from earlier... and also that of Miguel. Both of them were people I respected, but the idea of a rat-devil that walked on two legs like a man seemed hard to swallow. While rationally I couldn't conceive of such a thing, Miguel's simple belief seemed a whole lot more plausible now that the sun had gone down.

Just because you haven't seen it doesn't mean it doesn't exist

"Are you ready to leave?"

I nearly jumped out of my skin, and whirled around, frantically groping in my purse for my pepper spray. It was only Lou standing against the bar, a towel slung over his shoulder, regarding me tiredly. "You all right?"

I took a deep breath. "Of course. You just startled me."

He smiled. "Sorry about that. You're probably half-deaf anyway. Those boys sure had that jukebox jumping tonight, didn't they? I don't know how they didn't wear it out." He leaned over and straightened a pair of salt and pepper shakers.

Lou was in his early sixties, a short, round little man who still retained not only his Marine discipline but his Marine haircut. His white shirt under his apron was always crisp and straight, and his kitchen was spotless to a fault. I liked him a lot... his stories were funny, and he had been flexible with my summer school schedule, always asking about my homework and health like a surrogate father. I didn't know much about his history. There were rumors that he had an Asian wife and daughter back in California, but he had never spoken of them to me, and I had never asked. This place was his retirement, an inheritance from an elderly aunt, and in the five years he had been here, he had remodeled and revitalized the place, making it one of the nicest little eateries on the lake.

I decided to tease him a little. "You don't like that kind of music?"

He made a face. "That ain't music. All the boys in those rock bands today wear more makeup than a Chicago whore—'scuse my language." He sighed. "You young kids don't know what good rock and roll music is. None of that sissy stuff in my day. We had music you could sink your teeth into." He thought for a second. "Course, I do like Van Halen. They're pretty solid. And that ol' black girl with the legs... she's pretty good too."

"Tina Turner?"

He nodded. "Listened to Casey Kasem the other day... he says she was beat up by her husband. You think that's true?"

I shrugged. This was typical of one of our conversations, all twisting and meandering. Lou was often all over the map, especially when he was tired or had had a few beers at the end of the night. We had hashed over some pretty odd things after hours, everything from politics to movies to even a few stories about his time in Vietnam that left me shaky inside. Usually, Miguel would sit with us, but tonight he had gone home, and frankly, I was feeling pretty weary as well. Lou must have seen it in my eyes, because he motioned with his head towards the door. "Come on, Miss Beth. It's late, and you've put in a full day. I'll watch you walk to your car."

When he opened the back door, the heat of the night struck us full force, and he switched on the back lot lights. Remembering my mother's advice, I reached into my purse and found my pepper spray, curling it in my palm to have it ready, but for some reason, not really wanting Lou to see it. "G'night," I said bravely, glancing out into the night.

The walk to my car seemed a thousand miles, and I paused.

Lou noticed my hesitation. "Beth, you all right?"

I swallowed, struggling with a quick cover story. "Oh yes. I was just trying to remember if I locked the cooler."

He shrugged. "Well, I'll check it before I leave." He looked at me closely. "Is that all?"

"Yes." I nodded my head, smiling weakly. "I'll see you tomorrow."

Taking a deep breath, I started off briskly across the pavement. The odd feeling of being observed was not with me this evening, but I still didn't tarry, and my white Nikes whispered across the concrete. Overhead, a night bird—possibly a bat—swooped down at my head and flapped in the dark before disappearing again. Its sudden presence startled me... I choked back a scream, and my heart fluttered.

I hated this, *hated* this interminable walk in the dark. All the tips in the world weren't worth these few moments of terror. Not for the first time did I resolve to ask Lou to change my schedule to breakfast and lunch to avoid this nighttime business... it would mean fewer tips; of course, breakfast patrons *never* tipped as well as supper patrons, probably because there was no beer served at breakfast, but that was all right, I would get by.

A car suddenly turned into the parking lot and headed towards me. I froze, hearing the soft puff of its engine as it got closer; from its interior, I could hear the faint thumping sounds of Corey Hart, explaining that he wore his sunglasses at night. *Damn, how appropriate*, I thought in my panic, and just as I turned to bolt back to the safety of the diner, the car—I saw now it was a dark-colored Jeep—did a fancy little turn, and I saw the driver.

It was him, the boy from the painting crew—Bobby Barnham—and if I had had a baseball bat in my hand, I would have busted out his lights and then hit him over the head. We stared at each other in the gloom, and I still wasn't sure if I had reason to be afraid or not.

"Hey!" I heard Lou shout from behind me. "What in the hell—Beth! You all right?!"

"Evening," Bobby said, idling his motor. He grinned at me over the edge of the door. "What's a nice girl like you doing in a place like this?"

"That's the best you can do?" I managed, finding my breath. I gaped at him, looking at his goofy, handsome smile and deciding that while he probably wasn't dangerous, he was at the very least obnoxious. I turned back to see Lou heading in our direction at a fat man's gallop, and I held a hand up, waving him off. "It's all right, it's just the idiot from the painting crew. They were in earlier."

"Wow," Bobby said, looking shocked. "*That* hurt."

"Shut up," I said fiercely. "I first thought you were a chupacabra."

Bobby frowned. "Isn't that one of those Mexican monsters that eat chickens?" I nodded briefly, and he chuckled to himself. "And the hits just keep coming..."

Lou pulled up short, just outside the edge of the Jeep's headlights. I saw that he had picked up the axe handle he kept at the back door, in case of trouble. He had another one just like it under the bar, and I suspected he had others squirreled around the diner as well, in case anyone ever got out of hand... one thing about Lou was that he liked to be prepared. "Beth, you all right?"

I was still trying to catch my breath and trying desperately not to appear like the damsel in distress from some bad gothic novel. "I'm fine."

Lou pointed the axe handle at Bobby. "You got business here? Why are you snooping around my parking lot after hours?"

Bobby looked momentarily worried... Lou was using his best military voice, and it sounded authoritative and no nonsense. He blinked a few times. "I'm not snooping around," he struggled. "I came to... pay Beth here a tip."

"A tip?" I looked confused, and Lou snorted.

"Well, yes." Bobby found his charming grin again, and absently he swatted at a mosquito. "I don't believe I tipped you earlier, when the boys and I were here."

"You and the boys never do, according to my hostess," Lou growled. "From what I hear, you all are decidedly cheap, and you all do it on purpose."

Bobby nodded embarrassedly. "A situation I'm here to correct." He reached into his pocket and dug out a five-dollar bill. He handed it through the window to me, but I hadn't taken it yet, watching him closely. "I felt bad about it, so I came back here to fix things up." He noticed my hesitation, and said, "Go on. It's the best a chupacabra can do for the night."

"A what?" Lou leaned forward. "Boy, you on drugs?"

Bobby actually looked offended. "Course not." He made a face. "Damn, I'm trying to make a romantic gesture here, and you're spoiling it."

Lou and I exchanged a look, and I couldn't believe my ears. "*Romantic?*" I repeated.

Bobby shrugged. "Well, I'm not very good at this, I guess." He reached down next to him and pulled up a bouquet of flowers—the kind that are easily bought at the grocery store, wrapped in cheap cellophane and faded from sitting in a bucket of water in the heat.

And the first flowers anyone had ever brought me. My heart tugged at the sight.

"These are for you," he said, handing them to me. "Sorry for us being rude, and all. I guess I was an ass."

"You still are," Lou muttered under his breath.

I looked at the bouquet. Daisies, some greenery, and a few lilies. Wilted and tired, nothing expensive. And yet somehow it was undeniably sweet and genuine, and I swallowed hard and gave a shaky little laugh. "Well, thank you, I guess."

"I promise I'll be better tomorrow, and my friends will too," Bobby promised. "Any of them that get out of line, well, they'll answer to me." His voice was so firm that there was no doubt he meant what he said. Lou made a sound in his throat, but I couldn't tell if he was pleased or not at Bobby's determination.

We stood there awkwardly for another long moment before any of us spoke.

Lou glanced over at me, probably to see how I was reacting to any of this, and he cleared his throat. "Well, the diner's closed for the night," he finally said. "And Beth here is heading home." He looked at me to make sure that I was, and then glared back at Bobby. "So, all right, you did your bad Romeo impression. You better go on now."

Bobby grinned. "Yes sir. What's for breakfast in the morning?"

Lou blinked a little. "Whatever you want, I reckon."

"Well, I'll take two eggs—fried hard, no drippy yolks—and sausage links." He flicked his gaze at me; I know he had seen the pepper spray clutched in my hand as I held the flowers, and amazingly, he winked at me, apparently not at all fazed that he had nearly gotten whooshed—a wink so quick that I don't think Lou caught it. "And toast with marmalade. But only if I sit in Beth's section."

"I'm not scheduled for breakfast… I have a morning class." I noted his look of disappointment, and to my amazement, I heard myself say, "But I'm on at lunch."

"Lunch it is." He looked over at Lou. "Cancel that last order. I'll have tuna salad on wheat, onion rings, and ice tea."

"I'll make a note of it," Lou said sarcastically. "Good night," and Bobby contented himself by cockily tipping his hat at us. We stepped back as he put his Jeep in gear, and he roared off into the night. At the end of the drive, he gave a friendly toot of his horn; we heard his engine fade away. I smiled.

Lou harrumphed. "You're not gonna let a bouquet of cheap flowers and a fast tongue swoop you off your feet, are you?"

I shook my head. "No, no, of course not. Don't be silly." I picked a dead petal off a daisy and admired the rest of my flowers. "Shut up, Lou."

"Oh hell." He followed me to my car and held the door for me. "Good night, Beth."

"Night, Lou." I wasn't so loopy that I didn't forget to lock my car. I waved at him through the closed window, and not worrying about chupacabras or dead fraternity boys, I drove home with a smile pasted on my face.

IV
CHAPTER

1864

One of the orderlies was an old man named Huffman. He had a crooked back and long swinging arms but was strong and tough. He had spent most of his life on a tobacco farm in southern Alabama. He wasn't actually an overseer, definitely not a landowner, but still above the slaves he worked alongside. The army hadn't wanted him because of his age and deformity, but he still had tagged along behind Lee's army and had insinuated himself in the hospital. He held patients down when the doctors commenced cutting, wheeled carts full of dismembered arms and legs out to the large mass graves; he performed these tasks with the same cheerful eagerness that he displayed when he wrote letters home for the boys or swapped stories with recovering patients.

The boys all liked him. They held him with no malice over their missing body parts, and as he was a rabid Confederate, he was also popular with the officers. He was always friendly, always available, and usually sober, and his face was the last smile that many of the boys saw.

"Tell me about Doctor Crane." Charlie struggled to sit up, but the pain made him dizzy, and he fell back against the cot. Huffman made a face at the effort, and patted Charlie on his good arm. "Doggone, that hurts."

"Not surprised. You lost a hoof... yer balance is all off, not to mention yer painin'. How is the pain, by the way?"

"Awful," Charlie admitted but wasn't going to be deterred. "About Doctor Crane..."

Huffman shrugged. "Outta N'awlins, I think. One of them ol' distinguished Creole families, that's got more money than sense. Good doctor, though. He can take off a leg—" he snapped his fingers, "just like that."

"Do you like him?"

Huffman lifted his bushy eyebrows. "Do I like him? That don't matter, do it? Do I respec' him? Yep. Is he a good doctor? Yep. That's what's important, boy, not whether or not I like him. He saved your arm, you know."

Charlie was nastily startled. "What?"

"You didn't know?" Huffman nodded. "He sure did. You came in that day with your arm all mangled, like it's been through a sausage maker. Doc took one look at that an' said, 'This boy will not lose his arm, just his hand.' Sure did."

Charlie digested this information, confusion dancing in his mind. He had spent a sleepless night, despite the heavy whiskey, trying to process what he thought he had seen. Had he seen Doctor Crane sucking on a bandage? He wasn't sure. After looking at other doctors in the hospital sniffing bandages for gangrene, all of them did it—the doctors, the nurses, the attendants—and he was even less certain. There was a certain smell of corruption—a horrible, nasty, rotten smell that was like no other—that the doctors had learned to identify early on.

And if Huffman gave his approval to Sebastian Crane...

"One more thing," Charlie said slowly, thinking this over and feeling better with all of this, "Have you noticed anything peculiar about Doc?"

"Peculiar?" Now there was a note of caution in Huffman's voice. "How so, peculiar?"

Charlie allowed himself to blush. "Well, I don't know. Peculiar, maybe?"

"Now look here." Huffman pointed to him with one horny forefinger. "Everybody's got his ways, the doctor included. I don't know what peculiar ways you're talkin' about, but I don't think I want to hear nothin' bad about the doctor. He not only saved yore life, he's saved a bunch of others. Salt of the earth, he is."

Salt of the earth. Charlie looked thoughtfully down at his bandaged arm, and then back up at Huffman. All right, perhaps he had it all wrong. Maybe through some combination of fear, pain and fever, he had experienced some wicked, tortured dreams.

Huffman was staring back at him worriedly and then said quickly, "It looks like that wound is seeping a little bit. We'll be sure to get it changed before dark, don't worry."

There was something in his voice that sharpened Charlie's senses, and he frowned slightly. Indeed, the bandage was a rosy pink from the bleeding, but it didn't look all that excessive to him. Still, Huffman seemed to be bothered by it, and worriedly, he asked, "Do you think it needs it?"

Huffman nodded gravely. "Absolutely. It would be a real shame if Doctor Crane comes in tonight and sees you bleeding like that..."

Charlie stared at him, not sure what to say.

"In fact," Huffman observed thoughtfully, "There's no telling what Doctor Crane might do, if he sees you bleeding like that..."

1985

Several television news teams were set up on campus the next day and stationed at various spots around the university. I was surprised when I saw them, confused as to why they were there, but then I heard someone talking about the missing boys, and it was pretty clear what the reporters were after. They were interviewing students on their way to class, but since everyone seemed stunned and shocked at the news—things like this just didn't happen in our little college town—no one seemed all that willing to go on camera and offer an opinion on the situation.

Still, the odd circumstances of the crime had caught the attention of the media, and they were anxious to follow up on every lead. One crew had set up a location outside the Delta Xi house, attempting to talk to everyone who came and went, but apparently someone higher up in the organization had cautioned the brothers not to talk without a lawyer or a representative, so the reporters had little luck there and branched out to other spots on campus.

One reporter and his cameraman stood outside the campus bookstore and tried to speak to people as they came out of the store, while two others stood at opposite ends of the student center and competed for attention. As best I could tell, as I took alternate routes to avoid the media, no one really seemed comfortable talking to them, except for the inevitable few who are always impressed by a television camera. The reporters interviewed a few giggly sorority girls who knew absolutely nothing but liked the idea of being on camera. They were full of drama, with nothing to say, but their scared pretty faces looked good on television.

There was other activity as well. Every type of search operation was conducted, with volunteers going out in organized groups and search parties every hour on the hour. Boy Scouts, together with other civic groups as well as the National Guard, were called in to search, but nothing—not even a trace or a hint of a trace was ever found, even using the cadaver dogs. The lake was searched as thoroughly as possible, but as Lou pointed out, no one knew how deep it was, and so that avenue was closed. "Besides, anyone wanting to get rid of a body in the summertime merely has to throw it into a body of water where there's wildlife… fish, crawdads, turtles will do the rest. If they're in the lake, they ain't gonna be found."

Both boys' parents also descended on campus, conducting interviews, and pleading in front of the cameras for any sort of information that would lead them to their boys, and it was them I felt most sorry for. Chris Giorgio's mom, in particular, was especially heart-wrenching. She was a well-spoken woman with pain-filled eyes who showed baby pictures of her son to the cameras, crying and begging for anyone with information to come forward. "Just any little piece of information would help," she said, standing at the top of the steps in front of the student center. "Chris, if you're out there, we love you, Daddy and I are waiting—waiting for you to come home to us…" But if Chris was out there, he was apparently unable to contact her, because her desperate pleas went unanswered.

Within twenty-four hours of searching, posters and pictures of the two boys were posted on every available bulletin board, wall, street corner, and window on campus and in town. Scott Partridge's fraternity brothers apparently got permission to pass out flyers at intersections and paste flyers on windows, and they turned out in full force, traveling in groups and passing out posters and handouts with the missing boys' faces on them.

I got three such flyers just walking across campus, and found another stuck under my windshield wipers on my car in the student parking lot. We were swamped and inundated with reporters, pictures, parents, and volunteers, but of the missing boys themselves—nothing, not even a clue of their whereabouts.

The police were stymied and frustrated, and from their terse comments to the press, it was apparent that they had no clue as to what had happened. The blood in the car was analyzed and the lab determined that it belonged to both boys, but other than that, little was known about what had happened that night. There seemed to be little sign of struggle—no broken glass, no obvious weapon, no torn or ripped clothing. There were no identifying fingerprints, either on the car interior or on the door handles, that amounted to anything, and nothing was found in the car that would indicate why the boys had been out on the lonely access road. No beer cans, no pornography, no stolen property... absolutely *nothing* to indicate that they had been involved in anything illegal or shady. A thorough search turned up no drugs, paraphernalia, or even residue, anywhere on the scene. With the total lack of anything to go on, the police's official line turned from "We're working on several possible leads and theories," to a very bleak, almost pleading, "If anyone has any information, we are asking you to contact our department. You don't even have to give us your name."

The day after I had received my rare gift of flowers, I showed up to work earlier than usual. As I was clocking in, I noticed Paulina sitting in Lou's cramped little office, watching her soap opera while she smoked a cigarette and drained a diet pop; we weren't friends but we were friendly, and as I put my little card back into its slot, she gave a low, teasing wolf whistle.

"Well, well, lookee you," she said, pointing towards me with one red taloned finger. "You did something different with your hair, didn't you?"

I blushed but managed to shrug noncommittally. "Oh, I just pulled it back, that's all. It's cooler off my neck."

"Uh huh." She peered at me through a cloud of blue smoke. "And you're wearing makeup... mascara, and you *never* wear mascara. Who are you trying to impress?"

"Oh nobody, geez." I stepped back from the smoke. "Lou doesn't like you smoking in here."

She made a nasty face, but stubbed her cigarette out in a little plastic ashtray and shoved it into a desk drawer. Taking a can of air freshener out of the same drawer, she spritzed the room a few times... now the smoke smelled like orange blossoms, and I coughed. "Better?"

"Not much." I tied my apron around me. "Well, nice talking to you Paulina—"

"Not so fast." She popped a piece of gum into her mouth. "You never said why you're looking so hot today, Missy."

"Nope, I didn't." I steadied her with a look. Paulina had made it plain that she didn't like the summer help, so most of the girls avoided her as much as possible. Some thought that she was mad because we were poaching on her territory, and she hated to share the tips, but I thought it was deeper than that. At the end of the summer, most of us would go back to school and various futures and leave her there, stuck in a waitressing job. She was jealous of us. She didn't exactly hate us; she hated not *being* us, though this was a theory I had yet to advance to anyone.

She studied me for a second. "Well, if you're looking to get on television because all of those reporters are here, I think you're sick. What's wrong with you?"

I stared at her. "What are you talking about?"

She smiled smugly. "Well, if it's not a man, I guess you're looking to be on television. What a story, huh? Pretty local waitress gets her big break during an interview for Double Murder in Podunk, Indiana. Let's face it, honey, Brooke Shields you *ain't*."

I didn't know how to even respond to such jealous craziness, and I could only blink at her. I couldn't decide if she was serious or not, and then I decided I didn't care. I glanced at my watch, pretending great impatience, and pushed past her. She smiled triumphantly to herself, but let me pass, and as I reached the doorknob, I paused and looked back at her.

"Thanks for the advice, Paulina." I gazed at her, a vision in teased-up, bleached rocker hair, and smiled. "And speaking of television… very David Lee Roth of you, eh? Might as well jump." She began to splutter, and before she could muster a reply, I laughed mockingly and pushed past her.

The diner was busy, and as I threaded my way through the tables to the waitress station, I kept an eye out for Bobby and the painting crew. It wasn't that big of a place, and a quick scan told me they weren't in yet. Still, there was a local news crew from WVIM in the corner and a group of middle-aged summer people, pink and sunburned from a day on the lake. Luckily, they were in my section and not the news crew—I really didn't want to serve them, and besides the reporter, a local beauty named Savannah Parker, had a reputation for being bloodthirsty and persistent. I really had no desire to meet her or risk being on camera. I could well imagine her getting her cameraman to turn the camera on me for an impromptu, ambush interview, and so I grabbed a stack of menus and I headed in the direction of the summer people.

They were a jolly group, three women and a man, and since the women all had a similar physical likeness, I assumed they were related somehow. They smelled of lotion and were brightly dressed in colorful tee shirts and flip flops, and they sounded like a tree full of sparrows as I approached their table. I smiled. They were the kind of customers I liked, on vacation and easygoing, and I was pretty sure their demands would be few. They would be at least an amusing diversion until—*if*—Bobby Barnham showed up.

Of course, they were full of idle gossip about the missing boys. They seemed to be quite interested in the whole situation. "We're from a little town down near Kentucky, a little farming community," one of the women told me. She fanned her flushed, excited face with a menu while she popped an onion ring into her mouth. "Nothing like this *ever* happens where we're from!"

Her sister grappled in the basket for an onion ring as well, but came up with a cheese stick instead. Happily, she dunked it into the marinara sauce and swabbed it around. "Reporters everywhere, police barricades, search parties! And we're right in the middle of all of it! We're not used to such excitement." She pushed her pink sunglasses back on top of her head and looked at me, as if I were the one responsible for all of this.

"Well, we're not either," I agreed, refilling tea glasses. "This is usually a quiet little town. Nothing like this has ever happened in my remembrance."

The first woman nodded. "We know. We come here every summer—Phyllis here," and she pointed to the third woman, "has a cabin on the opposite side of the lake. We come for a few weeks, go antiquing and boating, usually until the middle of July or so." She shivered deliciously. "Now, we might go back early, don't you think?"

"Oh no!" The woman named Phyllis shook her head vehemently. "Absolutely not! We should stay! How often do we get to experience something like this!" She waved a fork around her. "Just think, one of these people, in this very diner, might be a killer! Doesn't it just give you chills?!"

They all agreed that it did, even the man, and out of the corner of my eye, I saw Bobby and his crew come in. My heart soared. He wore a tee shirt with the sleeves cut off and a Yankees cap on backwards; sunglasses hung on a lanyard around his neck. I could tell he was looking for me as he casually scanned the diner, and when he found me, his face lit up and he raised a finger at me in greeting.

Making sure my summer people were all right for the moment, I casually made my way to his table; Dawnette was seating them, and I saw that it was a smaller party than usual, just Bobby and only two of his regular cowboys. Dawnette looked at me knowingly and gave me a wink as I walked by her, but I paid her little attention. "They're ready for you," she giggled, and I shot her a dirty look. She was a high school senior whose wardrobe looked like it had been pulled from Madonna's back closet; lots of rubber bracelets and crosses, and lacy fingerless gloves. We had little in common, and I had no time for her speculative insinuations.

Bobby smiled up at me as I served them their water and pointed out today's specials... dear Lord, his eyes were so expressive, bluish gray like a spring day, and full of life and energy. "We're a little late today," he apologized. "The police had Cooper Street blocked off, so we had to go around the long way."

"Cooper Street?" I frowned thoughtfully, and then nodded in understanding. Cooper Street, also known as Fraternity Row, was no doubt a center of activity for both the police and media today. I didn't want to think about it.

"Totally blocked off." He shrugged, dismissing it. "Hey, do you remember my order? I told you last night—"

"Tuna fish on wheat, onion rings, and ice tea." I stared at him coolly, and he blinked in surprise.

"Wow. I'm impressed." He looked around him, his eyes widening in surprise as he recognized Savannah Parker. "Isn't she the reporter?" His friends craned their necks to get a better look, and I nodded.

"It is. She's looking for people to interview, but I'd be careful. She has sort of a reputation."

One of Bobby's friends laughed. "Well, good, so do I. We should talk." There was some laughter, though Bobby flashed him a warning look; apparently, he had told them to be on their best behavior, as he had promised, and now I realized why there were only two other guys with him instead of his usual posse. He had weeded through them and brought the two who he thought would be the least offensive. Of course, it was *also* true that he could have come alone, but had wanted moral support and hadn't wanted to come alone. I wasn't sure if I should be flattered or worried that he considered me someone from whom he needed reinforcement.

Before I could fully answer, the sorority of summer people signaled for my attention, and I had to excuse myself to go see to them. One of them needed more salad dressing while another needed to change her order, and I had to listen to a whole new set of worries and theories they offered about the missing boys.

"You know," one of them said casually, pointing with her fork to the eldest of the trio, "If the police *really* want to know what happened, they should just talk to Harriet here."

"Oooh, stop!" Harriet insisted, while the others at the table nodded and chirped in agreement. She looked flushed and flattered and I raised my eyebrows in polite confusion.

"Harriet is a psychic!" The man confided in me. He beamed over at her proudly. "She can predict things before they happen, and whenever I go out to the horse tracks, I always let Harriet look over the names of the horses first. She tells me which ones to bet on, and I usually come home a little richer."

"Not always!" Harriet demurred. "Maybe it's just luck."

"Luck!" The man looked horrified. "Gosh, no, it's not luck!" He looked at me. "I tell you, my wife's sister is a true miracle! Just last year, before the weather turned cold, she said to me, 'Harold, you better get your furnace checked, because I'm getting one of my feelings.' Well, I had just won a hundred dollars at the races a week before because of one of her feelings, so I called the furnace company right away to come out and have a look, and they said, yep, there was a problem. Something was clogged or something, or there was a backup or…" he shrugged. "Well, *something* wasn't right; I'm not sure what. But anyway, the repairman said if we had turned it on, carbon monoxide would have gone through our house and killed us in our sleep!"

He tapped his fork on the plate and shuddered for emphasis, while the others looked suitably impressed. Harriet waved him on, but she looked pleased with herself, and I had the feeling this was an oft told story in the family.

I didn't know what to say, and wanted to get back to Bobby's table, but I made all the appropriate noises of admiration. "That really is amazing!" I managed. "That must come in handy when you lose your car keys."

Phyllis nodded enthusiastically. "We tell her she should open a little shop or something and do readings… there's just an amazing interest in this sort of thing, you know. When we were on vacation last year, we drove through an artsy little village that had several psychic shops…

Tarot cards, crystals, books and such." She looked at me, suddenly inspired. "I know, Harriet could do a reading on you!"

"Oh, no," I said, keeping my smile fixed on my face. "I don't think—"

"She'd do it for free, don't worry," the man promised. "And it's just for fun. Don't you believe in this sort of thing?"

I looked at their little group, four plump faces smiling back at me, waiting for an answer. I realized it didn't matter what I believed; it mattered what they believed, and I didn't want to lose a tip, or worse yet, anger them and have them complain to Lou about bad service. Weakly, I nodded in agreement.

"Well, to quote Shakespeare, I guess there are more things in Heaven and Earth than are dreamt of in philosophy," I said, and shrugged. "Or something like that. That's pretty close, I think."

They laughed with me, or maybe *at* me, and Harriet suddenly said, "Well, I can maybe have a look at her and see if I get a feeling or a vibe or something." She shrugged. "I mean, if she wants me to, that is."

"Of course, she does," Phyllis answered. She reached for my hand... charm bracelets on her fat wrist jangled musically, and I suddenly felt a moment of panic. She glanced at my nametag, confirming my name. "It's all fun, you know. Come on, Beth, let's see what Harriet can predict for you!" I glanced around me, hoping that Dawnette or Miguel were close by, hopefully needing something that would pull me away from here, but the place was nearly full with the lunchtime crowd, and they were busy with

their own tables. I sighed.

"All right," I surrendered, offering my hand. "Let's see if she sees someone tall, blond, handsome and covered in white paint is in my future." Harriet assumed the attitude of modest authority as she beamed expectantly at me. "Now, I'm the first to admit my powers of divination are puny compared to others," she tittered. "I'm no Oracle of Delphi, so don't expect too much."

"Don't believe a word of it," the third sister, whose name I had yet to catch, countered. "Harriet is a wonder, you'll see."

Harriet took my hand and stroked the back of it thoughtfully. I wasn't sure if she was searching for vibes or emotions or maybe she just liked my watch, but I submitted gracefully. Actually, I sort of had an idea as to what she was doing… I had seen a documentary on television about psychics who found lost children, and they always requested an item of clothing or something the child had touched. As it turned out, this was exactly what she was doing as she ran her finger over my knuckles, tracing the blue veins gently. Then she turned my hand open, and gently studied my palm. Other tables were beginning to notice and were watching, and I began to feel embarrassed. I saw Bobby watching interestingly, and I wondered what he must think of me.

"You have an interesting lifeline," she mused, following the lines and creases on my palm. "I don't believe I've ever seen one quite like this one."

"Well, I guess it's better to be unique than be lost in a crowd," I said, but I saw now that she was frowning slightly, and had leaned forward for a better look. I stirred.

"It seems to be interrupted in places, so faint I can barely see it, and then it gets strong—very strong, in fact—here." She seemed to be thinking. "A purposeful existence is what this means, but I've never seen it like this. Like you are destined to do something great, but even you don't understand it yet." She grasped her forefinger over my vein, as if she were taking my pulse, and then closed her eyes. The table had gone silent, and from the looks on the others' faces, I knew they had never seen a reading like this.

Suddenly, I was incredibly sorry I had ever allowed this to happen, and I wanted to bolt… yet her gentle grasp was as strong as chains.

And all at once, she let go. She took a deep, shuddering breath, and opened her eyes, focusing them on me. "That was really something," she said, reaching for her tea glass.

"Harriet," the man said, looking uncertainly at her. "What did you see? I've never seen you do a reading quite like that before."

"That's because I never have." She shook her head, and I thought she had gone pale.

I looked at her, feeling my heart race in my chest. "What did you see?"

She sighed, and I could tell that like me, she wished she had never started this either. I bet this would be the last impromptu reading she would ever give. She seemed to consider her answer and then shook her head. "Tell you what. We probably should talk about this, but this probably isn't the place, and I know you're working." She dug into her purse and pulled out a little notebook and a pen. She scribbled an address down on a piece of paper, tore it out, and handed it to me. "Here is the address of our cabin. Give me a day or so to sort it out, and I'd like to make a few phone calls too, to ask people who are far smarter and better at this than I am, just how to interpret it." She smiled weakly. "I'm just a parlor seer, you understand. Usually, I just predict trips over water, coming into money, new romances, that sort of thing. I'm in way over my head here."

I gaped at her, wanting to pour the whole pitcher of tea over her head for scaring me. "What's wrong? What do you mean, you have to call people? What people?" And as much as I didn't believe in this kind of thing, she had really spooked me, and I hated both myself for allowing it to happen, and her for doing it to me. "Am I going to die? Just what did you see?"

She smiled reassuringly, but it was a weak smile at best. "Few days, honey. You'll be all right."

I looked worried, and tried to smile, but clearly, she wasn't about to say anything else, and I hurried away. I saw Miguel looking curiously at me as he wiped down a table, but decided if I confided in him, he would only chide me for doing it in the first place. He was such a strong believer in such things that he probably had a whole list of do's and don'ts, and I had probably broken every one of them, so he was not the person to go to with my woes.

I found myself back at Bobby's table, on the pretext of checking on them and taking their orders. "Is holding hands with the staff part of the service I get here?" he asked. "Because if it is, I think it's a great customer service."

I tried to laugh. "Oh, you saw that, did you?"

"Yep." He brushed a lock of blond hair away; I was pleased to see that like a gentleman, he had taken his baseball cap off at the table. Someone had trained this boy right. "Was she taking your pulse, or what?"

"Well, sorta, I guess." I shrugged. "It's nothing. Do you want lemon with your iced tea?"

He pretended to consider. "Well, of course. But is it all right if we change tables?"

"Change tables?" I was confused, and glanced at the table, looking for a spot of food or grease that Miguel had missed when he had bussed. There was nothing wrong that I could see. "Where do you want to sit?"

"Well, down by the beach." He grinned at me so sweetly that I felt my heart flutter. "It's a little more private there; it's hard to have a first date in a noisy diner, and besides, you're working." His friends exchanged amused glances, but my eyes were only on Bobby.

I cleared my throat. "Is that what we're having? A first date?"

"Well, sorta. Except you were holding hands with that old woman earlier, and I'm the jealous type. I guess I gotta get you all to myself." He pretended to sigh. "Though, I have to admit that you serving me is a positive for my chauvinistic side."

"He's a caveman," one of his friends snorted, looking at me. "Tell him you'll do it, for the love of God. You're all he's been talking about for two days now."

"Really?" I was surprised and flattered. I looked back at Bobby.

"Well, not two days," he muttered, pretending a great sulk. "Maybe just a few minutes is all. So, what do you say, Beth? Me or the old lady, which is it?"

Once again, I saw another table had been listening to this conversation, and I realized I was becoming quite the spectacle today. If nothing else, I was good for entertainment, and I felt like I had been a source of amusement for the whole diner the minute I stepped out onto the floor. It was an older couple, also summer people, and when I looked back at Bobby and nodded, they laughed and smiled at me. The old man even clapped along with Bobby's friends.

"You've made a good choice," the old lady told me, while Bobby beamed and his friends high-fived each other. "He's a good-lookin' little bastard—cocky, but good looking, just like my Franklin here. Have fun."

"I'm sure we will," Bobby said. "I'll take good care of her, you have my cocky little bastard word on that." He grinned at me. "So, it's a date?"

I nodded. "Yes. It's a date."

Smiling, I walked back to the kitchen to put in their orders, and as I went, clapping and cheers still ringing in my ears, I saw that Harriet's party had left during the excitement, their food uneaten. Dismayed, I was worried that they had skipped out without paying—a common enough occurrence, and every server's nightmare—but I noticed a twenty-dollar bill tucked under a glass, which more than covered their tab and a generous tip for me. I scooped it up and tucked it into my apron, signaling for Miguel to come over and start bussing when I suddenly saw the words scribbled on the back of the bill. I looked at them, feeling the blood pound in my ears, as I felt a chill trickle down my back.

Beth... please call me as soon as you can. I feel you are in terrible danger.

I crumpled up the note and stuffed it into my pocket, and when Miguel asked me what was wrong, I couldn't answer him.

V
CHAPTER

1864

Charlie could only look at him, and though the man's face was inscrutable, there was a hint of fear in his voice, and Charlie knew he was giving him a warning of some kind.

He shook his head, fear creeping into him. "Well, he's a doctor. I guess he would know what to do, wouldn't he?" He looked at his wound again. "It ain't bleedin' all that bad anyway."

Huffman nodded. "The doc... well, you're right. He would know what to do with that. Yes, Lord, he would... I'm just trying to remove temptation, is all. Maybe in a day or so, you'll be healthy enough, we can move you out of here, get you back to Tennessee with your family." He looked seriously at Charlie. "But in the meantime, I think it's best if you stay quiet and keep to yourself, and we keep those bandages as clean as possible."

Silence fell between them, and Charlie suddenly remembered the image of Crane, sucking on the bandages. He began to feel dizzy.

"Mister Huffman," he whispered softly, "am I safe? The doc ain't gonna hurt me, is he?"

Huffman shook his head stubbornly and looked away. "Like I said, Doctor Crane has his ways, yes indeed, and his own peculiar taste—"

suddenly, he sighed as if burdened with a heavy secret. "I'll do what I can to help you, boy," he promised.

"Then it's true." Charlie's voice was tight. "I know what I saw, then. Doctor Crane was sucking on that bloody bandage... oh my God..."

Huffman shot him a final look and then, almost imperceptibly, raised one shoulder, as if in helpless agreement with what Charlie was saying. Out of the corner of his mouth he whispered, "He can only hurt you at night, boy. Watch yourself."

And then, pushing his cart of bedpans, he slowly shuffled back down the aisle of wounded men. Charlie watched him go, fear spreading over his entire body as the shadows in the hospital tent grew long as night approached on silent feet.

1985

Even though I usually share most things with my mother, I decided not to tell her about my strange encounter with Harriet and her scary predictions, at least until I had more information. Frankly, I wasn't sure that I wanted to call her to even pursue what she had discovered after she had spoken to her people. She was clearly a weird lady, maybe with emotional problems, and I had enough to worry about without inviting trouble into my life. Still, she had seemed so shocked and worried about what she had seen in my palm and felt when she had grabbed my wrist, that I was worried. It was like an emotional Pandora's Box... which was better? To know, and be expecting for the truck to hit me, or to *not* know, and when it came suddenly think, *ahh, it's about time...*

About Bobby, I was a little more open. I didn't get asked out on many dates, so I was pretty giddy when I went home. I guess my mood was light enough that it didn't take long at all for my mother to guess what had happened at work. When I finally confessed to her that I had a date—and not just any date, but a date with a boy as handsome as Bobby Barnham—I felt like a little girl talking about her first trip to the circus.

Even though the hour was late, she fixed us both a big bowl of ice cream, and we sat at the kitchen table and giggled and talked like silly children. I realized I didn't really know all that much about him yet, but what I did know, I filled her in on—what he was doing in town, where he lived, his blue Jeep, the way he wore his hair; I guess it was pretty immature, but I was smitten and flattered that he had asked, and I wanted to share my happiness. And my mother, bless her heart, sat right there and asked questions and egged me on and grasped my hand to show how very happy she was for me. She didn't give me any advice but just listened, long past our bedtime, until I got the hint when she began to playfully hum the song "I Could Have Danced All Night" from the musical *My Fair Lady*.

"Wow," I exclaimed, looking at the clock on the stove. "It's so late. You've let me babble and chatter away at you for hours. And we both have work in the morning."

She shrugged, rinsing out the ice cream bowls. "I'm glad to see my girl so happy. This boy better treat you right, or I'll break his neck."

"Well, it's just a date," I reminded her. "We might not even like each other after we go out."

She shrugged. "Maybe. But I have a feeling about this… like this is the start of something special."

Like you are destined to do something great, but even you don't understand it yet…

I cleared my throat. "Mom, do you believe in fortune telling?"

She looked at me strangely. "Like gypsies, you mean?" She curled her hands out, palms up, and croaked, "As in, cross my palm with silver, dearie?"

I laughed with her. "Well, sorta." I thought of Harriet, and couldn't see her working out of the back of a gypsy caravan. She was more of a mini-van sort of woman, and an air-conditioned minivan at that. "Just telling the future."

She shrugged. "My grandmother knew an Italian woman from the old country who could supposedly divine the future by looking at chicken guts."

"Gross." I wrinkled my nose as I considered that.

"And my mother could witch for water... strangest thing in the world." She sat back down across from me. "If I hadn't ever seen it, I wouldn't have believed it. She would take two metal clothes hangers and bend them into right angles, one for each hand. Holding them loosely in her fists, she would walk across the field, and when she would hit underground water, I swear to God those clothes hangers would turn outward, each time. It was incredible. I couldn't explain it, and neither could she."

"But have you ever... had your fortune told? By someone who supposedly really could?"

"Well, I read my horoscope in the paper every day, if that counts. And, I always break open those little fortune cookies and read the little slip inside, even though those are pretty vague." She shrugged. "I guess not, no. Why, was your date foretold by somebody in the know?"

"Oh, no, nothing like that. They were talking about it at work, that's all. I just wanted your opinion on it."

She looked thoughtful again. "Well, I don't really know. I suppose it is possible to have... vibes, or little flashes of the future. Have I ever told you the story of your cousin Ronnie? On my dad's side?"

I shook my head. "Wasn't he killed in Vietnam or something?"

"He was." She cleared her throat. "Well, he was due to come home the week before Easter. He was the baby of the family, and the only one of the boys who hadn't managed to escape the draft. The others had, you know, including your dad. There were ways to do it: getting married, keeping your grades up in college, enlisting in the National Guard. Well, Ronnie went off to college, and I guess he partied too much and he flunked Algebra. So, the Army got him, and they shipped him off to that awful jungle on the other side of the world where he joined in a fight he didn't really care a thing about."

Her voice had grown husky, and she looked away. I really didn't know the story of my second cousin... no one had ever really spoken of him, except to say that he had gotten killed in Vietnam. My grandmother had some medals on display on her mantle, and that was about the extent of my knowledge. I leaned forward to listen.

"Well, he was to come home, and we had planned a party. The family was coming together. It was turning into a reunion of sorts. Your father and I were pregnant with you, and we had just bought this house. Life was good." She took a deep, heavy breath. "Well, about a week before Ronnie was to come home, I started having funny dreams and thoughts about him. A few times I thought I had seen him around me—at the market, at the laundromat, on the front porch. I would just look up, and there he'd be, standing quietly close by, watching me."

"Like... a ghost?"

She shrugged. "Possibly. I actually began to see him a week before he was killed. I don't know what I was seeing exactly—maybe an image of what was to come, maybe his wandering spirit wanting help—I just don't know." She sighed. "And after he was killed, maybe it was his way of coming home."

I felt the creeps settling in. "Have you seen him since?"

She smiled sadly. "Occasionally. When I'm sad, or when something really awful has happened." She looked away. "The week before your father left me, Ronnie was here quite a bit. Again, when my mother died. Moments of stress, I guess."

I looked around nervously. "Er... you don't see him now, do you?"

She laughed quietly. "No, all quiet on the western front. And really, since you have a new male friend, why would he be hanging around? It looks like life is going well."

Beth... please call me as soon as you can. I feel you are in terrible danger.

"Yeah, I guess." I thought of Harriet and frowned slightly.

"Beth?" She looked hard at me. "Is there something about this boy you're not telling me?"

I shook my head. "Oh no, I'm not worried about him at all."

She took my hand. "Are you sure? If it's not that, something seems to be chewing on you. What is it?"

Like you are destined to do something great, but even you don't understand it yet...

"Just tired, I guess." I managed to yawn, and I really wasn't kidding. "You're right. It's late." She stood up, leaning in for a kiss. "Night, sweetheart." She seemed to remember something, and then paused. "Oh, by the way, you had a phone call earlier today."

"I did? Who was it?"

"Well, not sure. I picked it up, and a man asked for you. When I said you weren't here, he merely hung up." She smiled. "Is your Bobby a shy one?"

"I don't know if he has this number," I said thoughtfully. "I didn't give it to him."

"Ooooh, two suitors at once," she giggled. "It never rains but it pours in your romantic life, is that it?"

"It might have been Miguel, asking me something about work," I said, but wasn't sure what it could possibly have been about. *Hey Beth, did you fill the salt and pepper shakers?* Probably not. Besides, Miguel had a trace of an accent, and my mother would have picked up on that immediately. I realized she was looking at me curiously as I pondered, and I gave a careless shrug. "I have no idea. I guess if it's important, they will call back."

"Keep me posted, things around here haven't been this romantic since we went and saw *An Officer and a Gentleman*." She looked at me naughtily. "Your young man isn't military, is he?" There was hope in her voice.

I shook my head. "I don't think so."

She sighed. "Damn. I like a man in uniform." She grinned at me again. "And does your Bobby Barnham look like Richard Gere?"

I thought of Bobby's sunburned blondness and shook my head. "Not really, Mom. I'd say he's more Christopher Atkins."

She sighed. "Not bad, not bad. I'm sure he's hunky nonetheless. All right, g'night, love." I watched her walk out of the room, finally headed to bed, and I felt a pang of guilt that she had stayed up so late with me and would have even less sleep than she normally did. Still, we had a good time, something our respective work schedule didn't allow us to do anymore, so maybe that made up for it a little bit.

Without turning on the hall lights, I walked to my bedroom and slipped in. Here was my sanctuary, my own little place with my things, just the way I liked them. On the bulletin board over my desk hung my 4-H ribbons and school awards, certificates of achievement and even a little plastic trophy proclaiming me winner of the fifth-grade spelling bee. My typewriter, books and school things were stacked messily across my desk, and a few teen idols stared down moodily from posters taped to the walls. It was a comfortable room, still a good mix of childhood and adolescence, with the hints of young adult. Lesson plans were scattered over the desk, while a few cherished stuffed animals, battered and well-loved, lay across my bed: a bear, a pink rabbit from many Easters ago, a silly looking mouse my father had once given me. Old friends.

I pulled off my clothes and quickly got into my nightshirt, sitting down in front of the mirror to take down my braid. The nightlight was bright enough for me to see by, and really, after the excitement of the day, the dark helped me to unwind. The house was quiet and still, the only sounds being the nameless little tune I hummed as I brushed my hair. I gazed at myself in the mirror sleepily, counting the brush strokes, and suddenly got a nasty shock.

There was a silhouette of a man in the window behind me, caught in the silver reflection of the mirror.

Clutching my hairbrush, I whirled around. My mouth prepared to scream as I scrambled off the dressing stool. My elbow hit the edge of the bureau hard, and I felt screaming flashes of pain, but nothing was as important or as terrifying as the man who was watching me.

When I looked back, the window was empty. He was gone.

I could feel my heart beating rapidly as I hesitantly took a step in that direction, foolishly holding the hairbrush like a club. The air conditioner kicked on then with a comforting hum, moving the curtains gently in the breeze as I peered into the darkness, looking out the window into the night beyond.

Running my fingers around the edge of the window showed that it was empty, and quickly I made sure it was locked. It was. I scanned the backyard, looking for a dark figure to go dashing across the lawn to the safety of the fence, but all was silent. A few late fireflies were still calling to each other in the grass, and I could hear crickets singing their night symphonies. I listened for the Murrays' dog, Harry, to start barking at whoever I had seen. He was a great neighborhood watchdog, sometimes too much so, barking at everything and nothing all night, but for now he was strangely silent. However, standing at the window looking out, I had the feeling that my watcher had moved away and was hiding farther off into the yard, under the bushes perhaps, and was observing me looking for him. I moved away from the window quickly, and sat back down on my stool, catching my breath.

The dim glow of the orange number on my clock radio said that it was several minutes after one in the morning. It was certainly late for me, but did a pervert have such an appreciation for late hours? Despite my fear, I had a moment of hysterical giddiness as I imagined a peeping tom punching a time clock. Would someone really stay up at such a late hour in hopes of getting a look at me in my nightshirt? And where had he gone now? If he had seen me notice him in the window, he would have had to have moved pretty darn fast to get away and hide before I had reached the window. Most importantly, why wasn't Harry barking? The Murrays had gotten complaints from the neighborhood association about their idiot dog barking and keeping people awake at all hours of the night, but now that he really had something to bark at, he was strangely, unusually quiet.

All right, so maybe I *hadn't* seen anyone there after all. Perhaps it had just been a shadow, or a reflection of my own self in the glass. And it was indeed late... admittedly I had been very, very drowsy, sitting there at my dressing table. I suppose it was possible that I had something of a waking dream, perhaps caused by stress and excitement and exhaustion. I felt my body relax as I pondered this explanation, and even though it sounded reasonable and logical, my mind reluctantly rejected it.

Oh, by the way, you had a phone call earlier today. A man asked for you. When I said you weren't here, he merely hung up.

Somehow, instantly, I knew these two things were somehow related, though I wasn't sure how. A prickle of fear went down my back as I tried to somehow link these two events together. And, as I pondered this, my exhausted brain—which wasn't nearly as tired as I had hoped, offered up *another* nasty tidbit and reminded me of the man I had seen observing me the other night as I had walked to my car, and I wondered if that was yet another link in this chain of crazy events.

Keeping out of the line of sight of the window, I crawled to my purse and pulled out my pepper spray. Curling it in my fist, I slid into bed. My eyes were dry and alert as I stared at the ceiling. Every sound in the house, every creak and squeal of woodwork popping, of the air conditioning shutting off and on, of my mother's snores from down the hall seemed ominous and scary as my restless mind tossed and chased itself around all night.

Sleep was long in coming, and when it came, it was restless and uneasy.

VI
CHAPTER

1864

After Taps and Vespers, as the camp was settling down for the evening, Charlie lay on his bunk. He had eaten a little stew—unknown meat, woody vegetables—and the pain was talking to him. He had never imagined anything hurting so bad... he had once fallen off a horse and had broken his leg in a couple of places, but this pain was like nothing he had ever experienced. Worse than that, the fingers that weren't there seemed to hurt, and the stump was itching maddeningly. One good scratch across it produced such sparks of pain he was left gasping, and so all he could do was stare at the watermarks in the canvas above him and hope for the pain and itch to subside.

He dreamed of home for a while. He remembered his parents' little farm in the Tennessee hills, the lowing of cows on a dewy morning and of his mother ringing the triangle to bring her boys in for breakfast. He remembered her biscuits, her spicy sausage, and most of all her homemade jam: raspberry, pear, wild strawberry, but his favorite had been blackberry. Dark, thick and rich, it had been a staple in his home his entire life, and in his sleep, a tear trickled down his cheek.

All of the valley knew that Mabel Barnham made the best blackberry jam. At every social event, every funeral, wedding or church function, people asked after her jam; over the years, it had become her calling card, and while she was glad to share her jam with her neighbors, sometimes even putting a colorful ribbon around the jar for more festive events, she was never willing to share her recipe as to how she made it.

To Charlie, its sweetness was pure heaven. All his life, he had it nearly once a day, at some meal, on his biscuits, or on a heel of bread; spread over a hunk of venison to take the gamy tang out of the meat, or even straight out of the jar, if his mother wasn't looking. The bushes from whence came the berries grew abundantly in their north pasture, and every summer it was a race to get them before the birds picked them clean. He and his brothers would be released from their routines for a few days, and sent to the woods with large baskets and pails to collect the dark little fruit. It was definitely a festive time, not a chore at all. Sometimes they would compete as to who could gather the most, and even better, Mabel would pack a picnic lunch for them, or sometimes even join them herself in the cool woods to escape the heat of the kitchen. There would be laughing and singing and joking and good-natured teasing and though Charlie didn't know it at the time, he would never have a better time in his life than those lovely times with his family.

He dreamed of those times now, sometimes almost smiling in his sleep, or twitching a little as he remembered his mother's voice.

And then the dreams dissolved and were jerked away, because the whispering had startled him awake.

1985

I wasn't exactly sure where Bobby was taking me for our date. He had been vague about it, and I wasn't sure if this was because he had meant for it to be a surprise, or if he was just being typically male. When my mother asked me about it, and I had shrugged noncommittally, she had given me an amused, sympathetic look. "Men," she huffed in an exaggerated voice, and then collapsed in giggles, which wasn't like her at all. When I shot her a look, she merely shrugged and patted me on the hand. "Even when a man makes plans at his most thoughtful and generous moment, it usually turns out to be exactly opposite of what the woman wants. So just paste a smile on your face and enjoy."

Because I didn't have many First Dates, I certainly didn't have a First Date Outfit, and added to the fact I didn't know where we were going, it made it a crapshoot. I stood glaring at my closet for quite some time, mentally debating this outfit or that one, before I decided on something I thought would work in a variety of places: a dark denim skirt, a cranberry-colored silk blouse, and several necklaces of different lengths, a la Madonna. I considered shoes and finally decided upon a pair of sandals with a small heel. My hair I just moussed back and held with a comb, and when I came out into the living room, my mom nodded approvingly. "Not bad," she nodded. "If this boy Bobby touches you, I'll kill him. But you look very nice, dear."

"Mother—"

"Unless you want him to, of course. And then I don't want to know about it." She grinned at me wickedly, and then glanced at the clock. "Do I get to meet this young man?"

I shrugged. "If you want to." I tried to appear nonchalant, but in truth I did want her to meet him, if nothing else to show him off. He was certainly a handsome boy, the most handsome boy who had ever asked me out, and a part of me I really didn't recognize wanted to show him off. Silly, perhaps, but nonetheless true, and I wondered what my mother's reaction would be upon meeting him.

Bobby had told me he would pick me up at six thirty, but as we watched the clock tick away to seven o'clock and he hadn't shown up, a sick feeling began to creep into my stomach. I kept a smile pasted on my face, but suspicious thoughts began to play through my head, and I thought about all of his friends back at their house, laughing at me. While not necessarily a cynical person by nature, unfortunately, I had seen enough meanness… I hadn't exactly been the most popular kid in high school, being on the wrong side of the economic divide, and college hadn't been a whole lot better. And while I hadn't really ever been the brunt of cruelty or pranks, I had seen enough done to others to know that people my age could be vicious. I could well imagine Bobby and his crew of boys sitting around laughing at me. Maybe one of them had dared Bobby to ask me out—poor stupid waitress in a poor stupid diner—and then not show up. Probably Bobby was drunk even now, curled up in the arms of some sorority girl he had met on the lake...

My thoughts were interrupted by the doorbell ringing, and my mother and I exchanged relieved looks. We got up at the same time, but I waved her off and went to the door myself; my low heels clacked on the hardwood floor like castanets... I knew my mother's eyes were on me at every step, and taking a deep breath, I opened the door.

Bobby was there with his blond hair neatly parted and yet shaggily combed; he looked like a rock star, just off the stage. His jeans were clean, his polo shirt with the collar popped fashionably chic, and he wore loafers without socks. Very *Miami Vice*. Mother would be pleased.

"I'm sorry I'm late," he said quickly. "Razzy had to borrow the Jeep to go into town—" he paused for a second, appreciating my appearance. "Wow, you look great. But anyway, Razzy had to go—"

"Who's Razzo?" I thought of his group of friends and had no idea which one he was talking about.

"Razzy, not Razzo. His real name is Razzini, but we call him Razzy." He grinned at me. "Just one of the Neanderthals in the fraternity where I live. They all sort of blend together after a while."

Nervously, we looked at each other, and then we both gave sort of an awkward little smile. The timing was so perfect and so unexpected that I felt a flush of pleasure as I knew we had just shared a moment. I cleared my throat. "Well, why don't you come in? My mother is waiting to interrogate you."

"I'm not good under torture," he whispered. "I usually break."

She was waiting for us in the kitchen, trying desperately hard to look like she was *not* waiting for us; she was working a crossword puzzle, her pen poised thoughtfully to her lips while she muttered, "Hmm, a six-letter word for fisherman..."

"Angler," Bobby said immediately and stepped forward. "Does that fit? And I'm Bobby Barnham."

I swallowed an exasperated comment as she penciled it in the boxes and pretended to be surprised. She had an extensive vocabulary; I had seen my mother work a crossword puzzle in pen, in less than five minutes, from corner to corner. She certainly didn't need any help, and yet she suddenly looked delighted and smiled coquettishly at her visitor. "Why, that's it! It *does* fit! It's a pleasure to meet you, Mister Barnham. I'm Beth's mother."

"Good to meet you." He flicked a lock of hair out of his eyes, and I could feel my mother mentally sigh in approval. "I'm Beth's date."

She laughed in delight. "Oh, a sense of humor! Good for you. You'll need it to keep up with that one." She jerked a thumb at me and then tapped the crossword puzzle with the butt of her pen. "So, you like words… are you a literature major?"

"Well, no." He glanced at me, almost embarrassed. "Actually—and I don't think Beth knows this about me yet. She thinks I want to be a house painter all my life—I'm a pre-med major."

I was indeed startled by this, and made a small sound in my throat in surprise… it certainly showed me there were a million things about this boy that I didn't know, a million conversations we hadn't had yet. I looked at him in surprise.

My mother, however, was less discreet. Her mouth flew open in happiness, and I could imagine her already putting together my dowry. "Really? A doctor?"

"Hardly." He waved her off. "Years from that. Just pre-med at this point. I've got my med school applications to do this next semester, and we'll see then."

She wasn't deterred, and I could see the gears and wheels turning in her head. "Med school! I don't know how your parents are going to manage that. I tell you, we've scraped and pinched every penny we've got just to get Beth through school… med school is so expensive, I hear." She was unabashedly prying, disguising it as small talk, and wouldn't meet my eye. I wanted to crawl into the floor.

He looked rather embarrassed and tried to shrug. "Well, I guess. So far, my undergrad has been all scholarships… I've got a few promised for med school, too, if my applications are accepted—"

"Bravo!" Mother shouted. Bobby jumped, and I glared. "You must be quite the smartie to have gotten this far, then. Those scholarships don't come easy."

He smiled weakly. "I guess. I just do the best I can, really."

"With an eye to the future, and a good goal ahead," Mother said, tapping her pen again, this time for emphasis. "Not to mention you've got good hair."

"That's it." I cleared my throat and looked at Bobby. "If you want to take her tonight instead of me, I fully understand." My voice was exasperated, and I wasn't really faking it.

My mother managed to look offended. "We're just making conversation, Beth, I have a right to get to know the young man who is taking my daughter out, don't I?"

I nodded. "You do, and now you've met." I turned to Bobby. "Are we going, or are the two of you going?"

He looked amused. "I guess we're going, then."

"Good." I gathered up my purse and glanced at my mother. "Don't wait up."

"Of course, I will," she countered. "I always do. I intend on making some popcorn, opening a bottle of wine, and curling up on the couch to watch an old movie." She smiled at me, and I saw she was no longer teasing us; in fact, I saw nothing but love in her eyes, and I thought of all the nights she had done this to make sure I had gotten home safely. There was no use in even trying to talk her out of it. I knew it would only be a waste of time, and I gave her a small smile back to show that I understood.

"I'll have her back at a reasonable time," Bobby promised and took me protectively by the arm. It was a surprising gesture, but I wasn't displeased by it.

And just to show that she wasn't totally beaten, my mother gave one final parting shot as we walked out the door. "Reasonable time? Wow, you're a fast worker, eh?" I rolled my eyes as she cackled at us, and red-faced, I hurried a chuckling Bobby out the door.

* * *

I wasn't sure where we were going and was afraid to ask, but as it turned out when Bobby got into the Jeep—after helping me in and closing the door, like a true gentleman—he didn't either. He started the engine, but then looked at me and confessed, "I don't know what kind of food you like, so I'm open to suggestions."

"You mean that you didn't plan this out, to the last degree?" I took a page from my mother's Book of Sarcasm. "I guess with all the medical school applications, you didn't have time."

He looked momentarily abashed. "Well, that would have come up eventually. I was going to tell you. It's just that some girls get all freaked out about it. I didn't want to ruin... I mean, if you think I'm such a brainy guy, it might scare you off."

I frowned. "Because you think I'm an idiot, so therefore I wouldn't be able to keep up with you?" Even as I said it, I realized that I was guilty of the same thing; just as I knew nothing about him, he knew nothing about me either, and upon agreeing to go out on a date with him, our conversations had been nil and our mutual attraction was the only thing we had going so far.

He looked sideways at me as he turned a corner, gently accelerating. "Well, no. That wasn't it at all. Just... it's a daunting thing to talk about, is all." He cleared his throat. "And since I'm not sure if... if you're in school, I didn't want..."

"Not that it matters," I said icily, "but I'll be starting my senior year in college in a few months. I'm an education major."

His blond eyebrows raised in interest. "You want to be a teacher?"

"Yep. Not bad for a hick waitress, eh?"

"Beth..." he sighed and eased the Jeep over to the side of the road. I had visions of him ordering me out, and I'd have to walk home in these stupid heels. No way would I humiliate myself and call my mother... maybe I could get to a phone booth and call Lou, or maybe Miguel. I wasn't sure if he was working tonight, but maybe on his break, he could come and rescue me...

But Bobby only turned the key in the ignition and looked at me levelly. "Let's start over. I think it's safe to say we both have a lot to learn about each other, and isn't that what a first date should be about anyway? Geez, this is our first fight, and we haven't even had our first kiss yet. Somehow, we're all backwards about this."

Despite everything, his words struck me as funny, and I tried to cover a smile. "Who says there is going to be a first kiss? It seems like you were more interested in my mother anyway."

He grinned a little. "Nah, I'm just her Thesaurus, that's all."

"I hate to burst your bubble, but Mom was just pulling your leg. She's done more crossword puzzles than you and I ever will. She was just testing you."

"Oh, I know." He shrugged. "I thought so. I was just playing along, and I think she knew it." He glanced at me. "I see where you get your fire."

I gazed out across the cornfields, watching the heat shimmering off of the green leaves. It was early evening, a beautiful summer night. Usually, this time of night I was busy serving beer and putting together onion ring baskets, but instead tonight, I was out on a date. A First Date. But so far, a date that was not going so well. I wasn't sure what to do, and the prospects of the First Kiss that Bobby had mentioned seemed far away.

A long silence followed. Finally, I ventured, "I think we're both trying too hard here."

He nodded. "Yep." Absently, he drummed his fingers on the steering wheel. "I gotta admit, I really didn't plan this all too well. I wasn't sure what kind of food you like... and then I figured since you work in a diner all day long, you're probably sick of food, so I was afraid to make plans without asking you." He shot me a sideways look, to see how I was receiving this, and seemed to be encouraged, because I thought it was a really thoughtful consideration, and I nodded my appreciation. "So... what *do* you like?"

I smiled. "I dunno. Let's just start the car and see where we end up."

His grin got wider as he turned the key. "Yes, Ma'am."

He started in the direction of the lake, which is where most of the restaurants in our town are. There are dozens of places to eat there, everything from hotdog stands, to little comfortable diners like Lou's, all the way to the members-only Yachting Club, which sits on the far east side, by Cassler Hill. Lambert Lake is actually a series of several lakes connected together and is the heart of a great deal of the economy in our town during the summer months. Along with all of the eateries and antique shops, there are two swimming beaches; a restored paddle boat, *The River Queen*, does excursions on the Big Lake three times a day; and there is also a water-skiing show on Sundays. There are a lot of fishermen and boaters, but they're usually found in the two smaller lakes, where the fishing is better. Of course, the county fairgrounds are there, with the boardwalk making the perfect Midway, and on the Fourth of July there is a beautiful firework display over the lake at sundown. Bobby's instincts were good, but I was curious as to where we might end up.

Along the way, we talked. It was admittedly stiff at first, but within a few minutes the walls began to break down, and I remembered why I had agreed to go with him. He was naturally funny, and a good listener. He turned the radio down as we told each other about our schools, and our classes, and before we knew it, the sun had gone down and we were hungry.

I was amazed at how fast time had gone by. The daylight had just melted away, and night had set in. Across the lake, we could see the multi-colored lights on the *River Queen* as she came into the dock from her final trip; laughter and voices floated across the water as happy, sunburnt Summer People clattered across the gangplank, headed for shore.

"Are you hungry?" Bobby asked me, and inopportunely, at that exact moment, my stomach growled. I was horrified and embarrassed, but he burst into delighted laughter, and after a second, I laughed with him.

"I guess I am," I agreed. "Any ideas?"

I pointed to a hotdog stand by the lake. Garishly painted, its logo was a laughing hotdog—never mind the Freudian implications—doing a jig with an ice cream sandwich with legs. Colorful plastic pennants flapped in the wind. "How about that?"

He looked skeptically at my choice. "The Happy Hotdog?"

"Sure, why not?" I have to admit my reasons for this choice were mixed. Partly, I was trying to be sensitive to his wallet. Being a house painter paid by the County, he probably couldn't pay that much, and I wasn't going to have him work all week and then blow his weekly savings on a Saturday night, like a cowboy entertaining a saloon girl. "I like hotdogs, and we can sit by the water."

He looked at me again, trying to read my true intentions. I put on my most earnest face, and he shrugged. "All right. But don't blame me if you get heartburn later. Come on."

He parked the car and held the door for me. As we walked across the lot, he surprised me by taking my hand, and I surprised myself by letting him. His fingers intertwined with mine, almost as if they were made to fit there, and my heart thumped a little harder.

We waited in line behind a family of Summer People, parents and four small kids who kept changing their order, but we weren't impatient. I liked standing close to him, feeling his hands in mine, and smelling his cologne. From the loudspeaker blared Madonna's burblings... *Like a Virgin*. Another omen? I smiled to myself and pushed the thought from my mind.

While we waited, I scanned the menu and told Bobby what I wanted, and he ordered for us. One of the little girls in line ahead of us skipped around us, singing to herself, and then seemed to notice we were holding hands. She stopped in front of us but stage whispered to her mother, "Are they on a date, Momma?"

Her mother shot me an embarrassed, apologetic look. "I think so, sweetie. And it's not nice to stare."

The little girl ignored that last remark and regarded me thoughtfully. Turning back to her mother, she said, "I thought people went to *nice* places on a date. That lady is awful dressed up for hotdogs, Momma."

Bobby, who was picking up the tray of food, snorted at this remark and tipped me a wink. I blushed a little, but I realized she was right— the hair, the jewelry, the heels—I could have gone into the Yachting Club and been served, but here I was at the Happy Hot Dog. And this was the other reason I had chosen to come here: this was real life. The Yachting Club and the other expensive places up on the other side of the lake weren't me... I wasn't champagne and petit fours by any stretch; I was beer and pretzels. This wasn't to say I was cheap, because I certainly wasn't, but I was simple and easy to please, and I hated to be fussed over. And while I had dressed up a little for tonight, definitely pleasing my girly side, I would have been just as happy in a baggy tee shirt and shorts.

I smiled at the little girl and nodded a little, indicating that I agreed with her, and followed Bobby to one of the tables closest to the lake. Strands of white lights had been strung around the railings, and petunias and other planting flowers lolled in big pots, making it feel like a garden. The Happy Hotdog shared its seating area with another eating establishment, Nate's Taco Stand... they were obviously owned by the same man, who recognized that while his eateries were one step above fast food, the dining area was at least comfortable and pretty. We settled into our wrought iron chairs, and I surveyed our dinner, laid out on the red plastic tray. Standard beach fare... hotdogs, onion rings in greasy little baskets, and two big fountain soft drinks, their sides already moist with condensation. It looked wonderful. Bobby unwrapped the foil on his hot dog and squirted on ketchup.

"Food for the Gods, eh?"

"Not bad," I agreed. I was strangely, cautiously happy. After our initial spat, things had been going very well. He was so easy to talk to, and more than that, he was a good listener. As we ate our dinner, listening to the gentle waves lap on the beach, I learned more about him. He was from Tennessee, which accounted for his light accent, and had been raised by his grandparents on a small farm. His parents had been killed in a train wreck when he was very young. He really didn't remember them at all, which I found rather sad. He had graduated valedictorian of his class and had won a bunch of scholarships; otherwise, he would have been stuck in a little do-nothing of a town with little prospect. "There was nothing for me there," he told me quietly. "Of course, I go back to see my Grandma Lucy, but that's about it. I don't feel like I belong there anymore."

"You don't want to live there someday?" I took a sip of my drink, rattling the ice a little.

He shrugged. "Well, I didn't say that exactly. My Gran thinks I should come back one day and be a doctor there. Help the people who live there." He looked out across the water. "Bisby is pretty economically depressed, let me tell you. If I were to go back there, I know I'd be doing a lot of people a lot of good."

I studied him. "But yet you don't want to?"

"I don't know." He frowned thoughtfully. "My family has been in Tennessee for over a hundred and fifty years. We have deep, deep roots there. But I don't know that it's necessarily a good place for us. We've always had trouble there."

"Trouble? Like what?"

He shrugged. "Oh, I dunno. It seems my family is prone to terminal bad luck. We've seen more than our share of accidents, deaths, tragedies. I can't tell you the number of family members who have died over the years. We've lost uncles, cousins, brothers, all to terrible things: war, hunting, farm accidents, and car wrecks. There's even been a few disappearances over the years…"

I looked at him closely. "Disappearances?"

He nodded, and took a deep breath. "Yep. Like… I dunno. Amelia Earhart. Or Judge Crater. Over the years, without reason, members of our family have just… vanished. Gone. We have no idea what happened to them." He smiled thinly, but I knew this was something that weighed on him, and I nodded for him to go on.

"An extraordinarily high amount of… just *odd* things. Not sickness or illnesses. As if there was something genetically wrong, passed from one generation to another, no faulty gene or trait. Just a high propensity for bad things to happen. My Gran says we're cursed, and she laughs when she says it, but sometimes I wonder if there is something to it." He smiled sadly. "I'm the last of the Barnham male line, except for my cousin Aaron, and he lives in Ohio."

I shuddered. "Well, I can see why you're not crazy about going back there."

He nodded. "But the land, even if it is bad, pulls me back, you know?" I glanced at him, but his face was stone now and unreadable. His gaze was fixed far out across the black water. We could hear voices laughing and talking from far down the beach, but somehow silence had fallen between us. I sensed there was more to the story, more that he knew and wanted to tell me, but wasn't able to yet.

Just as I was desperate for something to say, a ketchup packet flew across the table, and hit Bobby right in the chest. We jumped and spun around to see a boy with long hair, longer and shaggier than Bobby's, laughing at us from another table. "Need any ketchup?" he called and flipped us the finger.

Bobby's face was a mixture of amusement and embarrassment. His face lit up when he recognized his friend, but then instantly he remembered me and therefore was on his best manners, and he raised a hand in greeting. "Razzy, what the hell are you doing here?"

"Same as you, getting a bite to eat." He pointed to the girl next to him, a vacuous looking creature with a mountain of teased blond hair and buckskin fringe. "Brandi wanted a taco. You guys want some company?"

Bobby glanced at me again, and I shrugged. "Of course, they can join us," I offered, and relieved, he called them over. Razzy stepped over the swinging chain dividing the two seating areas, and then with a lot of giggling and cawing, helped his girlfriend over.

I looked him over. Like Bobby, John Razzini had shaggy rock star hair, just a few inches longer and a shade or two darker. He was skinnier and taller than Bobby, with the same dark tan from spending all summer on a painting ladder. Though I specifically didn't remember him, he said he had been to Lou's Diner with Bobby, part of the loud and boisterous group that had under-tipped and been so obnoxious.

"We cleaned up on Pancake Night!" he proclaimed, and then when he laughed, I remembered his voice calling for more pancakes, and I laughed with him. As for his date, Brandi, she looked barely out of high school. If that was one of the girls that hung around the boardwalk in the summer, screaming with her friends, smoking cigarettes and trying to look older, Razzy would have to be careful or he might be going to jail for playing with a baby, no matter how willing that baby might have been. Brandi and I looked at each other and quickly decided we hated each other.

Still, Razzy was fun, and it was impossible to be with him and not laugh. He and Bobby clearly were good friends, so close that they finished each other's sentences and roared with laughter over their stories and comments. I was glad he had shown up... not because I was glad he had interrupted our date, but because Bobby had been telling such a dark story about his childhood and Razzy's stupid, infectious laughter quickly brought him out of his slump. We sat there at the table for a good while, the music pumping merrily away from the loudspeakers atop the telephone poles: Bruce Springsteen and Simple Minds, Dire Straits and Duran Duran, and Huey Lewis. There was talk about going to a movie... I had already seen *The Goonies* and was eager to see *Back to the Future*, but Razzy was insistent upon *Rambo*, which showed the sort of entertainment he was partial to. Brandi didn't care, as long as she was with Razzy, but I was mindful of my mother, waiting up for me. Also, I worked the next day, and it was already after ten thirty.

Bobby wavered, but of course he sided with me, if he wanted a Second Date. He yawned impressively, and I tried not to look smugly over at Razzy. "I guess we'll have to take a raincheck."

Brandi popped a huge pink bubble and looked prettily at her Swatch. "Razzy, baby, if we're gonna go, we probably should get going. I *hate* to miss the previews." She looked at me, and inwardly I rolled my eyes.

Razzy stood up reluctantly. "You sure you don't want to go with us?" Clearly he liked a party, liked the company of his friends and from I could tell, Brandi served only one purpose—and that wasn't her mind. She hadn't been able to contribute much at all to our conversation but had sat popping her gum and twisting her hair like the predatory idiot she was.

"Naw, we're gonna call it a night," Bobby demurred, and pleased me again by reaching for my hand. "Although I thought we might take a quick walk down the beach before heading in. Beth? You up for that?"

"Absolutely." Razzy and Bobby gave each other a brotherly high five, while Brandi and I coolly ignored each other, and in a few minutes, I had my sandals swinging from my hands by their straps and we were walking along the shoreline. There was a summery breeze blowing over the water, ruffling our hair, and the stars were reflected in the lake like a silky mirror. It was a perfect night, and I was having an even better time than I could possibly have imagined. We walked along in companionable silence until Bobby offered, "I'm sorry that Razzy sorta intruded into our evening."

"Oh, that's all right, I don't mind," and I really didn't. Razzy was fun and goofy, and I hadn't been offended by him being there. "But I think that Brandi is a little light in the brains department. I don't think she'd fare well on Jeopardy, to be honest."

He laughed silently and squeezed my hand in agreement. We kept on walking, enjoying the night, enjoying each other until, as if we had planned it, we both stopped. Lake water lapped at our bare feet, and his blond hair shone in the moonlight. The time had come, we both knew it, and as he lowered his lips to mine, I could taste the cheap supper on his lips, and I didn't think that life couldn't get any better.

"How was that for a First Kiss?" he whispered, and gently stroked my cheek with his fingertips.

"Not bad," I sighed back. "But maybe we should do a Second Kiss to make sure we're doing it right…"

So, we did.

* * *

My mother was indeed waiting for me when I got home, sitting blearily-eyed in front of the television. I felt a pang of guilt, wishing she hadn't insisted on this, but one look at my happy face and she wanted to hear all about my evening. She made us each a big glass of iced tea, and while the big circular fan in the kitchen spun lazily above our heads, I filled her in on as many details as I thought prudent.

"I like him," she finally proclaimed. "He's a nice boy, with nice manners. And he has good hair. Not as good as Don Johnson, but not bad either."

"He does," I replied dreamily, and she laughed at me.

"Whoo, girl, you've got stars in your eyes," she said, picking up the glasses and putting them in the sink. She kissed me on my forehead as she headed towards bed. "I'm wishing you well, sweetie. I hope it goes well."

"Me too." I watched her disappear down the hall, and I sat in the dark quietly, reliving the evening. I went to my room, creamed off my makeup, brushed out my hair, and snuggled into my comfortable nightshirt. I laid with my head on the pillow, thinking of what a beautiful night it had been... things were exactly right and good. Everything in the world was perfect.

But apparently, the world wasn't perfect and bad things still happened, because that night, John Razzini disappeared.

CHAPTER VII

1864

He wasn't even aware that he had drifted off. He had fallen into a dreamless, light sleep, and he jerked awake. He lay in the darkness for several minutes, needing to pee, sickened by the pain in his stump, when he heard the whispering again.

"—lovely, yes, how lovely... that's right, ah, a Texan, are you? Just the faintest tinge of pepper, yes."

Charlie strained his eyes in the dark, trying to place where this voice was coming from. He struggled up on one elbow, and saw the dark outline of Sebastian Crane straddling the prone body of one of the new boys, one aisle over. McGraw, his name was; a young, redheaded lad with a strong accent and ropy, taut muscles. He hadn't been wounded, but had fallen sick with fever; they had brought him in the day before, out of his head, but in the past twelve hours the fever had broken and he had taken a little food.

Doctor Sebastian Crane had the limp, pale wrist of Thomas McGraw to his lips, and this time there was no doubt. He was not smelling for gangrene, he wasn't examining something closely. He was drinking blood right out of McGraw's arm. A dark line ran down McGraw's arms, and every now and then Crane would lift his head from the wound he had made in McGraw's wrist and lap at the blood like a cat.

"Oh, dear God," Charlie whispered, his eyes filling with tears. He shrank back against the cot, frozen with terror, not able to believe what he was seeing. He twisted his head side to side, unable to take his eyes off of Crane. The doctor slurped at the wound like he was partaking of a delicious, hot soup; he even made little mmm's in his throat of satisfaction. Charlie squeezed his eyes shut, unable to look away, trying to convince himself that this was just a dream.

And then he felt cold, dead fingers touching his chin.

1985

The next morning, I found myself up and early at work, floating on a cloud. I wanted to share the news and details of my date with someone other than my mother, but I wasn't sure exactly with whom. I knew I could tell Lou... he would listen politely, but he wasn't really the romantic type, and Paulina would view it as an act of hostility, so that just left Miguel. I found him in the kitchen, slicing cucumbers and tomatoes as he did the prep work for the salad bar. To give him his due, he listened attentively while I regaled him with all the minutiae of my evening, though I suppose it was out of loyalty and not genuine interest in my suddenly active love life.

Still, he had his opinions and wasn't shy about sharing them. "Hotdogs?" he wrinkled his nose. "He's a cheap one, eh?"

"Oh no, actually, it was my choice," I assured him, running my knife through a bunch of carrots, scraping them artfully. "It was real nice, there on the beach... the water, the music..."

Miguel rolled his eyes. "Who woulda known a house painter would have got your motor running, eh? Better slow down, chica." He snapped his fingers, suddenly remembering something. "Oh, by the way. Last night, you had a visitor come in, looking for you. They asked me to give this to you." He dug into his shirt pocket, and handed me a folded piece of paper.

I froze, thinking of the man I had seen at the edge of the parking lot—and the one I thought I had seen in my window the other night. Now, in the light of day I wasn't sure if I had dreamed it or not... it could have been caused by exhaustion, overexcitement, a reflection... or anything at all.

But another part of me—a nagging, suspicious part—argued that I knew *exactly* what I had seen, and that not only that, the two encounters were somehow linked. I just wasn't sure how yet, and quite frankly, I didn't want to think about it.

"Oh?" I tried to keep my voice casual. "Who was it?"

Miguel shrugged, uninterested. "The old spooky lady from the other day, the bruja. Maybe she wants to read your palm again, I dunno."

I had almost forgotten my palm reading, being so focused on my date with Bobby and trying *not* to think about the other strange things that had been happening to me lately. I unfolded the piece of paper, glancing at it in what I hoped was a casual way.

Beth...

Still looking to talk to you. We are leaving tomorrow at noon to go back home. We are at the Stillwell Motel on the highway, Room 148. If you would like to stop by tonight, I would be glad to talk to you then.

It's very important.

Harriet

Miguel looked at me curiously. "Well? What is it? Secret bruja stuff?"

I shrugged. "Something like that. Maybe she wants to give me a broomstick or something."

He looked at me closely. Like my mother, I had forgotten how well he knew me, despite my nonchalance. "Elizabeta," he singsonged. "I think you're full of something warm and brown. Did you forget who you're talking to?"

"Nope." I tossed a cherry tomato in his direction, and then popped one in my mouth. "You're the Emperor of Salads. And you better get that cabbage cut up before Lou comes back here and finds you loafing around." I fixed him with a stern eye. "You know how he tends to take his salad bar personally."

The morning passed fairly quickly. We were steady but not swamped; a few families of Summer People drifted in, mommies and daddies and kids in water wings with sun-screened noses, and later, a group of middle-aged women who were bent on hitting all the antique shops. I kept one eye on my tables and one eye on the clock, and just before noon, was rewarded with the sight of a familiar blue Jeep come roaring into the parking lot, Van Halen blared from its speakers. Over the grill, Lou looked at me and nodded approvingly. "At least he has good taste in music," he commented, "Though his volume is a little much for my taste." He gave me a wry little smile, waggled his spatula at me, and then returned to his burgers.

Bobby—blond, energetic and full of life—came into the diner with two of his crew. I hated it that most of the women in the place cast their eyes admiringly in his direction, but I did feel a stab of happiness when I saw him search the room, and then smiled when he found me.

"Hotdog Boy is here," Miguel whispered. "Good thing I filled the ketchup containers."

I shot him an evil look but stuffed my order pad into my apron and walked over to Bobby's table. He was pretending to look at a menu, and when I set down his glass of water in front of him, he said in an awful British accent, "Miss, what is good in this establishment?"

"Waffles. But it's not Waffle Wednesday, so I'd recommend the chicken basket."

He grinned up at me. His eyes were beautifully blue, like the waters of some tropical island, yet today they looked troubled. "That's good. I'm not really in the mood for pastries today anyway."

One of his friends peered over the menu at me. "But I'd be careful about asking him what he *is* in the mood for—"

Bobby looked sideways at him. "I'm in the mood for you to shut up," he barked, and there was enough warning in his voice that his friend disappeared back behind the menu. He glanced at me. "Sorry about that. Some of us have no sense of manners."

I shrugged. "It's okay." He had little paint spatters across his tee shirt, and he smelled like sunshine. I tried not to stare, but in doing so, I noticed a cloud over his features, and I whispered, "Are you all right? What's wrong?"

He frowned slightly, troubled. "Razzy didn't come home last night."

I inwardly shrugged. John Razzini hadn't struck me as someone who was good at checking in or minding a curfew, and nearly said so. But Bobby's face was clearly anxious, and his friends glanced at each other worriedly, so I knew this was more serious than I had imagined. "Well, did you call Brandi?"

"Not yet. But you saw them last night. Did you think he was all that interested in her?"

I chewed on my lip thoughtfully. "Well, no. Actually, from what I could tell, he seemed kinda annoyed with her at times." I cleared my throat, choosing my words carefully. "To be honest, I could agree with that... she didn't seem like... well, I doubt that her SAT scores were all that high."

"If she took it. I know. That's typical of Razzy's dates, blonde and boobs and no brains." He glanced at me. "Sorry. That was crude."

"Yeah, it was." I shrugged. "But that's all right." I glanced behind him, and saw another table of patrons waiting, giving me impatient looks. "Tell you what, Bobby. Give me a few minutes, and I can take a quick break. If you want, we can eat out on the back patio. There are some wrought iron tables out there, overlooking the water..." I glanced significantly at his friends. "It might be a little more private."

"Are we cramping your style?" one of his friends asked, in mock surprise, and I rolled my eyes.

"You won't if you're in here and I'm out there," Bobby fired back, and smiling I walked away. Ten minutes later, I had taken off my apron and was sitting next to Bobby; he had ordered a tuna melt and fries, and we each had an iced tea. Lou's back patio was nearly empty except for a pair of elderly ladies in sun hats, chatting over salads and a National

Enquirer. Above us, large striped umbrellas, open to shield us from the June sun, rippled lightly in the breeze.

"It's not like Razzy is a saint or anything," Bobby said, chewing around his sandwich. "But even at his worst, he wouldn't miss work. He was poor as a kid, and so a strong work ethic was just something his father instilled in him. I've even seen him show up at work with a fever of over a hundred degrees. He certainly wouldn't have missed work for some little trampy girl he just met a few days ago."

"Well, I hate to bring this up…" I cleared my throat. "Have you checked the hospital yet? Maybe he had a wreck or something."

"Not yet." He shook his head. "And I haven't called his parents yet either, though I know I probably should, if I don't hear from him tonight. I don't want to worry them if I don't have to, but I also don't want to wait too long, if something really is wrong." He played restlessly with his straw, swirling a few ice cubes. "And I'll tell you what keeps bothering me. I keep thinking about those two guys that got killed a few weeks ago."

A chill went down my back as I realized he was right. I hadn't even considered a connection between the two situations, and looking at Bobby's worried face made me realize there were indeed similarities. There had been no further developments on that first case, though it was still fresh in everyone's mind.

Every day on the news, there was still some reports about it, but no real answers: the searchers were looking in a different part of the woods. The boys' roommates had been re-interviewed, and there were more tearful pleas from the mothers. The university had even collected money and offered a reward for any information, but even that had failed to turn up anything solid. No arrests, no bodies, not even any new clue. Those boys had just been wiped away, leaving a bloody mess behind them, and now *another* boy—someone who was close to me—had gone missing. I swallowed hard.

"Bobby," I said, taking his hand, "I don't know Razzy that well. Actually, I don't even know *you* that well," and I watched him smile a little. "But I don't think that anything's happened to him. I bet that he's probably just holed up with that girl and will be slinking in home tonight."

He shrugged and focused on a speedboat zipping across the lake; a skier, bright in a neon green flotation vest, waved at people on the shore and whooped to them merrily. He smiled, and I could almost read his thoughts. Here it was, a beautiful summer day, and while some people were carelessly squandering their time in useless frivolity, other people were distraught over missing—or dead, God forbid—loved ones. And so, the world kept spinning.

"All right, you could be right. Razzy is a wild child; he always has been. Maybe he's just on a bender." He tried to smile, seeing if I believed what he was saying, and I smiled back. We sat for several minutes in pleasant silence, so long that the speed boat made several more passes back and forth on the lake.

"Hey," he said suddenly. "What do you think about going out tonight? Maybe a movie?"

There was nothing I would have loved more, but I remembered Harriet's note in my pocket, and I shook my head. "Bobby, I can't... I already had something planned."

His face fell, but he nodded graciously. "Oh, it's okay. I mean, I just thought... not that we're exclusive or anything... that is..."

I shook my head, secretly thrilled that he seemed jealous. "Oh, it's not another date with someone, don't worry. It's just something I have to do, that's all." I crossed my fingers. "A family thing, is all."

He raised his eyebrows. "Everything all right?"

I waved carelessly. "Oh, of course. You know, nothing serious. It's no big deal."

Beth... please call me as soon as you can. I feel you are in terrible danger.

"All right." He played with his straw a little more. Apparently, he was too preoccupied to eat, and now I had just given him another worry. "I didn't mean to pry. Sorry."

"Bobby..." I hated to lie to him about this—and another part of me reminded me that I was starting a relationship out on a lie, and that is *never* a good idea—but I also didn't want to tell him that the reason I couldn't see him tonight was that I had been summoned to a secret meeting because a palm reader hadn't liked the curvature of my hand. It just seemed too crazy. What would he think of me? Heck, it *was* crazy, I recognized that.

And yet, she had been so insistent, so sincere and almost scared by what she had seen that it had worried me enough to go and see what had made her so flustered. "Bobby, it's no big deal. Don't worry, I like you. I just can't go tonight. Ask about any other night this week except for Wednesday—I work then, and Friday night too—and I'm free."

He nodded. "Ok. Fair enough. I just wanted to make sure—"

I stood up and kissed him, moving so fast it probably startled him. Behind us, I heard the two little old ladies twitter and chatter among themselves in a mixture of giggling approval and embarrassment, and then I sat back down and faced him levelly.

"Make sure of that. Okay?" I suddenly couldn't believe my own boldness and blushed to the roots of my hair. "And before I make an even bigger fool of myself, I better get back to work. My break is about over."

He looked pleased and then glanced over at the two ladies, who were watching us. "The service here is excellent!" he assured them, and while they all laughed, I hurried back inside, tying my apron back on as I went. I didn't tell anyone about going to see Harriet, probably because I was too embarrassed. Looking back, I realized this wasn't a good plan, if reading my palm hadn't really been their true agenda. For all I knew of these seemingly friendly summer people, they could have been white slavers, prepared to slip a needle in my arm the minute I walked into their hotel room. They could spirit me away, and I would never be seen again... but then I decided my life was already crazy enough without adding extra embellishments, and so I went.

* * *

I drove out to the Stillwell Motel after work, almost hoping that Harriet and her family had changed their itinerary and had gone home early. The motel was all one story, laid out in spokes from a main central office, and I parked my car along the spoke known as Tourist Way. For a moment, I paused outside Room 148, staring at the numbers in gold on the door, wondering what it was about them that bothered me. And then I realized that, added together, they totaled thirteen.

As if I needed another omen, this was just getting better and better by the minute. I shook my head, deciding what to make of this, when the door opened and there stood Harriet, decked out in a flowered sundress and big colorful, plastic jewelry. She looked like a walking Afghan when she greeted me.

"Beth! I'm so glad you made it, come in, come in." She moved out of the way, letting me pass. "Everyone else is out to dinner… I kicked 'em out, to be honest, so we can be alone."

"Did they go to Lou's?" I asked, worriedly.

"Oh no, not on your life. Harold found a cute little steakhouse on the other side of the lake. They serve all-you-can-eat French fries, so I'm sure Phyllis is in hog heaven." There was a little occasional table in one corner, littered with playing cards and magazines; she swept them off with one generous sweep of her arm, and then indicated a chair. "Go on, sweetie, sit down. We have a lot to talk about, I think."

Nervously, I took a seat. I was tense and alert, ready to bolt out the door the very second I sensed danger. I could still imagine Harold and Phyllis hiding in the bathroom and bursting in on us the minute I let my guard down…

"—have to admit, I've never experienced *anything* like what I felt that day I touched your hand," she was saying, and I jerked back to attention. She looked at me closely. "Beth? Are you following me?"

I nodded. "Of course. Sorry. I'm just curious about all of this, is all."

"Just curious?"

I shrugged. "Well, all right. Maybe a little freaked out, to be honest."

"Well, you have reason to be freaked out," she nodded. She picked up an embroidered cigarette case. "Do you want a ciggie?"

I shook my head, ready to scream. "No, I don't smoke."

She flipped open the case. "Well, I do. Nasty habit, though. I wish I had never started. They're more addictive than heroin, or so I hear." She lit one with the expertise of a long-time smoker, and then exhaled slowly, obviously savoring the taste as it entered her lungs. Like a dragon, she exhaled through her nose, sending twin plumes of smoke back out of her body.

"All right, my dear, the time has come, to speak of the whys and the howcomes of all of this." She took a deep sigh. "And first, I need to admit to you that mostly I'm a fraud."

I jerked. "What?"

She shrugged. "A fraud. Most of what I do, I've read from books. I've got quite a collection at home." She smiled sadly. "Some hobby, huh? I never took to gardening or crocheting. I hate exercise, and I'm allergic to pets. So, I cast about, looking for something to keep me busy, and I found that fortune telling, palm reading, and the like is all very easy. I've always had a particular interest in things like that, you see. Maybe my interest isn't even healthy, I dunno," she shrugged. "But I've always liked ghost stories, witches and spooky things. I'm the one in the group that always likes scary movies, y'know?"

I smiled politely, imagining her at one of those slasher movies, screaming her head off and jumping at every chance.

"I took an interest in the occult, and like all who work in the industry—palm readers, ghost hunters, and the like—I quickly figured out that a little touch of flash helps the show. In high school, I was an actress, and half of what I do is pure hokum. I give the paying customer what they want, see? A little spicy romance for the women, maybe a mysterious gentleman they're about to meet, or fortune and coming into money for the men, with different variations; traveling over sea, maybe visitors from old friends, maybe a gentle warning here or there about things that aren't really all that scary. I might remind an older person who I assume is on medication not to forget their pills in the morning, or maybe a college kid the dangers of drinking and driving, because I can see twisted metal and a mother crying in their future. That sort of thing."

I frowned. "I'm not sure why you're telling me all of this."

She smiled, reached out and tapped her ash into a little ceramic dish. "Because I want you to know that what I saw when I touched your hand was the pure truth. No hokum, no little show, none of that." She took a deep breath. "In fact, Beth, to be honest, most of what I do is crap.

I make up stuff, just for fun, and rarely, if ever do I get a true psychic flash. But when I touched your hand, I didn't get a flash, but a whole explosion of lightning."

"But Harold said… the whole furnace story…" My head was spinning.

She nodded wearily. "That's the funny thing. Occasionally, I *do* get it right. Not often, and never planned. That furnace story—that's true. Three years ago, I was at a Tupperware party with some of my neighbors, and they wanted me to do some readings on them… to be honest, we had all been nipping at some homemade wine Bonnie Hunter had made last spring, and we were all a little screamy. But I read their fortunes anyway, and when I went to take ol' Florence Carmichael's hand, I immediately said, 'Get into the doctor tomorrow, Florrie, you've got a nasty-bad blood clot down in your leg.' Well, *that* shut the room right down, let me tell you, and pretty much ended the party, but the next day Florrie did go to the doctor, and sure enough, she did have a blood clot down in her left leg, about as big as a grain of salt that was moving its way upwards. She called me from the hospital, crying and blubbering, carrying on that I had saved her life, and blah blah… '*How did you know, Harriet?*' she kept asking me, and I pretended it was some Mystery of the Orient and I would be doomed if I told her… but of course the truth is, I have no idea." She looked at me levelly through the smoke. "No idea at all, Beth."

I observed her for a second, and then said shakily, "So most of the time, you just make things up, saying whatever you like for entertainment purposes—just vague, random things, to please the mark, right?"

She nodded. "Yep. Random is a good way to put it. If what I say comes true, then I'm a success. If I gave warning and they do something to correct their behavior, I'm a success *that* way too. Get it? It's a foolproof way of always being right. But every now and then, I do get it right, I get a dead-on hit, like that game *Battleship*. Do you understand? Most of that game requires groping around, casting hopeful probes onto a blank grid. But every now and then you get a direct hit, and girl, yours was a doozy."

I nodded. It was a good analogy, floundering blindly around in the psychic netherworld for a bullseye, mostly missing, but occasionally getting lucky. But then that meant the obvious: that something about me had twitched her supernatural antenna, and I wondered what it was and what she had seen.

"So... no trips over water for me, no coming into riches?" I tried to make my voice light and carefree, but she smiled bitterly.

"No." She took a deep lungful of smoke and blew it out again. "More than that, I should say. Quite a lot more."

My nerves broke. "Harriet, please tell me! This is awful, this verbal cat and mouse... if you know something or think you know something, please tell me."

She looked sympathetic and concerned, but I also noticed she took care not to touch me. "I'm sorry, sweetheart. I don't mean to cause you trouble or stress you or anything. But I do think you have a right to know what I saw, keeping in mind that maybe I'm totally, completely wrong, and these are all the products of an old woman's overactive imagination and too much beer." She flicked another ash and took another deep breath. "All right. That day in the diner... it was more the vibe I got off of you that raised my suspicions than what I saw in your palm."

"My... vibe?"

"Sure. Your psychic aura... your spiritual cloak, so to speak. Your *energy*. Everyone emits different psychic signals, though to different degrees; some seers think of them as colors or vibrations. They can touch someone and will be able to pick up a variety of things about that person based on just a touch. It's kinda like a search and rescue dog sniffing something that belonged to a person; they get a smell from that person that helps them find them. Well, it's similar, except when I touch someone, if that person's vibe or energy is strong, I can get a bead on them, and I *know* things about them."

Skeptically, I challenged her. "So, when you touched me... what did you get a bead on?"

She smiled thinly. "Well, you sure project, so some of it was easy."

"Like what?" I wasn't about to let her off the hook.

"You have a sadness about you… you've lost a parent, though not lost to death. And you come from a family of scholars, either educators or teachers, though I don't know exactly what or whom."

I stared at her. "Those are all things you could have easily found out, simply by asking people at the diner."

She shrugged. "But I didn't and I didn't need to, because I already knew." There was such a finality and certainty to her voice that I believed her. "But here's the thing… when I get a bead on things, it's never like a whole picture. It's like a movie screen, with part of it blacked out. You know how you can look out of the corner of your eye and see things… what's that called? Perri…"

"Peripheral vision," I said softly.

She snapped her fingers. "That's it. That kind of vision. Well, it's the same. I can never see the whole picture all of the time. I know you're from a family of scholars, but I don't know who or what they teach. I know you've had a rough time of it growing up, but I don't know which parent left you… and when I mean left you, I don't think they died, but really left you."

"My dad," I whispered. "He left me and my mom a long time ago."

She nodded. "I see." She stubbed out her cigarette, considered the pack, and then shook out another one. "Damn things. Whenever I get stressed, I can't lay off 'em." She lit it and then observed me frankly. "Beth, I have to be honest. There is more I picked up on…"

"I figured." My throat was dry. "Well, go on."

"Well, all right. I guess you deserve to know." She looked away. "All right, here it is. The next few months are going to be the best *and* the worst in your life. I saw polar opposites, totally different ends of the spectrum. Sadness and happiness. Black and white. Fear and contentment… but intense, Beth. Intensely so. Forgive me, but are you in love?"

I blushed. "I don't know… I've recently met someone, but it's too early to tell…"

"No, it isn't. This young man, whoever he is, is going to be the one great love of your life. In fact, he is going to change your entire life… the very course you thought you were on—because of this young man—has changed. Your direction... hell, Beth, your purpose, your life's very *purpose*, has been altered forever because of this boy."

I looked at her crazily. "That's absurd, Harriet... this boy, I just met him a few days ago. We've only been out once. How could he change my life so drastically?"

She shook her head. "I don't know how, but I just know that he will. Everything you think you want to do, the direction you think your life is going—well, it's not, honey. It's all about to change."

A chill went through me, and my stomach dropped. "Do you mean... teaching? I'm not going to be a teacher?"

She looked away, and I saw her chin quiver. "No. You will never see the inside of a classroom."

I gaped at her. "But that's all I've ever wanted to be! It's what I've been saving and scrimping and studying for... for years! And now you're saying that because I went on one date, it's all going to be wiped away?! That's crazy, Harriet." I stood up, grabbing for my keys. "I'm leaving."

"Don't." Her voice was pleading. "There's more."

"I don't want to hear any more of this." I turned to go, my head spinning, and headed for the door. But my footsteps were heavy, and my heart was pounding, and as I reached for the knob, she said, "I know about the missing boys. And how they're connected to you."

I froze.

Slowly, I turned back to look at her. "What did you say?"

She smiled sadly. "The missing boys. There are three of them now, but that's not for general information. So far, only two have been reported, and the third one soon will be."

Razzy didn't come home last night... I haven't called his parents yet either, though I know I probably should if I don't hear from him tonight.

"What do you know about this?" My throat was so dry I could barely speak, and I wondered if this woman and her clan had something to do with these disappearances after all. My hand remained on the knob, prepared to flee at the second, the very *second* she moved towards me.

But she only sat there, a fat old woman in a colorful caftan, smoking her cigarette and regarding me sadly. "I don't know a lot. There are holes in the screen, remember? I just know that somehow, they're connected to you, to what course you have now become set upon."

"Those boys... they haven't even been found. They're just missing, at this point, and the last one... well, that just happened. Are you saying they're all dead?"

She sighed heavily, a sigh that seemed to come from her very soul. "Yes. They're all dead."

Tears sprang to my eyes as this sank in. "I didn't even know them... two of them, only slightly, the third, not at all." Helplessly I stared at her. "I don't know what you're talking about. I swear I don't!"

"I know." She shook her head. "I don't either, really, and that's the hell of it. But what I can tell you, though, is this: somehow, these three deaths are connected to you. Something is stalking you, though it's not really you it wants. It's hunting someone close to you, hunting them for its own evil reasons and purposes far beyond our understanding."

I thought of the man in the parking lot and the face in the window, and suddenly, I *believed* her. Oh my God, I believed her, and I felt my knees weaken.

"Harriet, you're scaring me..."

"Good. Fear causes awareness, and you need to be aware." Suddenly fire came to her eyes. "Beth, whatever is stalking you... it's aware of you, but it doesn't seem to consider you a threat, only a curiosity. It might be using you as bait for what it's really after, or it might only be observing you, the way a scout observes another team before a game. But however it falls, I know that you've raised its interest, and it is sniffing you out. You will have to be very careful."

"But what—or who—is it? Is it someone I know? Someone from the diner? Someone from school?" A thought occurred to me. "Could it be my father?"

She shook her head. "No, to all of those. It's no one you know, and certainly not your father." She firmed her jaw. "I wish I could tell you more, so you know what to watch out for."

I looked closely at her. "You keep referring to this not as a person, but as a thing."

She nodded. "I would say that's fair. Because I'm not sure that whatever it is that's chasing you—or rather, chasing someone close to you—is a person. It's something spiritual, I think."

She looked thoughtful, as she tried to articulate what she was seeing. "Alive, but not anymore. A predator, certainly," she spread her hands helplessly, and from the look on her face, I could tell she was honestly distressed. "More than that, I'm not sure."

"Something spiritual... like a ghost? What does that mean?" I looked at her, mouth open, and she blew out another plume of smoke.

"All I can pick up on is that it's like a moving storm front, coming your way—an entity, maybe—but it has intelligence and a purpose. Possibly demonic... I don't know. That's the closest I can come—a demon, perhaps—but even *that's* not quite right. But whatever it is, you have caught its attention, and probably by proxy, I now have too. That's the real reason we're leaving tomorrow—to get as far from here as we can. But I thought I should tell you, before I leave."

I looked at her trembling, at the ashtray full of butts, and I realized she was afraid. "You're scared," I said softly, and she grunted.

"I'm not scared, my dear; I'm terrified out of my mind. In all my years doing this, looking at palms, casting tarot cards, and reading and learning about such things, have I ever experienced *anything* like this. And when I do get that occasional vibe, it never has anything to do with me. But this time, I feel like I'm in the way of something bad, and it terrifies me—this feeling of a truly evil force, hunting and searching and single-mindedly intent on destruction." Her voice broke, and I thought she was actually going to cry. "I don't know what to do except to get out of its way, to run away as far and as fast as I can."

I looked at her, horrified. "And me? What do I do?"

She smiled, a truly sad, regretful smile. "Beth, my dear, I don't know that you can do anything except to pray. There is power in prayer, you know..."

"That's it? You don't have anything else for me? You drag me here, you scare the bejeezus out of me, and you don't tell me what to do now?"

She shook her head. "But I did. I'm telling you to pray. At this point, I don't know what else to tell you."

Then she turned away, and I knew I would get nothing else out of her. Shaking, I turned the knob, my head spinning, and went out into the night.

I'm telling you to pray. At this point, I don't know what else to tell you.

VIII
CHAPTER

1864

Charlie Barnham opened his terrified eyes to see good Doctor Crane standing over him, smiling indulgently. "Well, good evening there," he said, his voice silky and quiet. "How's the arm?"

"For the love of God," Charlie whispered, "What kind of thing are you?"

Sebastian cocked an amused eyebrow. "Just like you, in most ways." He caressed Charlie's temple, his fingers lingering over the pale vein that pulsed under Charlie's fair hairline. "But in some ways different. I am, you see, not only a doctor, not only a gentleman from New Orleans, not only the man who saved your life." He leaned closer to Charlie, to whisper in his ear, "I am Vampyr."

The word meant nothing to Charlie. In his backwoods of Tennessee, he had been exposed to plenty of folktales; haints, ghosts, goosalums and restless spirits had been all the talk of the hillfolk. There had even been an Indian legend of a creature named a wendigo who resembled a large crow on a baby's body... but the term vampire had never been mentioned.

The concept was very clear, however. Whatever sort of creature Crane was, he was something that drank blood off of the living, something old, evil and dangerous. Crane studied Charlie for a second, realizing he had no experience with the word, and he gave a cold smile. "Vampyr," he said, "is something unholy, something removed from God, though usually without the Vampyr's permission. No man willingly wants to be a Vampyr, you see. Unlike you, my dear friend, I will never grow old, never sicken, never die."

"You drink blood!" Charlie whispered. To his horror and shame, he was still crying, but he was unable to stop. "You drink blood!"

Crane nodded. "Yes, that's true. In peacetime, I hunt the streets and parties at night for my victims, and in wartime? How perfect!" His eyes gleamed dully in the night. "Oceans and oceans of blood... I love wartime, my friend. The War for Independence was something. It was a feast indeed. But this! There's never been anything like this! Thousands and thousands of men slamming into one another, killing without abandon! I realized at Manassas what potential this War held... but I had no idea how marvelous Antietam could possibly be, or Gettysburg! I fed for days!" His eyes glassed over, as if in rapture. "How marvelous! As a doctor, I attach myself to an army—usually the losing side, of course, since there are more wounds—and then..." he gave a Gallic shrug. "This little conflict, I hope it never ends!"

Charlie looked at him in horror and tried to inch his way back from Crane, scooting his body on the canvas cot. Pain flared along the stump of his arm, and he gasped in pain. Crane cocked his head hopefully.

"You must be careful," he said, his eyes gleaming, "That you don't injure yourself, and re-open that wound."

And as he said it, he involuntarily licked his lips.

1985
....

Every day Bobby would pick me up after work, waiting outside Lou's in his battered blue Jeep, baseball hat cocked jauntily backwards, and smelling of sun and hard work. He became browner every day, and his hair bleached out the color of cornsilk; he was achingly handsome, and Paulina was overheard saying, "What the hell does a babe like that see in her?"

I often wondered that myself but was afraid to ask. But evidently there was *something*, because within a week of dating, I was with him practically every moment I wasn't working. His friends, after our first meeting, calmed down considerably—I suspected he had a few strong words with them—and I met all of their girlfriends... though, granted, most of the girls in the group came and went, depending on the day and how much beer had been consumed. Their beach house was a regular case of musical-chairs-around-the-bedroom, which scared me at first because I didn't want to be just another name on the list. When I finally got up the courage to ask Bobby that, he looked at me gravely and kissed me on the nose. "I'm not like that, Beth. I never... well, you're different. You're special... I wouldn't do that to you." His words made my heart swell; my eyes misted over as he held me tight, and I knew he was perfect.

My mother was both amused and thrilled by the whole situation, and she and Bobby became good friends. She took to baking again after learning he liked oatmeal cookies, and in return he did odd jobs around the house for her. He nailed on a few loose shingles, carried a bunch of junk from the garage to the corner for her, and even gave the back fence a lovely coat of Continental White. She began to talk to me about the joys of having blond grandchildren, and I don't think she was really kidding. "Hold on to that one," she would tell me. "He's too good to let go." And I agreed.

John Razzini was reported missing on the second day of his disappearance, though the story never quite generated the same interest the way the other missing boys did. Partly, I think, was that there was a definite crime scene in the first case; a bloody, abandoned car. Razzy had just disappeared, which according to the police, really wasn't a crime. He could be reported as a Missing Person, and he was, but as they pointed out, he was young, white and over twenty-one. He could do what he liked, and the supposition was that he had grown tired of his menial job and taken off for greener pastures. Bobby and his roommates argued this theory with the police, and Razzy's parents did too, but to no avail. "He's just rambling around somewhere, probably chasing a girl, or weed, or something," one of the police officers opined. "He'll turn up when the money runs out, or we'll get a call from some little police force in Arizona or somewhere that picked him up for vagrancy or public intox or something. You'll see."

The other reason I think Razzy's case didn't generate the interest the way other one did was because of money and familiarity. Partridge and Giorgio had been local boys of some standing from affluent families. John Razzini was an Outsider; not much better than a Summer Person, and therefore thought of as little more than transient. His parents didn't have the money or the wherewithal to organize the media the way the other families had, and so his story never generated more than a third page little blurb in the newspaper. Bobby and the roommates passed out flyers one Saturday and I helped them, but nothing ever came of it. Razzy was just Gone, and according to Harriet—and this was a theory I kept to myself, never sharing with anyone, especially Bobby—he was already dead. It was depressing business.

But we tried not to dwell on it. Oddly enough, the whole situation helped Bobby and me to get closer. Off days were spent on his boat. Sometimes we water skied with his friends, or sometimes just the two of us went off into some of the coves for private time for us. We searched for crabs and mussels, picnicked on the rocks, or kissed and made out in the trees. He was very gentle and very patient, and when I finally allowed him to go as far as he wanted—as we both wanted, really—it was a beautiful July day without a cloud in the sky. I lay on the blanket, and for several of the sweetest hours of my life, I stroked his hair, felt his weight on me, and startled the birds in the trees by crying his name out loud.

It was a regular routine for us to build a bonfire on the beach and gather with his friends. We spent our nights watching the waves roll across the sand, and the sounds of the loons were never able to drown out all the laughter. Bobby was very careful with his alcohol... I never saw him drink more than a few beers at any one time, even when his friends became puking drunk, which I appreciated because I had already had my share of drunken college boys. It was a sweet time for us... we were stupidly in love, and for a brief time, I was sure the world was perfect.

I tried not to think about Harriet and her strange predictions. In defiance of what she had said, I poured my energy into my final assignments for the classes and was rewarded with good grades and heaps of praise from my professors. One project had me incorporating children's literature into a multi-disciplinary unit, which earned me high marks and an encouraging note from one of my instructors. *"Looks like a wonderful, well-thought-out plan, Beth. You've done a good job making this fun and meaningful for your future students. Can't wait to see it put into place."* And truth be told, I hoped I would be able to.

Things were going so well. My life was so sweet and perfect that I began to think that everything Harriet had said was wrong and crazy. I was happy; my schoolwork was going well, and I was stupidly in love. Harriet's wild predictions were a million miles wrong, and my feet were perfectly set on the path I had chosen. For the first time ever, my life was blessed.

I had no idea how wrong I was.

The world had its share of evil, and it was closing in on us.

* * *

There were two men in my life that summer, and now it is time to tell of the second.

I first saw him one night, well after dark, at the diner. Paulina and the other two waitresses—*servers*—had been scheduled to work, and I had been scheduled to be off, but somehow Paulina had managed to convince Lou that she needed the night off, and both of the other girls had already left for the night since business was slow, so I was nearly alone when he walked in.

He was a slender man, with black, curly hair slicked back from his forehead. He wore a black cotton shirt, open to reveal dark whorls of hair on his chest, and his shoes tapped expensively on the tiles as he made his way to a corner booth. He was obviously an Out-of-Towner… he was no one I had ever seen before, but that was not uncommon. It was the height of tourist season, and lots of people from the larger towns came this way to vacation or to go antique shopping. He was clearly just another Summer Person, down to the lake for a weekend of fishing and antiquing. Still, the thought crossed my mind that for a vacationer, he was dressed very well, especially to be eating supper by himself in a diner.

With the grace of a dancer, he slid lithely into the seat, opened a menu, and ran one thumb thoughtfully down the items. I pasted a smile on my features and headed his way with the coffee pot. Truth be told, I was in a grumpy mood. I could imagine Bobby and his friends down on the beach, even though he had told me he would wait for me and pick me up later. Still, I was missing the bonfire, the laughter, and most of all, him. I certainly didn't want to be serving grilled cheese and fries this evening to strangers.

"Evening," I said politely. Before I could pour him a cup, he raised one casual hand to halt me.

"Hello, Beth." He looked up at me, his dark eyes gleaming. For a second, I felt my heart race.

"How did you know my name?" I stammered. The hair on my arms rose, and I heard my voice pitch a little. It was silly since there was no reason to be worried or afraid... yet I was. Being this close to this stranger had sent electric chills through me for some unknown reason, and I tightened my grip on the plastic handle of the coffee pot.

He smiled and nodded to my chest. "Nametag," he said. I caught a hint of a southern drawl, but I couldn't fine it down more than that in just the few words he had spoken.

Relief flooded me, but not totally. I laughed nervously. "Oh, of course. But I thought you knew me, the way you... oh, never mind." I motioned to his coffee cup. "You want decaf instead?"

He gave a Gallic shrug, and I saw again how very handsome he was. It was an unconventional handsomeness... his nose was slightly overlarge, but his skin was flawless, and his jaw was strong and blue from a recent shave. Dark, feathery eyebrows floated over his eyes... and what eyes they were. They were of the darkest blue; so blue they were almost black, like perfect spheres of coal. They brimmed with intelligence and a knowledge—no, an *understanding* of things—that made me nervous. "Perhaps not. Coffee keeps me up at night," and he offered me a little half smile, but somehow, I sensed it was more of a private joke, and I didn't care to understand its meaning. Again, I caught the accent... there was a hint of Southern in his voice, but not white trashy Southern... classy, old aristocratic Southern, from what I could tell.

I cleared my throat. "All right. Can I get you something else then?"

He looked at me closely again, as if bemused, and then looked out the window into the night. "Do you love, Beth?"

I was nastily startled. "What?"

Without turning his head much, he flicked his eyes in my direction. "Do you love, Beth?"

I took a step backward. I had had my share of men coming on to me since I had worked at Lou's, of course... touristy husbands sneaking gropes when their wives were in the restroom, other college boys writing their phone numbers on napkins and pushing them at me, even pimply middle school kids trying to look down my blouse. I had handled them all with different degrees of tact and good humor, but I had never, ever felt alarm until now—just disgusted annoyance. But this man, staring at me, made me afraid. Somehow, this was different, though I couldn't say just how. I just knew that in some way I couldn't explain, this man was dangerous, and he scared me.

"Look," I said, trying to control my voice. "I don't know what you're getting at, but I... I've got a boyfriend, and he..."

He looked at me smugly. "Ah yes. *That* is the one you love. The affable Master Barnham. Lives in a big old house on the lake, with a bunch of other young men... drives a blue Jeep, if I'm correct?"

Desperately, I looked behind me, hoping to see Lou watching us from over the counter, but I heard the clanking of pans and water running, so I knew he was away and would be able to offer no help. I looked at this man again, knowing if he took one step in my direction, I would throw the entire pot of hot coffee in his face and run like crazy.

"How... how did you know..."

He shrugged again. "Small towns. You know how they are. Everyone is in everyone's business, Beth. Everyone knows all the dirty little secrets, even those like me who are new here." He looked back into the night and watched the moths batting against the window. "Everyone knows everyone's family, everyone's past. The things that should be kept secret aren't secrets at all… who is ill, who is dying, where the bodies are buried…" he flicked his eyes at me again, this time with smug knowledge. "Who goes to the hidden coves on the lake, and what they do there…"

My skin crawled, but I found my voice. "Get out. Get out of here before I call—"

He laughed, and it was a cruel laugh, a laugh tinged with arrogance. "Who would you call, Beth? The police? I've dealt with enough officials and soldiers in my life so that it seems nothing more than a mere annoyance at this point. Would you call your old, fat cook behind the counter? He doesn't appear to be very intimidating, if you forgive me." He smiled at me. "Your gentleman friend? Mister Barnham?"

I nodded, too afraid to speak, and he cocked an eyebrow. "Yes. That would be good. Please call him. I would like very much for you to call Mister Barnham… I would so *very* much like to meet him."

He stood up so fast I had to move backwards to avoid hitting him, and I couldn't even imagine touching him. For a second—though it seemed longer—we were only inches apart, and I could smell the very nearness of him.

"Don't worry, Beth. I am leaving. You won't have to call anyone." I moved back, and he sidled past me. I watched him walk leisurely toward the door, and then he paused, one hand on the push-bar.

"Love is a funny thing, isn't it? One day it's here, and the next, it's gone." He considered me for a second, and then tipped me a wink. "It was lovely meeting you, Miss Beth. I've no doubt we'll meet again, and soon."

And then he was gone into the night, and I was shaking.

CHAPTER IX

1864

Charlie moaned deep in his throat. "But you're a doctor... you saved my life."

Sebastian smiled. "Yes, for a while. When I was amputating your hand, my saw hit an artery, and a gout of lovely, fresh blood sprayed me. To a doctor, this is nothing new; to the layman this is disgusting... but to me? Ambrosia!" He grew quiet for a second, savoring the memory. After a second, he continued. "And I tasted you, took you into me." He leaned forward, interested. "Tell me, friend, where are you from?"

"Tennessee," Charlie whispered.

"Ah, yes, Tennessee," Sebastian repeated thoughtfully. "That's why I didn't immediately recognize it. It was thick and heady, with just the slightest taste of... I'm not sure what. Do you live near an orchard?"

Charlie shook his head. "Blackberries," he said softly. "Lots of 'em... my ma raised 'em to sell, made jams and jellies, wine... I was raised on it."

Sebastian sighed happily. "That's it," he nodded. "Blackberries, ah, delicious." His eyes flickered down to Charlie's stump, and his tongue flickered out uncontrollably. "I kept you aside, friend. Like a patron of fine wine, I put you aside, nursed you back to health, while I fed on others. Men *from all over your Confederacy, all with different tastes and bouquets... but none like you, friend. None as sweet, or as heady as you."* He smiled chillingly in the dark and raised the bloody stump that had been Charlie Barnham's hand to his lips. He sniffed it, and his tongue tasted the bandage approvingly, while Charlie trembled.

"And you see," Sebastian whispered, as he prepared to drink, "see how convenient I left it? No biting, no breaking the skin. I simply removed the bandage," and he did so, with a flourish, "Immediate access! How easily I can feed!"

And after a while, "Ah, blackberries..."

1985

I told Bobby all about my terrifying encounter later that evening. The fire in the firepit on the beach had burned down to low embers; his friends had gone in for the night, so it was just the two of us, propped up against a large rock, cuddled under a blanket. He was so warm, and I was so afraid that I couldn't get close enough to him, and he held me tight and stroked my hair.

"He was just a nut, that's all," he said, and I could tell from the casual tone in his voice that he really wasn't that alarmed. "Just some psycho getting his kicks off." He kissed the top of my head and stared into the fire. His profile looked so handsome in the firelight that my heart flip flopped, and I reached up to stroke his cheek. He took my hand and kissed my fingertips. "But you didn't see him, Bobby. He was..." I shook my head, unable to articulate it. "He was *scary*. Like bad scary. And he *knew* things."

He shrugged under the blanket. "Well, one thing that he said is true; it is a small town... everybody around here knows I drive a blue Jeep." He kissed me again. "You just shouldn't be such a cutie, guys wouldn't hit on you like that."

I poked him. "He wasn't hitting on me." A sudden thought occurred to me. "It wasn't like that. He was... polite. Creepy, but polite. And he wanted to know about you." I considered. "Actually, it was like he was hitting on *you*, through me."

Suddenly, I thought of Harriet, and her words echoed in my brain.

Something is stalking you, though it's not really you it wants. It's hunting someone close to you, hunting them for its own evil reasons and purposes far beyond our understanding.

He laughed a little. "Great. I've got my own private stalker. Maybe I owe him money or something."

"Bobby, I have to tell you some—" a sudden sound from the trees startled me, and I lifted my head. "What was that?"

He laughed quietly. "The boogeyman?"

My heart was thudding, and I frowned slightly. "Don't joke. It's not funny. I know I heard something." I pointed to the dark row of trees off of the beach.

He cuddled me closer. "It's nothing, Beth. Probably just a dog or something." He turned my head to kiss me, but this time we both heard the insistent sound of a branch snapping, and we both froze.

"It's Larry, I know it is." He cupped his hand to his mouth. "Hey Larry, joke's over; come out, you dip!" He grinned at me a little… Larry was one of his roommates, the loudest and definitely the goofiest of all the boys in the beach house. He was always either drunk or getting drunk, and I had never, ever seen him serious. We both looked in the direction of the sound, and then, to our surprise…

Snap. More crashing sounds, like someone who was deliberately trying to be quiet, but not too quiet. And oddly enough, this time it came from a *different* direction.

"I heard it too," Bobby whispered, when I opened my mouth to speak. He shook his head slightly, and he stood up. The blanket fell away from us, and I saw him silhouetted in the fading light from the fire. His blond hair shone in the night like a helmet, and I saw the rise and fall of his bare chest as he scanned the trees. The night birds had grown still, and there was no sound except for the gentle lapping of the waves on the sandy beach.

And then we saw him. Walking out of the darkness like he was part of it, never making a sound as he came towards us.

It was him. The man from the diner.

"Bobby, that's the man," I whispered. He looked at me as if he couldn't believe it, and then he raised a casual hand.

"Hey man." But there was a note of uncertainty in his voice, and I slipped my hand in his.

"Evening." The man stopped at the edge of the firelight, his hands in his pockets. "Nice night, isn't it?" He smiled at me and nodded, but I saw the smile never reached his eyes. "Hello there, Beth."

Bobby's voice was sharp. "Do you want something, man?"

The man seemed to ponder the question. There was a long, terrible silence before he spoke. "Do I want something? Do you think there is anything I want that I couldn't just take?"

Bobby reached down and picked up a stick from the firewood pile. "I don't know who you are, or what you want here. But I'm gonna give you five seconds to clear out or I'm gonna beat your ass."

The man eyed the stick disdainfully. "In five seconds, the world can change. Babies can be born, children can grow up, a life can be extinguished." He smiled at us. "But come. We need more time than that to discuss our mutual business."

Bobby's voice was high in his confusion and nervousness. "We don't have any business, man. I don't know you at all."

The man smiled. "Then let me introduce myself. I am Sebastian Crane, a physician from New Orleans. At one point in my career, I attended to a patient who happened to be a member of your family." I saw Bobby's face register more confusion as he tried to work this out, but before he could speak, Crane went on.

"A charming young man. Correct me if I am wrong, but your family hails from Tennessee, isn't that right?"

Bobby nodded. "Yes. Who was your patient again? I didn't catch the name." There was clearly confusion in his voice.

The doctor closed his eyes for a second, seemingly pleased. "Tennessee. Yes, I *have* found you. I have been searching for so long, so very long, you just don't know." He opened his eyes again. "And all the other pretenders—all the ones I thought were you! Foolish of me, but then I had very little to go on, so I suppose that is to be excused." Bobby glanced at me, uncertainty passing between us, and then Crane clapped his hands delightedly. "But success! Here we are! Together, at last!"

"Together?" Bobby's grip tightened on the wood, and I could feel him telling me to run, run and get help... but I couldn't leave him. "And what do you mean? I know I've never seen you in my life. You've got the wrong guy, so why don't you just leave?"

"Oh no, you're the *right* guy, no doubt about it." The man still had not moved, but he was watching us intently, and I saw his eyes were bright and feral. "My once and former patient was a distant relative of yours whose bedside I attended. We spoke of many things before he died, but what strikes my memory the most... was his love of blackberries. Tell me, Mister Barnham, do you like blackberries as well?" He licked his lips, and I felt myself tremble. "Because I do. I like them very, very much."

I felt Bobby jerk. "All right. This is bullshit. Come on, Beth. We're leaving." He reached down to pick up the blanket, never taking his eyes off of Crane, and then Crane said, "Do you love, Mister Barnham?" And then, quicker than I could register, quicker than *anything* I have ever seen before, he had moved away from the perimeter, had leaped over the fire, and in one stunning blow, slapped Bobby so hard against the face it echoed in my ears. No, not a slap... a clubbing. It sounded like someone hitting a side of beef in the freezer, and Bobby gave a startled gasp and collapsed to the sand, his legs twitching... a thin trickle of blood snaked a crooked line down his cheek. I was too stunned to scream out, too stunned to even move... and then Crane bent down while I watched with horrified eyes, flicked his tongue out and lapped at the blood trail like a dog.

"Oh my God," I whispered, feeling the terror rise in my throat. I looked at Bobby, and then at Crane, who was kneeling over him, and I knew I had to run, I had to help Bobby, I had to...

Crane stroked Bobby's cheek tenderly, then flicked his eyes up at me. I saw they had inexplicably gone red—two flaming pinpricks in the darkness—and his voice rang out in the stillness of the night. "Do you love, Beth?" And then quick as a snake, he battened his mouth onto Bobby's tanned neck.

I heard Bobby scream: high, desperate and hopeless—the scream of the damned—and then awful, wet sucking sounds, as Crane licked and sucked. A dark arterial spray of blood, powerful and hot, shot out across the sand, and Crane moved his face in its path, like a man enjoying the warmth of a shower. The flames from the bonfire illuminated the hellish scene... I saw Bobby's bare feet beating helplessly as Crane chewed at his throat, and I tried to scream. But I was so terrified, no sound came out except for a whistling cry.

Crane stood up, brushing the sand from his knees. His lips were black with blood, and his eyes were crazed, as if in ecstasy. "It's similar, yes. But, not *quite* right. Did you know, Beth, that I have traveled the world, have hunted down generations of his people," he nudged Bobby's still form with his shoe, "and yet I can never quite duplicate the taste of the first, no matter how hard I may look. I'm afraid that now I never will, but I swear to you, I shall keep looking." He looked down at Bobby again and sighed. "I had hoped he might be the one... he looks like him, though, of course, you wouldn't know that. My dear Charlie." We might have been speaking of a cheese or a wine in a grocery store, and I shook my head, confused.

"But still..." Crane looked down at Bobby in the firelight and smiled almost tenderly. Bobby was moaning softly, and Crane reached down and lovingly stroked his hair. "It is close enough—closer than some of the curs in his family. I shall enjoy him, I'm sure." He smiled, and *dear God*, this time I saw his *teeth*. I saw that they had grown long and pointed and gleamed in his mouth like sabers. I began to cry, and I closed my eyes.

And then... I felt his hand, as cold and lifeless as something from the grave caressing my neck, and I cried aloud in absolute fear. Leaning forward, he nuzzled my throat, and from the dark, his whisper came like a stiletto. "But first, my dear Beth... I shall enjoy *you*."

He smiled at me lovingly... no, *hungrily*. "You shall be my aperitif."

* * *

It was unspeakable.

Hours later, when the police found me and the drained corpse of Bobby Barnham, I was unable to give them any answers. I was in shock; barely alive, and had been tortured and raped and abused time upon time.

I remember the ambulance ride, and the sirens, and I remember screaming. I have struggled to put this out of my memory. But no matter how hard I try, no matter what medication the doctors may prescribe for me, I cannot forget the silky sound of Crane's voice as he stood over me, forcing my mouth open as he ran his bloody fingers—Bobby's blood—across my lips.

"Tennessee blackberries, my dear. My goodness, but there's nothing better in the whole world."

PART II

CHAPTER X

The hospital—or more correctly, the *Rehabilitation* Hospital—she always thought of it like that, in italics, as if that made it any more important—was very well known for admitting low-level celebrities with emotional or chemical dependency issues and putting them back together after a protracted amount of time.

Though its clientele was famous, or at least infamous, discretion was assured. The staff was superb and made to sign confidentiality agreements. Summer students, only those at the top of their class, interned there from various universities and after a rather well-known British rocker with a penchant for cocaine and heroin had granted the hospital several million dollars, a new mental health wing had been added on the grounds.

It was where they had taken Beth, not because she was a celebrity, but because every other treatment center had already admitted and released her, since her case was of interest among the psychiatric and law enforcement communities. She had been screened and evaluated a dozen times and written up in several medical journals, and had been the subject of a keynote speaker in New York at a Psychiatric Convention. Her diagnosis had been changed half a dozen times in over a year, and with each new finding had come new problems.

It had first appeared to have been a standard rape and murder case. She had been brought into the emergency room, more dead than alive;

her boyfriend, a house painter, had been viciously murdered. "He had been cut on and bled out like a pig!" One of the Emergency Technicians had whispered deliciously to the nurses as they had worked on her, "Bled out white... and this one, near dead, too."

"Poor thing, I don't think she'll make it either, from the looks of her." And Beth had struggled to open her eyes and had felt the blessed prick of a needle in her arm. The dark clouds moved in on her, and that was a relief because it hid the horror of what *he* had done to her.

But she hadn't died. Despite last rites being said over her, she had rallied that first night, much to the surprise of the doctors; they had had to give her nearly six pints of blood, and several surgeons had worked for hours over her mutilated body, stitching her back together. She had been on a ventilator, in a drug-induced coma for fifteen days while she had healed, and when they had begun to wean her off the medication, waking her up, no one had been prepared for the girl that had woken up.

Early on, catatonia and self-injurious behavior; hallucinations, both visual and auditory, and protracted bouts of insomnia. Intravenous medications from the Thorazine group had helped there until she had physically healed. Later, more diagnoses had followed: Acute Depression. Suicidal Tendencies. Post-Traumatic Stress Disorder. Neuroses. Hallucinations. Fugue-like behavior, where she would focus on a spot on the wall, seeing nothing, yet moving her lips silently, saying nothing.

Psychotherapists and counselors had worked with her, both individually and in a group setting, but she had responded little to the treatment. Words such as *hostile* and *deeply angry* began to appear on her chart, later to be replaced with *I am nervous to be around this patient. Her eyes are hollow and bottomless.* And while she never made a move to ever harm anyone, those in contact with her would come away vaguely uneasy and uncomfortable because of her dark, penetrating stare.

She spoke little and made poor progress. Occasionally, she was seen praying in the hospital chapel, and much was made of that, for it seemed to be the only thing that would comfort her. This behavior was encouraged by the doctors, until small items began to disappear from the rectory: small statues of saints, holy candles, vials of holy water, even communion wafers. These were eventually found stuffed at the back of Beth's closet, and when she was confronted with the evidence and asked why she had done such an odd thing, she had merely glared at them helplessly and ferociously, and another sub-diagnosis of kleptomania was added to her chart.

She had very few visitors. Her mother visited faithfully every day for several years, until she suffered a mild coronary while at work, and then she was forced to scale back her visits to only three times a week. When she died six years after Beth's hospitalization, there had been talk of letting Beth attend the funeral, but an attack on a staff member for moving her religious items around on her desk canceled the possibility. The few other visitors she had dried up over the years, and eventually the only people who ever came to see her were the occasional police investigator, intent on opening the cold case, or perhaps a therapist with a new treatment plan.

Her story, while a sensation for a while, eventually dropped from the newspapers. No suspect had ever been caught, and though she had been interviewed a dozen times by the police as to what had happened that night, there was little information to work with. There seemed to be no clear motive—not drugs nor a robbery—and neither of the victims had any known enemies. It spoke mildly of a crime of passion, and more unsettlingly, it appeared that the boyfriend, Bobby Barnham, had been the target, but the theory was weak at best and eventually discarded.

Crime scene photos showed an awful scene, and hardened police officers with thirty years of experience had experienced nightmares about it. The victims had been found by an early morning jogger, just after sunrise. It was difficult to believe that such a thing had happened in a friendly little community, but overnight, FBI agents and profilers, and eventually the media, descended on the town like a plague. While one victim was dead and the other in a coma, agents worked feverishly to piece together the crime scene. The incident appeared completely random, with all the hallmarks of earlier serial killers. The Night Stalker and Son of Sam were both mentioned in an interview written by a journalist who had his five minutes of fame by giving his opinion on the case on *Good Morning America*. The Crime of Passion Theory was scrapped for lack of evidence, and investigators changed tactics; they theorized that possibly an opportunistic drifter had stumbled on the pair that night at the beach and had surprised them. The crime had happened in a secluded spot on the dunes, and away from interruptions, the killer had been leisurely taking his time with his victims, torturing and raping them both before eventually killing the boyfriend. More ghoulishly, while it was obvious that both victims had been drained of blood, there was little blood on the scene, causing the police to draw the conclusion that the killer had collected the blood and taken it away, possibly as a trophy. This detail was kept from the public but was well-known among the police and the physicians, and naturally, rumors inevitably spread.

Of course, there had been other crimes that summer—at least three missing persons cases, all young males, all presumed dead. This was in a community where no one *ever* went missing, and so the police and community were frantic in their search for answers. Investigators were certain that there was a link between all these cases and Beth, but nothing was ever determined.

Despite the best efforts of the police, no suspect had ever been arrested. The killer had left behind little physical evidence behind—no blood, certainly, and despite the fact that both victims had been repeatedly sexually abused, no semen whatsoever was found. Obviously, the killer had used a condom, but there was also the absence of latex residue in and on the victims, which puzzled the investigators. Also, while the victims had been swabbed for foreign blood, hair and even latent fingerprint samples, the tests came back inconclusive. The lab blamed the police, the police blamed the lab, and an important piece of evidence was lost and useless.

The newspapers and media had a field day with this. There was a rise in the sale of weapons and security systems in the Midwest, and a well-known crime writer flew in from New York to start gathering material for her next book. And, while profilers spoke of possible repeat occurrences and the public nervously waited for the next attack, none came. The case became cold. It was assumed that the killer had either hunkered down, spooked by all the publicity, or had moved on to another area. Beth, as she was known in the psychiatric community—no last name, of course, was ever given due to patient confidentiality—languished in the hospital as a strange, silent figure. She has become a woman with a dozen diagnoses and no positive hope for the future.

She was known to have said only one word in nearly a year, and she had been asleep at the time. A nurse on the night shift had been doing her hourly rounds and had checked the unit, only to have found Beth moaning in her sleep, obviously in the grip of a nightmare. The nurse had been prepared to alert the doctor, for Beth was thrashing around violently and clawing at her blankets, and just as the nurse had begun to back fearfully from the bed, edging toward the door and the safety of the security guard in the hall, Beth had sat up in bed, eyes wide and horror stricken, and she had thrown her head back and screamed one word.

"CRANE!"

* * *

"This is a new day for you."

Beth glanced up. She was packing a small overnight bag with a few things the hospital social worker had gathered for her. Some jeans, tee shirts, a new pair of Nikes. Toiletries. And of course, a plastic baggie, filled with her prescription bottles. Mustn't forget those.

The social worker sat down on the edge of the bed. "You must be excited."

Beth looked away through the window. It was bright outside, with the promise of a beautiful summer day. She could hear cars driving, birds singing, faint laughter from the quad, where a group of adolescent substance abusers, under the careful watch of their counselors, were doing a team-building activity. They were passing a large, red medicine ball among them without using their hands; it bounced off a tall boy's head and rolled away, causing shrieks of hysterical laughter. Beth smiled.

It was good that it was sunny. Sunlit days were the best, of course. As long as the sun was shining, the evil things were kept at bay, hidden in corners, under floorboards, down cellar. Away. Light and warmth were like bleach to evil things, it kept them away, kept them from encroaching on her. Only when the sun dropped would the danger become real again, when the evil things would waken from their sleep, to start...

"Beth?"

She shook her head, realizing she had tensed her body at her thoughts. "Yes."

"Are you all right?"

She nodded. "Of course."

"Good." The social worker was watching her carefully. "I was saying this is a big day for you. You must be excited."

Beth nodded. "I am."

"Good. Nine years is a long time... to be away." Beth glanced at her. "Away?"

The social worker looked mildly flustered. "Well, yes. Away. From the rest of the world, I mean." She sighed. "You've been through it, I know. You survived an awful experience, suffered a tragic loss. But you made it, girl. You pulled through to the other side." She took Beth's pale hand in hers; Beth jumped, but allowed her to hold her hand. "You gotta go on living, again. We talked about this in group."

"I know." She looked through the window. The teenagers had resumed their activity and were starting the medicine ball down the line of extended arms again, amidst more laughter. *Stupid children. You wouldn't laugh so hard if you knew what I knew.*

The social worker squeezed her hand and stood up. She had a Female Self-Mutilators Group in ten minutes, and she had to use the restroom before she got started. Besides, Beth was certainly not one of her favorite patients... usually, she connected on some level with her clients, but this girl had always remained aloof and distant. Inwardly, she shrugged. Maybe her meds weren't right; maybe she had been a bitch even before her accident. Didn't matter. She was leaving today, and that was that.

"You'll be fine. The halfway house is expecting you before noon. Call when you get there."

Beth nodded agreeably and grabbed her bag. "I will." Without a backward glance, let alone a word of thanks, she walked out the door.

The social worker watched her go, quite certain that Beth would never make it to the halfway house.

She was right. Within an hour, Beth had flushed all her pills down the toilet in the bus station, had bought a ticket, and boarded a bus headed south.

* * *

She had never been to Tennessee before. It was a land of rolling hills and deep valleys, of good food, deep history, and tranquility. That was what struck her the most—the tranquility. Even the larger cities had a quiet rhythm to them; the people never seemed to get excited or anxious. They were polite and reserved—friendly enough, but reserved. That was all right with her.

She rented a car at the bus station in Nashville and then turned further south, headed down I-65. She had wanted to get further on the first day, but there had been a delay on the highway, and now it was getting dark. The thought of being out in an open area on her first night alone was terrible. She found a string of hotels, and checking her dwindling wallet, pulled into a nearly empty lot.

She didn't think she would be recognized. It had been years since her picture had been splashed across the television screens on the morning news shows, and she had changed since then. There was nothing remarkable about her; she was merely another traveler, somewhat pretty, dressed in jeans and a tee shirt. Still, she thought the woman at the desk at the Best Western had given her a thoughtful look as she handed over her key, and Beth had hurried away to her room with her heart beating.

She doesn't recognize you. Don't be stupid. Your Hoosier accent alone invites a second look down here… maybe you look like her sister, or a friend, or maybe she's gay. Don't be paranoid; it means nothing.

Once in her room, she didn't even unpack, but merely put the bag in the chair. She stood for a moment, looking around her; it was a typical room with a large double bed, a bureau, and a television attached to the wall. A nightstand with a lamp and a telephone, and a hideous picture on the wall. She opened the nightstand drawer, fearing she might be unlucky enough to land in the one hotel room in the nation where the Gideons had missed… but no. It was there. With a sigh of relief, she pulled the Bible from the drawer, looked at it, and then began to rip pages out of it.

She had stolen a roll of bandage tape from the hospital, and quickly she began to fasten random pages of the Bible to the windows, and to the door. Over the lock, by the jamb. She paused for a second, considering, and then put a few over the air ducts, just in case.

The Bible was the word of God. It would keep evil things at bay, keep her safe at night. She was certain the Gideons, or the hotel wouldn't mind.

You're safe now.

She pulled her clothes off and put on an old, overlarge men's white tee shirt. She kept the light on in the bathroom, but turned out the light in the bedroom, and pulled the covers to her chin.

Her sleep was restless and uneasy.

* * *

There was a stand of free brochures and maps in the restaurant, and over a cup of coffee and a sweet roll, she did some quick research. She remembered Bobby had told her the name of his town—Bisby—and while she hadn't wanted to spend the night there, she had decided that one town over was close enough. From the calculations she had made, she determined it was less than an hour away. She scribbled out the directions, paid her bill, and quickly left before the housekeepers discovered the ruined Bible in her room.

It was late morning when she made the last turn off of the highway, onto a narrow, two-lane road that meandered in and around endless farmland. The sweet smell of summer corn pleased her nose through the open windows. Once she had to pull over to the side to allow a tractor to pass, and another time she nearly missed a hairpin curve that would have sent her over the edge, and into a creek. She shuddered, thinking how long it would have been before she had been found, or how long the walk back to town would have been if she had had to seek help.

A battered mailbox proclaiming the name BARNHAM signaled that she was close, and she paused for a second, feeling her heart race. Heat shimmered off the road, and she slapped at a mosquito while she found her nerve. Then, taking a deep breath, she made the turn into the long driveway and headed for the house.

It was a wide, two-storied farmhouse, white with green shutters and a long front-over porch. A pair of rocking chairs and an old washing machine crowded the porch; clothes and sheets flapped from the clothesline. A middle-aged man wearing suspenders was running a weed eater by the ditch. He paused from his work to look at her curiously when she drove by; she raised a hand to him in greeting, and politely he waved back, though he didn't smile. She came to a slow stop, so as not to raise dust and ruin the laundry, and then stepped out of the car and shielded her eyes, looking up at the house.

A solid woman, drying her hands on a towel, banged the screen door. She was gray-haired and smiling in polite confusion. "Help you?" She took a step down the stairs, keeping one hand on the railing. "You lost, honey? Most folks don't get this far off the road."

Beth took a deep breath. "Are you Lucy Barnham?"

"I am." The woman tilted her head. "Do we know each other?"

"Not officially." She suddenly felt as if she wanted to cry. This woman was exactly as Bobby had described her, and she could remember him telling her of his childhood, of this kind woman who had raised him.

Best cookies in the world, Beth... someday, I'll take you there.

"Missus Barnham..." Beth took another step forward. "I'm Beth Franklin..."

The woman's eyes widened in recognition, and she seemed to freeze. One trembling hand rose to her mouth, and her eyes seemed to glisten in the morning sun. "Ohhhhh," she whispered. "I should have known..." She swallowed hard. "The doctors called us a while ago and said you might be getting out..."

Beth was unsure of her welcome. "May I talk to you?"

There was a long silence while Missus Barnham evaluated her. Somewhere off in the trees, a crow called, and then further off, an answering cry from its mate. Finally, she replied, "I've been waiting for you. I guess you better come in. I think we got a lot to talk about, Beth."

Beth felt as if her throat had sawdust in it. "Thank you…" she glanced behind her at the man cutting weeds. He had stopped his work again and was watching them. Lucy waggled a dismissive hand towards him to let him know she was all right.

"That's just Karl; he's the handyman. I still need a man around here to help me out with the heavy lifting. But as to *this* business… he ain't got no part in it. Come on."

And Beth followed her up the porch steps, and into Bobby's childhood home.

* * *

The kitchen was clean and well-used; it was clearly the hub of the household. The chairs around the table were old and scarred, and there was a fresh bouquet of summer zinnias in a Mason jar in the middle of the table. Light poured in from the kitchen windows, something that Beth approved mightily of. Windows faced both east and west on opposite walls, so the room was always bathed in light and immediately, she felt slightly more comfortable.

Lucy shooed a cat out of her chair, and poured them both a cup of coffee. She raised her eyebrows questioningly at Beth, handing it to her, and Beth shook her head. "Just sugar, please."

"I like a little milk in mine. And more sugar than is healthy, I suppose. Doctor is always after me to cut down, but I do have a sweet tooth." She sat down heavily in her chair, brushing imaginary crumbs from in front of her. "Whoo boy, that feels good to sit down, let me tell you." She studied Beth. "So…"

"So," Beth repeated. "It's nice to meet you."

Lucy nodded slowly. "You too, darlin'. I wasn't sure if we ever would." She ran her fingers over the rim of her coffee mug. "Bobby had written and told us he had met someone special that summer." She studied Beth frankly. "So, you're Beth."

"I'm Beth." She nodded.

Lucy swallowed hard. "It's good to meet you… well, to be honest, I had seen you once before, but you don't remember. When… when we were told about the accident, we flew up there, of course, to… to bring Bobby back." She swallowed hard. "The police asked us to look in on you, to see if we knew you, if that would help the case at all, and we did. You were in a coma, more dead than alive…" she trailed off.

Beth nodded.

"Those were such bad, bad days," Lucy sighed. "The story was all over the news; reporters and police everywhere. They were even at the funeral," she shrugged. "But things eventually settled down, of course. They always do." She looked at Beth. "Drink your coffee before it gets cold."

Beth did.

"You know my grandson loved you, don't you?"

It was a surprising question, but Beth was ready for it. "I know. And I loved him."

Lucy nodded. "I know. He told me, before he died. He said he had met the most wonderful girl in the world… I had never heard him talk like that before. Of course, there had been other girls… Bobby was so sweet, so handsome, but none had ever lasted. I think you were in it for the duration, honey."

Beth swallowed hard. "I… I loved him very much. You'll never know how much… or how hard this has been…" she blinked and looked away.

"It's been hard on all of us, in different ways," Lucy agreed. She sighed. "I lost a grandson, you lost a lover, the world lost a beautiful person. The person who did this awful thing will never know what he took from us all that night."

Beth cleared her throat. "That's sort of why I'm here." Lucy looked sharply at her.

"How so, darlin?"

"I want to catch the person who did this to me, to Bobby."

Lucy sighed and sipped her coffee. "Last time I talked to the police, they weren't any closer to catching the suspect. They said it's gone cold, become a cold case, like that television show. They said—"

"Does the name Crane mean anything to you? Sebastian Crane?"

The reaction was immediate. Lucy stiffened as if her entire body had gone on alert, and she nearly spilled her coffee. She fixed Beth with a suspicious, wary look. "No. Should it?"

"Missus Barnham..." Beth leaned in closer. "Please listen to me. I've spent nine years of my life locked away in a psychiatric hospital, trying to sew the rough edges of my sanity back together. I've had a thousand nightmares, a thousand dreams and a thousand bad nights over what happened. I've been the subject of psychiatric reports, been discussed in journals and workshops, been probed and prodded and medicated and over-medicated and studied and examined. My mother died, probably of heartache, while I was in that awful place, and my childhood home sold away to pay my medical bills." She locked eyes with Lucy. "My life was taken from me that night; Bobby was taken from me that night, and all I want are some answers. Please, for the love of God, help me."

Lucy took a sip of her coffee with a trembling hand, and then set it back down on the table. "You don't know what you're asking..."

Beth nodded. "Yes, I do. I'm asking for information. And for justice." Silence fell in the kitchen.

"Please help me."

Lucy closed her eyes, as if in prayer. "Tell me what you know. I'll try to fill in the rest."

"Not much." Beth shrugged helplessly. "The police operated on the theory of a random attack on us that night. No suspects. But I remember that night... it was so horrible... but it seemed that while Bobby didn't know the person who killed him, the person seemed to know Bobby. Someone named Crane."

"*Crane.*" Lucy shivered, as if a cold wind had swept through her kitchen. "That's what I had thought, too. And, of course, I never mentioned it to the police... they woulda thought I was crazy, a crazy old woman."

"But you're not." Beth took her wrinkled, liver-spotted hand in hers. "You're not. And neither am I." She paused. "So, who is he?"

Lucy wiped at a tear. "An old legend, my dear. A ghost story, a haunt tale. It goes as far back as the Civil War, nearly a hundred and fifty years old, and probably farther. If I tell you these things, you'll have to suspend all rational thought and reason."

Beth nodded. "I know. The things I saw that night..." she shuddered, "were not of this world."

Lucy looked closely at her. "No, they're not. Crane is a creature from hell... he's a demon..."

"No." Beth's voice was steady. "He's a vampire."

Lucy sighed deeply. "Yes. That's what he is." She took a deep breath. "All right. According to family legend, Sebastian Crane was a doctor, attached to the Reb Army who followed the troops from battle to battle. By some reports, he was a gifted surgeon; he even removed some wooden splinters from Jubal Early's leg after a shell exploded too close to a fence he was standing by. But, the real reason he was there... can you guess? Him, being a vampire and all?"

"To hunt." Beth felt a chill descend over her, like a cold blanket. "That's what I always figured, too. All those wounded men, dead and dying and helpless in the hospital tents. They couldn't escape. They were easy prey for a creature like Crane to go down the rows in the hospital tents, picking and choosing and taking what and who he liked."

She stood up. "Just a minute." She smiled weakly and hurried from the room. Beth watched her go, worried that she had upset her, but after a minute, Lucy returned, bearing a stack of photo albums and notebooks. She opened one and flipped to a photograph in an old, gilt-edged cardboard frame.

"Here. Have a look. Does that remind you of anyone?"

Beth gazed wonderingly at the picture. It was an old tintype of a sturdy, blond teenager, dressed in a Confederate soldier's uniform. In one hand, he held a rifle, and in the other, a large bayonet. It was typical of the period, melodramatic and maudlin; the boy's eyes looked fierce, but she thought she could see a glimpse of a smile beneath the scowl, as if he was just glaring at the camera because the photographer had told him to.

And yet, despite the period clothing and the age of the photograph, she recognized the family resemblance.

"He looks like Bobby," she said, wonderingly.

Lucy nodded. "Yep, he sure does. The Barnham genes are good, aren't they?" She laughed quietly. "These two could be brothers, born over a hundred years apart. Not twins, not that close, but clearly, they're family."

Beth touched the photo behind the glass, feeling her heart squeeze in sorrow. "He has Bobby's eyes."

Lucy nodded. "Well, that's old Charlie Barham, an ancestor of Bobby's. About five generations back, I think. He's wearing the uniform of the Tennessee Scarlet Rangers, a local militia that joined up with the Reb Army to go off and fight the Yanks. He never came back, you know. He was wounded down at the Battle of Dark Hills, and that's where he met Crane."

Beth couldn't take her eyes off of the tintype. "It's uncanny."

"Charlie's friend, Manny Draper, was there at the battle with him, and was wounded too. He's the one who came back and told the folks what happened... course, he wasn't fully believed. Some thought he was tetched in the head... lots of boys came home that way, you know. Not right. They call it shell shock today, I guess. Thousand-yard stare and all that. And he came back and told everyone that Charlie had been wounded, and that was the end of that... but if he had a jug in his hand, and got to drinking, his story would change, and he would tell what *really* happened to Charlie there in the tent."

"Tell me." Beth looked up, imploringly.

"Well, apparently Crane was there at the hospital where they had taken Charlie, working on the boys, hunting among them like a vicious predator. They were easy pickings, of course, and Crane was able to have his choice among them... apparently, he even had certain favorites among the soldiers based on how... how their blood tasted." She looked pale and put a hand over her heart. "And that's where he met Charlie, and that's where Charlie..."

Beth felt sick. "Oh, my God."

Lucy smiled weakly. "Charlie was a young, healthy farm boy, raised on the best fruits and vegetables here in the valley. Good milk from the family cows, butter, cream... grapes from the arbor, apples from the orchards here on the property, and berries of any number in the forests.

Something must have appealed to Crane, something that Charlie had in his blood, because he sort of became a... a favorite of Crane's. He fed on that poor boy for at least two nights before he eventually killed him, satisfying himself... but it was the case of the goose that laid the golden egg. Once Charlie was dead, there was no more of that intoxicating blood he loved so much, and Crane was left wanting more."

Beth took a steadying, calming breath. Her stomach was fluttering, and she felt sick.

"Crane became obsessed with the Barnhams. He thought he could find that same... same flavor he had experienced with Charlie. So, he became a hunter. After the war, he made his way to Tennessee under a different name, of course, and began to pick off Charlie's brothers and his two remaining uncles. Five Barnhams mysteriously died in three years; more than ever died in the war... Cyrus was found in the barn, drained away, and Nathan just simply disappeared." She shrugged. "The others died similarly, all pale and wasted away... people thought it might have been the plague, or just a series of accidents and bad luck, but that wasn't it."

Beth remembered Bobby's words and felt a chill.

We've seen more than our share of accidents, deaths, tragedies. I can't tell you the number of family members who have died over the years... we've lost uncles, cousins, brothers, all to terrible things...

"No one tried to stop him?"

Lucy shrugged. "Of course. The remaining brothers fought, but they didn't know what they were fighting, and they were easy pickings. Crane is ancient and cunning; he's seen a thousand tricks in his time and knows the game. The Barnham boys, as dashing and as brave as they might have been, were no match for a creature like that."

I've dealt with enough officials and soldiers in my life so that it seems nothing more than a mere annoyance at this point...

Beth nodded. "I seem to remember him bragging about something like that—that he was untouchable."

Lucy sighed tiredly, looking at the photograph in front of Beth. She stroked the frame lovingly. "And over the years, there were others, of course. Cousins and sons and nephews... all male. The women were never bothered." She looked pointedly at Beth, who nodded.

"I know. I figured that Crane's preferred victims are male," Beth sighed. "Although he... abused and raped me, I was merely an appetizer," her breath caught, and her voice cracked. "That's what he said. That's what he told me."

Lucy looked thoughtful. "But I don't think it's a sexual thing... that is, I don't think that Crane is a homosexual. I think he's an addict, actually, and he's always trying to repeat that first taste he had with Charlie. He believes that only the males of the family could possibly come close to duplicating... well, whatever it was he tasted." She looked sad. "No, he's not preferential to one sex or another; he's an equal opportunity killer."

"Lucy?"

The old woman flipped open another notebook. "I've kept track of him over the years," she said. "At least, in cases where I think he's been. Random killings, unexplained missing persons..." she shrugged. "Some of them might not be his fault, but after a while, there is a pattern. The victims are usually young and savagely abused, both physically and sexually..."

Beth made a sound in her throat. "That's right." She looked away. "The summer Bobby was killed, three other young men disappeared within weeks, right before we were attacked. I've thought about it, and I think now that Crane was hunting Bobby, looking for him; somehow those other three boys were mistakes. He knew he was close—very close, actually—when he got to Razzy, Bobby's roommate. But either he was just warming up or he was truly mistaken when he went after those other boys." She shrugged. "I guess it doesn't matter. The end result is the same, isn't it? And I can tell you... that night he killed Bobby... he raped me repeatedly, over and over... before drinking my blood..."

Horrified, Lucy looked at her. "I can't imagine the terrors you have experienced, my child." Her voice was quiet. "It's never gone away, you know. Each generation has been affected. My own husband, nearly thirty-five years ago. It was right out there in that field. I found him just after sunset, with his throat ripped out."

"Oh, dear Lord," Beth said, feeling her eyes well up.

"Crane got to Bobby's father when Bobby was just a baby, and we—my daughter, Rachel and I—thought if we sent Bobby away up North to live, we could hide him. That Crane wouldn't be able to find him." She smiled sadly. "But of course, it didn't work... it took him over twenty years, but that bastard got to him. His patience is endless... I think he has gotten to the point where he actually enjoys the hunt, enjoys the search for Barnhams. When the call came that night, saying Bobby had been killed, that despite what the police were telling me, I knew it was no random murderer, no drug deal gone bad, nothing like that. I knew it was Crane, that he had finally found my grandson."

Beth wiped a tear away. "Have you ever seen him?"

"Crane?" She looked thoughtful. "Just once. But I've *felt* him more than I've ever seen him. It's quiet out here, you know, but it's never totally quiet, if that makes sense. The animals make noise, the wind whistles through the trees... nature and life are all around this place. But sometimes, things seem to pause, and I can feel something watching me from the tree line. And on the night my husband was killed, when I ran down to the field because the stillness was so overwhelming, I knew; just *knew* something had happened... and I surprised him."

Beth looked at her, horrified.

"He was standing over my David, hunched over him like a rutting dog. His head was buried in his throat, like a lover kissing him deeply, and I heard the sounds, and I saw David still struggling weakly, but I could tell that it was too late. And Crane stood up and looked over his shoulder at me, surprised but not worried. His shirt was covered in blood; it ran down his chin, dark and thick, and his hands were drawn up in claws. We stared at each other, and then he licked his lips one final time and winked at me. He *winked* at me, as if we were old friends, sharing some secret, and then he was gone, disappeared into the rows of corn like a shadow." She shuddered. "I stood there, not believing what was happening, not believing what I had seen, not believing that my David was dead... and then, I heard the laughter over the stalks of corn, long and slow and even... it shook the early night, and I knew that every living thing within range had heard it and was afraid."

Her story was over. They sat looking at each other, bound by their common horror; the coffee was forgotten. Finally, Lucy stirred herself. "Where are you staying?"

Beth shrugged. "Nowhere, really. I'm supposed to be at a halfway house; the hospital set it up for me. But I came here instead."

Lucy nodded. "You were right to do so. I think Bobby would have wanted it."

"I think so, too." Beth smiled faintly. "The whole way here, I think he was steering the wheel."

Lucy tipped her head. "That's a nice idea, actually." She looked closer at Beth. "Do you know that we had his Jeep sent back here?"

"Really?" Beth looked startled. "The blue Jeep?"

Lucy nodded. "Well, he loved it so much. He bought it in high school, paid for it by mowing hay and working on people's farms. He was really proud of it, and I just couldn't let it sit in some police impound." She jerked her thumb. "It's out in the barn."

"Well, I'll take a look at it later," Beth decided. She took a deep breath. "It might be too much right now, to be honest."

Lucy stood up, clearing away the cups. "More coffee? Lands, I guess I should offer you some lunch, you must be hungry." Quickly, she slapped together some ham sandwiches and spooned up some homemade potato salad. "And the pickles are some I put up last fall," she chattered, and Beth had the idea she was eager to be speaking of simpler, less nefarious topics. "I did dill and sweet both… and that's sweet pickle relish in the tater salad there, too."

"Lucy," Beth said softly, "After lunch, though, I need to get going—"

Lucy blinked at her in surprise. "Going? Going where?"

Beth shrugged. "I don't know, really. I guess back to Indiana, maybe. I just needed some information, and maybe some confirmation that I wasn't crazy. I know what I saw, I know what killed Bobby that night… your stories and information did all that."

Lucy bit into another pickle. "And if you go back… what then?"

Beth shrugged. "Well, I can tell the halfway house people I got lost…I'll have to do a drug screen to get back in, I guess, but I'm going to need a place to stay. And they said they could find me a job, too…"

Lucy harrumphed in her throat and pushed the Ball jar of pickles over towards her. "These are really good," she decided, chewing one thoughtfully. "Now then, about this foolish leaving business. Why don't you stay here for a bit?"

"Here?" Beth frowned. "I couldn't ask you to put me up. You just met me... I could never impose on you like that..."

Lucy shrugged. "Well, if you was good enough for Bobby, that's good enough for me. You know, he wanted to bring you back here, don't you? After school, he wanted you to meet me. Wanted to show you off, is how he put it. You being here... well, it's natural."

Beth looked doubtful and nibbled at her sandwich. "I don't..."

"You've got nowhere else to go, am I right?"

Beth sighed. "Well, that is blunt, so I will be equally blunt. No. I don't. I have no other family... my father, according to the hospital, came exactly two times to see me in all the years that I was there. I don't even know if he's still alive, and I guess I don't really care." Her voice broke, and she put down her sandwich, looking away.

Lucy looked at her for a second, and then reached out and took her hand; Beth, who was wary of people touching her, flinched for a second but allowed the gesture.

"Bobby spoke of bringing you here one day," she said quietly. "You were the only girl he ever thought well enough of to even do that. I suspect if things had worked out, if life had been kinder to you both, you would have ended up being my family one day." She looked away, out past the window, into the green yard beyond. "You are welcome to stay as long as you like, sweet Beth. For a day or a year, I don't care."

"There is no way I could intrude on you... you just met me, for God's sake," Beth whispered. She pushed back a lock of stray, blond hair, tucking it behind her ear.

"If you were good enough for Bobby, you're good enough for me." She looked grandmotherly and clucked her tongue in distaste. "And don't use the Lord's name in vain in this house, darlin', if you please."

Rather than be offended, a small smile played at Beth's lips. "Oddly enough, that felt nice."

"Eh?" Lucy frowned.

"Being told what to do. Being scolded. I haven't had that in years... the only interaction I've had with people has been in therapy groups, where they don't tell you what to do; they *suggest* things, and you're supposed to figure them out. Get in touch with your *feelings*, and all that crap. Being reprimanded and told what to do... well, it was kinda nice. It reminded me of my mother."

Lucy laughed. "Well, let me know how nice it is when you're ready to wring my neck. I'm a tough old bird, set in my ways, and I like things just so. You might decide you can't take it after two days and head out. And you're free to do so. But in the meantime, we've got peaches to put up tomorrow and blackberries the day after that. I had Karl get the buckets and pails out of the barn just this morning. You know anything about canning preserves?"

Beth laughed helplessly and wiped at her eyes. "No. I'm a city girl. I always got my fruit out of a jar. I don't know the first thing about living on a farm."

Lucy stood up, wanting to hug her, but knowing it was too early yet.

"Well, you'll learn, I suppose. Now help me with the lunch dishes, and after that, I'll show you around the property; show you the garden and the orchards. And you can meet Karl. I know he's just beside himself with nosiness out there. Like I told you, we don't get many visitors. Get a move on, girl; we've got things to do."

And Beth nodded happily, and if she didn't speak right away, Lucy understood the reason.

CHAPTER XI

True to her word, Lucy had Beth up early the next morning, cleaning and pitting peaches. She was especially particular about the way she wanted it, too, with each peach cut into eighths and put into the jars just so. They did nearly thirty quarts the first day, in between the other chores, and by dinner, Beth was exhausted. Lucy also insisted on taking Beth's rental car back to Hertz to avoid the cost of another day and followed her in her old pickup truck, no faster than thirty miles an hour. "It'll get me there, and this ain't the Indy 500, so who gives a whoopdedee?"

A "whoopdedee" was just one of Lucy's expressions, and she had one for every occasion. While she never swore or took the Lord's name in vain, she certainly skirted around the edges and came close. When her knife slipped and she nicked her thumb, she burst out with an enthusiastic, "Heckatootie! Dadgumbed knife nearly cut off my thumb! Wouldn't that be something special in a pie this fall, eh, Bethie?" And when they were coming home, another driver veered in suddenly and cut them off. She stuck her fist out the window, shaking it mightily at the speeding car. "You worthless RudiePoodie! Go on around me, I don't care, you and your stupid little rice-burner car! Who made that thing, the Emperor's grandmother?"

Still, despite her crustiness, she was generous and helpful, and she proudly showed Beth around her farm. She showed her the barns, the orchards, and the garden, where much of her produce in the summer came from. She still raised turkeys and chickens and had a small flock of guinea fowl on the place that she claimed were better watchdogs than any hound could be. Beth acknowledged this thoughtfully, considering the prospect of guarding the property, and wondered if it worked on all manner of creatures. She met Lucy's eye, and the older lady gave a quiet, insignificant nod of her head, and no more was said about it.

Lucy also introduced her to Karl Kopinski, her hired man. He was a huskily-built man, somewhere in his sixties, who lived in town but worked at the Barnham farm six days a week. He was quiet and kept to himself, and after he had met Beth and was reassured she wasn't a tax collector or a surveyor, he decided she was harmless. He didn't ask any questions when Lucy told him that Beth would be staying there for an indefinite time, and in fact, was patient when Lucy took Beth out with them to do the chores.

There were beans to pick, snap and can, grass to mow, eggs to collect, firewood to gather, and fences to mend. The chores were endless, but it was better therapy than anything she had ever received in the hospital. The sun, the green grass, and tending to the animals seemed to rejuvenate her; she was as thrilled as a ten-year-old at finding a litter of kittens in the barn loft, and the first time she drove the tractor by herself, tilling up fresh, wonderful earth to put in a second planting of beans, she found the smell—the whole experience, actually—intoxicating. Lucy seemed to know this was sovereign medicine too and pushed her with just the right mixture of sternness and compassion. While she sometimes scolded Beth for various things: not cleaning the eggs properly after gathering them, not locking the shed, cutting the grass with a dull blade, she was also patient and eager to share her wisdom and lore of fifty years of farming.

The property itself was interesting as well. The farm still had a working orchard and a luscious arbor of grapes, and Karl showed her a stretch of land where he had planted over a hundred fir trees to be harvested for Christmas trees in a few years, and from which they expected to make a tidy profit.

Karl was an excellent tour guide and showed her the various outbuildings on the property and what they were used for. He explained the difference between the Big Barn and the smaller Horse Barn, and proudly pointed out the new John Deere tractor locked away in the giant garage. Less excitingly, there was an old corn crib, mostly unused now, and a fenced poultry coop that had to be cleaned daily. And while Lucy kept most of her canned vegetables and fruit in her basement, keeping them close at hand, she also had an ancient root cellar by her garden for storing vegetables. Its design predated refrigeration and was simple: it was merely a cave-like structure, built into a small, man-made hill with a door like a hobbit door that was so low that Beth had to duck her head to get through. Lucy kept all manner of things there, for it was wonderfully cool: apples and potatoes, cabbage, squash and pumpkins in the fall. Bundles and swatches of dried herbs hung from the ceiling, as well as gathers of flowers—Sweet William and pink clover and hollyhocks and dozens of wildflowers that Beth couldn't even begin to identify. They were used to make homemade potpourri and contributed to the pleasant, earthy smell of the place.

One aspect of the root cellar amused Lucy immensely, and she was eager to share it with Beth. "During the fifties, when everyone was running around worried about Russian rockets and commies, David's parents recognized this place could also be used as a bomb shelter, if we were ever attacked. They even stored provisions here, for a time, but of course after a while, when the invasion never happened," she shrugged. "It just became a root cellar again, which is what it was intended for in the first place. People can be silly sometimes."

She also decided that Beth needed to learn how to cook. Before what she had come to call "The Incident," Beth had been a survivalist cook at best, but to be fair, there had never been all that much of a need. Her mother had done the cooking for the two of them, and as a college student, Beth had picked her way around quick and easy food between classes: tuna salad and canned soup and fried egg sandwiches. Lucy, who had been used to cooking for a growing farm family and its complement of farm hands, was affronted by this and made it her mission to not only teach Beth how to cook but also how to cook Southern, which, according to her, was a whole different style of cooking altogether: cheesy grits and pork chops, pot roast with rooted vegetables, chicken and dumplings with mashed turnips, fried okra and black-eyed peas. She was particular about rolling out her pie crust, insisting that "it is never more than a quarter inch thick, girl, and make sure you roll it out from the middle," and nobody was more delighted than her when Beth's first attempt at baking, a blackberry pie, came out delicious and near perfect.

But it was other information that Beth craved—a darker knowledge that she wanted to acquire. One afternoon, she drove into town by herself, found the local library and situated herself at a large oak table in the stacks. The librarian raised her eyebrows over her choice of books but said nothing, for she found the blond girl intense, and she made her slightly uncomfortable.

For several hours, Beth poured over a large stack of books that were rarely circulated, making notes in a three-ring binder and cross-checking her information. Her system was simple: nothing was written down unless it could be verified in three references, and four was actually better. Some points she highlighted, others she merely scribbled down in her own form of shorthand, and within a few hours she had quite a lot of information.

Lucy was sitting on the front porch, waiting for her and pretending not to be worried, when Beth rattled the truck down the driveway. Although she hated to sew, she was mending the pocket of an old apron and gratefully, she put it all back in the basket as Beth walked up the steps.

"Well, did you get all the learning you could stand for one day?"

Beth shrugged. "I don't know. I did find out some things, I guess. I'll show you what I've got, after dinner." She sniffed the air. "And speaking of which, something smells good…"

Lucy heaved herself to her feet and grabbed her basket. "Chicken casserole, and I was waiting until you got here to put the biscuits in. I expect by the time you wash up and refresh yourself, *and* set the table, supper will be ready."

Beth nodded and stood on the top of the steps for a moment after Lucy had banged the screen door behind her. She looked out across the driveway, down the green expanse of lawn, to the dirt road. The summer sun was a brilliant red ball setting in the west, and the evening was warm and pleasant. A slight breeze blew over the porch, raising her hair, and she lifted her nose, smelling the rich, earthy farm smells the wind had brought. It was incredibly serene and tranquil. A few chickens were scratching in the dirt by the ditch, and beyond that, in the woods, cicadas hummed and droned in the trees. Karl had gone home; she had passed him going out as she was pulling in, and they had each raised a hand in greeting as they had driven by. She was glad he had not stayed for supper. As Lucy had said, what she had to speak about tonight was private.

As to this business... he ain't got no part in it.

Off in the distance, a dove looed softly, and in answer, its mate called back. Even further out, she could hear the faint mooing and bellowing of a cow, well beyond their own pastures. It was a sweet sound, and she smiled. Another quiet, peaceful evening in the country.

Still...

She had learned to be aware of her surroundings, had learned to be aware of places where someone might hide, and where she could be ambushed. Nature itself had taught her lessons about how to tell when she wasn't alone—startled birds in the trees, a shift in the wind bringing some unfamiliar scent, or worse yet, the *quiet*, when all of the world seemed to stop when it sensed something was about to happen. Perhaps it was a sixth sense or an instinct that she had developed since the attack, but she had come to trust it, and so she paused now.

All was quiet, yet she lingered for another minute, scanning the trees, looking for movement. Nothing. Nothing at all. Reassuringly, it was daylight, and according to all lore, creatures like Sebastian Crane were married to the night.

It was lovely meeting you, Miss Beth. I've no doubt we'll meet again, and soon.

With a final, thoughtful look, she followed Lucy inside.

* * *

Dinner was every bit as good as it had smelled, and when the plates were pushed back and the coffee poured, Lucy said quietly, "I don't want to pry, but are you all right?" Beth looked up at her, eyebrows raised in question, and Lucy looked embarrassed. "I mean, you were gone most of the day. I figured maybe you had gone and seen a doctor, or maybe..." she trailed off, not sure how to finish her question.

Beth gave a half-smile. "You mean a psychiatrist or something? Like I was having trouble... flashbacks or something?"

Lucy shrugged. "Well, something like that. I would think that counseling would be a good idea after all you went through." She cleared her throat, reaching for her coffee cup.

"The truth of the matter is," Beth said slowly, "I've had enough therapy and counseling and introspection crap to last me a lifetime. I was pretty sound and whole before Bobby was killed, and to be honest, a lot of the time I was in... the hospital wasn't because I was nuts, but because I was afraid." She shook her head. "And maybe that's crazy in itself, but you see, in the hospital, I was locked away, and there were guards and nurses and therapists and volunteers there, and so I was always surrounded by people. I figured Crane couldn't get at me, and so I kept finding reasons to stay there, especially after my mother died. I would pick fights or pretend to be self-injurious, or threaten to kill a staff member and guarantee myself another six months."

Lucy was silent, watching her. There was a great sadness in her eyes. "And then one day..." Beth gave a mighty sigh. "One day, I was in the hospital courtyard—the *locked* courtyard, of course—and this squirrel climbed right over the fence into our side. He just zipped along the fence, grabbed an acorn, and then back over. The fence didn't even stop him; he was free, just like that." She snapped her finger. "And I began to wonder what was on the other side of the fence. In nine years, it's amazing how things change—hairstyles and fashion and movies. When I went in, Reagan was president, and now it's two presidents later. I missed a war and two different Olympics and books and holidays. I missed *living*, and I decided, watching that stupid squirrel go back over the wall, that if he could go out there and live in the world, I could too."

Lucy nodded.

"And so, I played the game, the stupid psychiatric game. I hit all the goals they set for me in therapy. I became more social, more cooperative. I made all the right noises and gave all the right responses. I made progress, and everyone there was proud of themselves, and said they had finally found the correct combination of medication and therapy for me and made a big deal about it." She gave a shaky little laugh. "But it was nothing they did at all, it was that stupid little squirrel that set me on the path to getting the hell out of there."

"I'll make sure Karl never goes squirrel hunting again," Lucy promised solemnly, and then looked at Beth, who burst into sudden laughter. "What? I meant it!"

"I know you did," Beth laughed. "And I'm sure squirrels everywhere will appreciate it far more than I will."

Lucy shrugged. "Karl isn't that good of a shot, to be honest. They'd probably be safe anyway." She pushed her plate to one side and folded her napkin. "All right, so you weren't at the doctor's today… may I ask where you were, then? Since you were using my truck and all, I suppose I do have a right to know."

"Sure." Beth shrugged. "I was at the library."

"Oh?" Lucy cocked an interested eyebrow. "I like to read, too, but running this farm leaves me so little time. Partial to Agatha Christie, sometimes, or maybe a good juicy romance if—"

"I was doing research," Beth said flatly. "On vampires."

"Oh." Lucy's eyes widened in surprise, and she sat back in her chair. "I see." Her face reddened, and after a moment she said, "And what did you find out?"

"Well, I was on a fact-finding mission, that's for sure," Beth said. "And the Bisby library isn't the best research resource in the world, but they did have some things I think were helpful."

Lucy nodded weakly; clearly the subject of Crane was something she wanted to avoid altogether. They hadn't spoken of him at all since Beth's first day there by mutual consent, though the topic had always floated unspoken in the air between them like a heavy cloud. Worriedly, she folded her hands, waiting.

Beth said suddenly, "I looked up ways to kill him."

Lucy was startled. She stirred a teaspoon of sugar into her cup and watched the bubbles come to the top. "You know, it's said if you have bubbles in your coffee, you'll come into money soon," she said thoughtfully. "Never knew it to be true though, it was just something my mother always said."

Beth said nothing; just listened and nodded. She knew that sometimes Lucy took a while to come to the point, rather like a dog turning around several times before it makes its bed. She waited.

After a while, Lucy sighed. "I don't know, to be honest. I don't know that he *can* be killed, or otherwise somebody would have done it by now. And there are a hundred old things that are supposed to do it... but maybe that's just in the movies, I dunno." She shook her head. "When I was a little girl, my older brother took me to see the original *Dracula*, with Bela Lugosi. You know the one I mean? Black and white, lots of shadows, stirring music." She chuckled softly. "I tell you, that movie scared the padookie outta me. I wasn't but eight years old, just a little girl with pigtails and penny loafers. I had no idea someday I would be fighting my own nightmare, eh?"

"Well, all of it is assuming that a vampire can even get to you," Beth said. "A vampire can't even get into your home unless you invite him in."

"What, does he have manners?" Lucy frowned, and Beth chuckled.

"In a way, I guess he does. I think it goes back to the formal, ancient Laws of Hospitality. Most cultures respect that, so just remember. Never invite one in, no matter what."

Lucy sipped her coffee. "I'll remember that," she said sarcastically. "I just hope that Crane is a polite old bastard as well, and he remembers his manners too. All right, so now what?"

"In the movie, they staked him," Beth mused. She reached over and pulled a spiral notebook out of her backpack. "But not just any old stake. According to legend, it has to be an ash stake... I'm not sure if the movies ever really say that, but from what I've learned—"

Lucy leaned over to peer at the pages. "What is all this?"

"Research. I made notes on everything I could on vampires, and the undead, and so forth. Where they came from, who they are, how to kill them…"

Lucy chuckled. "You did homework on vampires?"

"Sure, why not? Know thy enemy, and all that. We have to know what we're dealing with—"

"Whoa." Lucy held a hand up. "*We're* not dealing with anything, Bethie. As far as I'm concerned, it's over. There are no other Barnhams here for him to hunt, and he's not interested in a fat old woman like me. I married a Barnham; I wasn't born one. He doesn't want me, and I don't think he wants you. You act like you're about to go to war against him, and I'm telling you, that's dangerous. Leave well enough alone."

Beth said nothing, but her eyes darkened in pain. "On the way here, I have to pass by that school in town… that new consolidated elementary school. It has lovely new playground equipment, and sometimes I park a little ways down and watch the children. I sit there and I watch them, and I listen to their laughter, and I think of all the things that could have been." She cleared her throat. "I was going to be a teacher, before Sebastian Crane came into my life. He took so *many* things away from me: Bobby, my life, my career… my sanity." Her voice broke, and she shook her head.

"Honey—"

"So, yes, I guess you could say I do wish I could go to war with him. And that's what today was about, a little intelligence gathering. I wanted to see what I could find on the topic, see where legends and folklore and stories meet." She looked up at Lucy. "You don't have to help me, I know that. I would never bring you harm, not after all you've done for me. You're about all I have in this world, to be honest… but Lucy… what he did to me was *wrong*. What he has done to your family, for all of these years, these generations, is wrong. And someone has to put a stop to him."

Lucy looked at her for a moment, and then stood up and went to the cabinet. She took down a bottle of Jack Daniels, and then came back to the table. She poured a decent swallow into each coffee cup and then took a deep breath. "All right. Let's see what you've got."

"Thank you." Beth took a deep breath and opened a notebook. "First of all, from what I was able to gather, there are ways to keep vampires at bay, and there are ways to kill them."

Lucy frowned. "What's the difference?"

"Well, keeping them at bay means they are repelled... they can't come around. Interestingly, from what I've found the things that keep them at bay are natural, while the things that kill them are from man." She scanned her notes. "Garlic, for example... that's an old one, everyone knows about that. But did you know white roses supposedly are also a deterrent?"

"Roses..." Lucy made a surprised sound in her throat. She put a thoughtful hand to her chin, deep in remembrance. "About twenty years ago, I had a rose garden out by the clothesline. We were in town one day, and when we came back, someone or something had torn it up. The bushes had been cut off or pulled out of the ground, and the roses had actually been trampled into the dirt. It never made sense to me, who would do such a thing..."

"Was it during the day?"

Lucy nodded thoughtfully. "It was."

"Well, then it couldn't have been Crane. He wouldn't have been able to stand being that close to the roses, and besides, he can't move about in sunlight. I bet he paid someone to do it, though. A derelict, maybe, or a hobo from town. Twenty bucks will pay for a lot of wine if you're thirsty." She consulted her notes. "There's a lot of mention of people who are controlled by vampires... they're referred to as day-walkers, familiars, or just servants. They do the vampire's bidding during the daylight hours. Remember the character in Bram Stoker's *Dracula*? Renfield, the crazy man who ate bugs?"

Lucy made a face. "I do. And let me tell you, it's almost as bad, knowing I had a crazy man out here on the property, at Crane's bidding."

"I doubt he even knew why he had been hired to do such a thing. Usually, a vampire will pick someone who is very suggestible, and has nothing to lose—someone with severe mental issues, maybe, and certainly drug and alcohol abusers. Sometimes daywalkers are with their master for many years, but I get the impression that usually they're disposable, hired for only one or two assignments, and then quickly dispatched." She tucked a lock of hair behind her ear. "If you remember exactly *when* it was your rose garden was destroyed, I can go back to the library tomorrow and check the microfiche—they have all the old newspapers on file, you know—and sure as the world, I'll find an unexplained derelict death within a week of that incident."

"Ain't necessary," Lucy grunted. "Don't trouble yourself at all."

Beth looked thoughtful. "You know, Manny Draper, one of the boys from Bisby who made it home, later wrote a book about some of his adventures in the war. It's a collection of stories, memories, and a pretty good account of the Battle at Dark Hills, and later, his time in the army hospital. There's a non-circulating copy at the library. The librarians let me look at it in the reference room, but they watched me like a hawk, and made me wear a pair of surgical gloves when I handled it."

Lucy nodded. "Yes. I know it. *The Draper Papers*, if you'll excuse such a terrible name."

Beth smiled thinly. "I know. Well, I went through them very carefully, reading and combing through the parts when Draper was in the hospital, especially looking for mention of our boy Charlie. They were close friends, and Manny spoke emotionally about losing his friend." She cleared her throat. "What I'm getting to is this. Manny also mentioned an orderly in the hospital, a man named Huffman, or maybe Hoffman; apparently, he was crippled somehow—hunchback maybe, some physical deformity that Manny wasn't very clear about." She looked thoughtful. "I think this man might have been Crane's daywalker."

Lucy looked at her. "But I thought you said a daywalker was supposed to... what, help his master during the day..."

Beth nodded. "Yes. A daywalker's job is to clear obstacles, to help his master have easy access to his victims, even procure victims if he's able. But that wasn't necessary here. Crane already had all of his victims helpless and wounded, he just had to walk up and down among the rows of patients, picking out who he wanted."

"So why did he need a daywalker?"

"To help keep his secret, to keep the patients content and unafraid. Think about it. Those boys were far from home... the reality and horrors of war had set in, and some of them were never going to see their families again. Those that made it, like Manny, surely suspected *something* was wrong with good ol' Doctor Crane and may have been suspicious of what was happening. Crane needed someone to keep them happy and preoccupied, to tell them stories and read to them, to offer comfort and be their friend. In his memoirs, Manny writes of this Hoffman as "a cheerful fellow to be around, helpful and pleasant despite his monstrous deformity." She scanned her notes, running a finger down through the lines she had written. "He also mentioned that Hoffman was 'very protective of his friend the doctor, never allowing anyone, not another nurse, orderly or patient, to ever utter a cross word about the good doctor, defending him vociferously against complaint or criticism.'"

Lucy shuddered. "What happened to him?"

"No idea." Beth shrugged. "He was lost to history. I suspect he was eventually killed by Crane after he outlived his usefulness when the war was over. It wouldn't do to have any witnesses lying around, you see, and Crane had to move on after the Confederate defeat and find safety. Hoffman was only a minor mention in Draper's memoirs, but an interesting one, as if he was leaving a clue for readers to figure out about so many of the deaths under Crane's watch."

"What a horrible man," Lucy muttered. "Keeping those poor boys in the dark and off-balance about Crane… I hope he's burning in hell right now."

"Probably is." Beth shrugged. "All right, so where were we… okay, white roses. And garlic. And look, like all evil things, vampires can't cross running water. That little ditch, at the north end of the driveway? Believe it or not, that's a good thing. Crane, or any like him, cannot approach from that direction. He would have to go around to the back of the house and come in from the fields."

"That makes sense too," Lucy nodded. She looked slightly paler now, as each piece of information fit into her own experience, and she took a healthy gulp of her coffee. "Charlie's brothers were all found south of the house, in the barn, or the fields… and my own David, of course, also in the fields." She looked sadly down into her cup, and then poured another finger of whiskey in it. "And Bobby's father, my son Michael. We found him in the garden, right next to the house. The official autopsy report said it was an aneurysm, but of course we knew better. We knew better..."

Beth decided the old woman could take no more for a few minutes, so she pushed her notebook aside and set about clearing the table. Lucy stood up to help her, but Beth waved her off, and for several minutes, each woman was absorbed in her own memories and thoughts. As Beth was wiping down the table with a wet rag, Lucy stirred herself, and pointed to the pie safe. "There's a pie in the cupboard, if'n you're wanting something sweet. Sour cream and raisin, my grandmama's recipe. I bet you never had nothing like that up north." She got up and took down two pie plate and forks from the cabinet. Cutting them each a big piece, she licked her fingers and smiled sadly. "A little bit of sweet always makes the world a better place, at least for a little while." She sat back down and pointed to the notebook. "All right, what else you got?"

"Well," Beth said, forking off the point of her pie, "there are several ways to kill a vampire, though all of them involve getting up close and personal, and of course that's the danger. I mentioned staking him in the heart—ash wood only, though I'm not sure how accurate that is—and sunlight." She bit into her pie, nodding appreciatively. "Wow, this really is good."

"I told you that you'd like it," Lucy nodded smugly. "All right, go on."

"Well, then there's the religious component. Apparently, it's very much tied into the vampire legend, largely based in the Catholic Church—"

"Catholic?" Lucy snorted. "Not a lot of *them* around here. Baptists, mostly, good ol' fire-breathing Baptists. Maybe some Lutherans and a few Methodists, but hardly any Catholics." She considered. "Prob'ly in Memphis, or Nashville. Bigger cities. None around here that I know of."

"Remember much of the vampiric legend supposedly originates from eastern Europe, especially Romania. Of course, it extends outward from there... there are legends all over the world about vampires: in France, England, Russia, and so on. But I really believe that true vampiric origins are much older than that, and possibly started when Jesus Christ was still alive during Roman times."

Lucy looked doubtful. "Oh?"

Beth flipped a page, and then pointed to some of her scribbled notes. "Here's something interesting I found. There's another part of the vampiric legend, much lesser known, that I think is very important. I haven't seen it in a lot of places, but apparently, vampires are also affected by silver—"

"Silver! I thought that was just werewolves," Lucy took a bite of pie, and waved her fork in the air authoritatively. "I seen the movies! A silver bullet stops a werewolf, right?"

Beth shrugged. "Yes. Actually, there is a theory that silver is used against *all* evil things. It probably dates back two thousand years, to the Last Supper... you know, Judas and the thirty pieces of silver." She flipped through some pages. "In fact, there's a theory that vampires actually *originated* from Judas, because of his betrayal of Christ. Let's see... where is it..."

Lucy looked skeptical. "You mean Dracula was at the Last Supper with our Jesus?"

Beth chuckled. "No. At the Last Supper, Judas Iscariot was still a man, still a human... it's only what he did there that caused him to be... the terrible thing he became later." She thumbed down a few paragraphs, and then nodded. "All right, I found it. Now listen, there are several good reasons that support this theory. I'll paraphrase here, but I tell you, it *does* make sense..."

Lucy took a bite of her pie, listening to Beth with an uncertain look on her face. 'I've never heard any of this before," she muttered, and Beth nodded.

"I know, I hadn't either, but just listen... now, let's start with the Betrayer's last name, Iscariot, which apparently has several possible meanings. One source says that the name *Iscariot,* the last name given to Judas, actually had definite connections to a group of Jewish assassins named..." She flipped through another page, looking for the highlighted passage. "Here it is. A brotherhood named *The Sicarii.* Apparently, at one point, Judas, or at least members of his family, had been part of this fraternity of hired assassins."

"Hired assassins," Lucy breathed. Her eyes were very round.

Beth nodded. "This group was notorious for going around and sticking people with daggers, and that Judas, at one point, had actually been a hired killer himself. He met Christ, and for some time cleaned himself up, tried to cut ties with the *Sicarii*. But, after a time, either the lure of his former life was too great, or the *Sicarii* were not to be denied, and so he fell back into his old ways. The money he received for the betrayal might have been to possibly buy them off, or more likely, was something like a down payment, to be allowed back into the brotherhood." She flipped a page. "However, after the crucifixion of the Christ… well, it's not clear just what happened. One theory suggests after betraying Christ, guilt and shame overwhelmed Judas, and he committed suicide, while another theory has him being murdered by the *Sicarii* as punishment for trying to leave them." She took a deep breath. "At any rate, his body was found hanging from a tree. Legend has it that he was sent to Hell… but his crime of betraying Christ was so horrible that even Satan couldn't abide him and cast him out. His punishment was to be sent back to walk the earth for eternity, forever fearing the silver that he once coveted, with teeth similar to daggers. And, in that form, he was doomed to never stop killing." She swallowed hard. "*Teeth similar to daggers*, true to his Sicariian brotherhood."

"Dear Lord." Lucy reached for her coffee cup and took another sip. She was very pale.

"Well, there's more about our old friend Judas." Beth frowned slightly as she considered the page. "*Another* theory has the term Iscariot coming from an Aramaic term, which coincidentally means the color red." She looked up. "It all fits a little too close, doesn't it?"

"Red," Lucy echoed softly. "Blood red."

They looked at each other across the table, and Beth took a sip of iced tea. Her throat was very dry.

"So…" Lucy picked up some of Beth's notes and looked at them. "Are you saying that Doctor Crane and Judas are the same man?"

"Oh no." Beth looked thoughtful. "No, they're two separate people, born almost two thousand years apart... but I do think that Judas was the *first* vampire, and that Doctor Crane can trace his vampiric lineage back to Judas, who has made many vampires in his Undead life through some process I'm not yet aware of." She frowned. "To be honest, I was so busy piecing all of this Judas Iscariot business together, I haven't done much research yet into the origins of our friend Crane yet... you know, his *human* life, before he turned. According to the stories, the Crane family came from New Orleans, but that's about all I know right now. I'm not sure who turned Crane and why."

Lucy scowled. "Thirty pieces of silver," she muttered. "How terrible and yet interesting how that history has rolled down over the many years to touch my family." Her voice sounded shaky.

Beth sighed. "Interesting is hardly the word for it." She cleared her throat, deciding to get back on topic. "So, if all my suppositions are true, we know that silver is extremely harmful to our friend Crane, and why, based on the story of the Christ."

"Silver." Lucy thought sadly of her silver tea service on the buffet. If it came to it, did she have the courage to melt it down for weapons? She wanted to cry, even thinking about it. She cleared her throat, dismissing the idea from her mind. "All right, good to know. Anything else?"

"Well, Holy Water is lethal to vampires, according to all sources. And the old standby, crucifixes."

"Holy Water," Lucy muttered. "Catholic again, eh?"

"I think it works because they are blessed items. A priest is God's hand on earth, and the items therefore become touched by God. And since a vampire is removed from God, therefore it's repellent."

Lucy looked worriedly around her. "There is so much here to learn, so different from what you see in those movies..."

"Yep. And a cross is different from a crucifix, of course. A crucifix has the figure of crucified Jesus on it, while a cross is just two sticks crossing each other. Huge difference."

Lucy sighed. "All right, Beth darlin', I'm gonna recommend we call it a night on this. My head's swimming, and I doubt I'll get any sleep tonight because of it." She glanced at the clock. "Besides, it's Tuesday, and Rachel is supposed to call tonight."

Beth nodded. Rachel was Lucy's daughter, who worked and lived in California. Beth, of course, hadn't met her yet, but had talked on the phone with her a few times after Rachel had gotten over her suspicions as to just who she was and why she had moved in with her mother. Beth remembered Bobby talking about his crazy aunt, the activist, though he had spoken of her lovingly, laughing at her antics. Apparently, she visited once a year, and was planning a visit back home sometime the last week of August. Beth knew that Lucy missed her dearly, and she herself was eager to meet another Barnham. It would be another link to Bobby, and she also was curious to know if Rachel had any insight into the Crane legend.

Lucy went to gather the plates and laughed a little as she stood up. "Whoo boy, too much of that firewater," she giggled, grasping the back of a chair. "A little goes a long way, I guess. Never could hold my liquor. Next thing you know I'll be staggering around here like a dimwickie drunk."

"Dimwickie?" Beth went to put the pie back into the pie safe. "Is that bad?"

"Horrible, child, you just don't know!" She fixed Beth with a look, and then the phone rang. "Oh, there's my girl, right on time. She always was a punctual child. Beth, get the phone while I dry my hands, and don't you *dare* tell her I've been drinking. She'll start sending me pamphlets about twelve-step programs and making me go talk to a bunch of strangers while we all sit in a circle and hold hands."

"I won't say a word," Beth promised and walked to the phone. It was an old, black rotary that hung on the wall, the only phone in the house, but as Lucy pointed out, it was for service and emergencies, and not necessarily for gabbing. She picked it up, eager to talk to Rachel. "Hello?"

Silence.

She frowned slightly. "Hello? Rachel, is that you?"

The voice on the other end was silky and calm, and terrifyingly familiar. "Hello, Beth. I'll dispense with all the formalities, since we're old friends by now, and I'll just ask you a question I think you'll recognize as familiar... *do you love?*"

The room seemed to spin, and she fought for control. "Who is this?"

There was an indulgent chuckle. "Oh, Beth. Let's not play games with each other, shall we? You know very well who this is. After all, I posed that very same question to you several years ago, and I know you still remember it." Beth waved frantically at Lucy to get her attention, but she had her back to her as she ran water for the dishes.

"Tell her I'll be right there!" Lucy called out, squirting dishwashing soap happily into the water. "And remember, nothing else! That girl shoulda been born a Prohibitionist, I swear."

Beth gripped the phone tighter, afraid she would start screaming. The voice tut-tutted. "Ah, there's our dear, dear Lucy... she's in her cups again, isn't she? Shame she took to drinking, though who could have blamed her, after all the terrible tragedies that befell her family? Tragic, ain't it?"

Her voice was low, and she fought to keep the panic out of it. "Tragedies that *you* caused, you bastard."

"Bastard?" There was real amusement in his voice. "Now, let's not resort to pettiness, dear Beth, it's unbecoming. And just as a point of correction, my parents were very much married, so the stigma of illegitimacy certainly never fell upon me." He paused. "And just for the record, if I were you, I'd be *real* careful about throwing that term 'bastard' around."

"What?" She frowned in confusion. "I don't—"

"Never mind, *mon chéri*, just a trifling observation. Forget I said anything, at least, for now." He paused for a moment, waiting for her to say something, but she remained silent, and he sighed again, as if in exasperation. "And speaking of observations, dear Beth, you do know that all that nonsense you served up our Lucy this evening is pure tripe, don't you? Nothing more than fantasy and fiction? Judas Iscariot, indeed!"

Black spots of panic began to swim in front of her eyes. Dear God, was he close enough to have heard their conversation? If he was, then that meant he was close, *dangerously* close. Quickly she glanced at the kitchen windows, but they were dark and empty. "How did you—"

He laughed—a laugh that was terrible and low. "I know because I make it my business to know. And by the way, Beth, how did you enjoy your pie? It's a shame it wasn't blackberry pie… that's my favorite, you know." She gasped, but before he could answer, he whispered, "Good night, dear Beth. Adieu, for now."

I've no doubt we'll meet again, and soon.

And she was left with the phone in her hand, listening to a buzzing dial tone.

XII
CHAPTER

It was late at night, and her books were spread open in front of her. The poem was ancient, and disappointingly incomplete, yet she had read it so many times she nearly had it memorized.

Daemones antiqui;
ubi rēs tam atrōx susurrat historia, tremit animus.
Proditores hominis et Deī;
hominēs, sīcut lepores, venantur;
latens in tenebrīs quasi malae umbrae;
aperientes venas sīcut utrēs vīnī.
Daemones violentiae pleni sunt;
numquam misericordiam faciēns.
Invoca eōs bannum!
Redde incunctanter illōs ad inferos!

(Ancient demons,
where history whispers of things so terrible, it trembles the soul.
Betrayers of man and God both,
They hunt mankind like rabbits,
Lurking in the dark as evil shadows,
Opening their veins like bottles of fine wine.
They are demons full of violence,

Never showing mercy or pity.
Invoke the ban against them!
Return them to hell without a qualm!)

She glanced at her watch. Nearly one thirty in the morning. She had been working for several hours now, reading and checking her notes, and she tiredly rubbed her eyes, feeling a headache coming on.

"*Latens in tenebrīs quasi malae umbrae,*" she muttered. "*...aperientes venas sīcut utrēs vīnī...*"

Lurking in the dark...

Hello, Beth... I think you'll recognize this as a familiar question... do you love?

She had played back their conversation in her head a thousand times, remembering the confident cat-and-mouse way he had toyed with her. How she had managed not to start screaming at the phone, she never knew. Trembling, she put it back into the cradle, just as Lucy turned to her, with an inquisitive smile on her face.

"Was that my Rachel?"

Beth shook her head, struggling to keep calm. "No... it was just a telemarketer. You don't want new siding for the house, do you?"

"Hardly." Lucy gave an indignant snort, and then glanced at the clock. "Well, that girl is late tonight—"

And then the phone rang again.

"I've got it," Beth said quickly, jumping to get it. She wasn't about to let Crane speak to Lucy and upset her or maybe even mock her about her dead menfolk. With a shaking hand and ignoring Lucy's strange look, she picked up the phone. "Hello?"

"Beth?" Rachel's cheerful voice came over the line. "How are you? Is my mother available?"

Relief flooded through Beth; she nearly wept. "Yes, yes, of course. Rachel, it's so good to hear from you... here she is..."

That had been several hours ago, and now the house was quiet, except for the gentle hum of the box air conditioner in the window next to her. There was no way she was going to sleep with the windows open tonight—no way at all... in fact, she had put a wreath of garlic in both her and Lucy's windows, and for good measure, a wild rose as well. They weren't white, but they were wild, and one source said that was just as good. She hoped the author knew what he was talking about.

Beth scanned the verse carefully, considering the words as she copied them into her notebook. They were part of a poem—an incantational prayer, actually—regarding vampires and how to banish them. However, it was incomplete, merely an excerpt from a much longer tome, long lost. There was no help here.

She flipped another page, looking at her notes again. At the library, she had photocopied off a picture of Judas Iscariot, and she looked at it now. Entitled *The Kiss of Judas*, it was a famous portrait done by the Italian painter Giotti di Bondone. It was well over eight hundred years old and considered a priceless masterpiece. She clicked open the rings of the binder and took it out, looking at it carefully. She wasn't an art critic, but she had to admit it *was* a powerful portrait, with brilliant colors, depicting Judas kissing the Christ. Taking a sip of coffee, she thoughtfully studied it. Something about it nagged at her, something that was on the tip of her consciousness, and she frowned.

Kissing the Christ.

Kissing...

Kiss.

"Oh, my God," she muttered. "Of course... how did I miss this?"

Despite Crane's disdainful mocking of her theories, the more she dug, the more she began to realize she was correct. It was well agreed among Biblical scholars that Judas kissing the Christ was the signal agreed on between him and the soldiers of the High Priest Caiaphas, who was Pontius Pilate's creature. The kiss was a pre-agreed upon signal to point out to the uncertain soldiers just which of the assembled men was Christ. It was therefore regarded as the ultimate betrayal, and everything that followed, the arrest, torture and ultimate crucifixion of Christ were a direct result of the kiss.

"You *kissed* him," she muttered, "didn't you?"

And really, what was a kiss? Touching one's lips to another, in an act of intimacy and presumed desire... and then, depending on the circumstances, and the person, and the passion, couldn't a little more pressure be employed? A caress, a nibble...

A bite?

Of course to throw her off base, Crane had told her that she was wrong and that her information was absurd. Then again, she wouldn't have expected him to admit anything... his game, as she was beginning to piece together, was to dissemble, to lie and deceive. And why not? He was of his Father the Serpent, the Father of all Liars. But as each piece began to fit into the puzzle of what Crane was, and who he was, she began to realize she was on the right track.

However...

Clearly, somehow, he was on to her as well, was able to listen to her conversations, and was able to track her movements. And while at the moment she might have been only a passing curiosity with him, an amusing game, at what point would she uncover a piece of information about him that would make him feel threatened? She couldn't believe that she was the first adversary he had ever faced... Lucy had mentioned that other Barnhams had fought him, and he himself had alluded to the fact that he had outwitted and outplayed other opponents. She doubted that he considered her anything more than an interesting pawn, scuttling here, scampering there, asking silly questions like a silly girl. She was an insignificant nothing... he could kill her without even batting an eye.

Do you think there is anything I want that I couldn't just take?

She wondered how it was that he knew she had come to live with Lucy, and more than that, how he had been privy to their conversation. Her notes all spoke of vampires having extraordinary senses, and she supposed it was possible that he had indeed been outside the windows, listening in to their council of war... but how far away had he been? And how had he arrived at the farm? Because he couldn't cross running waters, it was impossible for him to drive down the long driveway to the house, which meant he would have had to come across the back fields, and that was no easy slog.

She closed her eyes, putting herself in his place. Thinking, thinking. To approach the house from the back, he would have had to park his car on the old access road by the far pasture and walk through the woods and come up through the orchards. She disbelieved the legend that vampires could fly; she was pretty sure that was only in the movies. No, he would have a car, and probably for the sake of practicality, a four-wheel drive, or a truck, to maneuver the dirt roads and gravel driveways.

"But where do you park it during the day, you bastard? Where are you hiding?" Her words were soft, and she flipped another page in her notebook, looking for answers. "More importantly, who is helping you?"

According to some sources—Bram Stoker's *Dracula* included—it was thought that vampires were required to not only sleep in coffins, but there had to be dirt in the coffins from their homeland. Beth didn't think so. A coffin would be cumbersome and nearly impossible to explain away, and she suspected that vampires—Crane included—relied on the ability to be as mobile as possible. Certainly, if a community started noticing a series of unexplained deaths the very day a stranger arrived in their midst, questions would be asked and investigations would be conducted. It was likely that a quick exit would be necessary and lugging a coffin around would be impossible. It might be a *preferred* method of sleep for them, but not necessarily required. No, she figured all that was needed was somewhere dark and private, possibly guarded by a daywalker.

And that also meant something else.

Who was protecting him, and where was he hiding? For him to have found her and to have overheard her conversation, he had to have his nest somewhere close by.

She thought about this. Bisby was the closest town, and it only had two motels. In her trips to town, she had also noticed a boarding house—kittenishly referred to as the Bisby Bed and Breakfast—but she didn't think Crane would risk staying at any of those places. And while it was conceivable that he was staying in a private residence, possibly a rental, somehow that seemed too easy. It didn't *feel* right to her. There were just too many risks with that scenario. Any stranger in a small town was immediately regarded as suspicious, especially someone who probably only paid with cash and who was only seen at night. The gossips would have a field day with that.

So, what did that leave? Old barns, outbuildings, or farm houses close by? Perhaps, even an abandoned home or above an old garage. More likely. The problem with that, though, was the risk of discovery, especially in the summertime. Such a place would be vulnerable to any hiker or rockhound passing by... an old farmer, perhaps looking for discarded tools or even a hopeful real estate agent looking for a property. As much as she interested him, she didn't think that he would risk his safety by sleeping in an unprotected place. And if he had employed a daywalker to watch over him during the day, who and where was that person? And to what lengths did they intend to go to protect their master?

The last thing he had said to her troubled her the most. She had mentally examined it, thought about it, and could come up with no explanation.

The stigma of illegitimacy certainly never fell upon me... I'd be careful about the term bastard...

He had dangled that in front of her, teasing her, mocking her, waiting for her frustrated questions. She had instinctively known that pressing him more would have furthered his enjoyment, so she had shut up, but it bothered her.

What had he meant? Was he meaning her father? She hadn't spoken to him in years—didn't even know if he was alive, and truly didn't even care, to be brutally honest—so any information Crane may have had on him certainly couldn't hurt her. And if, by chance, her parents *hadn't* been married, which was very unlikely, it didn't seem all that important now.

Still, he had mentioned it in a very obvious way, and in a way she knew he hoped it would bring her some amount of pain. And while on one hand, it could have been another mind game or a way of diverting her attention from what was really important between them—and she wouldn't have put it past him to employ such things—she suspected there was something to it. He knew something about her, some knowledge, and he was keeping it close to the vest. But why? It only meant he intended to torture her with it and then later reveal some troubling news, the best way to maximize her pain.

Forget I said anything, at least, for now

Questions, more and more, with very few answers. She put the cap on her marker and closed her notebooks. Tiredly, she rubbed the back of her neck and slid into bed. She reached out to turn off the light on the bedside table and then reconsidered. Better to leave it on.

The old tintype of Charlie Barnham was beside her bed, and she picked it up for a second. Fiercely, he gazed back at her, hiding his hint of a smile. Fondly, she touched the edge of the frame.

"Oh, Charlie," she whispered. "I wish I had known you. I sorta feel like I do, actually. You were the first—the first of your family to go up against that monster, but there were many behind you. You poor, brave boy," she swiped a tear away and struggled to control herself. "But don't worry. I'll get him for you. You can count on that."

She put the picture back on the nightstand and cleared her throat. She settled back onto the pillow, pulling the sheet to her chin, and closed her eyes.

Sleep was long in coming, but when it came, it was a blessing, and she welcomed it after she had whispered the prayer to herself.

…hominēs, sīcut lepores, venantur;
latens in tenebrīs quasi malae umbrae;
aperientes venas sīcut utrēs vīnī.
Daemones violentiae pleni sunt;
numquam misericordiam faciēns.
Invoca eōs bannum!
Redde incunctanter illōs ad inferos!

And outside, sitting on the peak of the roof, Sebastian Crane nodded slightly.

Earlier, he had gotten a nasty shock when he had heard her whisper the poem aloud and was still recovering from the unexpectedness of it. He hadn't even thought of that verse in years—couldn't remember the last time he had heard it spoken aloud, in fact—and despite being startled, he was actually rather impressed that she had managed to find it.

He frowned in thought. When was the last time he had heard it, and who had spoken it? He thought it might have been a French priest in a little village outside of Augusta, possibly in 1864… or perhaps '65. Yes, 1865, and the priest's name had been… he pondered. Hugo. Yes, that was it. Father Michaud Hugo: a skinny, rabbit-like man, who, like many underestimated men, had shown a surprisingly remarkable courageous face at the end. He had been nothing more than a parish priest, certainly not a Vampire Slayer sent from the idiots in the Vatican, but he had shown *heart*, and that had made him an interesting opponent. He and a band of villagers had chased and searched for Crane for about two weeks once they had discovered he was in their midst, and Crane had been impressed with his tenacious bravery.

Crane had fled to Maine upon the end of the War to hide and regroup. Through a series of machinations, he had wrested the deed to a house and property of an Army Colonel he had met at Appomattox, and had moved there to lie low. It was not a new move for him… he was used to doing this in peacetime, moving from place to place by swindling victims out of their inheritances and then killing them, and then moving on as the victims of his feeding frenzies began to be discovered. This time, however, he had met with a lot of bad luck. Either the citizens there were more suspicious of strangers in their midst, or more sensitive to their losses, or perhaps he had even left a witness to one of his attacks; he wasn't sure, but he hadn't been there more than a month before the townspeople had panicked and gone to Father Hugo for help. Worse luck yet, apparently the good Father had been something of a student of the occult, and immediately had known what he was up against and how to fight it. Crane remembered the little priest standing in the yard after he and the townspeople had finally found his sleeping spot and ousted him. The little fool valiantly chanted this poem at him, waving a crucifix at him with one hand and holding the Bible aloft with the other. It actually could have had a very bad outcome for him, except that Hugo's nerves disastrously had broken, and he had bungled the whole process, screaming and garbling the words and tragically mixing up the verses. Ironically, had he gotten it right and been able to finish the thing, there definitely would have been a very different outcome that night. But alas, despite a momentary brave face, Father Hugo's timid nature had taken over—his will had broken, and it had been his undoing.

And now, here was that damnable poem again, after all these years! It was unbelievable, but here it was... the Poem. He doubted if Elizabeth knew the true power behind the words or knew the *magic* in the prayer. Somehow, he didn't think so, not because she was obtuse but because incantational prayers were hardly spoken of or used these days, and were a lesser-known part of the lore that surrounded him. Still, in her reading and research, she had uncovered it, and that alone raised her estimation in his eyes.

"Well done, Elizabeth," he whispered. "Well done indeed. If nothing else, you are becoming... *interesting*."

However...

Poor Elizabeth. What a shame that she only had discovered *part* of the poem, not all of it. The most important pieces—the truly powerful words—were missing, and without them, he doubted what parts of the poem that were left could hurt him at all. It was incomplete now, nothing more than a collection of words... wasn't it? Could only *half* of the poem cause him harm? He wasn't sure, and it troubled him.

Because... what if he were wrong? This silly human female had stumbled on a weapon—a broken weapon, perhaps—but even a jagged sword could still cut. A trickle of unease stole over him, something he hadn't felt in years, and he stirred restlessly.

Daemones violentiae pleni sunt;
numquam misericordiam faciēns.

"Indeed," he murmured. "*Never showing mercy or pity*. Welcome to the game, my dear."

He gazed at her through the window one final time, and then, like smoke, dissolved into the night.

CHAPTER XIII

Thursday was Farmers' Market Day.

The first few Thursdays, Beth had shied away from it, mainly because she knew it would bring a lot of people, and crowds made her nervous. She watched Lucy pack up her eggs, her produce, and her various preserves, jams and jellies, load them up in her truck, and then come back hours later with empty boxes. Obviously, it had been a good day. She had traded for a few things, including a lovely watermelon and some early tomatoes, and she was in a good mood.

"I made nearly seventy dollars, and coulda made more," she crowed triumphantly. She peeled off a twenty-dollar bill and handed it to Beth, who looked surprised. "That's your cut of the peaches."

"Oh, no, I couldn't—"

"Don't be silly, you worked just as hard on them as I did." Lucy sat down and opened a beer. "Whew, that tastes good, you can be sure. No, really, your sweat went into making them peaches, and I won't hear another word about it. You ain't exactly got money fallin' outta your ears right now." She cocked a determined eye at Beth, who still looked uncertain. "I thought we'd put up some corn relish before next week, and maybe some more blackberry jam. You can come with me and sell 'em yourself."

Beth chewed on her lip nervously, thinking about all the people milling about and their loud voices, talking over one another... "I don't know. I'll help you with whatever you need, but going there... I'm not—"

"Oh, don't be a heckatootie, chicken-pie. You can't stay hidden from the world forever, darlin'. Besides, it'll be good for you."

By the following Thursday, they had loaded up five milk crates with produce, corn relish, and blackberry preserves, and Lucy was ready to go. She tied on her floppy straw hat and donned her favorite tee shirt, which read, "I'm So Old, I Fart Dust," though Beth decided she was not about to ask her to prove it. She lingered on the porch, but Lucy crooked a finger at her and pointed to the truck. "And I'll buy you lunch when we get there," which was a hint that she wasn't cooking, and that if Beth wanted to be fed, she had better get in the truck.

Farmers and gardeners from all around Bisby had their stalls set up along Main Street; the more experienced of them had set up awnings and card tables with tablecloths to make their wares more enticing. There was a good deal of excitement and laughter in the day; most of the vendors knew each other and joked and spoke to one another, teasing about the freshness and cost of their produce. Lucy's booth was on the end, shrewdly placed nearest the large parking lot just off the town square to maximize the number of people who walked by her stand.

Her handyman, Karl, had picked six dozen ears of corn, and the garden had provided any number of cucumbers and summer squash, both green and yellow. Lucy showed Beth how to arrange the vegetables at the front of the table and then artfully stack the relish and jam—in both pints and quarts—in attractive little pyramids. "It's about the presentation at first," she instructed, tying a little ribbon around the neck of each jar. "These people love this kind of country crap... most of these people coming through here probl'y have painted wooden geese in their home with stupid signs around their neck...'God Bless Our Country Home' Can you imagine such crap? None of 'em worked on a farm a day in their life, but they like to come out to the Market once a week, buy our stuff, and pretend they've spent a day out with the country folk. Makes you wanna puke, it does."

Beth nodded, not sure what to say.

"Still, it's profitable, so why—" she stopped suddenly as two middle-aged ladies, carrying big wooden baskets, stopped by her booth. "Good morning to you! Y'all fixin' to buy some corn? And we gots some lovely corn relish today, too, if'n that suits your fancy." Beth noticed her accent had increased as if for show, and the women—they were obviously tourists as she had seen them get out of a mini-van with out-of-state plates—giggled and ate it up. She remembered her own days at Lou's Diner dealing with Summer People, and decided this wasn't much different. She sat down on an upended milk crate to enjoy the show.

As the day went on, it became clear to Beth that Lucy was a favorite at the Market, both with the other vendors and the customers. People stopped by to chat, even if they didn't buy anything, and when they curiously looked at Beth, Lucy took it as an opportunity to introduce her. "This here is an old family friend, just down for a visit," she would say vaguely, which Beth thought was smart. As small as Bisby was, she figured that most people remembered that Bobby had been murdered nine years ago—after all, it had made the national news due to the savagery and peculiarity of the crime, and anyone who knew Lucy could also account for all her other family members. Even a fictional distant cousin would be suspect—Lucy had told her that to a Southerner, family was extremely important, and lineages and family trees played a big part in their day-to-day life. Calling her a family friend was probably safer.

Business was surprisingly good. It was a nice day, which, according to Lucy, brought people out to the market. And true to her word, Lucy bought Beth lunch… or at least she traded for it. Sometime after noon, she grabbed two quarts of corn relish and a few cucumbers and pointed to a stall several vendors down. "Take this down there to Louella's… tell her I'm offering all of this for two of her chicken salad sandwiches. And tell her not to be skimpy when she spoons it up, or she'll hear about it."

Beth looked uneasy. "I don't even know… Louella? I don't think I would feel comfortable telling a stranger all that."

Lucy waved her hand dismissively. "Oh, go on, Louella and I went to school together; our graduating class was so small we could all share the same schoolbooks. Don't worry, she won't bite," she cackled a little. "And even if she wanted to, she ain't got no teeth, so go on."

Beth sighed, but packed up her items in a box and took a deep breath. Lucy turned away and began chattering away to an older couple, who were busy sorting through the zucchini. As she walked away, Beth heard Lucy saying, "Why, you just fry that up in a little butter and onions, maybe throw in a red pepper, and you got yourself a good ol' summer stir-fry…"

Louella's stand had less produce and more lunch items: chicken and tuna salad, garden salads, several types of homemade cookies, and fresh lemonade. There were a few people ahead of her, but when Beth finally got to the front of the line, Louella had already marked her. "That Lucy Barnham's wormy old vegetables? Can't give the stuff away, eh?"

Beth felt her face flush. "I don't know about wormy… Lucy sent me down to trade this for lunch."

"I just bet she did." Louella peered into the crate, holding up an especially pretty cucumber. "Well, this one ain't bad," she grudgingly admitted, and then grinned. "And you're just the messenger, I know. I'm Louella Draper."

"Beth Franklin." She felt she should explain herself. "I'm visiting for a while, down from Indiana."

"I heard." Louella fixed her with an inquisitive eye. "Indiana, eh?"

Beth swallowed hard. "Did you want to trade? Lucy had wanted two chicken salad sandwiches, and she said, don't be skimpy when you dip them up."

Louella shook her head. "Demanding ol' thing, ain't she? Don't know how you're able to live with her… I'd be heading for home in about a day." She turned her head and called, "Wes! Two chicken sandwiches, and don't be skimpin' on the chicken. We got Lucy Barnham's corn relish riding on this."

For the first time, Beth noticed a young man at the back of the stall; he wore baggy khaki shorts and a white tee shirt. A shapeless golf hat was pushed back from his forehead. He was slicing tomatoes and glanced up when he heard his name. "We never do, do we?"

"Well, depends." Louella looked at Beth and jerked her thumb. "That's my grandson, Wesley. He'll take care of you. I'm gonna go jaw at Lucy, ask her why she grows such pitiful cucumbers." She moved around the edge of the table and waddled off down the row, waving the cucumber like a standard.

Wes watched her go, amused. "She's a character, ain't she?"

"Just like Lucy. Two peas in a pod." She looked at him again and then looked away. He was close to her age and skinny, with a lot of shaggy brown hair; a pair of sunglasses hung around his neck. He looked like a scholarly surfer, and she smiled at the thought.

"How do you want your sandwich?" He had caught her looking at him and seemed amused.

She shrugged. "Oh, any old way—"

He made a face. "Naw, that won't do. I've spent all durn morning back here, cutting up tomatoes and onions and lettuce. You're gonna have to put *something* on your sandwich, or my feelings will be hurt."

She smiled. "All right… tomatoes. And a pickle on the side?"

"Good call." Expertly, he built the sandwiches while she watched. It was cooler under the awning of his tent, and she saw that he had a great big ice cooler where he kept his perishable ingredients; when he bent over to scoop out the chicken salad, his shirt rode up and she saw the smooth, tanned expanse of his back. She looked away.

"There you go." He pushed the food over to her on a plastic tray. "The price is…" He picked up a quart of corn relish and held it up to the light, examining it. "The price is two quarts of corn relish. And two cucumbers. Sorry, no change."

"Deal." Despite herself, she found herself smiling… he seemed so carefree and light… just like…

I'm Bobby Barnham, Housepainter Extraordinaire… and you are…?

"I'm Wesley Draper." He grinned at her. "My friends call me Wes. My grandmother calls me Wesley Michael Draper when she's pissed. What do you want to call me?"

She shrugged, aware that he was flirting with her. She wasn't sure how it made her feel, and so she did her best to just ignore it and get back to Lucy. "Don't know that I have to call you anything, except Sandwich Boy."

His face crumpled dramatically. "Ouch. I might have to take back my pickle."

There was a pause for a second while she thought that over, and then she burst into sudden laughter. He blushed and then he laughed too, realizing what he said. "Like that wasn't Freudian," she said, grabbing the tray. "I'll see you around, Wesley Draper."

She paused.

Draper...

Charlie's friend, Manny Draper, was there at the battle with him and was wounded too. He's the one that came back and told the folks what happened...

She looked at him closely, her heart beating. "Did you say your name was Draper?"

He looked mildly confused. "I did. Do we know each other?" He took off his hat and fanned himself with it. "Heck, we couldn't; I don't even know your name yet."

"Beth Franklin." She stood in the sun, feeling a chill go down her back. "Look, this is crazy... has your family lived in Bisby for a long time?"

He shrugged. "Yep. Generations. No one ever gets out of Bisby, really. I mean, even I left for college, and I came back. Why do you want to know?"

Her head was spinning. "I'm doing some... well, some research on citizens of Bisby. From the Civil War era. That's kinda why I'm staying with Lucy, actually, and she had mentioned that a Manny Draper had gone off to war with Charlie Barnham."

"Oh, sure!" His eyes lit up. "The Tennessee Scarlet Rangers. Everyone around here knows about them—about twenty of Bisby's finest who marched off to war. They're famous, though only six came back, I think. Yep, you got the right Draper... ol' Manny was my double-great grandpa."

"Really?" She swallowed hard. "Well, like I said, I'm doing some research on the locals, gathering information, and talking to people." She cleared her throat. "I'd like to talk to you, ask you some questions about your grandfather, if you've got the time."

He nodded enthusiastically. "Sure. Of course, I never met the ol' boy, but I know all about him... Granny has talked about him so many times, it feels like we're old friends. I've got stories—maybe a few medals in a box somewhere, and a belt buckle. I can show you all of that, if you want." He shrugged. "Tell me when and where, and I'll be there."

"Tomorrow. At Lucy's house, we'll make you lunch." She didn't think that Lucy would mind, or at least, she hoped she wouldn't.

"Lunch?" He seemed amused. "That's a switch, people making me lunch. I'll be there. You want me to bring anything special?"

"Just whatever you've got on your grandfather. Paperwork, stories your family may have written down, photographs. That sort of thing. You never know what might be helpful." Behind her, the line was forming again, and she could hear throats being cleared impatiently. Beth smiled weakly and motioned with her head. "You've got customers waiting. I'd better go."

"Nice meeting you," he called, over the head of the woman who pushed her way to his table. Beth looked back to see him waving at her, and she offered him a smile.

He's nice, but don't get involved. People you get involved with usually end up dead.

Good advice. She squared her shoulders and went to find Lucy, but she couldn't quit thinking about his smile and his tanned back.

* * *

"Wesley Draper, eh?" Lucy nodded approvingly. "He's soft on the eyes, ain't he? Sort of hippie-like, maybe, but not too bad. Needs a haircut, but that's easy." She chuckled. "So, you enjoyed his sandwich, eh?"

Beth blushed. "It's not like that. I figured he could help us."

"Oh?" Lucy cocked an inquisitive eyebrow. "How's that? You want a recipe or something?"

"Lucy!" Beth laughed in spite of herself. "You're exasperating sometimes!" She folded the dish towel and sat down at the table. "Help us with… old stories." She nodded meaningfully. "You know what I mean; I know."

"Oh." Lucy took a sip of her beer. She sighed heavily. "Still on that, are you?"

Beth nodded. "Without a doubt. I figured Wesley might have something—maybe some family lore, maybe a clue—that could help us." She shrugged. "I guess any little bit will help."

"Beth, darlin', you're a smart girl, but you're not understanding me. We don't want to pursue this; we don't want to go after Crane. He's untouchable; he's lived forever, and he's far smarter than we are. And I'll be honest with you, it makes me nervous, even talking about this. If he were to know we were talking about going after him... Lord knows what he would do then."

Beth looked away, fussily rearranging the flowers in the cut glass vase. She hadn't told Lucy about Crane's phone call because she knew how the old lady would react. She would immediately demand that Beth stop her investigation, or worse yet, she would make her leave the property. The thought scared her. Besides having nowhere else to go, she honestly had to admit she had come to care about Lucy Barnham, about the farm and the land she worked alongside her. To leave her would break her heart.

"Beth?" Lucy's voice was worried. "I don't want anything to happen to you, you know that. This thing, this revenge thing... well, it scares me, it really does. Just let Crane go on—something or someone will eventually get him, or he'll run into a priest, maybe, or he'll bite the wrong person, or maybe he'll even meet another vampire, and..."

"I'm only asking questions, that's all," Beth promised. "I'm not doing anything else, I swear."

Lucy frowned, looking at her, and looking like she was trying to decide if she should pursue this further or not. With shaking hands, she took another sip of her beer and decided to change topics.

"Hope your boy likes egg salad," she grunted, getting to her feet and getting a covered plastic bowl out of the refrigerator. "This being a first date and all, I wasn't going to serve steak until you decide if you like him or not."

"It's hardly a date," Beth corrected. "We're having lunch, and he's going to bring some things about his double great-grandfather. We'll talk, I'll get some... *information*... and he'll go home." She looked out the window as Karl came walking up the back walk, carrying a hoe.

"Besides, you invited Karl, so even if Wes and I wanted to be alone, we couldn't."

"We're chaperones, is all." Lucy set out a big bowl of coleslaw and a bag of potato chips. "But only for a little while. And besides, Karl's not staying for lunch, really. He's just nosy. You know, I don't think I told you, but a long time ago, back in high school, he mighta had a crush on Louella, which is really funny, because at the same time, she had a crush on my David."

"Really?" Beth was intrigued. "Ooh, small town scandal, eh?"

Lucy shrugged. "No scandal, really; just missed opportunity. Old town gossip from when we were all young and dashing and stupid." She chuckled. "It all sorted itself out, for the most part. David didn't have a whole lot of interest in Louella and began to court me, and Claude Draper came along and married Louella within a few months of graduation."

"And Karl? Seems like things didn't work out for him."

Lucy suddenly looked sad. "I know. He never did have a whole lot of ambition or luck. He did get married eventually, but not to a local girl. When that hellcat Freida Mayes from over in Nashville showed up to manage the post office—forty years old and unmarried, with a face like a Rottweiler and a voice to match—I guess they both saw it as a last chance and hitched their team together. Nothing but unhappiness since, as far as I can see." She shook her head in disgust and sorrow and then looked at Beth sternly. "So, if this is a date with Wesley Draper, don't waste it by talking about unpleasant things, eh Beth, darlin'?"

Beth sighed. "We're gonna talk about… Civil War battles, is all." She looked thoughtful. "Really? Karl and Wes' grandmother?" She shook her head. "And then Wes' grandmother and your husband? And I thought the Depression was boring."

Lucy chuckled. "A regular soap opera, eh? Well, not much ever came out of it. Karl was too shy to be a serious suitor, and Louella wasn't interested in him anyway. She had set her cap for my David, which was unfortunate because he never was really all that interested in her. Oh, he was polite about it, but by then, he and I were already something of a couple, and so he let her down easy. Louella finally settled down with old Claude Draper, who was so dumb that he barely managed to graduate. I'm not sure if she ever really loved him, to be honest, but girls back then had to get married, and she was afraid of being alone."

Beth looked sad. "So, Karl and his wife were unhappy, and Louella and Claude were unhappy. It all sounds terrible, to be honest."

Lucy nodded. "I know. The only happy couple in the whole mess was me and David, and of course that eventually ended in tragedy as well, thanks to Crane."

"Thanks to Crane," Beth repeated softly, her features hardening.

Lucy reached for her hand. "But all of that—all the crushes and loves and high school drama—it's just ancient history. It happened nearly fifty years ago, so who cares? What's important is today, so let me tell you; if you're serious about Wes, don't let him linger and dawdle—"

"Lucy." Beth couldn't help but smile. "I'm telling you—"

Lucy looked out the window delightedly. "Don't tell me, tell him. He's coming up the back walk right now."

Beth looked startled. "Really? He's early..." Automatically, her hand went up to smooth down her hair, and quickly she brought it back down because she noticed Lucy looking at her with an amused expression. "Well, he is," she said defensively, and Lucy nodded enthusiastically, coughing away a smile.

Momentarily flustered, Beth hesitated and then cleared her throat. "I'll get the door."

"Good idea," Lucy agreed. "Don't leave that boy out there, get him on in here."

Beth shot her a dark look and then moved around the table lightly, headed toward the door. Taking a deep breath, she pasted a smile on her face.

Wes stood on the back porch, neatly dressed in faded jeans and a polo shirt. He peered out at her from under his golf hat, and she saw that though he looked clean and well-scrubbed, he hadn't shaved. Artlessly scruffy, and she wasn't sure if it was by design or neglect.

All words of greeting flew out of her head, and before he could say anything, she blurted, "I hope you like egg salad. Lucy wasn't going to make you a steak."

He looked surprised. "Well, that's all right, I guess." He blinked a few times, deciding on what to say, and then handed her a covered basket. "Here, I made some cookies... and I hope *you* like chocolate chip."

Lucy craned her neck around Beth. "Oooh, hoo, and you can bake too! Beth, you better tie this one up so he don't get away. I guess all them years working in Louella's kitchen has taught him a thing or two. Well, come in, come in; you're letting the flies in."

They moved inside, and Wesley hoisted the basket onto the table. "I brought the other stuff you asked about, too. I found ol' Manny's muster record, and when he was discharged."

Beth moved about the kitchen, putting bowls and paper plates on the table. For some reason, she felt very nervous, and she didn't think it was solely the topic; the very nearness of him was exciting, and he smelled very good, very clean. She fought to clear her mind. "Did you find anything that had to do with his time during the Battle of Dark Hills?"

Wes eased himself into a chair, taking a folder of papers out of the basket. He nodded. "Yeah, there's some stuff in here about that. Gran said I had to be careful with these, or she'd wear me out," he cautioned, and from the sink, Lucy snorted.

"She'd have to catch you first, and she ain't built for speed." She dropped ice in glasses and brought them to the table, peering over his shoulder. "But put your papers away for now, we'll eat first before you two start digging up old bones and giggling over boring paperwork that ain't seen the light of day in a hundred years."

Lunch was delicious. Lucy also sliced some tomatoes and had some vinegary, homemade pickles on hand, and they sat in her well-lit kitchen and talked. The conversation was halted and awkward at first; Wes didn't know the real reason he had been invited and wasn't sure if this was a date or just a casual lunch, and in all actuality, neither did Beth. She tried to keep her mind on Crane and keep her purpose business-like, but she kept glancing at Wes while he talked. Like Bobby, his eyes were blue—not Barnham blue, but a much lighter blue, like a pale winter, icy sky. And his scruffy beard... Bobby had been clean-shaven, but Wes looked like he perpetually needed a good shave and a haircut. No, he wasn't Bobby, and it wasn't fair to compare them. Bobby had been an All-American boy, an intelligent jock working his way through school, and Wesley was... well, a nerd. But an interesting nerd—a handsome nerd who made sandwiches and chocolate chip cookies.

"—never came back." A polite throat clearing of the throat. "Hey Beth, you with me?"

She jumped, realizing she had drifted off. "Of course."

"Woolgathering, eh?" Lucy smirked and took another bite of coleslaw. "Where did you slip off to, Beth darlin', and were you following someone with pretty blue eyes?"

Beth blushed. "I was just... thinking, that's all."

"I bet." Lucy snickered, and Wes smiled politely.

Beth calmly took a drink of her tea. "No, I really was. I heard everything you were saying, but I was thinking that this tea needs more sugar."

"Nothing wrong with my tea," Lucy frowned. She took Beth's glass, and sipped at it suspiciously. "Nope, it's fine. Nice try."

Beth glared at her and then turned back to Wes. "Sorry about that, Wes." She pushed back her plate and smiled politely at him. "Let me tell you the sort of thing I'm looking for—"

"By the way," Wes said suddenly. "You never really said why you are doing all of this research. Are you taking a class or something?"

She shook her head. "No, not anymore." She felt a flash of pain and mentally shook it away. Avoiding Lucy's eye, she said, "Actually, I'm writing a book—a book about Civil War soldiers who returned home, and what their lives were like afterward... if they had effects of post-traumatic stress disorder, which of course wasn't recognized and certainly wasn't diagnosed back then, but certainly it existed, and how they treated it—"

"Oh, whew," Wes sighed, and pushed the last bite of sandwich into his mouth. He looked relieved. "I was afraid you wanted to ask me about the vampire my ol' Grandpa Manny said he saw there at the battle. That's a story for strong hearts, let me tell you... I never did like scary stories, ghosts and vampires, and all that. They keep me up at night, to be honest." He nodded to himself and grinned widely. "Excellent egg salad, Miz Barnham, better than my Gran's, but please don't tell her that."

And Beth could only stare at him, her mouth open in astonishment.

CHAPTER XIV

The cicadas droned low in the trees, and though it was the heat of the day, Wes had proposed a walk around the small lake on the edge of Lucy's property. It wasn't anything like the huge lake Beth had grown up on, but the fishing there was good; Lucy had a paddle boat tied to the dock there, though it was partially swamped from recent rains. There was an old plastic cup hung upside down on one of the dock posts for bailing water out, and Wes pointed to it. "We can use that for scooping the water out," he offered. "Fancy a turn around the lake?"

Beth smiled, amused. "Think that thing is seaworthy?" She laughed. "I can see us getting out in the middle of the lake and it springs a leak. Can you swim?"

He shrugged. "Well enough. Let's try it." He grabbed the cup and knelt by the boat, quickly scooping water out and dumping it into the lake. Again, his shirt pulled up and she saw his tanned back. Flushed, she turned away, not wanting to admit the thumping of her heart.

"All right," he said, standing up and drying his wet hands on his jeans. "It might not be the QEII, but it'll stay afloat." He cleared his throat hopefully. "I think."

"That's hardly reassuring," she snorted, but offered him her hand and stepped into the boat. He followed her, and they readjusted their balance as the paddle boat tilted and rocked for a second as it settled into the water; shifting themselves, they both found the foot pedals and began to move away from the dock. The paddles splashed behind them, and Wes worked the rudder with his left hand, steering them gently but slowly out into the lake.

"If I had known we were going boating, I'd have brought my fishing pole," he commented, but she glanced quickly at his face and decided he really didn't look all that put out. "I bet there are bass in here."

"Karl says there are," Beth nodded. "Sometimes he slips off down here and drowns a worm or two... Lucy pretends she doesn't know he does it, but when he brings a string of panfish up for supper, she sure doesn't turn them away. She fries them in cornmeal and butter... absolute heaven, let me tell you."

He nodded absently, and then glanced at her. "Beth, tell the truth. You didn't invite me to dinner to ask me about my grandfather, did you?"

She was startled but managed to keep a straight face. "Not entirely, no."

They had stopped paddling, and the boat drifted slightly... small waves trailed behind them, and she dangled her fingers in the water. "I mean, that was partly the reason, don't get me wrong."

He looked at her curiously. "Oh?"

She swallowed hard. "Well, I did. That's true. But there was more to it than just old war stories... that is..."

He suddenly laughed. "Oh, Christ. You *do* want to talk about those old vampire stories, don't you? Beth, let me tell you, I never met old Grandpa Manny, but my Daddy said he was a drunk and had a case of the shivering crazies when he came back from the war. They said he didn't know where he was half the time, talked to people who weren't there, babbled and giggled about vampires." He tapped his head. "Completely crackers, you know?"

She said nothing.

He restlessly adjusted his feet on the pedals, giving it a half turn; against her will, her feet which were connected to the same rod, also turned. "So... that book you said you're writing... it's not about the Civil War soldiers returning home, is it? It's more about local folklore, urban legends—that sort of thing?"

"No, not exactly." She sighed. "All right, I'm not really writing a book, but I am doing research." He only gazed at her mildly, and she realized he was disappointed that she had lied to him. "Look, this is crazy and complicated—"

He snorted a laugh. "Just as long as you don't tell me you believe in all that old crap, do you? Vampires, Dracula, all that?" He suddenly affected a terrible accent and flapped his hands like a giant bat. "I vant to suck yore blood."

"No thanks," she muttered, without thinking. "It's not what it's cracked up to be, trust me."

Immediately, she knew she shouldn't have said it. He looked at her carefully. "What did you just say?"

She focused on a weeping willow across the lake, whose limbs were trailing in the water. "Nothing," she said softly. "Let it go."

There was a long silence in the boat while he obviously struggled with a thousand questions. He rubbed his palm on the knee of his jeans, and then said softly, "What exactly did you mean?" She looked over at him briefly, and saw that he was thinking—thinking so hard about which question to ask that he wasn't sure which question to ask first. "You've been... *bitten*? I've read about people in clubs who like that sort of thing... masochists, I think they're called..." he looked disgusted, as if suddenly the last place he wanted to be at that moment was in a small boat on a lake, with no clear way to escape her company.

"It wasn't anything like that," she sighed, suddenly tired. "I wouldn't ever do anything like that... trust me, what happened to me was against my will." To her horror, her voice quivered, and she swallowed hard.

"You can tell me about it," his voice was low and amazingly calming. "If you want to, that is."

"Wes..." She took a deep breath. "What if I told you that there was something to your Grandpa Manny's stories. That maybe, I believe he wasn't so crazy after all."

He goggled at her. "You can't be serious. *Vampires*? Come on, Beth..."

"I am serious. Very serious." She turned to him, and pulled back the collar of her tee shirt, exposing pink, faded scars; they were not new, but were clearly the outlines of a bite mark, and he blanched. "And I have others, just like this, on various parts of my body. My inner thigh, my breasts…" she shrugged, but was long past the point of embarrassment. "He really worked me over."

"Who? Who worked you over?" He pulled his eyes from her scarred neck to her face.

"Sebastian Crane." It gave her an odd tingle, saying his name aloud, and she realized that somehow, saying the name during the day took a little of his power away. "He was the vampire from your grandfather's stories, I believe. He's the man your grandpa saw, the one that killed Charlie Barnham and all those other boys in the hospital tent. Does that sound familiar to you?"

He nodded, stunned. "That's the name, sure. But Beth—come on, you don't *believe* all that, do you? I mean, I heard the stories too, about the crazy doctor who killed his patients, but I just figured that Crane was a Northern sympathizer posing as a doctor, who took the opportunity to kill those wounded men. A psychopath, maybe, I dunno, opening up wounds, letting patients bleed to death. There are stranger things in wartime. I sure don't believe he actually *sucked* their wounds, drinking their blood…"

"It's true," she said softly. "What your grandpa saw and came back and told is just part of it… apparently when Crane fed on Charlie Barnham, he became intoxicated by his blood. Enamored, fixated… maybe even addicted. Lucy thinks it's because Charlie had something special in his blood, though she's not sure just what it was. Anyway, Crane loved it so much that he hunted down Charlie's family after the war, killing off a lot of them, in hopes of duplicating what he had with Charlie that first encounter." She shrugged. "And he never stopped. My boyfriend, Bobby Barnham, was killed nine years ago. I was attacked that night, too—raped and beaten and… fed on. By the same man your grandfather saw at the Battle of Dark Hills, in 1864. Sebastian Crane."

He jerked, realization suddenly dawning on him. "Oh, so you're the one."

"Pardon?"

He studied her, making her nervous. "Damn. Of course." She frowned, and he shook his head. "You're the girl Bobby was with that night."

"You knew Bobby?" She had never considered this possibility.

"Of course, I knew Bobby. He was a year younger than me in school, and remember, Bisby ain't all that big. We all took it hard when he died. And the reports were so odd, but I remember something about there being a girlfriend of his who was attacked that night as well... not a Bisby girl, someone he met in Indiana... who ended up in a coma, or something..."

She looked away. Tears filled her eyes.

"So that was you." His voice was still gentle.

"That was me," she agreed.

"Dear Lord." He had gone pale beneath his beard. There was a long silence while he digested this, and then he said, "Well, I'll tell you what. If you're lying, you don't believe you're lying. Although I have to tell you... it's a hard business to swallow."

"I know it is," she agreed. "You have to suspend all rational belief and jump out there. It took me a long, long time to believe it as well..." she thought of the years in the hospital, and felt a small panic rising in her. *Deep breaths. Don't think about that.* "But I tell you, it's true. And it's not just me who believes it... Lucy does too. And her daughter Rachel, and I believe there's another cousin in Ohio somewhere... I don't know much about him, though. Crane hasn't gotten to him yet, but I'm not sure. But anyway, I'm telling you the truth about all this."

"That a vampire named Sebastian Crane is hunting down generations of the Barnham family," he said, keeping his voice dangerously neutral. "That he killed Bobby, and he—"

Not far off the boat, a fish jumped, startling them both, and he gave a small smile. "I told you there were bass in this lake," he murmured, and surprised her by taking her hand. It was warm and slightly moist; his fingers curved protectively over hers. And surprisingly, she allowed it.

"You don't have to believe me," she said. "It's all right. It's an incredible story, I know that. I just was hoping you could tell me something your grandfather may have said that might help me, some little bit of information..."

"About what? Why?" He frowned. "What are you talking about?"

She sighed in frustration. "About Crane." She shook her head. "Believe it or not, he's found me. He knows I'm with Lucy… apparently he's watching me, or having someone watch me, because the other night he called me and taunted me."

"A crank call," he offered weakly. "A bad joke…"

"It was him," she insisted. "I remember his voice. How could I forget it? I hear it in my head every day, from that horrible night he killed Bobby. It was the same voice, don't doubt me on that. And besides, he *knew* things, certain things that only he and I would know, and said things from before."

Hello, Beth… do you love?

He shook his head, not sure what to say. She could see he was wavering, struggling to find the balance between rationality and the supernatural. He glanced at her, and she said quietly, "Don't worry. I know I spent time in a mental hospital, but I'm not crazy. Don't think that."

Finally, he took a deep breath. "I don't. But all right, even if I suspend the idea that it wasn't someone pretending to be Crane—which is hard, because I still think it was just a crank call—then I'm not sure where to go from there." He gave a strange little chuckle which sounded just inches away from being frightened. "I mean, I don't know what to tell you. I don't think I have any new information to share with you, and even if I did, I don't know what you would do with it."

She blinked, surprised. "Well, sure you do. I intend on killing him before he kills me."

Shockingly, he laughed. "I knew you were going to say something like that. A regular little Van Helsing, aren't you?"

She pulled her hand away from his; fury and frustration flared up inside her, and she began to crank her feet, working the pedals. He yelped in surprise, and jerked his legs to keep up with her. "Hey! What do you think you're doing?"

"Heading back to the dock. I've got enough to worry about without you making fun of me." Her face was flushed with anger. "But just so you know… if Crane figures out that you're here, a descendant of

Manny Draper's, he may go after you too. How's that for a pleasant little thought?"

"Beth." He straightened out his legs, stopping the pedals. The boat churned to a stop. "Quit pedaling. Listen to me. There is no Crane. There is no such thing as a vampire. What happened to you and Bobby... What killed him and attacked you that night was some psychopathic crazy man. Maybe he just thought he was a vampire or something. It's in no way connected to any call you may have received last night. Someone here in Bisby obviously recognized you from the news all those years ago, and as sick as it is, they're just having their own sort of crazy fun."

"Move your legs," she said furiously. "Move them right now or I'm jumping into the water and swimming to the dock. I mean it. I'm done talking to you."

"Will you stop?!" His calm shell was starting to crack, though she thought it was mostly just exasperation. "Beth, just stop."

She glared at him. "No, I think it's you that needs to listen, Wes. I'm not crazy. I'm a victim... or rather, I was, but I'm done with that. Now I've decided to hunt what was hunting me. If you can't or don't want to help me, that's fine." She tossed her head back, reminding him of a high-spirited mare. "And just as long as I'm on this self-righteous path of indignance, let me go a little bit further, and tell you that not only am I *not* going to be a victim anymore, but I'm going to kill that sonofabitch that did this to me in the first place."

He gazed at her and started to grin. "Wow."

"What?" The color in her cheeks was high, and a flush was spreading down her neck.

"You. That was amazing." He pulled back a little, as far as he could, to observe her frankly. "That little speech made the hair on my neck stand up."

Her eyes narrowed dangerously. "Are you making fun of me again?"

"Nope." He shook his head. "First of all, I'm not stupid... the mood you're in, you're liable to push me into the drink, and I've already had a bath today, so thanks very much." He stroked his beard thoughtfully. "So, all right. You believe this all to be true, and according to you, so does Lucy Barnham, and that makes it a little harder to scoff at. And also, admittedly there *have* been a large number of Barnhams drop off mysteriously over the years, including Bobby—"

"And his father, Michael. And his father's brothers, and cousins." She looked determined. "And all the others that came before them, too."

He nodded absently, clearly remembering something. He looked at her, as if not wanting to bring something up, but then sighed and jumped in. "You know, there was a Barnham in my high school class... he musta been an uncle to your Bobby, now that I think about it."

She thought furiously, trying to remember. "Name?" She wished suddenly she had her notebook with her; in it were all the names, dates and occurrences of the Barnham deaths.

"Hmm... Ronnie-John." He chewed on his lip. "Big blond kid... football player, baseball too. More athletic than smart, but not a bad guy. We weren't really friends, but we were friendly, if that makes sense." He looked at her, and she nodded.

"And let me guess. Ronnie-John disappeared. Or was found dead, with no explanation. Or maybe even was diagnosed with some mysterious illness and died of a wasting disease within a week or so."

He frowned. "None of those, but he did die quite young." He looked as if he were reluctant to admit this, but then shook his head and looked out across the water. "He was coming home one night from a school dance, and for some reason, he wrapped his car around a tree... it was a terrible crash, twisted metal and broken tree limbs everywhere."

"I think I remember this," she nodded slowly. "Lucy mentioned it, but not in great detail. He wasn't an uncle... maybe a cousin of Bobby's dad, one of the last ones."

Wes nodded. "Maybe. The whole thing was very strange, a really weird mystery. Nobody could ever decide just *why* Ronnie had wrecked... he hadn't been drinking, and while it was assumed that maybe he had fallen asleep at the wheel, it really didn't seem likely because of the pattern of skid marks on the road."

"All right, I'll play devil's advocate here, not because I need to, but because you need someone to." She shifted on her seat. "We'll start with the obvious... were the weather conditions bad that night?"

He looked uncomfortable. "No, not at all. Actually, I had been at the same dance that night: it was a clear night, almost a full moon… well-lit, no precipitation…"

She nodded. "Check. So, weather certainly hadn't been a factor in the crash. Bad brakes? In movies, the brakes are always failing. That the case here?" He was quiet, and she poked him in the ribs with her finger, making him jump. "Come on, I already know the answer."

He swallowed, and for a second, she sensed a lie coming, but then he shrugged. "According to Ronnie's mother, he had been a bit of a mechanic and loved to tinker on his car, so that ruled out any mechanical failure. He had just… crashed, for no reason." He glanced at her.

Beth thought of Chris Giorgio and Scott Partridge, victims of Crane, long since dead, and shuddered. Another boy on a lonely road, inexplicably dead. She closed her eyes.

He cleared his throat. "Of course, maybe something had been in the road that had made him stop so fast—a deer, maybe, or something else, or someone." She could well imagine Crane hunting that young man; learning his patterns, his habits, determining his routes. Standing in the middle of the road had been a guaranteed way to force an encounter, and even if Ronnie hadn't been able to stop in time and had hit him, so what? Crane was already dead.

A thought occurred to her. "The body? They didn't find it in the car, did they?"

He looked at her quickly, seemingly amazed, and then looked away, "How did you know that? No. It was yards away from the wreck."

She nodded. "Right. And despite there being horrible wounds, there wasn't a lot of blood, if any, on the scene. Lots of broken bones, internal injuries, but any cuts and scrapes and superficial marks, I bet they were clean. Am I right?"

"Dogs," he said quietly, but she could tell he was struggling with the idea. "They figured that a farm dog had happened by and had licked him, cleaned him up…" he trailed off weakly.

"Don't be absurd, that's a weak explanation at best and you know it." She was becoming frustrated with his stubbornness. "A wreck like the one you described would have caused terrible trauma… he couldn't have walked away from a crash like that. So how do you think he was found, yards away from the accident site?"

He continued to look uncomfortable, and she had to admit she almost enjoyed it. "Well yes, that is a question… if he had managed to get out of the wreck by himself, he had done it with two broken legs, a broken arm, and a bunch of other injuries. Dad said the doctor had said it was adrenaline that had allowed him to do that, for lack of a better explanation, but it had always seemed like a poor excuse. Some people put forth the theory that maybe an animal had dragged him away from the wreck… coyotes, maybe—"

"An animal. Sure." Her voice dripped with sarcasm. "Maybe it was that same big mysterious farm dog that licked his wounds clean. Whew, that dog really was busy that night, eh?" He scowled, but she didn't care. "Come on, Wes, it stinks and you know it."

She could see in her mind how it had been, and she wanted to cry.

Ronnie-John Barnham, fresh from the dance… trademark Barnham blond hair, mowed into a crew cut, white sport coat gleaming in the night, pink boutonniere still pinned to his lapel, whistling happily as he came home from the dance… maybe he had kissed his girl, maybe did a little more, if she had allowed it, and so he was feeling good, feeling happy and young and alive… the radio had been on, oh, of course the radio had been on, because his heart was still full of music from the dance, and he had kept time to the music by tapping his thumbs on the steering wheel as he had driven home in the warm spring night, remembering the way his girl had smelled, thinking of the lights splashing on the gym floor while they had danced, and she had whispered in his ear that he was the handsomest boy there and she loved him… and then his lighthearted joy had suddenly turned to terror as suddenly there was a man standing in the middle of the road, the headlights shining on him but inexplicably through him as well and Ronnie had instinctively swerved hard and fast to avoid hitting him…

"He never had a chance," she murmured. "He was just one more innocent victim in the long string of victims."

He frowned. "But it doesn't prove anything. It was a car crash, certainly with a lot of weird, unexplained elements to it, but it doesn't prove that your Sebastian Crane caused it. You have to see that."

She frowned stubbornly. "But it is one more brick in my wall of proof, isn't it? Look, I've collected stories like this—*lots* of stories—of unexplained deaths in and around Bisby, since the end of the Civil War. All of them are connected to the Barnhams in some way, and most of them are centered *around* them. What is it you're not seeing? How much more proof do you need? I hope you're not wanting to meet that particular gentleman and ask him yourself, because God forbid, if you do meet Doctor Sebastian Crane, I promise you that you will wish you hadn't by the end of the encounter."

He sighed and focused his attention on a heron that was wading in the shallows. It was moving slowly, keeping one eye on them while it fished, poking its beak in and out of the water. Wes seemed fascinated by it. Silence fell, broken only by the cicadas in the trees and the birds working in the cattails. After several tense moments, he blew out his cheeks in a big breath. "Well, it's getting late. I'd say we head back for the dock." Without waiting for her to reply, he began to work the pedals, and she did as well, silent and miserable. He caught the end of the dock and pulled them in closer, and then got out, offering her a hand as well. He studied her for a second, and then without saying a word, they walked back up the path to the driveway, where he stopped and faced her.

"Thank you for lunch," he said formally. "Please offer my thanks to Miz Lucy as well. You're welcome to go through those papers as long as you like, as long as you are careful with them. You can just drop them by our stand the next Market Day."

She nodded. "All right, thank you. And I'll thank Lucy for you, also." He opened the door to his truck, and hoisted a leg in. "Beth Franklin, I'm not saying I don't believe you. I can tell you are very sincere about all of this, and I sure am sorry for what happened to you, and Bobby too. But I'm going to need a… a little more convincing, I guess, a little more proof, before I start running around, digging up coffins and staking things—"

"Never said he was in a coffin," she muttered. "Point in fact, I don't think he is—"

He laughed weakly, and held a hand up. "All right, stop! Damn, woman, how you do run on!" And before she could do anything else, he leaned in and kissed her, hard and fast on the mouth. She was too surprised to move, too surprised to do anything but kiss him back, which seemed like a good idea at the time.

Geez, this is our first fight and we haven't even had a first kiss yet. Somehow, we're all backwards about this

But this wasn't Bobby. This was Wes, which was a thought she had been repeating to herself all afternoon.

Finally, she pulled back. "What in the hell was that?"

He looked quite pleased with himself. "It was the only way I could think of to shut you up." He grinned widely, revealing white, slightly crooked teeth. "It worked, too."

She punched him in the arm indignantly. "Well, don't do it again. If you don't believe anything I have to say, you certainly don't deserve to kiss me. I mean it."

"If you say so." Humming to himself, he swung up into his truck, slamming the door behind him.

Rolling down the window, he beckoned closer to her. "Listen... I promise you I will think about what we talked about. All of it. That's the best I can do, all right?"

She studied him, and saw that despite his goofy smile, his blue eyes were serious and intense. "All right. Fair enough."

"See you at Market Day." He started the truck, and she moved back. "No, you won't. I'm not coming. I'll send your papers with Lucy."

He adjusted his sunglasses in the mirror and faced her cockily. "Yes, I will. I'll see you Thursday, Miss Beth. Can't wait." And without waiting for a reply, he pulled out of the driveway. She watched clouds of gravel dust billow in its wake. At the last minute, before he turned down the lane, he honked his horn at her, and a tanned arm shot out and gave her a jaunty wave.

"Cocky bastard," she muttered.

"But good looking," Lucy commented, coming up behind her. She had been watching them from the front window and had delightedly witnessed the kiss. She handed Beth a cookie. "But he bakes good—here, have a cookie, it'll calm you down—and his manners are good. I like him. And you do too, I can tell."

"Lucy!" Beth looked at her, mouth open in astonishment. "I do not! Don't tell that lie!"

Lucy watched her smugly and patted her on the arm. "Come on inside, it's getting late. It's almost time for Wheel of Fortune, and you know I can't miss that."

"No," Beth sighed, nibbling on her cookie… it was good, she had to admit—nice and sweet, with giant chocolate chips. "We don't want that." She scanned the property a final time, and then followed Lucy into the house.

I'll see you Thursday, Miss Beth. Can't wait.

She smiled.

CHAPTER XV

Lucy sat at the kitchen table, long after Beth had gone to bed. On the table in front of her was a nearly empty bottle of Jack Daniels' and an ashtray full of crumpled cigarette butts, and one more item which she had kept face down. Thoughtfully, she tapped her fingernails on the back of the picture frame, and then turned it over, examining the young face that stared back at her.

Charlie Barnham, in all his youth and glory. She studied the half smile on his face, nodding in appreciation... of course she had never met him, but he was her husband's grandfather, and the Barnham genes ran close. That crop of tousled blond hair, that mischievous mock grin... it was uncanny how close he was to her own Bobby, and she sighed.

"You damn little squirt," she muttered. "All this trouble sprang from you, you know that... you shoulda kept your head down that day, you never would got hurt and you woulda never have met that monster..."

He only grinned back at her, mocking her with his smug smile, and his dancing eyes. She reached over and unscrewed the lid on the bottle, poured another finger of whiskey into her glass, and tossed it down.

"Here's to you, Charlie, wherever you are." Her voice was quiet, and only slightly slurred, though she doubted anyone could really tell, unless they really knew her.

Not good to drink alone, she knew that, but it was nothing new to her. She had hidden it from Beth, not wanting her guest to know how much she drank, but she could tell she was quickly figuring things out. A beer or two—or three or four, sometimes—after supper, a toddy here or there, a quick nip in the pantry, or barn, or bathroom. She knew that Beth had noticed. A few times, she had caught her looking at her as if she were about to mention something and Lucy had stared her down. Beth had subsided, but Lucy knew that she knew, and she was embarrassed by it. Still, Lucy had an alcoholic's reasoning and mentality, and she had an answer ready, if needed… Jack had been here first, long before Beth had ever shown up. *He* had been her constant companion for so *many* nights, long after the tears had dried up and the emptiness in her soul was as endless and as huge as the universe itself. Beth, as lovely and as connected to Bobby as she may have been, was a latecomer. A runner-up. And though Lucy loved her, she didn't love her the way she loved Jack, and Good Lord, but that was the truth.

The house was still and quiet and dark; the only light came from the television in the kitchen, which she had muted. Its flickering images showed voiceless late night talk show guests screaming laughter at each other. About an hour ago, she had heard footsteps creak above her as Beth walked back and forth to the bathroom, and then the rumblings and gurglings in the pipes as she had flushed the toilet, but apparently, she had settled down for the night now because all was still. Lucy cast her eyes upward for a moment, listening for movement, and then reached for the bottle and poured herself another drink.

She liked this girl, she really did. It was easy to see why Bobby had fallen for her, and she wished that Fate had been kinder to them both. She could well imagine them sitting around her kitchen table, with several little ones scrambling about on a visit… and her husband David would be there, and her son, Michael… they would all be together, maybe for Easter dinner, or Christmas…

Don't think about that.

She tossed down another drink, and thought about Crane.

I've felt him, more than I've ever seen him. It's quiet out here, you know, but it's never totally quiet. But sometimes, things seem to pause, and I can feel something watching me from the treeline.

He had taken so *much* from her, this monster. She had lived in fear of him most of her adult life: avoiding the dark places, jumping at shadows, always watching over her shoulder. Of course, it was no way to live, but she had grown used to it because she knew no other way... but suddenly here was this girl—this headstrong, stubborn girl who was talking about slaying the dragon. Lucy didn't even think it was possible... Crane was an omnipotent demon, impossible to kill and dangerous to even approach. Beth's talk of roses and garlic and charms... silly. To kill a monster with a flower? Impossible.

She poured out another drink, feeling the familiar, comforting feeling beginning to settle in. She wasn't drunk, not by half, but she was starting to feel warm and mellow, and that was just fine. She picked up Charlie's picture, considered it, and then gave a mighty yawn. "Charlie, it's been wonderful drinking with you this evening, but now I think it's time I get my tired old bones to bed." She took one final draw on her cigarette, and then stubbed it out.

A whisper, as sharp as a knife, cut through the dark.

"Lucy..."

She whirled her head around, expecting to see Beth standing in the doorway reproachfully, or even Karl, maybe... sometimes after an argument, his wife kicked him out and he would come and sleep in her guest room... but not tonight. There was no one there. So, all right... was she crazy enough to believe that Charlie Barnham's ghost had just spoken to her? If so, he had never contacted her before, nor any of the other unfortunate Barnham souls that certainly had to be floating around the property. Heck, if it was true that ghosts stayed around the place where their bodies had died, it was likely there were enough ghosts hanging about to field a baseball team, and half the stadium. Cautiously, she looked around the kitchen again, but there was nothing. Of course not. She was alone.

All right... perhaps, it was just Jack talking to her. She picked up the bottle, swirling it around for a moment in amusement. "The likker's making me sicker," she muttered and put it back down. Great. Now she was hearing voices, hallucinations. They'd cart her away and put her in the laughing house if she wasn't careful.

"*Lucy... enjoying your drink, are you, my darling?*"

Shaking, she put her hands on the tabletop and pushed herself to her feet, where she stood for a second, tottering on her pins. All right, she wasn't crazy, she knew she had heard it for certain this time... there was no doubt. Cautiously, she looked around her, glancing around her kitchen, reassured by its familiarity and her things, just where she had put them...

"*Lucy... turn around, my love.*"

And suddenly, the knowledge of just what was happening here struck her, full force. It wasn't a ghost, and she wasn't crazy, and it wasn't the whiskey. It was something much worse, the fear that had dominated most of her life and stolen her family and driven her to the bottle... it was here; there was no mistaking, and in that instant, she was more terrified than she had ever been in her life.

The voice was insistent. It was impossible not to obey that voice. It slipped into her brain, cajoling her, enticing her, making her feel young again...

"*Lucy... I'm here for you, darlin'... aren't you going to greet me? There's a good girl... turn around for me...*"

And she did, knowing what she would see before she turned around, but unable, desperately unable to not do his bidding.

Sebastian Crane was standing in her doorway.

She opened her mouth to scream, but he held up a warning finger. "Lucy, come now... you always were a plucky girl, don't go on like that. You knew I'd be coming, didn't you?" He smiled at her, his teeth gleaming in the dark. "After all, I really never left."

Fumbling, she reached down for the crucifix she kept in her apron pocket, ready to hold it up and threaten him, but he gave a careless little wave of his hand—a dismissive gesture that told her he wasn't in the least concerned about any weapons she may have had.

"Don't do that," he advised, and his voice was sharp. "Things are interesting enough without bringing *that* ol' boy into it, don't you think? No, let's just talk for a bit, like two old friends." He tipped her a wink. "May I come in?"

A vampire can't even get into your home unless you invite him in...

"No." She was shaking like a leaf in a strong breeze. "Hell no. Of course not."

I think it goes back to the formal, ancient Laws of Hospitality. Most cultures respect that... so just remember. Never invite one in, no matter what.

His face twisted in disappointment. "Ah, Lucy, you know how to really wound me, don't you? Here we are, two old campaigners, and you're making me stand out here on your back porch like a peddler! I know you've got better manners than that... so what do you say? You let me in, and we can sit there at your kitchen table like two old friends and we can talk?" He licked his lips uncontrollably. "Yes indeed, we can talk."

"Go away," she whispered. "You can't come in... please, just go away... I'm an old woman..."

"Lucy, Lucy..." He was firmer now, like a schoolteacher reprimanding a naughty child. "You don't want to anger me, do you? Now go on and do the right thing for both of us, and invite me in. I just want to talk, I promise."

His tone was deceptively light, yet almost wheedling, and she sensed a livid frustration there and a fury at being denied. She felt herself almost nodding, and triumphantly, he smiled encouragingly at her.

Beth. She had to get Beth, and at the same instant this occurred to her, and she had turned her head to scream for her, he seemed to suspect what she was about to do. "Don't you do it," he hissed, his voice a cold grip on her. "If you call for that girl, I will burn this place down around you and kill you all as you come scuttling out to avoid the flames. Do you hear me, old woman?"

Helpless tears streamed down her wrinkled cheeks. "I hear you... oh, can't you just go away? Please, haven't you caused enough harm to my family?"

He sighed. "Always so melodramatic, weren't you Lucy? Damn, but your glass is always half empty, isn't it? That's the trouble with you—you just *never* were able to get over things and move on. You just want to whine and mope and carry on..." He glanced past her, up at the ceiling. "And look at you. Inviting strange people to come and live with you. I tell you, Lucy, you oughta be careful. That girl you got upstairs has loose morals, I fear." He leaned forward conspiratorially, mockingly eager to share some piece of gossip. "I think she and your grandson have had... *relations*, if you know what I mean. And now I fear she might have designs on that Draper boy! You know, young Master Wesley?" He put a pensive finger to his lips and gazed thoughtfully at her. "And now that I think about it, I may have known his granddaddy, actually... but never mind. Back to what I was saying. That girl you got upstairs... she's moving through your menfolk pretty quick, ain't she? What kind of girl is that, I ask you?"

"You killed them," Lucy said numbly. "You killed my sweet David, and you killed our boy, and you killed our grandson... you nearly killed that girl upstairs. You hurt her real, real bad. You're a monster, a demon..."

He shrugged. "Can you blame the tide from coming in? The salmon from swimming upriver, or the swallows from migrating to Capistrano? No, and they make no apologies for their behavior, and neither do I. They are what they are, and I am what I am." His mouth was set in grim determination. "Now, for the last time, I'm telling you to let me in."

"I can't..."

"Lucy." Demanding and harsh.

She sobbed harder. "Noooo..."

"Lucy..." His tone was different now... it had changed, and was now soft and caressing, the words slipping over her like warm water. "Lucy, darlin', look at me. It'll be all right. Just look at me, now."

She did, turning her eyes up to meet his, and was instantly glad she had done so. Why, he was beautiful, standing there in the framed doorway... why hadn't she noticed it before? His dark hair curled down over his forehead, like a Greek god come to life, and she had no doubt that she was willing to do anything this man asked her to do. His eyes were so understanding, so full of caring and of love for her that she immediately knew he had nothing to fear from him. She felt her legs tremble and her heart race, and she remembered a name for it... *hot-blooded*. That was the term she had heard used on girls back when she was young—girls who went with boys and let them do as they pleased... nice girls didn't and bad girls were hot-blooded, and she felt about fifty years slip away from her in an instant. Her mouth was dry and her head pounded and she was more than hot-blooded. Hell, she felt downright *dirty*, the way she had felt on her wedding night—when she and David had first lain together—and she had shocked him by playfully dancing for him, stripping off her clothes like some stripper whore on a stage and then taking him into her mouth and finishing him off that way, not because he necessarily liked it that way but because *she* liked it that way.

"Hot blooded," she murmured. "I'll do you like I did my husband, I swear I will, and you'll *love* it, because that's how I love it."

"There's my girl," he whispered appreciatively, and she moaned lustfully at the very sound of him. "I know I will... and so I'll repeat my question, Lucy darlin', can I come in now?"

Her will had crumbled like a sandcastle before a wave, and it didn't even seem to matter. "Of course," she rasped, and moved aside. "Please, *please*, come in. I want you to."

A look of triumph settled across his face, and he stuck a foot out and waggled it theatrically over the threshold. "Why, lookit that," he chuckled. "Funny how easy it is now, after you say those magic words." He stepped into the kitchen, looking around him curiously. "Quaint little cottage you've got here, Lucy. Now why don't you point me in the direction of Our Beth's boudoir, eh? We've got a little business to take care—"

"I'm already here."

Beth stood in the doorway, dressed in jeans and a tee shirt. Her hair was tied back, and her face was calm and pale. "You aren't nearly as cunning as you think you are," she said softly. "I knew you would recognize Lucy as weak and try to get to me through her. I've been waiting for this."

A look of surprise crossed Crane's face, but only for an instant. He paused, one hand on Lucy's shoulder and patted her protectively. "Well, look who's here! The circle is complete now, what? Beth, it's so good to see you! Last time we met, you were lying on the sand, bleeding and begging me to let you live. Do you remember that? And how's your day going today?"

She smiled thinly. "I only wish it were day," she said. "I wish it was full sunlight, about noon. Why don't you come back then—"

Suddenly she held her crucifix out, fast as a bowman drawing the string. "No, no. No you don't. Careful. *Don't move.* Stand where you are." She remembered how lightning fast he could move and she knew she had to head him off.

He had been drifting casually around the edge of the table, in her direction, but froze. "Oh, Beth," he whispered, keeping his tone light, "do you think that silly thing can stop me? You've been seeing too many old movies, haven't you?"

They faced each other, locked in a hatred that was so intense it was almost palpable while they took measure of each other. Lucy, now that Crane's attention was redirected, was loosened from his grip and with a small moan slid to the floor. Her hair hung in her eyes, and she lay crying, but neither Beth or Crane was about to take their eyes off of the other, and so she was ignored.

He didn't move, but he stood before her, taut like a coiled spring, and she sensed he was about to make a move. "That thing's just a silly symbol: a token of an ancient, dried up faith," he assured her. "Don't you think others have used that before you and failed? What is it really, nothing more than two sticks with a little figure glued on there for decoration. Come on, throw it down, and then you and I can get down to business."

"We have no business," she said, and brandished the crucifix again. His eyes were drawn to it hatefully, yet he hesitated, not moving. And in that instant, any doubt she had had was instantly dispelled.

He frowned, struggling to keep a straight face. "Beth... I must insist you toss away that silly object before—"

"It's more than that, and you know it," Beth whispered back. "This silly object's got you backed up and afraid to move. Come on then, Doctor Crane. If it's nothing except for two sticks tied together, then why don't you come and *take* it from me? Show me how silly it is, why don't you? Come on, I dare you. Come take it." Without warning, she took a quick step and held it out to him; to her delight, a look of miserable horror flickered across his face as she saw him flinch backward.

"Don't!" he barked, despite himself, and was shocked when she looked at him and laughed.

"What's wrong, Doctor? Does my little token of a dried-up faith bother you?" She held it out again, and his eyes narrowed in absolute hatred, for they both realized the same thing... he was showing weakness, and for now, at least in this moment, she suddenly had the upper hand.

"You will wish you hadn't done that before I'm through with you," he whispered, each word full of venom. "I swear to you, I will make you rue the day you ever met Bobby Barnham—"

"Lucy," Beth said sharply. "Revoke your invitation. Make him leave." Lucy looked up at her wearily, not comprehending, and Beth raised her voice. "I can't do it, it's not my house, but you can. Revoke your invitation, make him get out."

"You bitch," Crane hissed, not believing this. "You sly little bitch, how *dare* you treat me like this—"

"Oh, it gets better," Beth assured him. "Do you like poems? I've got a good one for you, Doctor."

>...*hominēs, sīcut lepores, venantur;*
>*latens in tenebrīs quasi malae umbrae;*
>*aperientes venas sīcut utrēs vīnī.*
>*Daemones violentiae pleni sunt;*
>*numquam misericordiam faciēns.*
>*Invoca eōs bannum!*
>*Redde incunctanter illōs ad inferos!*

Crane's face twisted, and his very body seemed to shimmer, and Beth said in a loud voice, "Lucy, that's got him on the ropes, but it's not enough! For the love of God, revoke your invitation! Get him out of here."

Lucy lifted her head slowly... her eyes were confused and not focusing. Her head hurts; from what, she wasn't sure, but it was a terrible pounding and she was *tired*—so very, very tired. She only wanted to sleep, to be left alone...

"—revoke your invitation, Lucy—"

The old woman licked her dry lips, hating that insistent voice, not understanding why it was yelling at her, demanding her... she wasn't sure why she was being asked to do such a ridiculous thing, but if that was what it would take to let her sleep, she would do it.

"I revoke my invitation," she whispered. "There, are you happy, damn you?"

As Beth watched, Crane began to tremble violently, actually jerking uncontrollably. His head tossed from side to side, like a swimmer fighting for air as a tide pulled him under, and then twitching like a marionette, began to move unwillingly towards the door. He swiped furiously at her, his hands grabbing nothing but air, and he screamed at her in hatred and frustration. He grabbed at chairs and the kitchen cabinets, but the magic that he was bound by was stronger and more insistent, and it pulled him fighting and clawing towards the door. He batted helplessly at the frame, locking his eyes on her one final time.

"You haven't beaten me, not for a damn minute," he snarled. "Just know, you better learn to love the night, because Bitch, I'll be coming for you."

And then, as if sucked out by a natural vacuum, he was gone. There was a soft, audible pop... and then the only sounds in the room were of Lucy crying as she scrambled to her feet.

Beth bent down to help her as Lucy pushed her hair back. "That was Crane, wasn't it?"

Beth nodded and helped her to a chair. "It was. Are you all right?" Lucy fumbled for a cigarette, found the pack empty, and reached for her bottle instead. "I think so. I don't know. I'm woozy... I don't remember..." She poured out a drink and looked blearily at Beth. "What happened?"

"Have you ever seen one of those nature shows where a cobra hypnotizes a bird, or maybe a rat? It sways back and forth, mesmerizing it?" Lucy nodded, a look of horror and realization dawning on her face. "Well, I think it's similar. I'm not exactly sure how he does it, but once he has you in his gaze, he's got you." She smiled briefly. "Lesson learned... don't look him in the eye."

"I don't want to ever look at him again, period," Lucy muttered. She glanced at the empty door, and into the night beyond. She could hear crickets and peeper frogs chirping, and she said, "Hurry, close that door, before he comes back."

Beth did so and came back and sat down. "I don't think he'll be back tonight, though. Didn't you see him? While I don't think I really hurt him, I do think I surprised him and made him think, at least for now. He wasn't expecting that." She looked thoughtfully at the crucifix, still clutched tightly in her palm. "Yes, I definitely think he's gone off somewhere to lick his wounds."

Lucy took another drink, and then looked worriedly at Beth. "When I was… well, you know. Not myself… did I say anything stupid?" She put a shaking hand to her temple. "I seem to remember a few things… but it's like a dream…"

Beth looked away, troubled. She had indeed heard what Lucy had said—had seen the way she was clinging and trembling like a desperate prostitute. But it wasn't true to her personality, and certainly wasn't her fault, and it would serve no purpose that she could see if she told her the truth. It would only upset her, and it had already been a traumatic evening, and so she smiled weakly. "Lucy, don't worry, you didn't embarrass yourself in any way. Anything you did or said, Crane made you do it, so you're blameless."

Lucy looked worried. "It was like… a dream, but not really. More like when the dentist gives you too much gas, or when you're waking up from a twilight sleep… little flashes of real things, like being underwater." She shuddered. "I remember him wanting to come in… and then he made me look at him…"

I'll do you like I did my husband, I swear I will, and you'll love it, because that's how I love it…

Anxiously, she looked at Beth, but she was still not meeting her eye, and she swallowed hard. They sat in silence for a few minutes, and then Beth sighed thoughtfully.

"If nothing else," she murmured, "we learned a few things tonight about our old friend Doctor Crane."

Lucy peered at her owlishly. She was strangely tired, exhausted even, as if she had run a marathon, and for some reason she still wanted to cry. "What's that? What did we learn tonight?"

Beth drummed her fingers on the tablecloth. "The poem I recited… do you remember? I found it in an old book, and I memorized it. I wasn't sure if it would work because the text said it was incomplete. Well, it *did* work—complete or not—and that's one for our side. That's the good news."

"Uh oh." Lucy looked worried. "And the bad news?"

"Wesley Draper. Crane mentioned him by name. He wanted us to make sure he knows about him, the bastard." She looked levelly at Lucy.

"I bet that's the last time he ever accepts a lunch invitation," Lucy remarked darkly, and whether it was meant to be a joke or not, a sudden hysteria burst inside of Beth, and she put her head in her hands and laughed until she cried.

CHAPTER XVI

The smell of coffee roused Beth from her sleep.

She ran her hands tiredly through her hair, sitting up. For a second, she blinked uncertainly at the unfamiliar setting and then nodded to herself, remembering. Rather than her own bedroom, she was in the living room, on the love seat. She and Lucy had agreed last night not to be separated and instead chose to sleep in the same room, Lucy on the couch and Beth just one coffee table away. As Lucy had put it, "I just can't bear the thought of sleeping by myself tonight... let's just have a girl's slumber party and keep the lights on. I'll make some popcorn..." she looked uncertainly at Beth. "We can talk about boys and play dominoes, but no scary movies, all right? Hell, nothing on television could compare to our night anyway, could it?"

Sleepily, Beth padded into the kitchen and sat down at the table, yawning mightily. Lucy, who obviously was able to do far more work and function on far less sleep, put a mug of coffee down in front of her and sat down as well. "Well, there you are. I thought you were gonna sleep the whole dingdanged morning away."

Beth peered at the clock on the stove. "It's barely half past seven," she grumbled. "Lemme alone."

"Me and the chickens been up for hours. We've all already had our breakfast... Karl too. And by the way, he won't be needing the truck today. I was going to send him into town and buy some fertilizer, but after last night…" She trailed off. "I think you need it more."

Beth sighed. "Probably. If I can get Wes to believe me. He didn't seem all that open to talk of the supernatural yesterday."

Lucy shook her finger at her. "I told you not to pester that boy with all that spooky talk. You shoulda listened to me and held off on all that." She frowned. "And I saw you had the boat out yesterday. That was Bobby's boat, by the way. He loved to fish."

Beth clouded over at the mention of Bobby's name. "I'm sorry… I didn't know…"

Lucy frowned. "I'm glad it got used. Doesn't do anybody any good tied up there, collecting water. I don't think he woulda minded too much." She stirred her coffee and peered hopefully down into the cup. "Damn, still no bubbles." She shrugged, and leaned back in her chair, fixing Beth with a resigned look. "You know you'll have to speak to Wes Draper today."

Beth nodded. "I know. Crane did mention him specifically last night… it was no accident, either. He wants us to know he's got us on the run, that somehow he has eyes on us." She took a deep breath. "And I've been thinking… how well do you know Karl?"

"Karl?" Lucy shrugged. "Almost all of my life, really. Why?"

"Well, it sorta stands to reason. Karl is always here, isn't he? Who better to spy on us and report back to Crane than him? He might very well be Crane's daywalker."

A doubtful look crossed Lucy's face. "Karl? I doubt it. He's just a good ol' boy, Beth, minds his own business, comes and goes…" she trailed off as Beth just stared meaningfully at her. "Which, I suppose are all things that would make him perfect for the job, eh?"

Beth nodded. "Well, it's just a theory. We're not sure yet. And it could be that either Crane is paying him very well, which makes him culpable and traitorous, or Crane has hooked him, and Karl is only following orders and doesn't know what he is doing." She took a thoughtful sip of her coffee. "If it's even Karl at all. He might be innocent, and Crane is getting his information from someone else altogether."

"What do we do? How can we tell?"

Beth shook her head. "Well, I guess we just watch him. I suppose we could feed him some bad information, and see if it gets back to Crane, but that might be dangerous because it means forcing another encounter with him. Do you think Karl's been acting strangely lately?"

Lucy grunted. "Karl is Karl. He's already strange. Just comes and goes, never says much. Probably afraid to... that hellcat wife of his never lets him talk, especially when they're together, the mean ol' thing." She considered thoughtfully, savoring her mouthful of coffee. "But if you're asking if Karl has been acting *differently*, then the answer is no. There haven't been any changes to his schedule, his routine, his habits, at all. He comes and goes like before... checks in with me in the morning, gets his chores, and maybe I'll see him again in the afternoon before he leaves. Sometimes I pack him a lunch, and sometimes if he's out in the fields, I might take him a fresh cooler of water, but he never asks for it. It's always my idea."

"Hmmm..." Beth pondered this. "Well, it doesn't sound like he's digging for information, does it?" She looked at Lucy. "Did he ever ask anything about me?"

Lucy laughed. "Well, I didn't say that. Karl is nosy, but then again, so is everyone else in this town. When you started living here, all of Bisby wanted to know who you were and why I was letting you stay with me." She shook her head. "Karl minds his own business, Beth, and he expects people to mind their own back. He never asked much about you, to be honest."

"Well..." Beth felt deflated. It certainly didn't sound like Karl was working for Crane, against his will or not. Yet it had made sense, and she had been sure he had been Crane's daywalker. Now, she wasn't so sure, though she intended to talk to Karl herself, to get a feel for his actions and reactions to her presence and own questioning.

A sudden knocking interrupted her thoughts, and she froze. Lucy stared worriedly at the back door, and Beth could read her mind. The last person who had come through that door had been Crane, and even though it was daylight now and therefore impossible for it to be him now, there was still a terrible sense of déjà vu about the moment. Lucy glanced at her, and then shook her head, as if embarrassed by her own nerves. "That might be Karl now," she said hopefully, and stood up.

But it wasn't. Wes Draper peered worriedly back at her through the window, and as she opened the door to greet him and ask him if he wanted breakfast, he said quickly, "All right you two. I believe you. I believe *all* of it, after last night."

A prickle of fear went down Beth's back. "What? Why?"

Wes looked pale, and he grabbed the back of a kitchen chair for support. "Because last night… Doctor Crane paid me a visit." He sat down heavily, a wild look in his eye. He glared at Beth accusingly as if it was her fault, and she could see how shook he really was. "It's true, every bit of it."

"Of course, it is," she said, refraining from telling him she told him so. In other circumstances, she might have, but he was too worked up to tease now, and she wasn't cruel. "All right. Tell us what happened."

Lucy had put a glass of lemonade in front of him and had briefly considered adding a good splash of whiskey to it. She actually had her hands on the bottle, but decided at the last minute that not only was it too early, but she didn't want to be responsible for corrupting Louella Draper's grandson, so she gave it to him unadulterated. However, it was never too early for her, and she added a healthy splash of faithful Jack to her coffee and came and sat back down.

"Crane sure is a busy boy," she remarked, taking a sip and relishing the taste. "He musta had his company shoes on last night."

Wes looked up sharply. "What does that mean?"

There was silence at the table, and then Beth sighed. "We had our own little visit last night from the good doctor." And she told him a condensed version, leaving out the part where Lucy had been enamored and entranced with Crane. He sat very still, only listening, and when she was finished, he looked accusingly at her again. She could tell that he was blaming her for all of this.

"Drink your lemonade," Beth said. She suddenly became aware that she must look horrible, and she excused herself and went back to her room and changed into a pair of shorts and a clean pink tee shirt. She ran a brush through her hair a few times, pulled it back in a quick ponytail, and then went into the bathroom and quickly brushed her teeth. She spared a quick glance in the mirror... even without makeup, not bad. Feeling more presentable, she ignored Lucy's sudden amused smile when she returned, and slid back into her chair.

"That was quick," Lucy said sarcastically, as Beth poured herself another cup of coffee. "Did you clean behind your ears?"

"More recently than you've cleaned behind yours," Beth shot back, and Lucy cackled in delight. "All right, Wes, don't mind her. Tell us what happened last night."

He shook his head, dazed. "It's the craziest thing I've ever experienced... and the most terrifying. Even now, I'm not sure that I didn't dream the whole thing, or that I've gone totally around the bend," he sighed, and ran his fingers through his mop of brown hair. "All right. After I got home last night, I didn't do a whole lot... I was too restless, too worked up over our conversation to really concentrate on much. I tried to watch a movie, but couldn't stick with it, and I couldn't focus on reading, either, though I've got a new one the other day and I've really been wanting to get into it—"

"All right, all right, cut to the part about Crane," Lucy said impatiently. "For the love of creation, this is like the previews before the movie starts."

"Only it's a horror movie," he agreed, and Beth shot Lucy a frown.

"So anyway, I knew sleep would be impossible, so I took a beer— one or two actually—and went out and sat on my back porch. It was a nice night; not real warm or too buggy, and I get a good view of the night sky from my deck. Anyway, I was out there for maybe an hour or two, drinking and thinking and trying to get sleepy, when I just decided to give it up and go on inside. I gathered my empties, slipped my feet back into my flip flops, and stood up. And when I turned around, there was a man standing at the foot of the steps leading up to the deck."

"Dear God," Lucy muttered. "That must have given you a turn."

Wes nodded. "It did. I never heard him come across the yard, he was so quiet. I don't know how long he had been there watching me before I noticed him."

Beth and Lucy exchanged a look. "What did he look like?"

"Good looking guy: black hair, black eyes. He wore a white shirt, black pants..." he gave a wry, tight little smile. "No cape or anything... he looked very normal, except for his eyes, and the way he moved. Damn he was fast... and that *voice*..." he shuddered. "Southern accent, deep south. I'd peg it as maybe Alabama or Louisiana... maybe even Creole..."

"That was him," Beth agreed. "New Orleans. When he was still human, that's where he lived."

"Well, it gave me a start to see someone standing there, let me tell you. Like I said, I sure didn't hear him come up through the yard... it was like he was just there. You know how it is, you think you're alone and then suddenly you realize you're not. I about yelled out, and I did drop my beer cans, and I asked him who in the hell he was, and what did he want... I guess maybe my yelling was a lot of bravado and macho posturing, but I tell you, I was spooked."

Beth swallowed hard. "No, go on."

"This guy just smiles at me, like we're old, best buds, and he says in that voice, 'It's a privilege to meet you, Mister Draper. Do you love?'"

Beth nearly fell out of her chair. "What?"

Wes looked at her closely, his face a mask of confusion. "That's what he said. "He asked if I love, though I have no idea what that means—"

"It's something he says to me," Beth said slowly. She suddenly looked very pale. "I'm not sure why he says it, but it usually precedes an attack." She swallowed hard. "You're very lucky." She looked down into her coffee, feeling her heart race.

"Well, even at that point I thought I was just dealing with a burglar, or maybe a psycho," Wes admitted. "I had no idea who he was, but I knew he was up to no good, standing there at that hour of the night. I began to walk slowly back toward the sliding door—I knew if I could get inside... well, I keep a .357 in my nightstand drawer for things that go bump in the night, and though I've only shot it at the pistol range, I had the feeling that this night might change that." He took a deep breath. "Well, so after he asked me that crazy question, he just stood there, grinning at me while I inched backwards, neither of us making any sudden moves. All of a sudden, I blinked… and damned if he hadn't flown up those steps and was between me and the door."

Beth nodded, remembering him attacking Bobby, and the incredible speed he had shown that night. She closed her eyes. "He can move very fast," she agreed, and felt her voice hitch.

"Well, I tell you, I couldn't believe it… it was impossible the way that guy moved. It was like lightning. And I stood there, trying to process it, thinking I was drunk, thinking I was dreaming, not believing *any* of it… and this guy just looked at me. Stared me down, there in the dark. We were close to each other, close enough to kiss each other, and I could smell his cologne. Beneath that, there was another smell—a horrible, nasty earthy smell, like wet dirt…" he looked away, feeling uncomfortable as he gathered his emotions. Beth let him compose himself, and then reached over and patted his hand.

"It's all right," she reassured him softly. "It's daylight now."

"I know." He nodded but smiled uneasily. "Anyway, as I pulled back, reaching for the handle on the sliding door, he took a step backward and tilted his head to one side, like a scientist looking at a bug. 'This is just a dress rehearsal, Mister Draper,' he whispers and then spreads his hands wide and steps back. He lets me go. Well, I threw that door open and got inside quickly, slamming it shut and flipping the lock. I look out at him, and he's still standing there, and we both know he let me go, that he could have killed me if he had wanted, and I'm wondering if I have time to get my gun or call the police or both… and then he points to me, and then to himself, and says—and I can hear him through the glass—'Just a dress rehearsal, Mister Draper. Next time we meet, it's gonna be Opening Night. You be sure to tell Miss Franklin her old friend Sebastian Crane said howdy, all right?' And then he opens his mouth… and Mother of God, his *teeth*. His awful, fanged, wicked teeth, gleaming in the night, like some horrible predatory animal. He curls his lip back, letting me get a good look—y'know, teasing me—and then he tapped on the glass… 'I knew your granddaddy,' he says, and sorta gives a laugh. 'You sorta look like him, through the eyes. I wonder if you taste like him, too?' And before I could say anything, before I could even really react and respond to that, he's gone. Just like that. I blink again, and the back porch is deserted... I flipped on the porch lights but didn't go back out there of course... but he was gone." He blinked a few times. "Sebastian Crane... dear Lord, you were right... he was right there in my face, within striking distance."

Beth said nothing. She glanced at Lucy, who sat quiet and pale.

Wes rubbed his jaw. "And you know what? I think... I think Crane was playing with me. Cat and mouse. Just toying with me, letting me go, making sure I *knew* he was letting me go, when he could have killed me just as easily."

The table was silent as Beth and Lucy digested his information, and then Beth looked at him. "You're right, he was toying with you, Wes. He's got an incredible ego, and he was manifesting it last night."

"It's true... he really is a damn vampire," Wes whispered slowly, and Beth recognized in him a bubble of rising hysteria. He rubbed his red-rimmed eyes. "Beth, those teeth..."

"I know, I remember them," she said softly, and he jerked.

"I'm sorry. Here I am, going on and on..." he suddenly looked ashamed of himself. "All right. So, what was his purpose last night? What did he hope to gain from all of this?"

"To show off," Lucy muttered. "To let us know how strong he is."

Beth nodded. "I agree." She drummed her fingers thoughtfully. "As Lucy says, he must have had his visiting shoes on last night, because he sure was busy. And clearly, he must have gone to your house before he came here," she mused, and when Wes looked confused, she smiled. "Well, after he visited us, I doubt if he wanted to go anywhere but back to his nest. He got a surprise here... he was expecting two helpless ladies..."

Wes raised his eyebrows questioningly. "What happened?"

She didn't want to get into the history of the poem, and just gave a casual shrug. "We were stronger than he expected, that's all. We didn't hurt him all that badly, I think. But I also don't think he was feeling all that spry after his visit, either. If nothing else, it gave him something to think about, and I'm all right with that as well."

"We kicked his ass," Lucy snorted, and when Beth looked at her, she cleared her throat. "Well, Beth did, anyway. I just helped a little."

For the first time, Wes cracked the hint of a smile. "It's like we're keeping score here," he said. "Like this is a great big game."

"That's a good point, actually," Beth agreed. "In a way, I think it is; at least to him. A great big chess game, and we're all pawns on his board, running around for his amusement." A faraway look came into her eye. "But the question is, how do we put *him* in check?"

"We find out where he is," Lucy said suddenly. A look of fierce resolution burned in her eyes. "What did you call it, a nest? We find out where his nest is, and then we smoke him out."

"Easier said than done." Beth stood up and went to the window, to look out at the bright day. Dew still sparkled in the grass, and Lucy's purple and pink morning glories were bright and cheerful on the fence. It seemed impossible that anything evil and murderous could be in play in the world, but of course she knew it was so. She sighed.

Turning around suddenly, she focused on Wes. "Does this mean you're joining us now? Think hard… yesterday, I was a Van Helsing wannabe, a crazy girl out of the nuthouse and you were humoring me while I told you ghost stories." She smiled faintly. "Funny how you've changed your attitude toward all of this."

He had the good grace to look momentarily ashamed. "What a difference a day can make, eh?"

"Indeed." She favored him with a look that was a trifle longer than necessary, and then sat back down. "All right. I'm open to ideas about where he is… how do we find him?"

"We can't just go from house to house, knocking on doors," Lucy said reasonably. "What would we say? Pardon me, can we go through your closets and basements while we hunt for bloodsuckers? *That* would go over well in Bisby, I'm sure."

"Besides—and no offense, Beth—but only Lucy and I would be admitted into people's homes anyway. You're an outsider around here." Wes looked embarrassed to even bring this up, but she waved it away in agreement.

"No, you're right. I'm a stranger… people have only seen me at Market Day." She frowned. Something seemed to be at the edge of her consciousness—something she was missing, and she closed her eyes as she mentally grappled with it. Nothing.

"Beth?" Lucy sounded worried. "You all right?"

"Yes, of course." She opened her eyes. "It's nothing. I'm just thinking, that's all. I thought I had something..." the others waited patiently, and then she shrugged. "I don't know. Maybe I'm just tired."

"Understandable. I'm running on nothing but adrenaline and nervous energy," Wes agreed. "But all right. I have an idea... maybe not the best, but it'll have to do, unless anyone has a better one."

"All right, I'm listening." Beth's stomach growled. Lucy chuckled, got up and quickly set out some zucchini bread she had baked the day before. "Here, have a bit of breakfast," she offered. Gratefully, Beth sliced a piece and spread butter on it. It was delicious.

"Well, we go to the people we know who have booths at Market Day. We say that we found a wallet, and we're trying to find its owner. A Summer Person named..." he looked at them. "Wait for it, wait for it... Sebastian Crane. Does anyone know this particular gentleman, know where he is staying?" He looked hopeful. "We might get a lead, if nothing else. Remember, he's a stranger too, and that alone would make him gossip-worthy."

Lucy looked at Beth, who could only shrug. "It's the best plan we've got so far," she admitted. "Although it might tip off Crane that we're looking for him."

"Good." Beth nodded eagerly. "Besides it not being that big of a surprise—I mean, he knows we're looking for him—it might make him nervous. And being nervous might cause him to make a mistake. We just need one little slip, one little error to go our way..."

Beneath that, another smell—a horrible, nasty earthy smell, like wet dirt...

She paused again. Why was that important? She thought furiously, but came up empty, and she mentally shrugged. She realized the others were looking at her curiously, and she sighed.

Wes took a bite of his own zucchini bread, nodding appreciatively. "All right... so let's say someone has heard of Doctor Crane—"

"Or at least heard of a stranger who only goes out at night," interrupted Beth. "It's possible he's using an alias."

He nodded. "All right. So, let's say we get a lead on somebody... then what do we do?"

Lucy looked worriedly at Beth, who smiled faintly. She dabbed politely at the corners of her mouth with her napkin and swallowed the last piece of food in her mouth. "Well," she said calmly, "then we go in and find him, make sure he's there. I doubt he'll be in a coffin, though it's possible. And after we find him... well, we stake him. Cut off his head. Throw it in the river." She smiled at them blandly. "Simple as that."

Wes looked pale. "Wow. All of that? There's a lot to it, isn't there?"

Beth looked at him levelly. "There sure is. It's the prescribed method of killing vampires. Technically, we have to turn the head over in the coffin *before* we throw it into the river... and the stake and hammer both have to have red ribbons tied around them when we do it," she frowned. "But I'm hoping those are minor points. I think the main thing is just staking and beheading him."

"Well, we can use the axe out in the barn," Lucy nodded. "And get a hammer from the toolbox... it's in the barn, too."

"And I've already got the stake," Beth said quietly. "Remember, it has to be ash... well, I've actually got several of them made and sharpened." She smiled grimly, and no one wanted to ask her when and where she had done such a deed.

There was silence at the table. No one made eye contact, and the only sound was the clock on the wall, ticking away the minutes.

"All right," Beth said suddenly, clapping her hands. "Let's get started. Sunset is about twelve hours away. We've got a lot of work to do, fast."

Lucy held her hands out to each of them. "Let's say a prayer first," she urged. "To help us on our way. Don't you think it's a good idea?"

Beth smiled. "I think it's an excellent idea, actually." She grabbed hands and nodded to Lucy. "All right, Luce. Make it a good one. We're going to need every bit of help we can get today."

No one doubted her, and three heads bowed dutifully and respectfully down to ask for divine help.

CHAPTER XVII

Kandace Grady leaned out the window of her car; oversized, dramatic sunglasses covered her eyes. A white plastic sun visor with the words *Bisby Little League* sat on top of her yellow Dolly Parton hairdo and a tank top like Dolly's, strained to keep its baggage in check. She was a mashup of soccer mom and barfly, and Beth could well imagine her swilling beers and singing karaoke on Friday nights while she bragged about her children's athletic accomplishments. Right now, however, she only had eyes for Wes, and she lifted her sunglasses up so she could have a better look at him.

"Why Wesley Draper, you sweet ol' thing, that's just like you, helpin' somebody out," she flirted. A squawk and a shout in the back seat interrupted her as several young voices began to fight over a ball, and she turned her head for a second to glare at them fiercely. "Shut up back there!" she bellowed. "Cain't you see Momma's talkin'!"

Wes smiled politely. Beth, wisely interpreting the chemistry here, moved away from the minivan and went and sat on a park bench. She uncapped her bottle of water and waited impatiently while Wes and Kandace chatted.

Kandace, Wes, and Brice—Kandace's husband—had all gone to high school together, though they had moved in different social circles. Kandace had been a cheerleader and had never outgrown it, and Brice had lettered in three different sports but had never been quite good enough to excite any college scouts. After graduation, he had impregnated Kandace in the back of his black Trans Am—with the obligatory golden eagle on the hood and removable T-tops—and then finding himself with no skills or college prospects, went to work for his family's farm before Kandace's father came looking for him with a shotgun. Now, twelve years out of high school, they were both bored and restless in their marriage. Wes had heard a lot of wild rumors about both of them. He figured they were just waiting for Brice's father to die so they could inherit the farm and take it over themselves.

The Grady Farm was one of the bigger vendors on Market Day, so large they actually pitched an open-air tent and set up long folding tables to better display their wares. Along with the usual produce, they also sold hanging baskets of flowers and trays of summer annuals, pumpkins and cider in season, and later in the year, Christmas trees and wreaths. Besides Kandace and Brice working the booth, there was a wide variety of seasonal workers they employed, most of them illegal and all of them underpaid. Kandace flirted shamelessly with them and with the customers as well, but Brice had long since given up caring because he recognized it was probably good for business... and as Wes felt her eyes crawl over him hungrily, he realized if anyone would know anything about a strange, nocturnal visitor in their midst, it would be Kandace.

"You always were a generous soul," Kandace observed, smiling prettily at him. "And here you are, out in all this heat, being a good Christian. You're putting the rest of us to shame, Wesley."

"Well," Wes said. "I dunno know about all that. I just know what a pain it is to lose your wallet, and I'm just trying to help some poor guy out. He dropped it by my Gran's booth and didn't notice it." He held up an old wallet of his—Beth had suggested this detail, since a visual lent more credibility to their story—and smiled charmingly. Kandace smiled right back while her brood grew impatient.

"The thing is, he mentioned he was staying in town for a week or so," Wes continued. Kandace nodded appreciatively and leaned forward, letting him get a better view of her cleavage. "But I don't remember where he said he was staying so I can get this back to him."

"Well, honey, I'm sure I ain't got any ideas, but if I hear something, I'll let—Bobby John, dammit, put *down* that ball bat before—I'll let you know." She clucked her tongue in exasperation. "Lord, but these children, I'd like to sell them down the river!" She glanced behind him at Beth sitting on the bench, and her eyes narrowed.

"That your new girlfriend?" Her voice had gone considerably frosty as she critiqued Beth's simple, All-American self. "She's the one staying with Miz Barnham?"

Wes blushed. "Yes, and no. Wait, I mean, no and yes."

Kandace's plucked eyebrows shot upward in polite confusion. "Well, which is it, honey?"

"No, she's not my girlfriend," he said, keeping his voice low so Beth wouldn't overhear. "And yes, she's staying with Miz Barnham. She's writing a book."

"Miz Barnham is writing a book?" Kandace blinked three or four times rapidly. "What about?"

Wes sighed. "No, not her. Beth is writing a book. About the Civil War… the Tennessee Scarlet Rangers, specifically. I'm just showing her around town today, killing two birds with one stone, while I try to find the owner of this wallet."

"Hmm." Kandace looked at him skeptically, and then flipped down her sunglasses. "You better watch out for them fast Yankee girls, Wesley Draper. If I hear about someone who's lost a wallet, I'll sure send 'em your way. See you at Market—oh, for the love of God, Misti, if you hit your brother one more time—next Thursday."

"Next Thursday, it is," he agreed, and stepped back from the rocking minivan. With a wave and friendly toot of the horn, Kandace pulled back out into traffic. He watched them go, and then shook his head. "If I'm alive next Thursday, that is."

Beth came up behind him and handed him an unopened bottle of water. "Any luck?"

"Thanks." He drank deeply. It was a hot day, and he wanted nothing more than to go and sit in the air conditioning somewhere and play his guitar. "Nope. Although I think I just got hit on by a Soccer-mom from hell."

Beth snorted. "She was rather trashy," she mused. "But expensive trash. I guess there's a difference." She started walking down the sidewalk, at least to get in the shade of the trees, and Wes followed her. Brimming with frustration, together they sat back down on the bench.

"I wonder how Lucy is doing," Beth sighed, tucking back a lock of sweaty hair. She glanced up at the clock on the town hall tower... 2:15. "I hope better than us, because we've got nothing so far."

He nodded, keeping his eyes straight ahead. "And time is ticking, isn't it?"

"It is." She struggled to keep the fear from her voice.

He swallowed hard. "All right... so, what do we do if the sun sets tonight and we don't know any more than we do now?"

She took a deep breath. "I know. Plan B. I've been thinking about that. Our choices are limited. Though whatever happens, we need to stay together. First rule of combat is to never divide your forces. We'll have to fort up."

"Gran, too."

She had forgotten about Louella. "Of course. Your grandmother, too. We can all gather together and get through the night as a united front. Or, we can all get in the truck right now and put as many miles between us and Bisby as we can... although that would only be a temporary solution at best. I guarantee that Crane would eventually find us, but it would give us a few days of breathing space."

Wes took off his hat and fanned himself. "But if we leave..."

She nodded. "I know. The balance shifts, putting us on the defense, and even if we're stymied at the moment, right now we're still on the offensive. We're hunting him, and he knows it. I don't want to lose that momentum."

He laughed nervously. "Well, it might be lost for us if things don't change, I'll be honest." She glanced over at him and read exhaustion, both physical and emotional, in his eyes. He looked one step away from bolting, and she reached out and took his hand.

"Do you want to hit the road? While I don't think it's really the best plan, I suppose it would allow us to regroup, get our heads together and get some rest. We can all be gone within the hour... we'll have to convince the old ladies to leave, and that might take a while. Your Gran, especially."

He sighed. "Oh, who am I kidding. Gran would never leave her home, and she wouldn't believe me anyway. She'd think I'm nuts, telling her all of this." Across the town square, one of the local churches was hosting a lemonade and bake sale; the banner tied to the bandstand proclaimed all money raised would be used to send the children's choir on a mission trip. It seemed like such a worthy cause, and they looked like they were having fun in the process; laughter floated over to them, and for a moment, he wished he had nothing more serious in his life than selling enough cups of quarter-cent lemonade to purchase a bus ticket to some place far away. Wistfully, he smiled.

"Last week, Lucy never would have left her farm either," Beth said. "But after last night, I bet she'd be willing to consider a vacation. Karl can take over and run the place for a while." She shrugged. "He's probably safe... I don't think that Crane is interested in him."

"Speaking of Lucy..." Wes lifted his head and pointed down the street. Lucy Barnham, visible in the crowd because of her floppy straw hat, was hurrying over to them, her face red and flushed.

"Any luck?" She was out of breath and panting, and Wes stood up to give her a seat on the bench. "Tell me you've found something out." She was almost pleading.

"Take some water first," Beth ordered. What was she thinking? It was nearly ninety degrees outside, and they were having Lucy Barnham run around like she was a teenager. They should have left her back at the farmhouse and gone on without her. She was clearly in distress and looked about five minutes from a heart attack.

Lucy gulped the water greedily like a calf at the teat, and Beth cupped some water from Wes's bottle and rubbed it on the back of her neck. "Just cool down for a moment, before you try to talk," she urged, but Lucy shook her head impatiently and pointed to the town hall clock. 2:31.

"We don't have time to cool down," she croaked, water spilling down her front. "Damn, now I need a bib." She pawed at her wet bosom, shrugging in resignation. "It'll dry. All right you two, tell me you haven't spent the whole afternoon holding hands and giggling. Tell me you've found something."

"I wish we could," Beth said regretfully. "We showed Wes's old empty wallet to about everyone we met, and no one seemed to know anything about any strange visitor staying in Bisby."

"Me, either." Lucy looked frustrated. "I hit the post office, the library, the bank and all along the square."

Wes nodded. "We did the high school; there is band practice going on and summer football conditioning, so it was pretty crowded actually. Then we hit the farmer's co-op, both hardware stores, the Wal-Mart parking lot and the McDonald's by the railroad tracks. Nothing."

"Damn." Bleakly, Lucy looked over at Beth. "Now what? Do we leave? I can have us packed in ten minutes... if we start now, we can make Louisville by dark and hide there."

"We'll be running forever if we do." Beth firmed her jaw. "No, the first thing we do is get you home, my lady. You need to sit in the air conditioning—" but Lucy was already shaking her head in denial.

"Hell if I will. I ain't going any dingdanged place, and you know it. Crane has been attacking and hurting this family for well over a hundred years. I'd say the time for running is over... I'd like to turn it around and do a little chasing."

Beth looked at her, not knowing what to say.

Lucy wiped a runner of sweat away with the back of her hand, and her voice choked a little. "For my David, and my boy." She smiled shakily at Beth and squeezed her hand. "And for Bobby, of course." Blinking rapidly, she looked away. "Damn, look at me, I got sweat in my eyes," she muttered, and no one dared challenge her on that.

"All right, then," Beth said, and glanced over at Wes, who gave a helpless little shrug. "All right. So, we stay." She looked up at the clock tower again, relentlessly watching the minutes tick away. "So, here's my plan, then. We have about five more hours of good daylight left... we keep looking and asking questions, sticking to the same story. But, if we don't turn anything up, we come back together and get ready for the night: Wes goes and picks up Louella, and we meet back at our place. Crucifixes in all the windows—and on everyone's person—and Holy Water as well. And I'll teach you all the poem that worked so well against him last night."

"Agreed," Lucy said, composing herself. Her voice sounded stronger, but Beth still looked at her worriedly.

"I really think you should go on home. We can handle this part of it, and you can get ready for the night… and stop by the grocery on the way home. Get all the garlic they have, and any roses in the flower shop. We're going to pull out every trick we've got tonight, every tool in our arsenal."

Lucy hesitated. "It still seems like you're getting rid of me."

"Well, we are," Beth said earnestly, and then laughed when she saw the look on Lucy's face. "No, seriously old friend, those are all things that need to be taken care of—important things. I'll check in every hour or so and give you an update, so you know how we're doing. And even catch a little catnap if you can… it's going to be a long night, I expect."

"Long night, indeed." Lucy shook her head ruefully and stood up. "And I'll make plenty of coffee, too. We'll need it to stay awake."

"Good thinking." Beth nodded in agreement but was just relieved that Lucy was cooperating. While she really didn't believe that Lucy would drop dead in front of her from a heart attack, she was worried the old lady might suffer from heat stroke or heat exhaustion. She could imagine the string of misfortune that would unfold then: Lucy in the hospital, their group divided and vulnerable, all easy prey for Crane to pick them off, one by one. No, get Lucy home, get her cooled down and give her a task to complete. It was a much smarter move.

Lucy looked at the clock… 2:43. "All right. See you at home in a few hours. I'll have everything ready." She hesitated again and turned to Wes. "Have you told your grandmother any of this?"

He looked uneasy. "Well, no. Not yet. But soon, we're going to have to, I know."

Lucy worked her mouth thoughtfully. "Do you think I should be there when you tell her? I've known Louella for sixty plus years, and you know how stubborn these old biddies can be."

Beth struggled to keep a straight face but caught Wes' eye and suddenly burst into laughter. Lucy looked from one to another, confused as to why they were laughing. "What? What did I say? What's so funny?"

Beth leaned over and kissed her sweaty old cheek. "Lucy, that's why I love you so much. Even in the darkest moments, you make me laugh." She wiped her eyes. "All right, we all better keep moving. There's a lot of ground to cover and only a few hours to do it in."

She heaved herself to her feet. She recognized her moment of gaiety for what it was, overtiredness bordering on giddiness and hysteria, and for a second spots swam in front of her eyes. All right, so the heat was affecting her, too… she drank some more water and tried to focus.

She watched Lucy hurry off to her truck, parked on the opposite side of the green, and drive away. She turned to Wes, taking another drink. "All right. Now where?"

He frowned thoughtfully. "Well, we could go find Gran and try and explain all of this. I don't know how… it'll take some doing."

She considered this but shook her head. "Let's wait a little while longer. I'd hate to waste these daylight hours by talking when we could be looking."

He shrugged. She was clearly the leader of their group, and it didn't offend his male ego in the least in letting her take charge of this operation. In a way, he liked it, found it reassuring, and he drew from her strength. "All right. You're the boss. Lead on."

"I only wish I knew where to," she muttered, but started down the sidewalk, headed towards the church lemonade sale. If nothing else, there was a crowd of people there; it was as good a place as any to start. And Wes, with his flip flops smacking the pavement, shrugged and started after her.

* * *

Lucy usually didn't run the air conditioning in the truck, mostly because she liked the freshness of the outdoors and the wind blowing in, but as she collapsed against the fabric seat, she decided to make an exception. She cranked the window up as she studied the dials, and then with a few flips, felt the unfamiliar rush of cold air on her face. Heaven.

She made the required stops at both grocery stores in town, and came away with several pounds of garlic cloves. As she put her plastic produce bags up on the scale, the cashier gave her an odd look, and Lucy felt her temper flare.

"If it's any of your business, young lady, I'm fighting vampires," she said loftily. She knew it would come across as a joke, but it was also a subtle way of tossing out a hint on the subject, to see if the girl had even an inkling of knowledge about the truth or had any information.

"Oh, I see," the girl nodded wisely. "Of *course,* you are. And by the way, I like roasted garlic as well… it makes a good paste on a roast or steaks." She laughed and winked. "But vampires are fun, too. Good luck with that."

Stomping out of the store and heading for her truck, she paused again to glance at the clock. 3:34. There was a feeling of impending doom of time running out, and uneasily she glanced at the afternoon shadows. Already they were growing longer, stretching across the pavement. The bank was closed now, the post office too. Within a few hours, most of the other businesses in Bisby would be as well. People would be finishing their work days and start heading home to supper; out at the ballpark, evening little league games would be starting as the lights on the field began to come on, and at dusk, the drive-in movie theater would start showing the previews.

And Sebastian Crane would rise from his sleep.

Despite the heat of the afternoon, she shivered, clutching her plastic grocery bag of garlic. Would he come right at full dark? Probably not. With the patience of a hunter, he would wait until well past midnight before he made a move. She had once read that humans were most vulnerable in the hours between three and six in the morning, when they were at their weakest for defense. Soldiers and terrorists alike knew this and planned their operations around this time. It was likely that Crane also knew this, at least instinctively, and would follow a similar pattern: he would wait until their consciousness was at their lowest ebb, when sleep was a blessing and staying awake was impossible, and then attack.

Just know, you better learn to love the night, because Bitch, I'll be coming for you...

She shuddered, and it wasn't from the cool air blowing on her.

She drove back through town using Kentucky Street, which paralleled Main Street. It was more residential here on the south side of town, though many of the homes were boarded up. Most of the residents had worked at the H and B Tractor plant, but when the company had pulled out of town three years ago—taking over three hundred jobs with them—people had been hard-pressed to pay their mortgages. Now this part of Bisby was almost a ghost town, a town within a town. As she drove, she counted fourteen boarded up or empty homes, and it suddenly occurred to her that Crane could very well be in one of them right now. Possibly, he had even spent a night or two in each of them, moving around a lot to avoid discovery. It made sense... here, he was at the heart of Bisby, but yet he could move freely from bolt hole to bolt hole like a giant, predatory rat, without fear of detection.

Pondering this, she pulled the truck over to the curb and paused at the corner of Kentucky and Cross, looking around her. She gazed up at one of the houses thoughtfully, wondering what secrets lay behind its boarded-up windows. "Doctor Crane," she whispered. "Are you in there?"

The house remained silent, mocking her. She put one hand on the door handle, steeling herself to get out of the truck and go and have a look for herself, but she hesitated again. Did she actually have the courage to go up to one of the houses by herself...

She considered this and settled back against the seat in defeat.

The answer was no, and for several reasons. Besides not having the nerve, she knew she didn't have the physical strength to pry the boards off one of the windows and crawl into a back bedroom like a petty thief where the dusty, stifling heat would be excruciating. She was already about flagged out and she knew it.

And what if she was wrong, and her search was in vain? She would waste precious time, frustrated and hot, as she went from home to home and finding nothing... or worse yet, opening a door and finding Crane there, asleep but yet Not, hiding behind a stack of old boxes. She could well envision him rising slowly, grinning and mocking her as he trapped her with his eyes before he pulled her to him.

"Lucy... I'm here for you, darlin'... aren't you going to greet me? There's a good girl... turn around for me..."

No. God help her, she couldn't go into one of these houses by herself. Tomorrow—if there was a tomorrow—she would bring Wes and Beth back here, and together they could all search. But going in solo? Impossible.

She started the truck and eased back out onto the street.

Once she crossed the railroad tracks, the neighborhood got better almost immediately. The homes here were occupied and well taken care of. Neat, manicured yards, colorful flower beds, the occasional American flag flapping in the breeze. A jogger ran past, with a large yellow retriever on the end of a leash, and four middle school boys whooped and hollered as they clustered around a skateboard ramp. One of them she thought she knew—Clara Partnam's grandson Travis, and he must have recognized her too, because he raised a hand in greeting as she drove by. Encouraged, she pulled the truck over and rolled the window down.

"Travis?" She hoped she had his name right, and the boys looked at each other and grinned.

"It's Trevor," he corrected, but didn't seem offended by it. He came closer, and she saw with distaste he had a little gold ball in his left earlobe. An earring! What was Clara thinking?

No time for that now. "Look, you boys seen anything funny around here lately?"

They all exchanged a look, and one of them burst into laughter, clearly interpreting her question as something with a sexual twist. She frowned at him disgustedly and snapped, "Remember, I know most of your mommas and grandmommas, so don't be cute with me. Trevor? You seen anything?" She shut the engine off and got out, to face them levelly.

Trevor looked blank. "Like what?"

She wasn't sure how much to reveal. "Well... just anything not right. Anybody sneaking around at night, skulking around maybe?" The boys looked at each other again, and she realized she had approached this wrong, and so she said quickly, "We had somebody break into our barn last week and steal a bunch of tools... chainsaw, log splitter, even the battery from one of the tractors. I'm doing my own detective work to find my stuff. Y'all know anything about any of that?"

Trevor shook his head. "I don't think—"

"My handyman Karl said he saw a tall, dark-haired man hanging around the place the day before we were robbed," she elaborated. "Spoke to him, said he had a thick Southern accent, maybe Louisiana thick. That ring any bells with any of you?"

There was more collective head shaking, and she could tell from their puzzled, earnest faces they were telling the truth. They weren't bad boys, really. They were just desperately *young*... each of them needed a haircut, and she spotted two more pierced ears—and dear Lord, one of them had a hoop through his lower *lip*—but she had always liked boys and decided these weren't all that bad. They didn't smell like they had been smoking, and she hadn't heard any cussing or taking the Lord's name in vain, and that alone was something. "All right, well I'll tell you all what. I'm offering a reward—fifty dollars, in fact," and she saw eyes widen in interest, "to anyone who can bring me information about that dark haired fella I spoke of."

One of the boys looked curious. "You sure he's the thief though? Just because he was hanging around your barn doesn't mean—"

"Oh, I'm sure he's the one," Lucy nodded. "Sneaky cuss... he mighta been high on something, needed the money. Karl said he was all pale and spooky-like." She inwardly smiled, proud of herself. Good. That had been a nice touch. The boys would understand the drug reference, and it also gave credibility to her story without explaining the whole vampire bit.

Nothing. One of the boys thoughtfully spun the wheel on his skateboard, producing a maddening, clicking sound as the ball bearings whirled and whirled, and another moodily picked at a pimple and shuffled his feet. Lucy looked at each of them in turn, smiling encouragingly, but no one seemed to know anything, and finally she sighed in defeat.

"Well, all right boys, I've gotta keep on moving. Remember, there's fifty bucks in it—"

"I think I seen this dude," the smallest boy suddenly said. All eyes turned to him, and he blushed. "But I ain't sure."

"You just seen your own shadow, and it freaked you out," one of the other boys said, punching him, and there was loud, goatish laughter. The small boy's face twisted.

Lucy gave them all her best grandmotherly, stern gaze. "Hush, you all, let him talk." She turned to the boy and tried to smile. "What's your name, son?"

"Evan. Evan Stoller."

She raised inquisitive eyebrows. "You Janey Stoller's grandson? Is your daddy Jimmy Stoller?"

He nodded, not sure if admitting this was a good thing or not. "Yes ma'am. He works down at Best Plumbing."

"Yep, I know your Daddy. He's a good boy. He and my grandson Bobby…" she swallowed hard. "Well, they went to school together. Bobby mighta been a few years younger… I think they played football together."

Evan brightened. "My dad was on the team the year they went to state," he offered proudly, and one of the boys snickered. Apparently, playing football these days was out, and skateboarding was in. She sighed.

"That was a good year," she agreed. "My grandson was just a sophomore that year… I remember it as a real good time." She nodded. "But listen, we can talk about all that later. Tell me more about that man you say you saw."

He glanced uneasily at his friends who were growing restless. Clearly, he didn't want to talk in front of them, and she pointed to her truck. "You wanna walk an old lady to her buggy? Your friends can wait here, unless they decide to get on those skateboards of theirs and roll outta here… but I'll bet they'll wait for you, won't you boys?" They nodded, and she looked at Trevor. "You tell your grandma I said howdy, won't you?"

He nodded. "Yes ma'am."

She turned and nodded to Evan, who reluctantly walked with her to her truck, out of earshot of the other boys. "All righty, Evan, you really think you saw the man I was talking about?"

He looked uneasy. "Well, I'm not sure—"

"Evan," she fixed him with a look. "Honey, it's pretty important. I know you don't know me, but our families know each other, and your daddy knew my grandson. Whatever you tell me, I'll believe you, I promise." She glanced at her watch. 3:51. "Evan?"

He swallowed hard. "Well, this dude you were talking about… I think I saw him a few nights ago, if it's the same guy." He frowned. "He was hanging around the square the other night… Thursday night, I think."

"Thursday?" She blinked in surprise. "Market Day? You sure it was then?"

He nodded. "Yep. I'm sure of it. I was helping my mom load some peaches into our van… she always waits until most of the vendors are packing up; they usually sell things real cheap then, so they don't have to take it back home. Also, after it's been sitting out in the heat all day, most of the stuff is pretty ripe at that point anyway, and she can get stuff cheaper that way." He looked away, embarrassed, and she suddenly remembered that Best Plumbing was on hard times, and was about to go under. Apparently, Jimmy's hours had been cut, and the family was struggling. She hated to hear it, but she had other things on her mind, and she made a hurrying motion with her hand to urge him on.

"Well, Mom wanted to can some peaches, so she waited until Mister Fleming was about to shut down for the night, and then she offered him a few bucks for all the peaches he had left, and I guess they were so ripe they wouldn't keep in the heat another day, so he agreed. Anyway, Mom made me carry them to her van, and when I did…" he suddenly looked upset. "That's when I saw the man you're talking about."

"What time of day was it?" She asked him to test him. Obviously, if it was still daylight, either it had been a different person altogether, or he was lying just for the attention.

He considered. "Well, late in the day. Market Day was about over..." he thought for a minute. "I remember the streetlights had come on, because I seen a giant moth or two flopping around by the lights, so I guess it was after dark."

"After dark," she said softly. "All right, go on."

"Well... I was carrying the baskets of peaches to the van, and was trying to get the hatch open when I dropped some of the peaches... they rolled across the pavement, and a few of them went under the cars, and I was fighting to pick everything up..." he paused, obviously struggling with the memory. "And when I turned around, there he was. This dark-haired guy, tall and scary looking. Standing in front of me, grinning at me and holding some of the peaches I had dropped. Well, it scared the hell outta me—oops, sorry, Miz Barnham."

She smiled faintly. "It's all right. It woulda scared the hell outta me, too. Go on with your story."

"And so, he's holding these peaches, but he's smiling at me, like some big ol' child molester, and I'm thinking to myself, 'Stranger Danger', which I know is for little kids but if ever there was a time to start yelling those words, it was right then." He swallowed hard. "And he says to me, 'You oughta be more careful with your groceries, my friend. Don't let the sweet things in life get away. Do you love?' Well, I just stood there. I didn't know what to say, and he was looking at me, and I was getting more and more uncomfortable. Grownups aren't supposed to *act* that way..." his voice broke, and she could see that despite this boy's skater friends, he had obviously led a rather sheltered, protected life, and was very troubled by this incident.

"No, they're not," she agreed, and imagined how upset he would be if he knew that Crane was not only a sexual, opportunistic predator, but also a vampire. The poor kid would probably have a breakdown right in front of her. "Can you tell me what happened next?"

He chewed on his lip nervously. "Well, it was like we were both frozen, both waiting for something to happen, and I didn't know if I should yell or run or throw the rest of the peaches at him, or what to do... when all of a sudden, Missus Draper comes walking across the parking lot with the rest of her stuff, headed for her car, and he sees her and gives me a funny look. 'As much as I hate to leave you, my friend—and after all, we haven't even been properly introduced yet—I must excuse myself. A thousand pardons, but one must always honor one's patron,' he says, and he turns and walks away... and I mean *fast*. So fast it was hard to keep up with him." He smiled, but there was no humor in it. "He walked right up to her, and she acted like she knew him... they talked, and she laughed and even touched him on the cheek. He got into her car, and she drove away." He shook his head. "And he left the peaches on the hood of a car, stacked in a weird little pyramid... stacked 'em so fast I didn't even see him do it, to be honest."

She frowned thoughtfully. There was so much to process in his story that she didn't even know where to begin, and she closed her eyes for a moment, feeling the dizziness sweep over her. She took a deep breath.

"Miz Barnham?" At the sound of his worried voice, her eyes flew open. "Are you all right?"

"Yes, I'm fine, sugar." She looked at him closely. "Did you say... Missus Draper? As in Louella Draper, the lady who sells chicken sandwiches on Market Day? Old lady..." she cleared her throat. "A lot older than me?"

He covered the ghost of a smile. "Yep, that's the one."

"Louella Draper," she echoed quietly, mulling it over. All right, so what was *that* about? There were only two options, and neither was very promising.

Either Louella Draper was dead, another victim of Crane, or he had another use for her in mind. Lucy thought the latter, unless he was desperate to feed. Louella seemed a trifle too old for his tastes; she was outside of his usual victim profile. And since Crane had referred to Louella as his patron...

Shamefully she remembered last night, and the way he had humiliated her. At first, the memories had been fragmented and random, but over the past few hours, she had begun to put them together, like scattered pieces of a jigsaw puzzle, and had remembered the things he had made her do and speak.

I'll do you like I did my husband, I swear I will, and you'll love it, because that's how I love it.

Just thinking of it made her nauseated. She remembered clinging to him—the killer of her husband and son and grandson—asking him, *begging* him to take her and use her like a cheap whore. However, he had done it, whatever he had done, it was obvious that he had bewitched and hypnotized her into helping him as well. And now, obviously, he had done the same thing to Louella. She felt a flash of indignant outrage, thinking about the poor woman… she had never been the sharpest tool in the shed anyway, and she doubted it had taken very much for Crane to get her to be his puppet.

But…

One must always honor one's patron…

What did that mean? How was Crane honoring her? What was he using her for…?

We find out where he is… We find out where his nest is, and then we smoke him out…

In an instant, she knew. Louella was hiding him. He had made his nest somewhere on her property, and somehow, against her will, poor Louella Draper was being made to help hide him. Sadly, Lucy remembered the young girl she had known in high school: all stringy hair and bony knees. And she thought of her now, selling sandwiches with her free, hippie grandson. She thought of Wes and how much she liked him… and how good he was for Beth. This would kill him, this knowledge that Crane had taken his grandmother and evilly manipulated her into helping and hiding him. When he found out, he would be out of his mind to help her, to rescue her from Crane's grasp.

"Miz Barnham?" Evan was looking at her worriedly. "Are you all right?"

She shook herself. "Yes, I'm fine, just thinking."

He glanced behind him, at his friends who were waiting for him by the skateboard ramp; they were talking among themselves, but it was obvious they were also trying to listen into the conversation, and he knew they were getting impatient. "I've gotta go," he muttered, but then hesitated again. "You don't think that man is gonna hurt Missus Draper, do you?"

"Oh no, 'course not," she said quickly, though her stomach was twisting and doing cartwheels. "He just probably was asking for a job, is all. Don't worry, I'll talk to her grandson Wes, let him know about it. You go on and play with your friends and try not to break your neck on that thing." She gave him a reassuring smile, and climbed into her truck, thinking, thinking.

All right... what to do. Drive to Louella's and warn her? Possibly, but what would she say? If she had been possessed by Crane, Louella wouldn't listen to her anyway. Under Crane's spell, she might order her off the place, or even call the police, despite their long history together. No, it would be better if she had help, especially Wes, who Louella might be more apt to listen to. Also, Lucy knew she had to follow the plan, which had been to return home and do the preparations there. Beth had said she would periodically call and check in, getting and receiving updates, and Lucy figured she could tell her everything then. Beth would know what to do... that girl was sharp, and Lucy had no problem in turning the leadership of this whole expedition over to her.

Still... what if Louella was in danger? Lucy paused again, leaning back in her seat. She wished she knew if Wes had actually seen his grandmother today... he hadn't said one way or another. What if Crane was holding Louella, possibly in the basement, possibly in the attic, without food and water, for her to watch and guard over him while he slept. He would have no fear of Louella; she was too timid to try and move against him, but she would be useful in protecting him while he slept, especially if he had bewitched her.

Firming her jaw, she made her decision.

She started the ignition and pulled away from the curb so fast her tires squealed. In her rear-view mirror, she heard the boys cheering in admiration, and a hard, determined smile settled on her lips.

Evan watched her go, a disappointed look on his face. "What about my fifty dollars?" he muttered plaintively, but she was gone.

CHAPTER XVIII

When Wes's truck turned down the long Barnham driveway, Beth immediately knew something was wrong, and prickles of worry began to travel up and down her spine. "Lucy's truck isn't here," she said worriedly, glancing around the yard. "And that doesn't make sense. She should have beaten us back here by at least two hours." She got out of the truck and stood with her hands on her hips, looking out across the yard for Karl.

"Well, she did have some errands, remember?" Wes mentioned reasonably. "She had to stop and get garlic, roses... maybe she thought of something else and stopped there too. And you know how she likes to talk—vampire crisis or not—if there's good gossip, Miz Barnham is right there to spread it. Bisby is still her town."

"Maybe," Beth frowned. She climbed the steps to the porch, looking at the long shadows under the eaves. 5:22. Her plan had been to reassemble at the farm, assist Lucy with the preparations, and then head to the Draper Farm as a group and collect Louella... and now there was a kink in the schedule. Hurriedly, she went to the kitchen to check the answering machine to see if Lucy had called and left a message, but the red light wasn't blinking, and she frowned. What was going on?

Wes came up behind her, sensing her nervousness. "Let's not start imagining the worst," he said. "We've still got a couple of hours to go before sundown."

"I know." She looked around the empty kitchen, noting how quiet the place was without Lucy's colorful presence. "It's just not like Lucy to not leave a message, especially on a day like today."

"Well, don't forget, she's had quite a shock the past few days," he reminded her, looking in the refrigerator. He came up with a plate of cold chicken which he popped in the microwave, and the rest of the coleslaw from their first date and stirred it up. "Here. You should eat something… we've got a long night ahead of us still."

"I know, but I'm really not all that hungry," she replied. She looked out the window again searchingly. "And where is Karl? It's not like him to have left this early."

The microwave dinged, and he took the chicken out, tested it, and laid out two paper plates. "Really, come get some food. I doubt you've eaten all day."

"I haven't." She poured out two lemonades and passed him one. "I just wish I knew where Lucy and Karl were." She sat down, mind whirling, as she thought of what had to be done still and how this new wrinkle would complicate the timeline. Grabbing a chicken leg, she gave it three or four bites, and then remembering something, she stood up quickly. "Excuse me, I'll be right back," she said quickly, and hurried from the room, and up the stairs to her room.

She took down her suitcase from the closet, and rummaged around in it, dipping her hands into the inner pocket. "Thank God," she muttered, finding what she was looking for, and triumphantly, she held them up for a better look. Five glass vials, similar to the ones that blood samples were collected in, snubbed tightly with rubber stoppers. They were all full; no evaporation had occurred, and she was pleased.

"What are those?" Wes asked, coming up behind her. She jumped, and he put a calming hand on her shoulder. "Sorry. Didn't mean to scare you." He peered at the vials. "What do you have there?"

"Holy Water." She handed him one for a better look. "When I was back at the hospital…" she trailed off, her voice breaking for a moment. He waited patiently, saying nothing, though he squeezed her arm supportively. "When I was in the hospital, right before I left, I stole these from the hospital chapel. I figured they would come in handy if

I was going to pursue... all of this." She gave him another one. "Here, we better divide them up." Her voice trembled, and he saw her hands were shaking at the memory.

"Beth." His voice was very even, but she couldn't look at him, was afraid to even look up. "It's all right. I'm here."

She took a deep breath. "You take two, I'll take two, and when we see Lucy we will—"

"Beth."

He took her by the shoulders, gently turning her to face him, and raised her chin with his finger. "Beth, look at me..."

"Don't," she said softly. "This isn't the time or the place. We're in real danger, and so are the people we love." Yet he was so warm, and he smelled like sun and fresh sweat and some other smell, a pleasant *Wesley* smell—all his own—that she felt herself wanting him back. She closed her eyes as he pulled her into him and put her head against his chest for a moment, feeling the beat of his heart, enjoying the very nearness of him before he kissed her.

She had never kissed anyone with a beard before, and even though she supposed his didn't really qualify as a real, full beard, she found it pleasant and ticklish. Bobby, of course, had been clean-shaven, an All-American frat boy, but Wes was hairy-faced and Bohemian and nerdishly handsome. And... he was also a good kisser, and not because she hadn't been kissed in years. He knew just when to apply pressure and when to pull back, both with his tongue and lips, and she felt herself weakening.

"We can't," she whispered, as she felt him pull her slowly towards the bed. "Wes, we can't... it's getting dark..."

He pulled back and looked at her, very seriously. "Beth, that's why we should, rather than why we shouldn't. We have time, and I want to make love to you, before the sun goes down, in case I never have the chance again." He kissed the corner of her mouth as she started to protest, and she felt tears on her face, but she wasn't sure just whose they were, and she supposed it didn't matter.

"Wes..." she began, but didn't know how to finish.

"I've never been so scared in my whole life," he confessed. "And if tonight, or the next, evil triumphs over good and Crane kills me... well then, at least I can die, knowing I had you."

She laughed shakily. "What a line," she whispered. "I bet you say that to all the girls," and he laughed quietly against her hair.

"Beth, I really—"

She kissed him fiercely, and held on to his neck tightly, running her fingers through his hair. "Shut up, Wesley," she whispered. "You're wasting time."

* * *

It was fast out of necessity and not because of lack of performance, but it was still intense and lovely, and for a few moments she forgot about Sebastian Crane, Lucy's disappearance, and frankly, much of the rest of the world. Later, she would wonder if it had been fast not only because of their time constraints, but also because of their mutual hunger and need for each other and supposed it didn't really matter anyway. She only knew Wes's sweet smell in her nostrils, the taste of him on her tongue, and his furry heaviness on top of her. When they were finished, she allowed herself a moment, lying next to him and she tearfully, desperately wished they could be like a normal couple, lying together to cuddle and kiss and talk, and whisper in the dark...

Whisper in the dark...

The dark...

Do you love... It was lovely meeting you, Miss Beth. I've no doubt we'll meet again, and soon...

She jerked awake suddenly, angry with herself that she had almost drifted off. She glanced at the clock on the bedside table... 6:10. Dammit. What had she been thinking? Thank God she hadn't dropped totally off to sleep but had merely comfortably drifted off into a light doze. But that was bad enough.

Her startled movements awoke Wes, who sat up with a frightened look on his face. He struggled to come awake, and she realized he had been even more asleep than she was. "What's going on?" he demanded, though his voice was slightly slurry. His hair was sticking up in spikes, and his eyes were wide.

"We fell asleep," she said acidly, grabbing up her clothes and throwing them on. "Idiots. We're total idiots. Two horny kids with the itch... the world is falling in around our ears, and we're up here slapping skins." She felt disgusted with herself, and with him. They were in a situation where there could be no room for mistakes, and here they were wasting time. More than that, she was allowing emotion to creep in over logic, and that was a huge mistake... emotions made you sloppy, made you make poor decisions, and she couldn't afford that.

"We shouldn't have done this," she said furiously, tying her shoes. "What was I thinking? Get up, I need to get the sheets off the bed." He blinked at her, not moving fast enough, and with an impatient grunt she pulled with all her might. The effect was not the same as a magician pulling a tablecloth off a table and leaving all the plates in place, and instead, he flipped slightly, moving with the sheets.

"Hey!" he said, surprised. For a second, he moved to cover his nakedness, and then decided she had seen everything already, and he moved his hands. "What are you doing?!"

"Pulling the sheets to put in the washing machine. Lucy has a nose like a staghound... she'll know what we've been doing here." She wadded the sheets up into a ball and made a face at him. "And put some clothes on. We don't have time for you to loll around naked, like some Greek statue."

He looked at her, amused. "Lucy has a nose like... like a what?"

"Like a staghound." Her impatience with him was growing. "Wouldn't a bloodhound be better? How many staghounds have you ever seen?" He put his arms behind his head lazily. "And I like being naked, the way God intended me to be."

She fixed him with her most furious look. "Good. Because you're probably going to meet God tonight anyway, so you can meet him anyway you like."

He swung his legs over the bed. "All right, all right, I'll get dressed. Kinda funny, though, we're getting ready to fight Crane tonight and you're worried about the sheets." He slid into his boxers and pulled his shorts on. She gave him another nasty look, and hurried from the room, her bundle of sheets in tow. In a minute, he heard the washing machine start up, and he chuckled and shook his head. Grabbing his shirt and his cap, he went to find her.

She was in the kitchen, flipping through Lucy's little phone directory, and didn't look up when he came into the room. "I'm calling Karl," she decided. "I don't know what else to do. I hate to think that something has happened to Lucy, but I'm at a loss. Dammit, I *knew* I shouldn't have split us up, I knew it."

"About what just happened... what we just did... I'm not sorry." His voice was quiet. "Not a bit." She flinched a little but didn't look up; she had been expecting him to joke some more, to get her to admit it was the best she had ever had, something. But not this. He was quietly defiant, and when she looked up at him, she saw strength and sincerity in his face. She softened.

"I'm not either," she agreed. "Maybe it was what we both needed at the time."

He raised a sardonic eyebrow. "Therapy sex?"

She shook her head, sighing. "No. Not therapy. God knows I've had enough of that to last a lifetime. Just... the finding of comfort of another person, you know? The mutual, soothing consolation of another person's arms. It made us both forget for a little while just how bad and evil this world can be." He sat down next to her, and she took his hand. "So, thank you for that."

He touched her cheek with his open palm, his eyes smiling at her. "My pleasure, Beth Van Helsing."

She actually laughed out loud, smacking playfully at his hand, when the phone rang. The moment was broken as she jumped up away from him, grabbing for the phone.

"Hello?" Relief flooded her face. "Oh, thank God, Lucy. I was getting worried."

He found the fried chicken still on the kitchen table, and tested it with his tongue. It had gone cold, and he put it back into the microwave for a minute, listening to her. "Really? You're with Louella? Are things all right?" He looked over at her and saw her frowning thoughtfully. "And Louella... yes. Uh huh. We're fine—"

"We're more than fine," he winked, and she covered the mouthpiece and shook her finger at him.

"No, that was just Wes, being silly. Even in moments of stress, he resorts to the humor of a second grader, which is why I can deal with him, I'm trained in how to handle seven-year-olds." Still, there was a hint of a smile in her words, and he chuckled and took the chicken back out of the microwave. "All right. What, there? Are you sure? Well... it's not the best... all right. I understand. We're leaving in five minutes then. We'll see you soon." She hung up and faced him.

"See? I told you she was all right." He pushed the plate over to her. "Here, have some chicken."

"She's with your grandmother," Beth said slowly. "Which is good, but we may have to change our plans... we're running out of daylight. I had wanted to fort up here tonight, but we're not gonna have time to go and pick them up and then get back here before nightfall."

"Is Gran all right?"

Beth shrugged. "I think so, but I know Lucy, and there was more in what she was *not* saying than what she was, if that makes sense. She musta not been alone when she called and couldn't talk."

Wes shrugged. "As long as we're all together tonight." He took a bite of chicken.

"Yes, but I wanted the safety of the running water on one side of the property," Beth explained. "That way we only have to watch three sides of the house. If we fort up at Louella's, we'll have to guard all four sides, and that's going to be harder."

Wes nodded. "Oh, I see. Wow, you shoulda been a General in the Army." He reached for the last wing, offered it to her wordlessly, and when she shook her head, he shrugged and bit into it. "Well, why don't we just have Lucy bring Gran back here?"

Beth shook her head in confusion. "Well, that makes sense, but Lucy says we have to come *there*, that she needs something for us to see at Louella's house."

Wes stopped chewing. "What does *that* mean?"

"I'm not sure." Thoughtfully she drummed her fingers on the table. "I can't think of anything that Louella needs us to see. Either she's trying to lure us into a trap, which I don't believe not only because I trust Lucy implicitly but also because she didn't sound in distress, or she's found something that will help us." She frowned again. "And I suppose it would have to be pretty freaking important to change up our plans like this. I wonder what it is…"

"Did she say why she's with Gran? Did she just run into her in town?" Wes asked.

"She didn't say." Her mind was working furiously. Lucy hadn't really sounded like she was in danger, but she hadn't sounded like things were perfect, either… she had sounded rushed and excited and clearly had something on her mind.

Restlessly, she checked the clock. 6:22. They were about out of time, and she took a deep breath. "All right. We can't wait any longer, we've got to get to Louella's and get ready for the night. We have less than an hour now, before the dark catches us." Fretfully she chewed on her bottom lip, looking behind her at the washing machine, which was still churning away. "I wish we had more time to put the sheets in the dryer… I'll get the Holy Water, and you put your dishes in the sink—"

He burst into laughter. "Beth, the chores can wait, can't they? I'd say we have bigger fish to fry right now than putting fabric softener in the washing machine, don't you think?" As he talked, he carried the plates to the sink, dropping the bones in the trash. He brushed his hands off, and then faced her.

"I don't want Lucy to come back in the morning and find a mess…" she stopped, and for a moment, they could only stare at each other in mutual understanding. To plan that there would be a morning at all was presumptive, and they both knew it.

"I'll help you both with the chores," Wes promised her. "In the morning." She stood up and went to him. He folded her in his arms and kissed the top of her head.

"In the morning," she repeated. "Absolutely."

They didn't move, and he kissed her again.

"Please God, let there be a morning," he whispered, and then there was nothing else to be said.

It was time to go.

Please God, let there be a morning…

CHAPTER XIX

The Draper farmhouse, much like the Barnham's, set some distance off of the road, down a long winding driveway that desperately needed some fresh gravel. Built originally in 1855, the house had been hit by lightning some twenty years later and rebuilt, and then added on and remodeled every so often that it looked like a set of child's stacked building blocks, all under one common roof.

Interestingly enough, most of the outbuildings—the barn, especially—were in much better condition. An errant tornado had ripped through Bisby in 1976, the year of the Bicentennial, and had destroyed not only much of the timber and crops on the Draper property, but also the barn, sheds and grain silo as well. Insurance had rebuilt most of the outbuildings, and after twenty years, they now needed a fresh coat of paint. Louella's husband Claude had died in 1987, and since his death, much of the farm's production had slowed considerably. She had even sold some of the larger tractor equipment, keeping only the most basic necessities, and every year was a struggle to just pay the taxes.

With a careful eye, Beth studied the ground and buildings as they drove in. She noted the poor condition of the roof on the house and the smaller barn with the low room, what Lucy would have called a milking barn. A large, sod-covered root cellar, similar to the one at the Barnhams, set into a small man-made hill, its hobbit-sized door, padlocked and painted a cheery red. A fence made of chicken wire encircled a well-tended garden, guarding its neat rows of cabbage and corn and tomatoes from hungry rabbits, while a whirligig windcatcher—designed for scaring birds—twisted and blew merrily in the evening breeze. Everything about the farm looked in order, but yet something about its stillness had raised her sensibilities, and she felt the hair on her arms whisper in dread.

"There's Lucy's truck," she pointed, and Wes nodded.

"And Gran's here too." He glanced at her. "I think everything is all right…"

"No, it's not. Something's wrong… I can *feel* it." She waited until he stopped the car, and then reached into the back seat for her book bag. In it was a collection of things: vials of Holy Water; two sharply hewn stakes, so recently made they still smelled delightfully of fresh sawdust; a small, pocket-sized version of the Bible, and a claw hammer. There was a musical jingling as she threw the bag over her shoulder and started up the porch steps. Wes was right behind her.

The screen door squeaked open, and Louella Draper met them, smiling and calm. "Wes! It's about time y'all got here, I was waiting supper on you two. Come in, come in…"

Wes bent to kiss her cheek. "You all right, Gran?"

She looked surprised. "Of course, I am, why wouldn't I be?" She patted his cheek, and then nodded to Beth. "Lucy's here… we wasn't expecting company, but it's nice to have good neighbors, all the same. We're having meatloaf and corn on the cob, hope that's all right."

"Fine," Beth said absently, quickly moving into the cool interior of the house. Her eyes darted here and there searching, and just as she was about to call out for her, Lucy came walking out of the kitchen, looking pale.

Quickly she went to Beth, grabbing her hands for support. "Crane is here, somewhere," she whispered quietly, and Beth jerked.

"How do you know?"

Lucy looked quickly at Wes and Louella, who were still talking by the front door. "I ran into someone who saw Crane with Louella…" she touched Beth on the arm urgently. "I think that she's hiding him here, somewhere on the farm."

An electric jolt went through Beth. "Louella is his daywalker?"

Lucy shrugged. "I think so, I'm not sure. But I don't think she knows what she's doing... I think she's like the way I was the other night, when he did his snake charmer act on me. Poor thing, she's—"

"We've got to tell Wes," Beth decided. She looked up as they came into the room; his eyes met hers, and she realized he looked desperately unhappy.

"What do you have to tell Wes?" Louella asked, waving them to the couch. "Here, please to sit down... y'all want something to drink? I've got some fresh peach tea, if you'd like." She settled down into her overstuffed chair and straightened a lacy antimacassar with the heel of her palm. Her smile was bland and calm. "I admit, I was surprised when Lucy came bangin' on my door right before suppertime, and then tellin' me that Wes was bringin' his new..." she paused, smiling knowingly at Beth, "...*friend* over too. Not that you're all not welcome, of course, you know that... I'm just glad I made a big enough meatloaf." She smiled sweetly at them. "Now, before I go put the corn on, why don't you tell me what this all about?"

The others looked at each other uncomfortably, and then Lucy said haltingly, "Well, Louella, we came to ask you something. And tell you something, also."

"Really? Do tell." Louella arched her eyebrows questioningly.

Lucy looked to Beth for support. There was silence in the room as Louella waited patiently, tapping her finger on the arm of her chair. Behind her, an antique clock ticked sonorously away; Beth glanced at it. 6:58. Sunset was just under an hour away. She took a breath.

"Miz Draper... I apologize for intruding on you at supper—"

"Oh, pish," Louella waved her away good naturedly. "Wes is always welcome, and anybody he brings with him." She grinned at Lucy, gesturing at her with a chuckle. "And as for my old friend here, she knows I'll always have a place at my table for her." Lucy smiled weakly and cleared her throat, urging her on.

"Well, thank you for that," Beth said quickly, moving ahead. "But listen, what we have to ask you about..." she glanced at Wes, who nodded encouragingly at her. "Do you know a man named Crane? Doctor Sebastian Crane?"

"Who?" Louella frowned thoughtfully. "Nope, who's that? The only doctor I know is ol' Doc Pierce in town... been going to him for about fifteen years now after Doc Patterson retired. Why should I know this other person?"

"Well..." Beth looked closely at Louella, looking for signs that she was under Crane's control. She thought of when Lucy had been bewitched, and she remembered the signs... the glassy stare, the halted, almost slurred speech, the feel of the person being underwater. There was none of that in Louella, and she was beginning to wonder if Lucy's information was correct.

"Doctor Crane has been around for a while," she said slowly, which was a good start. She looked over at Wes, who nodded encouragingly. "We think he might be responsible for some of the terrible things that have happened to Lucy's family over the years."

Louella frowned. "Why, what does that mean?"

Lucy leaned forward in her chair. "Louella, you know all the tragedies that have fallen to my menfolk over the years. Well, this Crane fella that Beth just spoke of... we think he's responsible. And we think he's hiding out here, on your farm somewhere."

Louella knitted her brows together worriedly. "What? Then just call the police, if you think somebody's been hurting your people, it's as simple as that. And hiding here? Lordy, this is like *America's Most Wanted*... I watch that show all the time, but I never see nobody on there in real life." She reached for the phone sitting on the end table.

"Wait, before you call," Beth said quickly. "Let me explain." Louella paused, looking at her, and Beth went on quickly, "This man we think is hiding on your property—this Doctor Crane—he's not a normal man."

Louella blinked a few times, waiting.

Suddenly Lucy burst out, "Louella, he's a damn vampire. And don't look at me like that, I'm as serious as I can be. He's the one that killed Bobby, and my Bobby's dad, and my David, and about every other Barnham male for a hundred and fifty years. And he wants to kill your grandson here, too."

Louella leaned forward in her chair. "What did you say? A vampire? There ain't no such things as vampires, you know that. Oh, Lucy, honey... you've been drinking again..." she looked embarrassed, and Beth suddenly knew that Lucy's alcoholism had been a poorly kept and obviously unmentioned secret between them for many years.

Lucy's face began to turn purple, and quickly Wes took his grandmother's hand. "Gran, no, listen. It's true. I saw it last night with my own two eyes. This Crane... he really is a vampire, and he threatened me." There was silence in the room as Louella looked from one of them to another, mouth working like a fish caught on a line. Finally, she said, "This ain't funny. Not at all. If this is some kind of a joke, well, let me tell you, I'm not finding it humorous, not one bit."

"It ain't a joke, Louella, and I'm not drunk," Lucy snapped. "Now listen... on Market Day, did a tall, dark-haired man help you carry your things to your car?"

Louella wrinkled her face. "No. Of course not. No one helped me at all."

Lucy looked at her closely, thinking of Trevor's words.

He walked right up to her, and she acted like she knew him... they talked, and she laughed and even touched him on the cheek

She glanced at Beth, and with the tiniest of movements, shook her head. There was silence in the room as Beth tried to decide which way to proceed next. Before she could say anything, Louella suddenly said, "Lucy Barnham, I've known you for years. This is pure craziness, and I won't have it in my house. And Wes..." she looked significantly at Beth. "I'm not sure I approve of your new friend here. If she's gotten you drunk and told you a bunch of fairy tales, I'm gonna have to ask her to leave, and I'm gonna be upset with you. Vampires! What in the hell has come over you?"

"Gran..." Wes tried to smile reassuringly. "I know this is hard to take in, but we really don't have a lot of time here. It's going to be dark soon, and we have to... well, we have to take care of something bad, before it gets worse."

Louella looked like she had just taken a sniff of something nasty as she surveyed them all with distaste. "You all have been watching too many movies," she declared flatly. "This is crazy. Wes, I'd always pegged you for being much smarter than this." Her eyes flickered to Beth, and then to Lucy. "And Lucy Barnham, I don't know what in the hell is wrong with you, or what you've been drinking, but you've obviously given it to these young people and now, look what you've done."

With an open mouth, Lucy looked at her incredulously, feeling her temper rise and letting loose of all attempts at diplomacy. "Now you listen here—"

"Shut up!" Abruptly, Beth stood up, reaching for her backpack; the two old women immediately stopped talking, momentarily stunned into silence, and Beth disgustingly shook her head. She had had enough of talking and had been watching the shadows growing in the living room with unease and impatience. As far as she was concerned, the matter at hand was not convincing Louella of Crane's existence, but to find him... they could show her his staked and beheaded body on her porch later if she insisted on such proof, but for now they had to keep moving. "We don't have time to talk anymore," she said urgently. "Crane is here... I can *feel* him, he's so close. But if we sit around here much longer, it'll be night, and it will be too late. I'm going to find him before that happens." Lucy nodded emphatically.

Wes firmed his jaw determinedly, getting to his feet. "All right... where do we start?"

She shrugged. "This is your farm, you know it better than anyone else. But think of what Crane needs... privacy, darkness and quiet. Where can he find that around here?"

"Not the barns," he said slowly. "Even in the loft, it wouldn't be dark... quiet and private maybe, but not dark."

"Wesley!" Louella's voice was starting to border on shrill. "Enough of this foolishness! What are you talking about? Sit down now, I mean it!"

He paused, looking at her sorrowfully. "Gran, we've got to do this, with or without your help... *with* would be better, but we've got to do this either way." He bent down to kiss her, and was dismayed that she turned her face away from him. Hardening his features into a mask of resolve, he turned back to Beth. "All right then. Let's go." They started at the front door.

"I'll stay here and try and talk some sense into her," Lucy called after them as she watched them rush outside. She felt her heart beating very fast, and she reached for her glass of tea. Across the couch from her, Louella was sitting with her arms folded, glaring at her, and Lucy decided to try and smile.

"All right, Louella," she began. "I've got a story for you, so you better settle in."

* * *

Beth and Wes stood on the front porch, leaning against the railing while she scanned the property. "All right, where do we start?"

"I don't know," he admitted. He looked toward the barn, seeing three or four pigeons come circling in, and knew that Crane could not be hiding there. He chewed on his lip thinking, and then turned to Beth. "Let's try the garage first. Gran's got some old cars in there she hardly uses anymore. It's the most obvious place… he could be curled up in a trunk of one of them, even."

They ran around the corner of the house, past Louella's swaying pink and red hollyhocks, and he threw up the segmented garage door. Though there was still light enough for them to see inside, he still flipped a switch, and fluorescent lights overhead buzzed to life. "All the better to see you with, my dear," he muttered, and Beth nearly cackled aloud with hysterical laughter.

"Wait," she cautioned, and peered around him cautiously. At the threshold, she reached into her backpack and took out a stake, and then handed him one as well. Making sure they each had a vial of Holy Water as well, she nodded to him, looking at the cars. There was Louella's minivan used for hauling her wares when she went to Market Day, but also two old junkers: an old yellow Plymouth Duster and an even older green Chrysler. He took a ring of keys off of the peg by the door and showed them to her, and then pointed to the cars with a question in his eyes. *Which one first?*

She pointed to the Duster, and he nodded. Walking quietly, they each took a side of the trunk, while he searched for the correct key.

Palming the others so they wouldn't jangle, he took a deep breath, inserted the key, and looked at her plaintively. She looked very pale in the fluorescent light. "God help us," he whispered, and tightened the grip on his stake. Quickly, he popped the trunk.

It was empty.

Beth made a gusty sigh and looked up at Wes, whose face was a mixture of disappointment and relief. "Nobody home," she whispered, and then moved to the other car. He nodded, quickly finding the correct key, and they took their positions again, stakes raised like batons. With a screaming, rusty creak, the Chrysler's trunk slowly opened… revealing nothing.

"Maybe Crane likes foreign cars," Wes muttered, and Beth shot him a dark look.

"You're hilarious, aren't you?"

He gave a weak smile. "Sorry. Moments of stress cause my sense of humor to work overdrive, I guess."

"Let's move on," she said grimly, slamming the trunk with finality. "Now where?"

They stepped out onto the garage apron; the sun was a red ball in the west, moving quickly and inexorably toward the horizon, and despite the heat of the evening, she felt a chill. Night birds were beginning their final songs of the day as they roosted in the trees, and anxiously she looked around her. "Tool shed?"

"As good as any," he muttered, and led her around the house. The grass was higher here, needing to be mowed, and grasshoppers and other insects moved in their wake; tall grass and foxtails whispered and tickled their legs as they jogged. The toolshed was a cinder block structure, big enough to back a lawn mower into; its metal door was padlocked with a sturdy combination lock. He spun the dial, finding the numbers needed, and then yanked on it hard, unclicking it. It fell with a metallic jangle to the ground. "Ready?"

She nodded. "Do it."

He swung the door open and she peered inside. The building was hot and stifling, and smelled of dry grass and gasoline. A few shovels and rakes were stacked in the corner, and a big red gas can sat between the riding mower and the push mower; a canvas grass catcher hung on the opposite wall in the middle of old license plates, and she shook her head in anger and frustration. But of Crane... nothing. She pounded the doorjamb angrily with her fist.

"Nothing here either. Dammit, where is he?!" Panic was beginning to trickle into her words, and she swallowed hard.

He bent to pick up the lock. "Don't worry..." His voice trailed off, as his eyes caught sight of the root cellar with its red hobbit door...

He straightened up quickly.

And I could smell his cologne, and beneath that, another smell, a horrible, nasty earthy smell, like wet dirt...

Like wet dirt...

The root cellar.

"Beth," he whispered, and pointed shakily to the root cellar. She heard the catch in his voice and followed his gaze. "Look..."

She felt her heart skip a beat. "Oh... Could it be that obvious? It's right next to the house. Louella would see him coming and going, or at the very least, find him during the day." A sudden realization dawned on her. "Unless..."

He jerked, not liking the terrible look in her eyes. "Unless what?" She looked away, and he touched her on the arm, turning her to him. "Unless what? Tell me!"

She swallowed and looked him in the eye. "Unless she was helping him." Although they had already established that Louella had been helping Crane, they had done it under the assumption that it was against her will, that he had exercised his terrible control over her, and she had no idea what she was doing. But what if...

What if Louella knew *exactly* what she was doing? What if she hadn't been put under his spell, but had been hiding him and helping him for some unknown reason. Another thought occurred to her, and she suddenly felt sick. "That's why she didn't want us to search the property, and that's why she lied about seeing Crane in the parking lot the other night. She's been helping him all along, Wes, she's his daywalker."

He could only stare at her in horror as the truth settled over him, as certain as the sun setting over the trees in the west.

XX
CHAPTER

The two ladies faced each other across the polished coffee table, not sure what to say. Louella was so angry her jaw trembled, and Lucy was in a similar state. The only sound in the room was the sonorous ticking of the clock, marking away the uncomfortable minutes until Louella put her hands on her knees and stood up. "Well," she said softly. "If my grandson and your…" she paused, fumbling for the correct word, "…*friend*, are gonna insist on rushin' around the farm, chasing fairy tales and ghosts, they're gonna be hungry when they come back in. I best get supper on the table." She cocked her head at Lucy. "You can help, if you'd like."

"Certainly." Lucy stood up, observing Louella thoughtfully. It wasn't as if her friend was waving the white flag in surrender, but neither did she look like she wanted to debate the subject either. She followed her into the kitchen.

"You can put out the plates and silverware, while I check on the meatloaf," Louella directed, grabbing an oven mitt and drifting towards the oven. Lucy nodded, and went to the cabinet, taking down plates; she and Louella had been in each other's kitchens for so many years that each of them knew where things were kept. On any other day, it was a comfortable feeling; today, however, she took no solace in it at all.

She cleared her throat, deciding she should say something. "You know, Louella, I know you think I've been drinking, but I'm sober as a judge… and I'm telling the truth."

Louella didn't seem to respond as she took a fork and broke a tiny piece of meatloaf off. She blew on it to cool it and then tasted it, nodding to herself. "Sometimes, I don't get enough catsup in there," she confided. "But I think I got it just right this time. That's pretty good."

"Louella!" Lucy looked at her in exasperation, counting out forks. "Did you hear what I just said to you?"

"Sure. You said you ain't drunk." She folded a piece of foil back over the meatloaf and put it back into the oven to keep warm. "All right, you're not drunk."

Lucy tapped a fork against a plate. "And did you hear what else I said?"

"Sure." She turned around and stared at Lucy, her eyes hard and angry in the dim light. "I heard *exactly* what you said, you said there was a vampire hiding here on my farm."

Lucy frowned, catching the sudden edge to her voice. "So, you believe me?"

Unexpectedly, Louella threw back her head and laughed merrily. "Of course, I believe you, silly Lucy. And you're right... he's here."

Lucy felt her world tilt. "What did you just say?"

"What, did I suddenly stutter?" Her face had drawn up into a hateful mask, witch-like and furious as she advanced around the table towards Lucy, who looked unaccountably startled. "Lucy. Stupid, stupid Lucy. Of course, I know Doctor Crane is on my property... I've been hiding him."

Lucy could only blink at her, speechless for one of the first times in her life.

Louella smiled tenderly. "He came to me months ago, when word came that your whore friend Beth might be getting released from the loony bin. He knew she would come here to Bisby, and he needed my help to get ready for her arrival..." she fluttered her hands in the air. "Oh, I was against it at first, but that's understandable. But the good doctor can be most persuasive, most charming when he needs to be, and it wasn't long before I decided to help him."

Keeping her eyes locked on Lucy, she pulled down the collar of her shirt, and there, low on her collarbone, was an angry, red bite mark.

The edges of the wound were ragged and torn, suggesting it was not fresh, but instead a wound that was not allowed to heal, as if it had been injured and then re-injured continually.

Lucy couldn't believe her ears. "What did you do?" She whispered in horror. "Louella, do you mean you let him bite you…"

Louella's eyes were suddenly misty. "He *loved* me," she corrected. She settled into a chair, folding her hands demurely. "When he first came to me, I thought it was a dream. And for a while, I was afraid because I kept having the same dreams over and over, every single night. But he would talk to me and reassure me, and would take me out into the night with him, to show me his world, and I learned not to be afraid of him." She smiled at the memory. "After a while, I began to look forward to his visits, and on the nights when he *didn't* come, I would cry and weep and wait in the dark for him, all the while hoping he was all right, and hoping he would come to me."

Lucy gulped and stared at her friend, stared at the woman she had known for so many years, but it was as if she was looking at a stranger. "Louella—"

"Oh hush, it doesn't matter what you say." Louella swiped at her eyes with the back of her hand and gave a shaky little laugh. "Doctor Crane is a wonderful man, Lucy. You just don't know him—don't know his boundless capacity for love the way I do."

"He's not a man, not anymore," Lucy corrected, her voice heated. "He's a vampire, and he's been killing my family for generations. What is wrong with you?!" She felt truly sick to her stomach.

"Nothing is wrong with me, nothing at all," Louella suddenly hissed, jumping up from her seat like she had springs in her legs. "Doctor Crane told me it would be this way with you, and he was right. He said you would be difficult and jealous and wouldn't understand—"

"The only thing I understand is that your new friend is a damn vampire," Lucy exploded. "He killed my husband and he killed my son and he killed my grandson… and quite frankly, he's after *your* grandson, as well."

"Doctor Crane wouldn't hurt Wesley," Louella said quickly, but she sounded less confident now. "He's promised me that…"

"Oh, Louella," Lucy said sadly. "He's a liar, don't you know that? He would kill Wes in a second and wouldn't think twice about it. Now please, please tell me where he is, and I'll go tell Beth—"

"No!" Louella's voice was like an icepick. "Absolutely not! What, hurt him? You want to hurt Doctor Crane, you and that damn slutty girl you dragged here? I won't allow it, no, not at all!" She faced Lucy, her eyes wide with anger and determination. "And the reason I can't allow it is that there is more to the story here, more than you know."

Lucy glanced worriedly at the clock. There was less than twenty minutes of daylight left, and she was stuck inside with this loon, listening to her ramble and prattle on about how wonderful Sebastian Crane was. She hoped that Wes and Beth had found his nest right now and were driving a stake through his heart... and once that was taken care of, she would personally whip Louella Draper's ass for her, for helping that evil bastard. "More to the story?"

Louella grinned at her, her face drawn up like a twisted jack-o-lantern. "Oh yes, indeed, Lucy old friend. You see, after Doctor Crane explained how I could best be of service to him, I realized that maybe—just maybe, helping him could benefit me as well." She glanced at Lucy, and saw a look of confusion on her face. She smirked. "How, you ask? Well, let me tell you, Lucy old friend, that there are many roads to revenge."

Lucy shook her head. "Louella, I'm sure I don't know what in the hell you're talking about. You've flipped your lid. Revenge? Revenge for what?"

Louella narrowed her eyes dangerously. "You really have no idea, do you?"

Lucy spread her hands wide. "No. We've always been friends, as far as I'm concerned."

Louella began to pace the floor, gathering her thoughts, while Lucy watched her warily. "Growing up, we had always heard the spook stories about the Barnham family," she began. "We never really knew exactly what to believe, and all of the grownups in our lives, parents and teachers and others, weren't talking. Because of that, I was always wary of meeting anybody from that family until I was fourteen, the first day of high school. Remember that day? All the little districts had consolidated into the high school, and that was the first day we all met... you, and me, and David Barnham."

"I remember," Lucy said softly, looking at the old woman in front of her, but seeing her as a young girl, wearing a hand-me-down dress two sizes too big for her, and shoes with holes in them.

"Everyone made fun of us... the kids from out of town, while you Bisby kids all knew each other and hung together and shut us out. Except for David." Her voice hitched a little. "Not him. He was kind to me, and decent. Sometimes he shared his lunch with me on the days I didn't have any, and he would always loan me a pencil or paper out of his composition book because he knew my folks couldn't afford such things. He was good and nice to me, and even though I had heard the stories about the Barnham men, it didn't matter, because I loved him. I loved him."

Lucy's hand went to her mouth in surprise and compassion for her. "Oh, Louella..."

Louella's face was a snarl. "No, don't pity me, don't you *dare*. Not one bit. I don't want your damn pity; I won't have it." She paused to look outside the window, at the setting sun. "It'll be dark soon," she remarked lightly, and Lucy could almost hear the joy in her voice. "And the good doctor will be up soon... good times then, eh?"

All of her empathy immediately dried up and blew away. "Tell me where he is before that happens!" She begged, but Louella didn't seem to hear.

"And so, I loved David, in spite of all those ghost stories, and I knew I could make a good wife for him. What other prospects did I have? Stupid, shy ol' Karl Kopinski? Ha, definitely not. And so, I did my best to get David to notice me; but he never did, not really. Not in the way I wanted him to, at least. No, he only had eyes for *you*, goody-good Lucy Marshall, with the home perms and the store-bought dresses and the good shoes, with the Cuban heel. And what did that leave me? Not much, not much at all." She shrugged and flashed Lucy a dangerous look. "Well, you know the rest. The man I loved, David Barnham, asked *you* to marry him after graduation, and the two of you skipped off to his family farm to start your family and your lives."

"But you had Claude Draper!" Lucy protested. "And you coulda had Karl Kopinski! You had *two* suitors, Louella—"

"Oh, I didn't want Claude Draper, I *settled* for him," Louella scoffed. "I never loved him, not really. But he had a farm, and nobody else wanted him, and he got me out of my father's house. So, I settled. But it was David I wanted… and you took him from me."

"Then why didn't you go with Karl, if you didn't love Claude?"

Louella made a disgusted face. "I didn't want him either, and he was worse than Claude. He has about as much backbone as a bag of flour… what would I want with a man like that? No, it was David I always loved: David, who was kind and good to me, and who never laughed at me." Her voice hardened. "And you took him from me, didn't you Lucy?"

Lucy looked at her, imagining the years of dissatisfaction and resentment and felt a tired pain deep within her. "I didn't take him from you, Louella, because he was never yours to begin with!"

Louella's face twisted as she sought the words to say. Her face colored nearly purple with rage, and she took several deep, calming breaths. She leaned forward to put her narrow face in Lucy's and hissed, "If David had been mine, I could have protected him better… he would still be alive. I could have persuaded Doctor Crane to spare him—"

"Oh, horse shit." Lucy glared back at her. "I'm sorry you're so bitter, Louella, and sorry you've led such a bitter life… I can't imagine all the years you've sat around being unhappy, but that's not my fault! David Barnham loved who he loved, and that wasn't you. And if you think you could have convinced that… that *creature* you're hiding, to do anything, you're mistaken! He's using you to get to Beth, and you're too stupid to even know it. He'll kill all of us before this night is over, including you, and won't think a thing about it, you stupid, stupid bitch—"

With a shriek, Louella launched herself across the table, claws outstretched like a furious cat. Lucy had almost been waiting for this and was able to meet the attack, her own arms up and ready to block the other woman. With a grunt, they locked arms about each other and fell back on the table, kicking and screeching. Unmindful of arthritic hips and rheumatism, they fell with a heavy thud to the floor, twisting like a tornado.

Louella was a dirty fighter, and with forty plus years of anger and resentment built up inside her, she had no compunction about hair pulling, scratching and eye gouging. Lucy had really never been in a fight her whole life, so her reactions and responses were purely and instinctively defensive as she smacked and batted away at Louella. She managed to keep from being hurt simply by her own reflexes and quickness and nearly had her pinned down, but Louella spit in her face and scuttled out from underneath her like a wriggling puppy. Breathing heavily, she scrambled to her feet, eyes flashing wildly.

"You bitch," she panted, and reached for the block of carving knives on the counter, "I'll cut you, get the blood flowing so the good Doctor doesn't have to work so hard—"

In desperation, Lucy picked a plate off the table and threw it at her, more of a blind toss than an accurate pitch, but she hit a lucky bullseye and the plate smashed into the side of Louella's head with a healthy bonk. She fell back against the counter, dazed but not beaten, and reached for the knives again.

"Stop it! For God's sakes, Louella, stop it!" Lucy pulled herself up to the chair and began pulling things off of the table, tossing it in the direction of Louella: silverware, glasses, plates and corn tubs. Louella screamed under the assault and tried to duck the objects, but they just kept coming, and she howled in frustration and anger as she began to realize Lucy was getting the upper hand.

"You're breaking my plates!" she shrieked, though she had no compunction about breaking them herself, as she picked them off the counter and threw them back. "You bitch, you're tearing up my kitchen!"

It zipped through Lucy's furious brain that actually, Louella was doing a pretty good job of this all by herself, not to mention trying to kill her in the process—but she didn't stop to reply. Louella's antique salt and pepper shakers, inherited from her mother as a wedding present, flew through the air like ceramic missiles. They exploded against a cabinet, sending spices everywhere. Louella began to sneeze violently, which might have been funny, except that Lucy saw she had finally gotten ahold of the knife block and had pulled out a rather large one. Its silver blade flashed in the dim light as she wielded it elatedly.

"All right, I'm tired of this!" She croaked, her voice rising in triumph. "I'm going to stick you and bleed you almost white, and then when the doctor rises, he will finish you off." She pulled a second knife from the block, and then like a gladiator, faced Lucy, holding a knife in each hand. She settled into a crouch, moving the knives in small, lethal circles while she looked for an opening. "So sorry, old friend—"

What happened then was pure luck, though not for her. She advanced forward, waving the knives in the air menacingly, when her foot slipped on a puddle of peach tea. Her eyes widened in horror and disbelief as she pin-wheeled her arms for balance, overextending herself. With a heavy crash, she fell backwards and hit hard; Lucy could actually hear the wooden *thwack* of bones breaking on the linoleum… probably a hip, possibly her elbow, maybe even more. The knives skittered across the floor, and quickly she tracked them with her eyes to make sure they were out of range of Louella's grasping hands. Slowly, grabbing the back of a chair for support, she pulled herself to her feet and stood over Louella.

"Lucy," Louella gasped. "I… I can't move my leg… I think it's broken." Pitifully, she began to cry; she held her head up, and gray hair hung in her face. "Can you help me, please?"

Coldly, Lucy regarded her on the floor, remembering her words.

Well, let me tell you, Lucy old friend, that there are many roads to revenge…

"Lucy, please…" Louella's voice was thin with pain. "I'm sorry for what I did and said… Please, help me. I take it all back, every bit of it…"

"I don't think so," she said softly, and Louella moaned softly; in pain or shameful regret, she couldn't tell.

I'm going to stick you and bleed you almost white, and then when the good Doctor rises, he will finish you off…

Careful to step around her, she headed for the back door while Louella began to splutter helplessly, and at the door, she paused and looked back. "You just lie there for a while," she advised. "I would send

Crane in to finish you off, which is the same fate you had planned for me, but it won't come to that, because I'm going to go out there and help them find him... find him and kill him."

"Lucy—"

"You know," she said thoughtfully. "You never were David's type anyway. He never went for the white trash type, and that's exactly what you are."

The back door slamming shut cut off Louella's pitiful cries, and anxiously she scanned the darkening yard looking for Beth and Wes.

The sun was nearly gone.

* * *

Louella Draper's root cellar was used for storing cabbages and pumpkins, beets and other rooted vegetables—or at least that was what its purpose had originally been. While she still stored the occasional foodstuff there, if the basement or pantry was full, Louella had mostly designated the root cellar for simple storage; Christmas decorations and lights in plastic tubs, broken furniture and old toys, clothes in plastic bags waiting to be donated to the local church for a rummage sale. It was, Wes realized as he ran, the perfect jumble of junk and rat's nest... and a perfect hiding spot.

They reached the red hobbit door at the same time, and Wes grabbed the combination lock, spinning the dial frantically. He knew the first two numbers, but the third one balked him, and when he pulled the lock down to open it, it stubbornly refused to move.

"Dammit!" he cried, trying it again. "Come on now... thirty-three... seventeen... five. Open!"

Nothing.

At his elbow, Beth was nearly frantic as she watched the last minutes of sunlight tick away. "What's the problem?!"

"I don't remember the combination," he muttered, sweat dripping from his nose. "Every shed and gate on this place has a different combination..." He closed his eyes in concentration, trying to sequence the numbers correctly.

"Hurry!" she gasped, handing him the hammer. "Here, if you can't get it, smash it, we're out of time…"

"Thirty-three, seventeen, *twenty-five*!" he suddenly yelled, flushed with triumph, and jerked the lock down. It obediently popped open with a metallic click, and he tossed it into the grass behind him. He flipped open the latch on the door, and then threw it open.

The smell hit them first, a musty, earthy smell. A dead smell, speaking of things secret and nasty. She flinched.

"This is it," Beth whispered. "He's in there…"

She reached into her backpack and pulled out her flashlight, clicking it on. Cautiously she took a step into the root cellar, playing the beam on what she found there. A cricket chirped somewhere inside, and she could hear Wes's heavy, nervous breathing behind her. She could feel her pulse, hammering in her ears.

Do you love, Beth?

Startled, she nearly dropped the flashlight. Where had that come from? She whirled around, shining the light on the row of shelves on the opposite wall, but saw nothing. Had it been only in her head? Possibly, she wasn't sure. The air was fairly crackling with magic and evil, and she took a deep gulp of air to calm herself.

"Where is he?" She muttered, desperation settling in. If they were wrong and he wasn't here, then it was likely the second they stepped back outside, he would be on them. No, he *had* to be here… they were out of time, out of options, out of daylight. She moved the flashlight back and forth, searching for something—*anything*—that would reveal him to her. The crucifix around her neck twisted in the yellow light of the flashlight, sparkling like the talisman it was, and for a brief moment, she felt better because of its presence.

Oh, Beth, do you think that silly thing can stop me? That thing's just a symbol, a token of an ancient, dried up faith… You've been seeing too many old movies, haven't you?

The terrible whispering voice again: mocking her, listening to her. She tried to shut it out as she peered behind a stack of boxes, coming up with nothing. She had been right about one thing; he certainly wasn't in any coffin because there simply wasn't room for one here. She took a step forward, glancing around her... the root cellar wasn't that big, and while it was possible he had burrowed into the walls, she found that unlikely... Suddenly she felt Wes stop. A small, whimpering sound escaped from his lips.

"Beth," His voice was soft, with an edge to it that bordered on panic. "Don't move..."

She froze, feeling his fingers dig into her arm. "What..."

"Beth, look above us... oh dear God, look up."

Quicker than Mercury, she jerked her head up, shining the light on the dirt ceiling.

Sebastian Crane's pale, dead face grinned down at her. Defying gravity and any ordinary forces of nature, he lay flat against the ceiling, arms crossed over his chest, instinctively protecting himself as he slept. He was still and unmoving—apparently still asleep—but the sun was down, night was settling in, and his time was nearly at hand.

"Hold the light," she whispered to Wes. She took out one of her vials of holy water and sprinkled it over the stake.

How best to do this? The angle was difficult... she had envisioned pounding a stake downward into his body, much like driving a tent stake into the ground. But this was different, this was more like the swing of a tennis racket...

"Hurry," he whispered, nearly dancing in his terror. "I don't think we have any more time—"

Crane opened his eyes.

With one swing of his arm, he swept his fist across Wesley Draper, sending him crashing into the shelves on the opposite wall. The stake flew out of his hands, buried in the rubbish and debris, as the shelves came crashing down upon him. Beth waited for Wes to stagger to his feet, to push boxes and junk and old books off of himself and stand up... but he didn't move. She saw his bare legs sticking out from under the pile of junk and felt her heart fall. Crane laughed triumphantly, the sound filling the small room like a tenor in the devil's opera, and then turned his gaze upon Beth.

"Well, well, my dear Beth... does our good friend Louella know what you're about, prowling through her root cellar like any common—"

She didn't let him finish. With a scream that surprised him and echoed dully off of the earthen walls, she brought the stake up in a flash. The movement was much like an underhanded softball pitch: deadly fast and accurate, but at the last second, he saw it coming and moved sideways slightly.

And the stake, aimed for his heart, missed its target and instead embedded itself into his stomach.

"You vile bitch!" he roared, clutching at the stake with both hands. His eyes rolled in his head as he twisted. "What have you done, *what have you done...*"

Black blood, cold and stinking, rained down upon her in a torrent as he screamed and twisted. He lost his grasp on the ceiling and fell crashing to the ground, writhing like a wounded bird. She knew her strike hadn't been deadly, but she *had* wounded him, and that was a start. Brushing bloody strings of hair out of her eyes, she frantically scanned the ground, looking for the stake Wes had dropped, but it was nowhere to be found, and desperately she dug into the pocket of her jeans and came up with the second vial of Holy Water. Uncapping it with her teeth, she splashed it across Crane's chest while he flailed. He screamed again—the scream of the damned—and scrambled to get away from her.

All of her life, she had been compassionate toward wounded things: people and animals both, but as she watched him kick in the dirt on the root cellar floor, she felt nothing but hatred for him. She knew she had to finish him off, not as an act of kindness as one would do to an injured animal, but out of revenge and retribution for every evil thing he had ever done. Blood poured from his wound, spraying across the room like a fountain as she kicked through Louella Draper's collection of junk, looking for Wes's stake. Crane gibbered and cursed, and she moved to get out of the way of his grasping hands...

And then she realized he wasn't coming for her at all but was clawing his way towards the door. He was so intent, so determined to get outside that she instantly knew what his intentions were...

He was trying to get outside: into the darkness, and the healing, rejuvenating safety of his Mother Night. He was wounded, perhaps wounded more severely than he ever had been in his whole existence as a vampire, but she was sure that if he were to make it outside, the night would somehow restore him.

"No," she whispered, but it was late, too late.

Straining like a man carrying a heavy load, his fingers reached the doorframe, and he pulled himself up. The stake was still sticking out of his abdomen, and it waggled obscenely in his struggles, like a lewd, wooden phallus. He turned his head to grin mockingly at her as he staggered: blood poured from his mouth, and his eyes were wild and feral, but he was standing again, dear God, no, he was back on his feet, stumbling out into the night with arms outspread, like a man seeking his first Baptism.

A wink of something caught her eye, and there at her feet was one of Wes's Holy Water vials. She bent to pick it up, wishing it was his stake but grateful for any little bit of luck tossed her way. She hesitated, knowing she should check on Wes to see if he was alive, but she heard Crane tearing through the grass, and she made a decision and followed him outside. After being inside the stuffy root cellar with its stink of ancient vegetables and dead blood, the cool night air felt wonderfully fresh on her face, but she knew that she didn't have the time to pause and enjoy it.

"Leave it alone, Bethie," he called over his shoulder, moving toward the barn. "Don't follow me... hear me now, girl. Leave well enough alone, you've done enough damage tonight. Go tend to the Draper boy... he might live, I think, if you take care of him now..." His voice was ragged and hard in the dark, but she thought she detected something else there, and that was fear.

"I'm coming for you, Doctor!" She shouted fiercely, watching him stumble like a drunken man towards the barn. "Don't even try to hide, you know this is it..."

Fireflies flickered in the grass as she hurried after him. Wounded or not, he was still incredibly fast, and within seconds he had reached the barn. With tremendous strength, he slid open the doors, gave her a final, hateful look, and then disappeared inside.

What now? Follow him and finish him off? He was wounded, severely wounded, but the night was restoring him, and that worried her. Also, she had no stake, no weapons save for a single vial of Holy Water and the crucifix around her neck. To go into the barn, to follow him inside would be madness… better yet to go see if Wes was alive. And if he was, return to the house, hide throughout the night with the old ladies, and start over in the morning…

But that wasn't her way, and with a quick prayer, she followed him into the barn.

CHAPTER XXI

The barn doors shrieked with protest in the still night as Beth Franklin pushed them open. The wonderful smell of sweet hay and old timber struck her nostrils as she paused in the doorway, peering inside, looking for movement. It was like a dark, monstrous cave inside, as still and solemn as a tomb. She could hear pigeons cooing softly in the loft above her, but they didn't sound like they were in distress or being disturbed, so she doubted Crane had gotten that far yet. No, he was somewhere close, hiding...

Watching her from some concealed spot. Bleeding and dangerous and full of hate...

But maybe... just maybe... he was *afraid* too, and that was good.

With horror, she realized she had exited the root cellar without finding the second stake or bringing the hammer. She fumbled inside her shirt and found her crucifix; it was small and hung from a chain, and she gripped it tightly; she patted her pocket and felt the last vial of Holy Water, so she wasn't totally unarmed, but she still felt like she was going to battle a raging forest fire with only a squirt gun. At least she had brought her flashlight, and she shone its yellow beam out in front of her, moving it quickly.

Remembering his trick of dangling from the ceiling, she moved the light quickly upwards, playing it back and forth across the wooden beams and rafter. There was a rustle of birds moving, and a few white feathers drifted downward like gently falling snow. But nothing else.

"Doctor Crane," she called, hoping her voice sounded brave. She took another step inside, looking in the shadows. "Where are you? I know you're here, I saw you run in... there's nowhere else to run. Come out."

Around her, the dark was silent, listening to her.

"You know," she mused, "You're not much better than an addict. Except your drug isn't heroin, or cocaine, or meth... and you're really not even satisfied with just blood, are you? No, you got a taste for Barnham blood all those years ago with poor Charlie, and you got hooked, just like some cheap crack whore junkie." As she talked, she moved silently from stall to stall, cautiously peeking in each one, holding the tiny crucifix in front of her like a sword.

"But the worst mistake you ever made, Doctor, was when you went after Bobby and me. You took my life and my sanity and my everything away from me that night, and now it's time for a little payback. Come on out, you leech, you sonofabitch..." She trailed off, suddenly remembering something, and a wellspring of hope bubbled up in her chest.

"Hey Doctor, you like rhymes? I recited my poem a few nights ago for you, remember? Didn't like it much, did you?" She dared a glance behind her, and then peered behind a pyramid of hay bales... nothing. "Well, how about I do it for you again...

"...hominēs, sīcut lepores, venantur;
latens in tenebrīs quasi malae umbrae;
aperientes venas sīcut utrēs vīnī.
Daemones violentiae pleni sunt;
numquam misericordiam faciēns.
Invoca eōs bannum!
Redde incunctanter illōs ad inferos!"

Shockingly, laughter filled the barn, a terrible amused chuckle, and she froze. It certainly wasn't the reaction she had been expecting...

previously, he had been seemingly horrified by it, and it had elicited a powerful reaction from hearing it, but now incredibly, he seemed amused by it. She felt a huge wave of unease settle over her.

"Oh, Bethie, Bethie," he said mournfully, and the voice seemed to come from all around her. She couldn't pinpoint its origin, and she whirled her head around frantically looking for him. Above her, the pigeons stirred restlessly, and she shone the flashlight up among them again out of desperation.

"As good as you are, you don't know everything…" the voice was mocking, and she twitched. "The poem you're so gallantly reciting is an ancient one, but it's got a couple of conditions that you don't know about…"

She had to buy time as she looked for him. Quietly, she kept moving about, searching for him. "Conditions? What conditions are those, doctor?"

He chuckled. "First of all, you don't have a complete poem there… it's like a recipe without half of the ingredients… you might have a cake at the end, but it ain't gonna be all that good without the sugar, if you follow my meaning." There was a scuffling sound as he moved, and she cocked her head, trying to determine its origin.

"And also, Bethie, the poem only works *one* time: its magic, you see, is a one-shot deal. And you, my dear, have already shot your wad." He laughed, amused at his own wit, and on silent feet she glided across the floor and quickly checked behind an old wagon seat. "After that, it's just a bunch of words, nothing more. The spell is broken, girl, you're too late, too late."

Still stalling, she crossed the floor to a pile of boxes, looking behind them, and then straightening up quickly. "Being late has always been the story of my life, Doctor—"

Suddenly, there was a yowl of protest and a scream as a startled cat jumped off of an old hay wagon, disappearing into the inky blackness. Instantly she was there, holding her crucifix in front of her, waving it like a baseball bat just in time to see Crane scuttling backwards in the darkness. Hate filled his eyes as he realized she had discovered him, and with a backhand toss, she threw her vial of Holy Water at him.

He shrieked like a fire bell and smacked at her ineffectually with his hand. Triumphantly, she stood over him. "Checkmate, Doctor."

Crane faced her, panting. A ribbon of blood was splashed across his face, and his lips were drawn back in a snarl. "You think that this is a checkmate," he hissed; she looked at him warily and hit him with another splash of Holy Water. He screamed.

"It's not only checkmate, it's lights out," she said, and then suddenly, he surprised her by moving fast and hurtling himself straight up and over her, as gracefully as a gazelle jumping over tall grass. She whirled to face him and saw that he crouched in the doorway: wounded, furious, perhaps even more afraid than he had ever been in his life.

"Lights out," he repeated. "Why, now I would prefer that to be honest, dear Elizabeth. I have always been more partial to the dark. Perhaps when we meet again, you'd agree to visit me at a time more amenable to my personal habits."

She spared a glance outside. The sun showed only a fingernail size clipping left over the horizon. Night was nearly here... she could sense him getting stronger despite his wounds, and as she watched, he reached down, and incredibly, grasped the end of the stake. Keeping his eyes locked on hers, yet saying nothing, he pulled it out slowly, *slowly*, with no more exertion than it would take to pull a straw from a glass. Black blood glowed on the stake, and after a second, he held it up to her triumphantly.

"There. Takes care of *that*." Disdainfully, he tossed it aside and faced her again. "And now, what do you want to talk about, Bethie?" He observed her frankly, and she saw that despite his bravado, he really was hurt. He was leaning heavily against the doorjamb, bleeding profusely; his fangs were out as dangerous and predatory as a wounded animal, which was ironic, because that's exactly what he was. And yet, wounded or not, he had leaped over her as if she were nothing, which reminded her of exactly how strong and terrible he still was.

Her hand reached into her pocket for another vial of Holy Water, only to discover a wet pocketful of broken glass. It had been her last weapon, and it must have broken when she fell. A flutter of panic rose in her throat.

His grin was a death's mask. "Ah, Bethie, come up empty-handed, did you? Pity, what?" Yet he didn't move, and it looked like he was trying to decide if he should attack her or escape. He seemed to be wavering... was he gathering his strength? Deciding to cut his loss, and run? She wasn't sure. She grappled for her crucifix.

"I'm not so empty-handed after all," she said, and held it up.

He visibly blanched. "Beth, you never fail to impress me, I'll give you that. Well, I'll tell you what. You've had your go at me and failed." He indicated his chest. "You pricked me, but you missed, and I'll get over it. But I'll tell you something... you came closer than anyone else has, in many a year. You almost got me, put me in check... but like I said, this ain't checkmate, not by far." He observed her frankly, as if considering what to say, and then narrowed his eyes, clearly making a decision.

"Tell you what, Bethie. Let's call this a draw tonight, what do you say? You put that damn thing away, and I'll just leave. And if you agree to that, I'll share a secret with you."

"Like I'd trust you with anything," she whispered. "No deal. I'm going to finish this and kill you for what you did to me, and to Bobby, and all the other Barnhams. There is nothing you can say that would make me change that."

He tilted his head. "Oh, there is. And since you mention him, let me tell you that my little secret involves your dear ol' Bobby, so what do you think about *that*?"

"I think you're lying." She held the crucifix out, and he shivered again. "I think you'd say anything at all right now to save your worthless skin."

He laughed hollowly. "Well, you're right about that, no doubt about it. I am rather fond of my skin, worthless or not. But trust me, Beth. You'll want to hear this secret. And if you'll forgive me a small pun, I can tell you I've been simply *dying* to tell you about it for ever so long." He laughed again, exposing his fangs, and she shivered.

She took a step backward. "So... if I let you leave, you'll tell me your secret? A secret about Bobby?"

He nodded. "That's about the size of it, Beth darlin'."

She gazed past him out into the yard. It was full dark now. She would have to make a decision.

"I don't want to hear it," she said suddenly, and advanced on him. If he had been waiting until he healed himself, waiting for the healing power of night, he hadn't had enough time yet because a look of fear came into his eyes as she walked toward him. He staggered backwards, holding his hands up to ward her off.

"There is a child!" he screamed suddenly. "Bobby Barnham planted a bastard in you... you gave birth in the hospital, but you don't remember a bit of it."

She nearly collapsed from the shock of what he had said. She paused, which under other circumstances would have been her undoing, except that he was wounded and scared... but also eager to inflict more pain at her reaction, so rather than attack her, he merely gazed at her triumphantly.

"What did you say?" she whispered. Her heart pounded.

He grinned at her. "Oh, I think you heard me well enough," he replied. "But I'll say it again, just because it's so much fun to say it. Another Barnham, one that you don't know about, is out there. Bobby's bastard son, born eight months after you and I first met."

The stigma of illegitimacy certainly never fell upon me, although I doubt if you could say the same thing...

Her head was spinning. "What... I don't believe—"

"Oh, it's true," he whispered, full of humor, and she realized that dear God, he was actually enjoying himself... he had saved this up just for her, just to amuse himself with her pain. "Darlin' Beth, it's very true... you naughty girl, you were six weeks pregnant when they brought you to the hospital that night. It was touch and go for a while, deciding if they could save you and the bastard—oops, sorry, the *baby*—but you're a strong little thing, and you pulled through. Course, you didn't know it... seems to me, you were out of the game for a while." He smiled at her.

"You're lying." Her voice trembled.

But she could see that he wasn't, and he grinned at her again, slowly shaking his head.

"It's an easy thing to find out for yourself, if you really want to. Simply request to see the medical records... you'll find out that next spring, sometime in March I believe, you were delivered of a healthy baby boy. But come on, Beth, tell me you didn't suspect? Even if you ignored the obvious physical changes on your body, you mean to tell me that some part of you, some instinctive maternal little voice never spoke up and told you that you had borne a child?"

She felt hysteria bubbling up in her. "My mother... my mother would have told me... or the doctors..."

"Nope." His smile was smug. "They didn't think you were healthy or strong enough to know the news. So, they kept it from you." He cocked his head at her. "Remember, Beth, you weren't quite yourself there for a few years. They had you so doped up on whoopee-pills you didn't even know your own name, and that's a fact." He shrugged. "Shame, too, once those drugs get ahold of a person—"

"Shut up," she said fiercely. "Tell me. Tell me where my baby is now!"

He cocked his head at her, shrugging. "Well, your momma took him and raised him up until the time she died, poor old thing. After that..." He shrugged again, but his look was sly.

She held the crucifix up, and he pulled his head back quicker this time, but with less fear... and with alarm, she also saw that he was standing a little straighter now, and the bleeding had stopped. He was clearly stalling for time as he healed, and she caught her breath in panic. The night... the night was restoring him, nursing him. Soon, he would be back to his normal strength, and God help her then.

"Tell me where my child is!" There were a few drops of Holy Water on her fingers yet from groping in her wet pocket, and desperately, she flicked them at him. He screamed in anger and pain.

"The authorities moved in, Bethie, what do you think? They came and took him and someone adopted him." He watched her closely, ready to dodge if she tried it again, and she had the uncanny thought that he was trying to catch her eye... if he did, he would be able to control her, and then...

"Where is he now?" She felt her heart begin to ache, an actual physical ache deep inside her as she suddenly knew this all to be true. A child. Bobby's child: a sweet, blond little boy, born in a locked mental hospital unit, never to know either of his parent's loving touch because of Crane. "And his name... tell me his name. What did my mother name him? Tell me—"

But she had waited too long. The power of the night had healed him, fully and completely. He smiled at her and began to rise.

"I think," he whispered. "That the time for you to make demands upon my person has passed. Too late, Beth, too late."

Suddenly, he stood up to his full height, tall and terrible. His eyes blazed fury and triumph at her as he spread his arms wide, as if to embrace her and pull her to him... and despite all reason and logic, she saw that he had actually drifted off of the floor as if *flying*, but no, that wasn't possible, that couldn't be happening, there was no way...

But it was. He hung in mid-air, several inches from the floor, and she saw that he was obscenely mocking her, in crude imitation of a crucifixion. His eyes gleamed at her, his fangs outstretched and glistening. Desperately, she waved the crucifix at him, but it hardly bothered him now, so great was his power and fury, and she gave a little cry of alarm.

"Now then," he whispered. "What to do now? Answer your questions, and then take my leave, as I promised, or..." he licked his lips hungrily. "Or do I forget myself, and you and I can revisit old times?"

"Tell me," she begged. "If you're going to kill me, go ahead and do it. But tell me first. Where is my baby? What is his name?"

"Patience, patience..." He drifted towards her, moving silently through the air, and one cool hand reached out to stroke her throat gently. "Ah yes, Bethie, that's what I always liked about you, your fire and spirit! My sweet, sweet Beth." She closed her eyes; a sob rose in her throat as he touched her on the chin, and then even though she knew it was going to happen, knew what he was planning to do and nearly died from the sheer horror of it, she allowed it to happen because she had no choice.

Dead, cold lips touched hers, as he bent his head to kiss her.

It was unspeakable. She trembled and fought to turn her head, but he held her chin, demanding, *insisting* that she kiss him. With a satisfied sound, he pulled back, smiling at her as he did so.

"There. That's how you oughta be kissed... I doubt if either your Bobby or your Wesley Draper ever kissed you like that, did they?"

A tear trickled down her cheek, and she fought to control herself.

"Tell me what I want to know," she begged. "Please, please tell me."

He observed her from above, and in a show of power he rose even higher, so high that for a moment his head grazed the ceiling. Slowly, slowly, he lowered himself, smiling at her, enjoying her pain, and then seemed to come to a decision. "All right," he purred, his voice dangerous and silky. "I will answer your questions... but only one of them. So, which is it? What do you want to know? Your bastard son's name... or where to find him?"

She wavered. What was more important? She would need a name to start a search, she realized, for if she only had a location, she wouldn't know where to start. Still, if she knew his location, she could possibly do a cross check, getting a list of all nine-year-old boys who had been adopted. Which way to go? And of course, all of this was dependent on her surviving this night.

"Hurry," he prompted. "tick tock, tick tock..."

"His name," she decided. "Tell me his name."

He smiled thinly. "And then what? Do you intend on finding the lost Barnham heir, hunting him down? Because I assure you... there are other interested parties as well."

She stared at him in horror. "What do you mean..."

He laughed. "Oh, come now Bethie. You know my little hobby... it's how we met, after all. I've traveled the country, crossed decades, in search of finding that same delicious ambrosia I first experienced all those years ago at the Battle of Dark Hills with sweet Charlie. Some of his kin were not even close to that taste, while some—like your Bobby, for example—reminded me of that first dear, delicious boy. Well, I've about come to the end of the line, as it were. Almost all the Barnhams are gone. I think there might be one cousin left somewhere, and this one. Your and Bobby's little bastard... but who knows? Maybe he's the one, eh? Maybe he's the one I've been searching for all these years... dear little Patrick."

"Patrick," she breathed. "His name is Patrick."

He closed one eye slowly. "Why, it is at that! Patrick Michael, though I must admit I don't know his adopted surname." He shrugged. "No matter. I'll find him."

"Keep away from him," she said fiercely. "You keep away from my son—"

He grabbed her fiercely by the neck, pushing her against the wall. Her head hit savagely, and explosions of pain burst before her eyes. "Careful now," he chided. "You don't want to start getting too uppity there, Miss Beth. You ain't exactly in a position to start making demands now, are you?"

She glared at him, though carefully, so as not to look him directly in the eye. "So now what? Are you going to kill me?"

"Well now, that is a good question, isn't it? What to do, what to do?" He frowned thoughtfully and then leaned in, nuzzling her again. "I think not, Beth, though I know you would not be so generous, given a choice about me. But you see, I think the world is a much more interesting place with you in it, at least for now. You've given me more fun and excitement than I've had in years. And, now that you know the truth about your bastard—about dear little Patrick—out there in the world somewhere, why, it's given you a new purpose in life."

She said nothing.

He pulled back from her slowly, drifting like a dark, evil cloud. "So we'll see, Beth. We'll see who gets to him first, won't we? Adieu, for now." And he was gone, out the door and into the safety of his blessed, protective night. Trembling, she slid down against the gate to one of the stalls, weeping softly from the horror of it all.

There was an ache in her heart, a physical hurt she had never experienced before as she thought of her son. Patrick. Patrick Barnham, Bobby's son. What a terrible, wonderful secret Crane had revealed to her. True, there was pain in knowing of it, but there was also hope which she knew Crane would not be able to ever understand.

Angrily, she wondered how she was never told of this. The doctors at the hospital, the therapists, the social workers... *all* of them had known about it. Besides it being in her charts and medical history, she couldn't imagine them ever discussing her care without discussing the ramifications of her knowing about her child. Certainly, they had argued about it back and forth at her coordinated care meetings, with the decision ultimately being not to tell her about it. It had been a wrong decision—a *bad* decision, and she hated them for it.

Shivering, she remembered Crane's hateful words to her.

You mean to tell me that some part of you, some instinctive maternal little voice never spoke up and told you that you had borne a child?

No, and that was the hell of it. Even in this matter, Crane's looming presence had shadowed over her life… any maternal instinct, even subconsciously, had been tamped down by the absolute terror of Sebastian Crane. Also, she realized, there had been the drugs: months and months of drugs. Drugs to keep her numb and compliant and biddable, drugs that suppressed feelings and emotions and had altered her personality. Bastards.

But there were more immediate concerns, and suddenly she shook herself and remembered Wes, still in the root cellar… was he dead? When she had left, he hadn't been moving, lying face down in the wreckage of his grandmother's stored things. And the old ladies in the house beyond… what if Crane went for them? She imagined they were easy prey. He had said he wouldn't go after her, would leave her because he found life more interesting with her around, but he hadn't mentioned not hurting the others, and she figured it would be just like him to go and kill them in some violent, messy fashion for her to find. She got to her feet, slipping a little and grabbing the railing for support.

She left the barn and hurried outside into the night. Crickets were in full song, and the stars were a magnificent display overhead. As a precaution, she held her crucifix in her hand, but she didn't think that Crane was waiting for her out here… she was sure he had been content to call it a draw this evening. Still, she shone her flashlight across the yard, headed for the house, and just as she reached the back walkway, she heard a weak voice calling to her from the grass.

It was Wes, staggering towards her, and she felt a rush of relief. In the pale beam of the flashlight, she saw he was bleeding from a nasty gash on his head and was looking dazed. Gasping, he nearly fell into her arms and they held each other. She kissed his bloody face, murmuring endearments and quiet exclamations.

"Where is he?" He asked, looking over her shoulder. "Did you get him?"

She shook her head. "No… but he's gone." She felt him start in panic, but she rubbed her hands soothingly over his back. "Don't worry, he's not here, Wes. It's just us. Trust me, I know he's gone."

He pulled back to look at her worriedly. "How do you know that?" She swallowed hard, thinking of his hateful words.

Maybe he's the one I've been searching for all these years… dear little Patrick… I'll find him.

"Because," she said slowly, "he said he had other things to do."

Printed in the USA
CPSIA information can be obtained
at www.ICGtesting.com
CBHW062031051124
16951CB00011B/174

9 781962 868556